SHE WAS FOUND IN A GUITAR CASE

DAVID JAMES KEATON

Perpetual Motion Machine Publishing
Cibolo, Texas

She Was Found in a Guitar Case

ISBN: 978-1-943720-52-1

www.PerpetualPublishing.com

Cover Art by Joel Vollmer
Interior Art by Tony McMillen

ALSO BY DAVID JAMES KEATON

NOVELS
The Last Projector
Pig Iron

SHORT STORY COLLECTIONS
Our Pool Party Bus Forever Days
Stealing Propeller Hats from the Dead
Fish Bites Cop! Stories to Bash Authorities

EDITOR and CO-EDITOR
Tales from the Crust: An Anthology of Pizza Horror
Dirty Boulevard: Crime Fiction Inspired by Lou Reed
Hard Sentences: Crime Fiction Inspired by Alcatraz

Some sections of this novel have been stripped, hosed off, or previously incarcerated in substantially different stages of undress in the following publications:

"A Vast Comic Indifference" originally appeared in *Carrier Pigeon #19*, 2021.

"Captain Mushfake and the Body Cam Crucifixions" was originally published as "Body Cam Crosses" in *Noir Nation: International Crime Fiction No. 7*, 2019.

"Vietnam Bug Hockey" originally appeared in *Our Pool Party Bus Forever Days* (Red Room Press), 2018.

"My Wife Was Found in a Guitar Case" was originally published as "El Kabong" in *Wrestle Maniacs* (Honey Badger Press), 2017.

"The Flowery" originally appeared in *Red Room Magazine*, 2017.

"Fasten Your Meat Belts!" originally appeared in *Great Jones Street*, Spring, 2017.

"The Ear Eater of Jasper Country" was originally published as "The Best Chicken in Jasper County" in *States of Terror: Volume 3*, 2016.

"Forced Perspective" originally appeared in *Taut Lines: Extraordinary True Fishing Stories* (Constable & Robinson), 2016.

"Sharks with Thumbs" originally appeared in *Lost Signals* (Perpetual Motion Machine Publishing), 2016.

"Taco Hell" originally appeared in *Junk*, 2013.

"Egg Tooth" originally appeared in *Chicago Quarterly Review Vol. 16*, 2013.

"Road Dirge" originally appeared in *Bluestem*, 2012.

"Beating the Living Shit" was originally published as "Mosquito Bites" in *Pulp Modern*, 2011.

"Is That My Sandwich in There?" originally appeared in *Flywheel Magazine*, 2011.

"73 Bad Reaction Shots" was originally published as "Reaction Shots" at *Burnt Bridge*, 2011.

"Movies for Milkweed" originally appeared in *Dark Highlands Anthology*, 2010.

PRAISE FOR
SHE WAS FOUND IN A GUITAR CASE

"There's romps, there's *romps*, and then there's *She Was Found in a Guitar Case*, from David James Keaton. If this book were a cereal box, it would be full of all my favorite cassette tapes, and probably a few of my tears, too."

—Stephen Graham Jones,
author of *Mongrels*, *The Only Good Indians*,
and *My Heart is a Chainsaw*

"*She Was Found in a Guitar Case* is a pitch-dark comic nightmare, replete with shocking twists and a narrative voice as sharp, fresh, and deadly as a brand-new razor blade. David James Keaton is a true talent."

—Alison Gaylin,
USA Today and International bestselling author

"David James Keaton's *She Was Found in a Guitar Case* is part James Ellroy, part John Carpenter, and part something else entirely. Keaton writes like he's stolen an ambulance and is driving ninety mph straight to hell. If you ever wondered what it might have been like if Warren Zevon had written a novel, here's your answer. Sprawling, exhilarating, gonzo, and batshit wonderful."

—William Boyle,
author of *Shoot the Moonlight Out*

PRAISE FOR DAVID JAMES KEATON

"The author's joy in his subject matter is obvious, often expressed with a sly wink and wicked smile. Decay, both existential and physical, has never looked so good."

—*Publishers Weekly*
(Starred Review for *Stealing Propeller Hats from the Dead*)

"David James Keaton offers an insightful riff on trend horror and contemporary pop culture very much akin to that of an early-'90s Wes Craven."

—*Fangoria Magazine*
(on *Stealing Propeller Hats from the Dead*)

"The universes David James Keaton creates have one foot in stark reality and the other in the oneiric realm of barroom stories and urban legends."

—Dead End Follies

"David James Keaton holds the lovechild of convention and expectations down to the hard, concrete floor, puts his hand over its mouth, and slits its throat."

—Michael Czyzniejewski,
author of *Elephants in Our Bedroom*

"Keaton's stories are as sickly exuberant and gargantuan as gothic dirigibles, tall tales of teleportation into urban myth and mystery, post-truth, anti-reality, they break every rule of regular fiction and good taste."

—Chuck Kinder,
author of *The Honeymooners*
and *The Last Mountain Dancer*

To all of the X's. And some of the O's.

“So full of artless jealousy is guilt,
it spills itself in fearing to be spilt.”

—William Shakespeare, *Hamlet*

TABLE OF CONTENTS

(order recommended but not required)

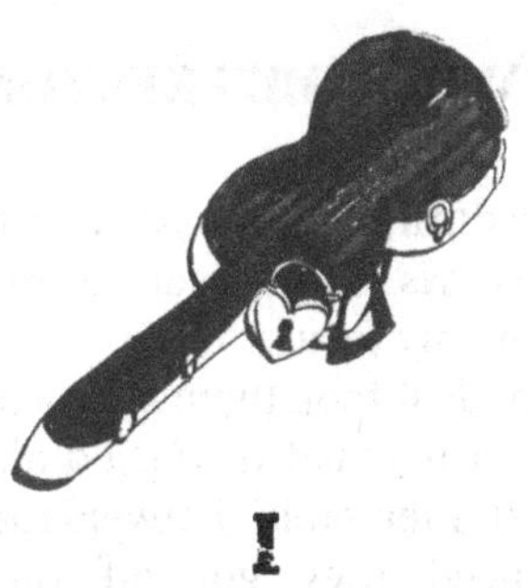

I

MY WIFE WAS FOUND IN A GUITAR CASE

WHILE I WAS still trying to figure out what to do with the mystery animal I'd rescued from the dumpster, cops were working my door like a speed bag, eager as hell to tell me my wife had been found dead in a guitar case. I opened up to stop the pounding and found three righteous knuckleheads perched on my porch, rocking back and forth on their shoes. One big, one small, with a medium-sized buzzcut standing in the middle. The two bookends were bright blue, wringing the hats in their hands real noble, while the middle guy was the porridge that was just "white" apparently, wearing the sharp suit, bright shirt with a starched collar, and a blood-red power tie that divided him neatly in half. He was clearly in charge. He looked me up, down, up, right, down, left, up, head twitching like a thumb memorizing a videogame cheat code. Because of this grim trifecta of foreheads furrowed like fists, as well as the rest of the insufferably officious body language being thrown at me, I knew immediately they'd come to report something horrible. Even though Angie hadn't been missing long enough for me to be fully prepared for the absolute worst, I'd actually watched a movie or two in my life and knew this scene well. So, in that moment, my certainty that these three police officers were going to be comforted later by loved ones dutifully impressed with their noble task of delivering tragic news to idiots such as myself had eclipsed any shock to become my focus.

In the five seconds it took them to square up and give me the *Always Sunny* ocular pat-down, I'd already imagined a decade of their dinner-table conversations, and I was thoroughly convinced they got off on these sorts of assignments. It might be difficult being some guy dealing with a murdered wife, but holy hell, how about the poor souls who have to inform distraught civilians about their spouse, child, or dog shattered on the highway? I pictured the cops making sure their wives caught them staring pensively at the horizon, or into their shaving mirrors, a silent countdown to a sympathetic back rub or blowjob. Okay, sure, I figured their training meant these guys were reasonably interested in my reaction, too. But only if it was a reasonable one. And it never was.

Suspense was emulating from them, almost like an audible hum (though this might have been coming from a walkie-talkie). I knew from my previous job closed-captioning a thousand true-crime shows that I, as the husband in the equation, was no doubt the prime suspect. They were watching for me to fuck up. And the detective in the middle, with his bottom-of-the-barrel semiotic strategies of interrogation (red power tie pointing at his groin, for example) had this objective written all over his scowl, causing what could have been an innocuous encounter to be blighted by expectation. Blame them, not me.

So, in spite of my confidence clocking their motivations at 99% accuracy (at least), and my very real horror at the prospect of losing the love of my life, none of this mental chess stopped me from being the most suspicious man in the history of bad news delivered on doorsteps. I could feel the misdirected rage boiling up and over and ricocheting in all the wrong directions before I could stop it, even if I'd wanted to.

"Mr. James . . . " the small cop began. "We're sorry to inform you that . . . "

SHE WAS FOUND IN A GUITAR CASE

Somewhere in the rumble of blood in my ears, I heard the words "wife," "murdered," and "guitar" rolling off the hot breath of this dude, and I had questions. But I couldn't stop thinking how they were relishing their roles as harbingers of doom. What kind of person does this nature of work? And who needs three of them to do it?

I was really stuck on all this.

Mainly because I knew they were watching me experience something I'd always found excruciating to witness in others: when tragedy becomes an excuse to be a monster. And if there were two things that captioning true crime and the occasional shitkicker Bigfoot hunting show had taught me, it was that monsters were ridiculous. And that a guitar-and-banjo duel could break out at any moment. Also, human beings didn't fit in guitar cases. Okay, that's three things.

But since we have a little time right now with my eyes closed and the thunder of my eardrums obscuring the scene on the porch, let's rewind to my first memory of the bad-reaction loophole I'd been cursed with forever. It goes back further but involves much lower stakes. In high school when I delivered pizzas, a co-worker got the mirror knocked off her car by some bump-and-run, and she came running into the shop yelling, "Call the cops, dummies!" But I hesitated, understandably wanting details, and she flipped out, upending the perfectly symmetrical pizza I was crafting, screaming inches from my nose. I remember thinking, "No *way* you're this upset. You just wanted to trash my pizza 'cause we broke up." See, I understood the urge to hurl a pre-cooked floppy disc of pizza dough across the room to see how it landed. And I understood that, in such a moment, you are hovering in a limbo of split-second understanding that you're going to take advantage of your newfound, tragedy-induced immunity in case the opportunity never arises again. But what I didn't understand was . . . you are also genuinely upset. So there on my doorstep, I finally appreciated why she'd launched my first geometrically perfect pie into a ceiling fan, and I opened my eyes and rubbed my ears red and ground my teeth in a vibrating crimson haze of despair that was still coherent enough to hope these cops gave me any reason at all to flip their metaphorical pizzas right the fuck out.

Later, I got more facts about the case, the horrible stuff, about how she likely survived in that guitar case for almost half a day, hogtied and folded up and running out of life while she listened to truck after truck piling the city's trash over her. But in that moment at the front door staring at this real-life representation of an Ascent of Man evolution poster, I just really wanted to hurt these guys. Future blowjobs be damned.

I scanned the big one, with his all-too-enthusiastic hat wringing, his lumpy blue shirt making his matching necktie practically invisible and therefore powerless, and I imagined him using these encounters to explain away impotence, alcoholism, maybe missing his lumpen, mouth-breathing spawn's big moment of sanctioned assault in a hockey game, probably when he hip-checked the first female player in the history of their school headfirst into the boards.

"When did this happen?" I asked, watching his mouth wriggling around so much that it practically ate itself, and now I was utterly convinced he'd definitely conceived a shitty, hockey-playing kid. I squeezed my doorjamb and watched my own knuckles turn as white as his face. I was extra strong in doorjambs, you see. Even though I hadn't gotten to the point where I could do 500 chin-ups on the bar I'd hung in our sagging bedroom-door frame, today I was squeezing this wood so hard all three of them heard the cracking. Though I couldn't be sure this wasn't just my knuckles.

"Well, sir, we don't know much," the detective in the middle answered, holding up a hand to keep Lumpy quiet. "But due to blood pooling in her right arm and leg, as well as the necrotic tissue frozen to the hinges of the guitar case, we believe, at this time, she was killed in another location, possibly struck by an automobile, and, subsequently, brought to the garbage dump."

"No shit," I said, not really asking, not really talking, just squeezing the door harder despite the cramps. "So, you're saying she didn't live there? At the garbage dump, I mean. So you're saying you got cutting-edge forensics telling you her day didn't start on a mountain of crushed beer cans and loaded diapers and gutted TV dinners? Thanks, supersleuth!"

"I'm sorry, sir, we're still trying to ascertain . . . "

"'*Ascertain*'? How about you stop trying to sound like some rent-a-cop on the witness stand bumbling over big words and just tell me what you know about my wife."

"We understand that you're upset." The little one stepped forward, screwing his hat back on his pointed head to exert some authority. "And you have our word, Mr. James, that we will do everything in our power to . . . "

"Now, can you tell us . . . " Lumpy started to say over him, and at that I stepped completely out of my house and into their arena, eyeball to eyeball with the disheveled one now, and, oh shit, he didn't like me in his bubble at all. But I figured I wouldn't get another chance like this, to toss their perfect pizza into the fan blades, so I stepped even closer. Today was my diplomatic immunity, before my depression or their defensiveness took over. I'd always wanted to get pulled over speeding when my wife was going into labor. They'd say, "Follow us!" and put on the sirens, and we'd all break the laws together, pizzas flying everywhere. All of us trapped together in this bubble, impervious in a shield of rising crust. And dangling heavy on the vine of a bending skyline, a nuclear explosion of tomato-red goodness.

"Listen, please don't use the word 'power' when you stand there twisting the sweat out of your lid," I said, right up his nose. I considered a quick bite on the booze-busted blood vessels at the end of his beak, but I kept it together. "You stand there fantasizing how you can tell this story over pork chops to your halfwit family of hockey players, and still I have to endure making you feel okay about making me feel bad?" What's weird is I loved hockey.

The big one blinked at this, getting a little fire back in his face, remembering I was just some citizen disrespecting him, and he went for his mirror glasses to push back with some steely-eyed sovereignty. But a hand appeared on his shoulder, then his hand appeared on that guy's shoulder, then on my own shoulder, then a couple more hands clapped over each other's chests, and miraculously this impromptu game of Twister calmed everyone back down. I looked around and started counting this weirdly comforting *Human Centipede* of cupped hands and wedding rings, and now it was impossible to blow up.

One, two, three, four, five, six, seven . . . wait, how many paws do these guys got?

"Sir, we know how upsetting this must be. But be assured, because of her pregnancy, we, as a result, now have ourselves, at this point, another homicide case to pursue."

"How did you know she was six weeks pregnant? I thought autopsies took days."

"This case is a priority," one of them said, mouth not moving.

"Okay, let me ask you a question," I said, then tried out a small shove against the big guy's chest. He stumbled down a step, and the other two held up their hands.

"Whoa, whoa . . . "

"Okay, two questions," I said. "When you guys run your mouths, how much do all those commas cost? More than bullets?"

"What?"

"Do you think I'm stupid? Do you think *I think* they really scrambled some special fetus squad instead of the usual team of incompetents? Maybe I'll follow you so I can watch you guys knock on five more doors and look sincere while you twist and fumble with your goddamn invisible ties. Or maybe we can just jump ahead to the TV screen that will read 'Ten Years Later,' because stay tuned, *maybe* you catch a break and finally catch a killer. Doubt it, though."

Hands were back on everybody's shoulders but mine.

"Let's go, Joe," the small one said, pulling the lumpy one away. I watched them get into their car, the detective looking like he still had a lot to say to me. So I pushed my luck and trailed them to the cruiser, knocking on the window good and hard. I'd always wanted to do that, too. The detective stood with his door open, and the big lumpy cop, the driver, rolled down his window, cheeks puffed in frustration as he held his breath behind pursed lips.

That's when I saw their hands hadn't been clapping each other's chests and shoulders to restrain themselves after all. They'd been covering up the electronic eyes of their body cameras, in case one of them snapped along with me.

A brave new world, I decided. *And a whole new type of restraint.*

"One last question," I said. "Have you heard of the Flynn Effect?"

He looked at his partner. Of course he hadn't.

"It was something my wife was working on," I explained. "Something from her doctoral research. It means every generation is smarter than the previous one. And it means our generation cannot think in the hypothetical. My unborn child might have been able to do this, but we have no chance. And one thing I now understand is I'll forever be unable to consider such hypothetical situations."

The big one shook his head at all this shit and started the car.

"Don't leave town, Mr. James," the detective said finally, pausing for effect as he climbed in. "Someone will be by to talk to you again soon."

I smiled. Even though I'd just found out my wife was dead and I was now beginning the second half of my cursed life where everything that made sense for half a minute when we were together and happy would no longer be recognizable and my previous life was just some bad movie we saw once where we had no interest in the ending. I smiled mostly because I could do something in that moment to make a cop feel foolish. And how often do you get the chance? The smile would cost me months of guilt and incrimination, and, eventually, something even worse, but it was probably worth it.

"Are you actually telling me you can't imagine anyone not thinking in the hypothetical!" I yelled like a fool as they drove off.

They didn't get the joke, and I may have laughed. Angie would have laughed. But laughing is something you don't do after cops tell you your wife was found dead in a guitar case. Something you definitely don't do if your wife died carrying your child. But lost innocence and laughing at cops was a combination as natural as chocolate and peanut butter, and, more importantly, there was no way I would let them record me crying.

But I didn't have to worry. They were gone, and any dashboard cameras or body cameras or covert plastic eyeballs would miss any honest reaction, even if it was no different from a manufactured one, or if I had no idea what that has ever looked like.

***

After the cops left, I may have stood there for an extra dozen deep breaths, even considered sticking around if I had any faith in the Louisville Police Department, or if I hadn't so effectively gotten the investigation off on the wrong foot by jamming mine in my mouth. And my feet continued to screw me up, as I stumbled around trying to figure out why my jeans suddenly didn't seem to have any leg holes, and I thought about my wife and our future baby curled up in a guitar case like grisly Russian nesting dolls. I thought about how much she would have enjoyed that doorway exchange, considering her recent anti-authoritarian research for her dissertation, but mostly I kicked at my elusive pant legs and thought about how we'd always joked about her height, about her being so short a hawk might swoop down to grab her on a jog. Which is kinda what happened after all. But she was no nesting doll. It just didn't make any sense. A guitar case? Even Angie wasn't that small.

"Matryoshkas," she told me once. "That's what those dolls were called." I'd mangled the word when we came across a pile of discarded playground hobby horses during our trip to France, stacked up high under an overpass and rusting away in order of decreasing size. She loved horses, even metal ones, even though she knew this was "expected of females."

I thought about how impossibly small a guitar case was, how there was no way to comfortably house a human body, alive or dead. I remembered the time we'd watched instrument cases playing musical chairs and chasing each other around a Louisville airport carousel, after Paris, as we stood waiting for our lost luggage. We were getting frustrated by the passengers breathing down our necks and elbowing us in the ribs, all waiting for missing bags, too. We got a good laugh when one stubby leather fiddle case got stuck on the conveyor belt and backed up the bags to upset everyone even more, until a guitar case finally slid down to knock it loose. It was brown, an artificial wood laminate, but covered in stickers of every kind of flower, mostly daisies? No, orange blossoms. I almost grabbed it, maybe to pull the guitar out of it and pretend it was mine as an excuse to abandon our stuff and be done with that long travel day. I told Angie about my plan, and she asked me, "What if you had to prove you could play it?"

But there was a padlock on the guitar case, thank Christ, so it was back to waiting. She was always three steps ahead of my bad ideas, and we stood there for two more hours, watching suitcases and boxes and musical instruments slide down the chute and around our sad cul-de-sac for at least four more flights before we found out from a sleepwalking employee that our luggage was safely on its way to Chicago, three hundred miles away. But while we waited for that surprise to ruin our mood completely, we relived our Paris trip there in the airport, laughing through the highlights. And

France was good for us, too, even while it was happening, which was rare. It rekindled things for a bit, as a trip to Paris is mandated by the United Nations to do, but our trip also benefited from her previous knowledge of the city. She'd been there for a conference on "composition and rhetoric," two things I knew little about (though I followed her blindly into a teaching career of my own). She'd already mapped out all the best places she missed the first time, so while I thought of the trip as a marriage life preserver, she thought of it in terms of "maximum efficiency." Either way, I told myself we both considered this trip a second chance to get something right.

But she really did map it out within an inch of its life, like a surgeon drawing dotted lines all across our bodies to get ready for the knife. We launched our tour at the heart, a.k.a. the Sacre Coeur, then the Eiffel Tower, of course, then next we hit those terrifying Catacombs beneath the streets and the millions of bones housed within, then the French Museum of Natural History and its notoriously chilling "spider cats"-in-jars exhibit. And finally, the Ugly American Abroad timeless tradition . . . we proudly clamped a "love lock" onto the Passerelle des Arts bridge.

We didn't have a real passion for that last adventure, actually, at least until a thinkpiece on NPR and an essay in *The New Yinzer* shamed Americans for doing this. Then Angie was all about it. "French love locks are vandalism!" the articles screamed. "Ancient architecture is being destroyed!" This got us curious enough to smuggle some padlocks into the country, like we were getting away with something. "Fuck the Patriot Act," Angie told the guy at the hardware store, flirting like she did, and she ended up buying a lock featured on commercials showcasing its resistance to a spectacular fireworks display of repeated, close-range shotgun blasts. Angie bought a ton of locks actually, since there was a sale and she loved to "get the deal." I still had a whole drawer of the suckers, which would remain forever unlocked. She put heart stickers on all their stubby keys and drew American flags on all their steel flanks, mostly because it was the most obnoxious "Freedom Fries" thing we could think of. Well, we tried to anyway. Not a whole lot of room on a padlock for artistry or identifiable flags, even if they do soak up gunfire real good. Just keep in mind that, when we vandalized famous bridges, my wife would spend three times the money so the locals couldn't scam us. And once we got to the Passerelle des Arts, we already had a variety of new theories about the recent online outrage to chew on:

First, we figured the internet scolds were probably just bitter because they didn't think ahead to smuggle a padlock into the country, and maybe he/she got ripped off by some local charging 50 euro for one, which was something like 947 American dollars and wonderful for the French economy. Or maybe the article was written by a bona fide "he/she," and the author could hold hands with itself and had no one to impress, let alone lock down. In any case, we were vindicated when, once on the bridge, we saw that 90% of the dewy-eyed lovers who were attaching these locks and snapping pictures after the fact were French as fuck. We knew this because, when they asked us to take their picture, we heard their unmistakable but adorably problematic Pepé Le Pew accents. Most Americans at least have the self-respect to selfie that shit and not ask for assistance.

"Gather 'round for some history!" Angie explained to whoever would listen. "Did you know this lock-bridge tradition is featured in the movie *Amélie*, an adorable whimsy-fest *and* the French equivalent of getting an endorsement by Uncle Sam herself? Of course you did. Because this movie was clearly what inspired you French to go nuts on these bridges. And now you're mad when the rest of the world takes you up on it? Case dismissed!"

Trivia note: the love-lock thing was also featured on an episode of *Parks and Recreation*, one of Angie's favorite shows, so she figured there was no way Leslie Knope didn't consider any and all negative implications.

She was all about this ritual for historic reasons, too. According to legend, her mom and dad had done this love-lock action, back on their own honeymoon. Or maybe it was her grandpa. Definitely not the brother, as he died young (speaking of locks, he was dumb enough to work in a prison and realized his poor choice of vocation way too late). But whoever it was, it was real important to someone in her family that we do this, and someone had called Angie when we were overseas and she got real serious about us getting it done. Come to think of it, her dad even had a job in the factory making the damn things. Or maybe it was prison. But despite the way Angie described it—like we were just being the Obstinate Americans—it was actually kind of a religious ritual for her family, though none of them were religious at all (at least as far as I knew). But I guess it could have been one of those new wacky religions, where you had no choice, or one of those *old* wacky ones, where you had no recollection.

We forgot to throw our keys in the river and finish her ceremony, though. Something distracted us, probably some French asshole trying to sell us ten more padlocks. It wasn't that I didn't want to litter in that river. Hell, I would have kicked a taxi's side mirror into the water for her if I could, because my love was a *beast* back then. But I just stuck the key back on my toy camera keychain—a gesture that at least one local scammer told me was bad luck for any relationship.

Proved him wrong today, huh?

Here's the thing, though, the real reason behind those internet haters and local swindlers: The parts of the bridge soaking up all our ugly tourist locks have never been ancient at all! Buncha spare parts, new materials, mostly replicas built back in the '80s, which makes romantic river walks only slightly more vintage than, say, a Sylvester Stallone movie, and with the same sag at the mouth.

"Who are they fucking kidding?" Angie said to our Parisian hotel concierge with the name I can't remember right now (but it was something so ridiculous you wouldn't believe me). "The panels with the locks? The 'ancient architecture' they talked about on NPR? Just a bunch of puke-green chain-link fence. The kind of fence you'd see at a Little League game. I ask you, Fabio, is there anything uglier than that? Remember those candy-coated fences from the 1800s? Yeah, me neither."

Our concierge who was totally named "Fabio" shook his head that day, but it was clear he knew she was right. And if that kind of hideous contemporary fence wasn't already catnip for attaching locks, then they'd probably have to put up the chain-link regardless, to stop love-struck locals from flinging themselves into the waves, which was infinitely dumber than throwing a key, right? Which I forgot to do. Throw the key or myself into the water, I mean.

But the point Angie was making was that padlocks looked way better than a rubbery split-pea barricade, and *my* point was she could talk any Frenchmen into siding with goddamn tourists, even Fabio. Just one of her skills.

So we stood there in the airport, watching nylon coffins crammed with tiny toiletries and even smaller plastic landmarks dance around the circle, while Angie got a little punch drunk, continuing to defend the tacky love-lock trend for anyone who was eavesdropping.

"You know, the Eiffel Tower is built with a lot of fence work and holes, so it looks pretty conducive to padlocks," she said, louder than necessary. "Coincidence? No way. The French love locks! A friend told me they dump off sections of fence to make room for more, so they're also job creators. Real talk? How hard would it be to make a lock-resistant bridge?"

"Who are you talking to?" I asked her, sighing. "I was there, remember?"

"You know, some of this same stuff about the locks I found in the Ohio archives while researching my dissertation. You'd know if you read it."

"I thought your dissertation was on prison."

"It's complicated, Dave. Cheap prison labor is on the rise,

especially for tourist junk. And out there in the Midwest, they have copycat bridges. Did you know that padlock panels and sectors of fences, some from all over the world, end up in a huge warehouse in Ohio? Mark my words, Paris will start recycling their locks soon . . . "

"That sounds awesome actually. It's much more romantic to have your padlock get squirrelled away in a dark warehouse *Raiders of the Lost Ark*-style. We're so lucky we kept the key."

We weren't really fighting, at least I didn't think so. And I *did* think we were lucky, at least at the time. So, as we watched all the unclaimed luggage continue to do their laps, hoping for more odd-shaped instrument cases to break up the monotony, I thought about how society ached so hard for us to put a lock on that bridge, how any article trying to shame us, or any hand-wringing Parisian government types, were all merely reverse psychology geared towards our contrarian Westernized brains. Like they were saying, "We *dare* you to show your love . . . " There was such a pressure by the Gypsies on that bridge for us to lock something, somewhere, anywhere, that I thought they were going to pull a pin on a grenade if we didn't participate. Or maybe the pressure was just coming from Angie. Or her family. Later, I would discover it was all three.

Earlier, when we were still working our way through customs, we'd gotten the giggles and asked the TSA agent if we could get the "real" French passport stamp, the one with "the tiny cartoon padlock on it," and we were almost strip-searched on the spot. Angie had already downed about a gallon of wine on the flight, so we were still flying kinda high, and it was tough not to tell dour customs agents about the graffiti we'd seen on *actual human corpses* in the Catacombs under Paris. Oh, and all the illicit flash photography, which was no doubt blowing those bones to dust after a million skeleton-scorching photos a year. Real, live bones down there, not '80s replicas like those dumb bridges.

"Someone writing shit on skulls?" I whispered. "Now

that's some real vandalism! And we got the skull selfies to prove it."

"Just keep the line moving, please, sir."

By the time we'd made it to the luggage carousel, we had stopped snickering, heads hanging low and the sleepy tail end of her wine buzz quieting us both down to some grumbles and teeth grinding. Then she pointed to a sign above our heads and laughed:

"Wouldn't it be more fun if that said 'Personal Baggage Claim' instead?"

It took me a second, but then I lost it, too, no matter how close to home that joke really was. I said to her, "Oh, you mean you'd rather watch a turnstile full of exes, neglectful parents, missed birthdays, broken promises, minor scandals, Electra and Oedipal complexes, all rolling down the ramp?"

"Yes. That," she declared. "Then these people might hesitate to swarm this carousel so damn close!"

It was officially the last thing she said on our honeymoon, then she snored through the Uber ride home. But everybody sure heard it. She always got away with stuff like that, maybe because of her height. And when she explained to me once how "Matryoshka" didn't really mean "nesting doll" at all, that it was just a name for little Russian biddies, any small but sturdy old lady, I realized this was her in a nutshell. Curled up in a nutshell, I mean, feet pinned over her head forever.

But that night at the airport, strangers backed up, clearing a path for her at the turnstile. She was small, but she had that kind of power.

***

Before I could come to my senses, I ran back inside our apartment and packed up all my stuff to leave town, jamming a couple soup-to-nuts changes of clothes into my suitcase. The Paris customs slips still dangled from the handle, and I thought about how a suitcase was almost too small to hold a reasonable stack of textile facsimiles of the average head-to-toe human being, let alone the entire thing, alive or otherwise.

And a guitar case was smaller than this? Insanity.

I patted my pockets and realized I'd lost my wallet somewhere in the chaos of the day, but a couple of my old driver's licenses were on the floor, so I gathered those up. I always saved my expired licenses, but the loss of my wallet and a valid I.D. (not to mention a visit from the goon squad), convinced me conclusively I was doing the right thing by getting the hell out of Dodge. Pulse pounding, I kicked my rubber horse head into the corner. It was a gift from Angie, but I was clear-headed enough to know there was only room for essentials.

But there was one final stop I needed to make.

I opened the bathroom door and stared for a good five minutes at the metal cage in the tub. The mystery creature was nosing the bars of its tiny prison.

Then I thought, "Fuck it," and gathered up my spirit animal and headed out.

***

The streets of Kentucky were quiet, even with my windows down, and I drove holding my breath in my throat. The DMV was right by our house, and I considered getting a new Kentucky license in spite of how strange that would seem after receiving news about a dead wife. This convinced me to do it.

But when I hit their lot, I saw it was the same spot I'd parked in the last time I'd lost my wallet, which was something that happened about twice a year. The same wizened old dude was smoking by the door, eyeballs clocking my car, and when I looked in my rearview, my beard was doing that same weird asymmetrical thing it did in my last license photo. It took me years to understand that this was simply because I drove with my head hanging out the window a little, like an animal. But this five-car pile-up of déjà vu changed my mind fast, and I pulled back out of the lot.

This is what a realistic Groundhog's Day *would look like,* I thought. *A straight-up horror movie with endless trips to the DMV. Nothing even close to a love story.*

SHE WAS FOUND IN A GUITAR CASE

I looked to the left and thought about Nashville, then to the right and thought about Ohio. Maybe I could stay with my dad in Toledo, tail between my legs. Ohio had its good qualities. And there must be plenty to do there, judging by how often Angie went back for research. Also in its favor was the fact that I couldn't remember seeing a single, solitary street musician staining the curbs or bridges of that state with their mediocre music . . .

Wait a second.

I steadied the cage in my passenger's seat and stomped the gas on my Rabbit, tearing ass down Bardstown road, back to the alley near the Keep Louisville Weird shop with the cut-out circus clown photo-op in front. This was the store where I used to make Angie laugh by trying on that same floppy rubber horse's head, but never buying it. It was always her idea to do it, and I would complain it would be terrible for a bank robbery because the eyes of the mask never lined up with my own, and she'd say, "Ride your horse for good, not evil."

It was funny enough, but I started to think it was a borderline fetish for her, because every Wednesday night, Angie and her girlfriends would head down to the Davis Arena for another Ohio Valley Wrestling Moron-O-Thon. The problem was Louisville's wrestling scene wasn't small enough for a bunch of smug PhD students to be there sarcastically, like Pittsburgh's ratty little Keystone State Wrestling Alliance had been when we'd hung out a couple times back in grad school. Her colleagues loved that nonsense, watching assholes munch light bulbs and press staplers and stick pins and thumbtacks into each other's heads. All the school supplies they could rustle up to press into each other's skulls with the ease of December porch pumpkins. But Davis Arena wasn't big enough to enjoy the full-on kitsch factor. Remember Arena Football? How embarrassing that shit was? Where it was kinda in the middle between NFL and college football? The porridge that was just stupid.

Angie's girlfriends would tease her because she'd root for

this big dude who was supposedly "half stallion." I hoped they meant his head. Seriously though, there really was this Mexican kid who called himself the "Lucha Horse," rubber horse head and everything. I even bought her the T-shirt. At the time, she was addicted to one of those Learn Spanish apps, and I heard her chirping "cabello this" and "cabello that." I don't think this was a coincidence.

Goofy horse heads everywhere, though! It was a popular item in a big Derby town. And Keep Louisville Weird was where I'd chat up a clerk I called "'90s Ex-Girlfriend" because she had that reddish Kool-Aid flavored hair so popular back then. I'd have that clerk repeat how much the horse head cost at least a dozen times because all I could ever think about while looking at her was everything I wished I would have said to my real '90s ex-girlfriend who unceremoniously dumped me, like, "You're welcome for all the Meat Loaf mix tapes!" or "Sorry for all the orgasms!" or vice versa. They also had a terrifying life-size Walt Disney, who was sporting half a moustache and disintegrating faster than the real McCoy. But they had cool stuff, too, like Spencer's Gifts stuff (the O.G. Hot Topic), back before shopping malls morphed into boat shows. But the only thing I ever bought there was an ant farm, which you can get anywhere. Any chance I got (when I wasn't working through baggage with ex-girlfriends), I spent working through memories of the horror that befell my first ant farm back when I was a little kid. Thinking about that shit was my own Vietnam flashback. Or so I've heard from actual veterans. They ship those ants from Cambodia, you know?

"For prison research," Angie said, thumping it into my chest, and I was confused but didn't argue, not ready to breach the subject of the ant-farm tragedy from my past, now or then. I realize it seems ridiculous I can ponder the death of my wife easily enough, but not my misadventures in ants.

Now that I think about it, Keep Louisville Weird was also positively *infested* with musicians. So there I was, circling their stomping grounds, but the musicians were gone. Calling them "musicians" was probably a stretch. In any warm state, they were a common infection, a topical rash on any establishment. Where Angie had grown up in Minnesota, they called them "buskers," and this word made me homicidal the first time I heard it, way before I suspected one of murder.

So during my drive-by with my mystery pet and memories, I stopped outside the store, staring at a clean spot on the street where a guitar case used to be. At first glance, this spot resembled the curve of a woman's hips, and I could picture this particular guitar case on this particular corner because I was always amazed how little money the guy always made. I got out of the car and crouched down in the gutter to touch the edges of the sidewalk outline unmolested by the stain of dust and oil and dried rain, still unable to comprehend how my wife could have fit inside it. I glanced up at the store and thought about the horse head, and not just because I wished I was wearing it right now. Angie had wanted it to cap off our last Kentucky Derby costume before we moved. "The Jockey and Her Steed," she called it, and all she'd need was her '90s Fly Girl hat to complete the illusion. But what turned out to be our final Derby had been such a fiasco that the idea was dropped.

Inside, I could see '90s Ex-Girlfriend rearranging the skin-tight hipster Mothman T-shirts for the window display, and I noticed she was about six months pregnant, but only three months from the Kool-Aid flavor growing out of her hair completely.

Okay, I guess that makes her more like '80s Ex-Girlfriend, I thought, watching that belly swing and remembering my own misadventures with birth control, both then and now.

Then I heard the unmistakable sound of a musical instrument thrumming low inside its coffin, strings protesting as the case rebounded around off someone's scrawny knees, and I spun to see a musician slinking through the alley. He turned the corner, top hat all askew, carefully manicured orange beard and ragged accordion under one arm, metal triangle around his wrist, heavy instrument case of unknown origin clipping his leg or the brick road every third step. He saw me and set up shop, unpacking and squeezing out a song in record time, tapping the triangle like Pavlov's dipshit between the compression of his fingers on that tuneless monstrosity, and suddenly I was convinced he'd switched to this accordion because something unspeakable had happened to his guitar.

I was on him in seconds, standing him up by scruff of his collar, sneering in the fog of his coffee breath.

"Were you here this morning?"

He smiled and croaked a mournful note from the harmonic rig around his neck, and it was almost enough for me to snap right there. But I kept it together. Then I remembered the triangle.

The man has a triangle.

I buried my fist in his teeth, then kneed him in the bread box, then one more in the squeeze box, java breath burping from his gut and covering us in its toxic cloud. I put the toe of my boot through the teeth of the accordion's grill, and both of them made the same tortured squawk, and they both kept smiling. I'd never worn boots in my life until we moved down south, but after six months or so, Angie and I both ended up with a half dozen pairs each. Boots were assigned at birth in Kentucky, even if it meant you slipped on the sidewalks when they were wet. But one benefit was made clear when I booted my first adversary with those sharp leather toes. The term "shitkicker" made a whole lot more sense now, and a boot in the teeth was even more effective than a boot in the ass as far as changing a street musician's mind about smiling. That's when I was swarmed by a bevy of stinky street maestros avenging their friend. I would have thought it was just one busker zipping all around me in a tornado of weed and onions, invisible if not for the colorful tinkling of the holiday baubles in their beards. But fashionable beard bling made for great targets, and my fists were finding them easy.

So much for never punching anyone in Kentucky. It was a good run.

They seemed to be multiplying around me. A whole goddamn band now, including jug and spoon sections, and I beetled up on the street for protection, worried the alley would hide our brawl long enough for me to get hurt pretty severely by these dudes. However, I was soaking up any shots to my face like they were barely there, their fists and hard-earned guitar-string calluses rebounding off my skull like balloon animals. I wrote this off as adrenaline, or maybe their vegetarian diets, but I was still nervous enough to reach into my jacket for my secret weapon.

More like secret *weapons*.

My hand went deep into my pocket, then past that pocket, where the lining had torn, and my fingers found the extra pouch sewn into the back of the coat. The pouch was for hauling waterfowl, as my favorite winter coat was one of those rough but roomy hunting jackets you'd find at Cabela's, a seasonal sale near the lifetime table reservation they maintained for Ted Nugent. Angie got it as a gift back when she still harbored dreams of me bonding with her dad over hunting someday. Her dad was one of those guys who practically lived at Cabela's, even before the Nuge celebrity sightings, and he had killed every animal that made the mistake of wandering onto his property, always trying to goad me into going out and "getting us some ducks." But I'd had my fill of adventure with him early on, after I stayed at their cabin for Christmas and her dad went out for groceries and hit a deer with his car. He ran inside asking someone for help, and Angie said, "Go with him! Bonding!" and I threw on my duck jacket and climbed in his car. Her dad asked me, "Do they sell men's clothes where you got that?" and together we rode back to the scene of his crime. Once there, my job was to aim the headlights into the ditch while he bumbled around the dark with the .22 he'd pulled from a haphazard pile of pistols in the glove box. Somewhere past the ditch, I heard a gunshot, then a "Shit!" then another shot, and finally a panicked "Pop the trunk!" He emerged back into the light, blood streaked all over his chest, dragging this limp, gangly thing by its hooves and a lolling snout. Her dad was a hairy motherfucker, seemingly hairier than the deer, and there were several times I'd seen him from a distance and thought, "Isn't it too cold to be sleeveless?" and then he'd turn out to be shirtless instead. This night was no exception. I jumped out and ran behind the car and did what I was told, and there in the trunk was a coyote so frozen you could pick it up by the tail. He'd forgotten about the last thing he shot or hit with his car, so he was staring at it just as confused as I was.

Anyway! That was Greg, my new father-in-law, always asking if I wanted to kill shit with him, needling me to take a road trip back to his hometown of Lovelock, Mississippi, someday soon to go blast the souls out of some marginally dangerous beasts. I wanted to explain, "I don't want to kill ducks, New Dad," because up until five years ago, I was still brooding over the pet duck I had in third grade. Shit, you thought having pet ants were bad? I couldn't even *feed* the ducks with Angie in Cherokee Park near our house, let alone blow their heads off for sport. But I did accept the expensive hunting coat from Angie regardless, pretending I might hit the woods with her dad one day after all.

Because there was a silver lining to all this. Literally.

See, Greg was always giving me weapons, and this pleased Angie and her mom, who suspected Greg was probably undiagnosed bipolar, or at the least a little unhinged, and maybe I could be the son he'd lost. One time, Angie told me he'd put a bullet in their water heater because it "looked at him wrong." The icebox, too. She said he spent the good part of an afternoon explaining there were "eyes on everything," especially "if there was water nearby," whatever the hell that meant. But Greg ran out of room at his cabin for weapons, or shooting appliances, so he started slipping things to me. And among these knickknacks and hand-me-downs was all sorts of fun stuff: a straight razor, an old-timey police blackjack, even a tin badge that identified me as "Indian Police," which I guess let him hunt throughout Minnesota casinos with impunity.

But I had my own toys in that secret duck pocket, too. And this day being a very special occasion, I went for my "wedding present" instead, meaning the brass knuckles. Well, more accurately, they were presents for my groomsmen that I ended up keeping because I knew they wouldn't be allowed on their flights home. My brother had told them to put a little sticker on the knuckles that said "five bucks," so if they got flagged by the TSA they could claim they picked them up at a garage sale earlier that day. He also scratched the word "paperweight" across the bottom with his car keys. He said these same tricks worked when flying with handguns. We had our doubts.

So, since I was hesitating on whipping out the blackjack due to its legality in Kentucky rumbles, I decided on the polished fists I'd procured for my bestest men, which were 100% illegal. But I figured if you could commit a crime against humanity like playing an accordion in public, there was no reason they could outlaw such a wonderful, natural extension of a man's hand. Sure, the brass knuckles were originally jokes, but I quickly realized there was a whole subculture of knuckles mania online, all custom made, all very serious. And once I secured some beautiful knuckles for my brother Lloyd, I couldn't just give everybody else the chickenshit tin versions. So everybody got heavy-duty knucks, forged from nautical brass and surrounded by all manner of disclaimers and warning stickers. But Lloyd's still cost twice as much as the rest. This was because, growing up, he was the first person I'd ever seen in a real fight. And on that day, he was smart enough to put in his plastic football mouthpiece before he ran into the mob, which was the next best thing to wearing a huge rubber horse's head in a brawl. So he was smart enough to hide the

Cadillac of Brass Knuckles from me whenever I came over looking to steal them back and complete my wedding collection, making me more of an "Indian Giver" than Indian Police, of course, despite my new badge.

Angie, she didn't mind the illegal weapon stash, as long as they were lined up on the curio cabinet instead, tucked alongside the Magic 8-Balls, Civil War straight razors and mustache combs, headless sock monkeys, and my prized handful of fake snow from the *Dark Knight Rises* shoot in Pittsburgh. All that stuff didn't fit in the duck pocket. Believe me, I tried. But when we were packing up our huge apartment back in Steeltown, trying to figure out how to cram all that shit into our smaller place in Louisville, I did use the mini-arsenal as measuring tools, and my unlawful weapon collection transformed yet another depressing relocation and subsequent Tetris challenge into a much more entertaining game of Clue.

"Hey, Dave, how big is that picture frame?"

"Three straight razors and a sideways blackjack!"

"You realize there's a measuring tape right next to you, right?"

"Shhh . . . "

I hope by now it's obvious there was all sorts of stuff hidden in the lining of my coat, waiting for just the right excuse. Also, Angie was a big fan of *The Iliad*, particularly when the narrative would stop for no good reason just to tell you the history of the stick that someone's getting brained with. So apologies in advance of future beatings, but this is a motherfucking love story.

Back at the fight, there really wasn't much else to it. This was because, during the Apocalyptic Busker Beatdown, I'd circled back to the blackjack after all. What a twist! Always the blackjack, though. It felt like home. It might not have been as cinematic as a golden fist, but it sure as hell sent people to slumberland. A few cracks across the temple and half the musicians were on the ground dreaming of album covers they'd never autograph, while the other half were running for their lives, long, thin beards trailing like silk scarves. It seemed like some of them were trying some old-school WWF moves on me during the battle, but maybe that was my imagination. Do buskers dig wrestling, too? They did have that sort of earnest sincerity that suggested they'd totally believe in anything. But even to a bunch of gullible one-man bands, there is one big clue wrestling is fake (and you have to have been in an actual fight to realize it):

When things end up on the ground in real life, they stay there for good.

Still, I tried some moves, some kicks, just for kicks, some stuff from when I was a kid, or probably just picked up watching the half-ass efforts of the Keystone Wrestling League. Angie would have loved it. Cross chop, forehand chop, Mongolian chop. Wrestlers were always using those open-fist hacks instead of punches to minimize actual damage, but all that changes when you're chopping down trees with a blackjack. In fact, if you handed every professional wrestler a blackjack instead of a feather boa, the sport would finally be more respected than *Rollerball*, or at least roller derby. Do they still have roller derby? Does it still use horses?

Oh, yeah, there were some "clotheslines." Now *that* was a great visual punchline on the television screen. Facedown on the street, though? With nowhere to fly off your extended arm? It breaks bones. But one move I definitely landed was the Bronco Buster, since it fit the theme. It's where you ride a dude like a horse. Only I was the horse. Another twist! There was probably a Mule Kick in there, too, but that's as close as I ever came to a signature move. I guess a blackjack counts as a trademark match ender, but, honestly, "Go to Sleep!" will always be universal, no matter the tool, and certainly not relegated to an arena.

It seems like a no-brainer, but the one thing I did *not* do was break a guitar over anyone's head. Remember the ol' "El

Kabong!" shout made famous by the cartoon horse Quick Draw McGraw? More specifically his vigilante alter ego and his patented guitar smash over all the bad guys' domes? I just couldn't do it. Guitars were now holy vessels.

After the bulk of the battle was done, I got up and blew some blood out my nostril, then crouched over Orange Accordion Man where he laid rigid. I grabbed him by his billy goat and gave him the open-palm "dicksmack" interrogation until he told me every corner where Louisville guitar players danced for their dinners. I wasn't even sure why I needed that info, because I'd driven by with the intention of leaving, not accosting the first singer-songwriter I saw. But suddenly I had this fantasy about being the seedy, sweaty fuck of a private eye right out of the movies, stumble-bumbling my way around Kentucky, beating the treble clefs out of hippies and hipsters alike. Then I remembered who I was sitting on again, and we played a little more blackjack with me as the dealer.

Whack whack whack, and another card for you, and another card for you, sir . . .

Afterwards, I returned to the guitar-shaped spot on the street. It was a huge mistake what I did next, but on the list of incriminating things I'd done since I'd received the news of Angie's death, it was barely in the top five.

I took out a piece of chalk and traced her from memory, drawing the crime scene I needed it to be. I outlined a guitar that wasn't there, and then the shape of my wife within it, just to see if she'd fit. Me, I fit inside easily this rendering. Even while standing. Even while walking. These lines were now my prison walls. I did this fast.

Quick Draw McGraw . . .

I guess I hoped this would help the police, too. Maybe one of the buskers was mad Angie didn't throw 'em a quarter? Or maybe she threw the quarter too hard. Or maybe our heated discussions outside Keep Louisville Weird about class theory and padlocks and cursed childhood ant farms drowned out all their terrible music and they'd had enough.

SHE WAS FOUND IN A GUITAR CASE

Then I saw Orange Accordion Man wasn't getting up, and the accordion wasn't smiling, and I worried they both might have stopped breathing for good. So I ran across the street to the Smoothie King and asked for some ice, remembering how Angie had done this weeks earlier when she went jogging too far and almost stroked out, calling me from the shade of a trash can, scared her body had stopped sweating. That was the most terrified I'd ever been. Until this morning.

I came back with the ice and poured some down the guy's shirt to see if he'd jump. Nothing. So I worked on the outline of the guitar some more, to make it perfect. I finished drawing us inside of it, then I collapsed on the sidewalk and put my arm around all three of us. I still wasn't entirely convinced my wife could fit inside a guitar case, let alone a guitar. But now everything seemed possible. And it felt like justice had sort of been served.

I might have blacked out.

***

I came to my senses and rolled toward the prone tunesmith, his shirt wet from the melted ice, my survival instincts kicking in. I was no doctor, by any stretch of the definition, and I couldn't even claim the rhetoric-and-composition PhD loophole, but my earlier ice-down-the-shirt diagnosis was good enough for me, and I got out my throwback '90s clamshell phone and called the police. I told them to check out some sidewalk art in the alley. Said it might help with their case, knowing full well it wouldn't. This, combined with skipping town before dusk on the same day I was informed of my new widower status, probably shot me right to the top of their most-wanted list. I imagined the head detective from my doorstep at that exact moment, taking my picture from the pile and pinning it to the tiptop of their pyramid of suspects, then, as an afterthought, grabbing a magic marker and adding a horse's bridle to my face.

I imagined the picture they'd choose was either my shittiest driver's license photo (good luck!) or my caller I.D.

image on Angie's phone, which was no doubt in an evidence locker by now. On her phone, I would forever be wearing the leering rubber horse head from Keep Louisville Weird, which would be how Angie and the police would always remember me. Because no way a mugshot like that ever gets demoted from the top of *The $20,000 Pyramid* in a cop's bullpen, even if I did manage to catch the real killer.

But if you need closure on this particular day, if not this incident, later I would read in a true-crime adaptation of this case that the cops did search that alley "real good." But instead of pondering the important revelations of my chalk outline, they simply found a street musician in a coma, triangle somehow locked around his neck in a permanent chokehold, and an accordion that would need braces to ever sing again.

They would also find the rubber horse head I was wearing throughout the assault, though I'd swear on a stack of telephone books I had no recollection of ever buying such a ridiculous thing, let alone sliding it over my face when I stepped out of my car. But if I closed my eyes, I could clearly visualize the black-and-white snapshot of my grinning horse head in the middle of that dog-eared paperback, right where they always tucked in exactly eight pages of "shocking" photos. An artist's rendering would follow, the double-splash sketch of my horse head askew on my shoulders, golden fist clenched tight, hunting collar up high. I would vow to find a horse's head that fit a little better than that one, with maybe a smile that didn't look quite so crazy, but I'd never bother doing this.

But the novelizations were yet to come. As I left Louisville behind me that day, all I knew unequivocally was that my wife was dead. And I was probably going to jail. But, as I would find out, this would be a completely different sorta prison. One that nobody had ever seen before, even the inmates.

II

PATIENT ZERO

THE DAY SHE DIED, I was already obsessed with the idea of serving time.

I never thought the phrase "serve time" made any sense until I kept hearing it over and over again. I always thought it sounded like an attempt to apply a noble description to the dull torture of incarceration, and Angie preferred "serve your sentence," maybe because it sounded like the endless writing advice she got in grad school. But when all the real craziness started, it seemed like I was hearing "serve time" every six seconds. Maybe this was so memorable because it was also when I discovered there was a place somewhere deep in the Ohio suburbs where kids role-played that they were inmates in a make-believe prison. Have you heard about the latest insanity these crazy kids are up to? Where the youth act out imaginary prison sentences like it's some kind of game?

Acting out imaginary sentences. This does sound like the worst writing advice of all time. But it was a lot like the infamous Stanford Prison Experiment, where students played Attica for a bunch of mad-scientist assholes, until everyone finally flipped out and started torturing each other for real. Only, impossibly, this fake afterschool version of a prison that

Angie had been researching before her death was way weirder than that, and somehow more dangerous.

But I'll get to all that. I want to back up a little, to the cat that wasn't a cat, who might be the reason things went bad. I was being all heroic and trying to save this thing from some villainous restaurant owner who may or may not have been serving cats for his lunch specials. Okay, perhaps he rescued stray cats and let them live rich, happy lives on his farm. I was never sure, and otherworldly (Martian?) stereotypes were too easy to fall back on, and I wasn't going to take any chances. So here's how the morning our life ended went down:

First off, there was the thing she heard in the dumpster. Well, it was *next* to the dumpster if you wanna get specific, and that "dumpster" was really more like a grease trap. But the day Angie died, I got this call from her, all shaky and frantic, and it woke me up fast. It was about noon, but I was unemployed, so noon was early for me. I was fumbling with my trusty outdated clamshell phone, almost snapping it shut on my bone-dry tongue, while Angie told me about this cat screaming behind Ramsey's Red Planet. It was touted as this "all-world" restaurant (that we called the "all-weird" restaurant), about three blocks away from our apartment, and it had nothing to do with Mars, except maybe the same lack of drinkable water. To this day, whenever I hear the name of that planet, I'll flash back to terrible corn bread: weirdly cold, with tumorous corn kernels everywhere. Now, this was all during the 2015 Cold Snap That Never Ended, back when that "polar vortex" deal came spinning down on our heads and temperatures in Louisville were dropping to five below. In Kentucky, that's like, well, five below. So Angie was pretty sure the cat was screeching so loud because it was frozen solid to something. She said on the phone that it sounded like a monkey it was so upset, which made sense later. But based on TV-show forensic evidence, and what I could remember from Stephen King's *Pet Sematary*, I knew it wasn't possible for it to be frozen to something if it was still alive. Days later on my porch, this movie trivia would be verified regarding a certain human cadaver. Still, it sounded like something was trapped, or hurt at the very least, and Angie was on her way to the bus and couldn't search the alley without being late. So I played the hero, standing up high in the bed, head dangerously close to the ceiling fan while my lips flapped with mock helicopter noises, telling her:

"Never fear! I love the smell of cat shit in the morning!"

Her bus picked her up three blocks from Ramsey's, so I knew right then, because of the timestamp of her phone call, there was no way she was going to make the bus anyway, and she'd probably have to walk the rest of the way to the University of Louisville campus. I figured the least I could do was lurch a hundred yards down to the alley to check out the monkey caught in a rat trap. No, seriously, don't clap me on the back for this. Even if it was the length of a football field I traveled before breakfast, it wasn't like I ran or anything. It was truly the *least* I could do. The *most* I could do would have been driving her to work in the first place.

Because that would have changed everything.

So I ran out the door toward Red Planet, not bothering to smooth down my Siberian Gulag-looking case of bed beard, and grateful for my shaved head, which was much easier to manage for any surprise calls to arms. "Institutional Chic," Angie called my patented look.

When I got to the spot in the back of the alley behind the restaurant, where the screeching was coming from, the first thing I saw was this huge, steaming, hot-grease tank and thought, "Oh, no, it's not in there, is it . . . " but then I spotted the storage shed behind it. The door to this shed was double hasped, double locked, one padlock was hastily engraved with a heart, and the other adorned with a skull and crossbones.

Talk about mixed messages!

I got down on my stomach. With my glasses askew I couldn't quite see under the door, but could just barely make out the tiny, inconsequential shape of some kind of critter in there pacing then mewling, pacing then mewling . . .

I pushed my head down against the cold street even harder, and my glasses bent to give me a better look. I called these my "fighting glasses," as they had springs that let them twist every which way if I ever had to absorb a punch to the face. I only wore them around the house, ever since one of my schoolmates heard my boasts and tested my claim with the smash of an ashtray. But even through the cracked left lens, I could still see some sort of animal doing little laps and chittering in the shadows. Then it got real frantic. It was certainly stressed, whatever it was, and the tone of its noises changed when it smelled me creeping around. But it was back against the far wall, not approaching the gap under the door where I could possibly grab it, and I couldn't see what was keeping it trapped in there. It seemed plenty small enough to squeeze out from under the door. A guitar case could hold a hundred easy.

I stood up and looked around to solve the mystery, and the animal's noises ramped up again, but oddly low and hopeless now, like the sounds a cat makes on the way to the vet. So this had to be a cat, right? These sounds were weirder than a cat, though, and I started panicking along with it, wholly convinced of the dire straits it was in. I rattled the door again and, based on the give, realized the entire shed was constructed of cost-cutting materials; particle-board and tin for most of it. So I took a deep breath to power up, then shouldered the door open like a champ. The door flew clean off the hinges and tumbled off into the dark, and when my eyes adjusted, I saw what appeared to be that long, wicked rat cage they strapped to Winston Smith's dumb fucking face in *1984*.

A few minutes later, I was sitting on our porch and calling Angie back, still groggy, but now keenly watching a squat, mangy quadruped impatiently circle its cell like those miserable lions housed in giant hamster tubes at the MGM Grand. It was an interesting looking animal, with some black-and-white racing stripes on its head, but so matted from filth and grease that I couldn't tell if I was dealing with rat, cat, or some Dr. Moreau combination of both. At least it wasn't a skunk. I'd seen enough cartoons to know there were no stink lines, and its dialect in no way resembled French. I thought about all those fake *chupacabra* snapshots, and how they turned out to be hairless dogs. Unfortunately, neglect can make any creature mysterious.

When Angie answered her phone, I verified from the traffic sounds that she'd missed the bus and was stuck walking to work, just as I'd predicted. Further in the background, there was no mistaking the passion-free, lackluster crooning of street musicians, always trying to sucker the lunch crowd with their hollow, impotent guitars and folksy banter. We called that insufferable stretch of Bardstown road "The Gauntlet," and only the foolish ever tried to run it without headphones or a handful of quarters.

"Hey, babe! So, yeah, I found that cat in a trap. I mean, I think it's a cat? Not sure what Red Planet was going to do with it, sooooo I kind of lost my mind and took it with me. So, um, now we have a cat thing! I didn't really think past the whole abduction part."

"What?" she laughed. "You took it with you? You're nuts. Did you check it for a microchip?"

"And where would I find that exactly? In its skull? Hold on, I'll get a wrench."

"Cats are microchipped these days."

"Hell, if it's a robot, we're keeping it for sure. We'll be rich!"

"It was in a trap?"

"Yeah a big, scary-ass cage! You ever see the movie *1984* where . . . "

"Aw, poor thing!" she cut me off. "Who knows how long he was in there serving time."

"Please don't say 'serving time.'"

"But it's so cold out!"

"Yes, it is, but speaking of 'servings,' there were a ton of cat-food cans in that shed. And a frozen can of cat food in the cage with it. I think this Ramsey the Red fucker eats cats. Do they do that on Mars?"

"He doesn't eat cats, jerk."

"I'm telling you, this dude eats cats like *Alf* eats cats."

"Maybe he was trying to catch his own cat after it ran away, scared his pet would die stuck frozen to something."

That's not a thing.

"Uh huh. Yeah, no, this ain't nobody's cat, Angie. I'm not even sure it *is* a cat. You should have heard the noises it was making. It knew the stewpot was coming! And you should see this fucking cage! You ever see *1984?*"

"Ugh, you mean, have I ever read *Nineteen Eighty-Four?* I'm spelling it out, by the way."

"Oh, excuse me. Is that the PhD talking?"

"No one's seen that movie, but the book's a classic."

"Okay, you're right. Actually I was thinking of the movie *Class of 1984*, which is where you'll be teaching next spring. Hold on, I'll call Mars and get back to you . . . doctor."

"I'm not that kind of doctor!"

"Damn straight."

***

The mailwoman came by while I was still getting busy signals from Ramsey's. I was kicked back on the porch, enjoying the creak of the ice in the trees, and she nodded at the cage on the steps next to me, big ol' grin. It was the first time I'd seen her smile, and I wasn't sure I liked it. The mystery animal's mewling was still going strong, even more monkey-like than before, but sometimes throttling down to an oily churr.

"What'd you catch?" she asked.

"A sewer rat!" I said, swinging the cage behind my leg as I got up to escape to the other side of our building. "I mean sewer 'cat.' I think it's trying to communicate."

"Funny thing about cats," she said, slowing way down to look but still walking. "Scientists say they don't meow to each other, to dogs, to mice, to nobody but us. So it's talking only to you!"

"Well, it hasn't really officially 'meowed' yet? Not sure what it's doing, to tell you the truth. It's been pretty patient, all things considered," I said, then I frowned. "So are you saying if you wake a cat up during a nightmare, you might get to hear its *real* voice before it switches back to meows?"

"Huh?" she said, shaking her head and stopping. She walked over to get close to the cage. "Aw, see? He's just biding his time till he's got somethin' to say. You're a patient little one, ain't ya . . . whatever you are."

Then she leaned over to me, locking eyes for the first time in our co-dependent relationship of her smashing only my most important packages. The bottoms halves of my fighting glasses steamed up, like they always did when I got nervous.

"One time, I had a cat that was dying," she said. "It went out the back door and I figured it was leaving to die. I didn't mind because I don't have a lot of money to put one down. Can't shoot it, and I'd rather do anal than be guilted by some capitalist vet. So it went away to die, then came back in two weeks later. *Fell* back in rather, like it had been in a refugee camp. I think it might have gotten locked in a shed. I loved on it until it died. Good kitty."

She blinked at the sun and shifted the weight of her mail bag before she walked on, and right then I knew I'd be keeping the creature.

So I took the "cat" and the rat cage around the back of our building to the basement steps. I'm not sure why I didn't just take it upstairs into the apartment, but I was feeling sneaky after smashing Ramsey's shed door and getting such an odd confession from my crazy lady mailman. I just figured I'd make sure the goofy little abomination had food and water, then try calling Ramsey's Red Planet again. The least I could do was inching towards "most." But our basement was a good place to lay low with any stolen mystery animals, all unfinished apartments and storage stalls. When we first moved in, one of the landlords had bullshitted us about the basement, weirdly proud that the stalls down there were "former slave quarters," as if people still had slaves in 1967, when the place was built. Actually, maybe they did in Kentucky. But the only ancient artifact I'd ever recovered down there was a tiny novelty camera keychain where you could click through sexy pictures of women. Remember those from the Civil War? Yeah, me neither.

I put the cage down in the middle of the only basement room with a door still attached, then closed it and stepped back to see what I was dealing with. I know I keep going on about this damn cage, but I'm not kidding about it being terrifying. Rusty, long as hell, and built like a brick shit house. I was pretty sure they caught baby Bigfoots in cages like this. Cat things, though? Seemed like overkill. I gave him the once-over and thought maybe it was one of those dime-a-dozen, pointy, grayish, blackish, brackish creatures? Sort of halfway between a kitten and the "Sumatran Rat-Monkey" from Peter Jackson's *Braindead*, but more like the ultimate representation of those awkward teen years you see in most newborn animals, where the head looks like a concussion and doesn't quite match the proportions of the body just yet. And the greasy fur wasn't helping it win any awards, either. Hunger or lack of ambition had stunted its growth to make it look as odd as those "goat sucker" hoaxes. Every time an angular, starving canine busted down a chicken coop, some idiot thought it was a demon. Maybe this was the source of those myths. I struggled with the gate on the cage to let it out, and it hissed and mewled louder, then stopped and blinked at me when I finally shook the rusty side hatch all the way open. The cat thing wouldn't come out at first, so I pulled out the cold tuna hockey puck from the corner of the cage and tapped the top to try and loosen up the food. But the Martian must have hosed the cage at some point, which froze everything up in zero point two seconds on a cold snap like today. No wonder the cat thing was freaking out, tongue probably got stuck on that ice kibble. I tried coaxing it from the cage with tribal clicks and hums, but it just backed up against a corner, eyes flashing, nose searching. Feeling rejected, I tried shaking it out in a calm, soothing voice that probably sounded something like *Hellraiser* to its flattened ears. *Rounded* ears framed that pointed face, actually, and the mystery deepened. Cats didn't have round ears, did they? I lifted my fighting glasses and rubbed my eyes, trying to see if the tips had been chewed off by dogs or if the frostbite had bobbed 'em like a Doberman.

"You're free!" I roared. "Come on! I vow not to eat you!" Nothing. Couldn't blame it.

Fine, stay in there then, dummy.

I wandered around the basement a while, to see if the creature would get bolder. On the wall in the next unfinished room, right around knee level, I saw a makeshift shelf crafted from a piece of cardboard and two coat hangers punched through its ends and anchored with a bent screw. A pile of papers were stacked high on the shelf, spilling onto the floor beneath it. At first, I thought it was junk from the painters that accidentally sealed all our windowsills shut the month prior. But looking closer, I noticed Angie's name on some mail. Then my own name. Then I found the birthday card I'd accused my sister of never sending.

What the fuck . . .

I rifled through coupons, junk mail, change of address forms, more junk mail, and some of those fake rebate checks. Then, on the floor underneath the shelf, I found a heap of receipts for Planters Peanuts stacked nice and neat, at least a hundred of them, all for just 99 cents each. This display of apparent mental illness suddenly made a light bulb go off in my brain. This was a bum stash I was dealing with. There must have been a homeless person hiding out in our basement for a long time. But for how long exactly? I mean, who makes identical 99-cent peanut purchases, but also keeps records? Of course, peanuts were a superfood, and the smartest bums probably knew this. If anything could keep a homeless person alive in your basement indefinitely on the cheap, it was fuckin' peanuts. Doing the quick math in my head ("If my sister sent me five bucks in that birthday card, that was five bags of peanuts he owed me . . . "), I started making this guy twice as homeless as I kicked through his belongings all over the floor. Deep in the receipts, I saw some color and unearthed some toys: a tiny gold camera keychain—which I knew had seedy porn from a bygone era on it without even clicking—half an alligator-shaped comb, and a doll's broken mirror with a dinosaur sticker on the back. Underneath all this was a brown postal mailer filled with more cards, junk mail, and bills, some opened and some sealed. Our address was on almost everything. I guessed the homeless person was saving the sealed ones to pass the time down there, like Tom Hanks did with that last FedEx box in *Cast Away*, but staring at the stash, it started to feel more and more like a violation. The cat thing rattled around its cage in the other room, and I took out my car keys and clipped the tiny gold camera onto it, then I stuffed all the paper I could gather into the mailer. I took this back over to the rat room and stuffed the mailer through the bars of the cage, reminding myself to sift more closely through everything later when Angie got home. She was probably missing a bunch of stuff, not just birthday cards, as she got way more mail than me.

She'd never get the chance, of course.

The mailer finally inspired the thing to creep out of the cage completely and sniff around the room. I watched it explore the corners for a few minutes, thinking about words like "Cat-Adjacent." It ran past my feet then flipped over onto its back and looked up at me, pupils dilated. This flounce revealed a furry peen with a tangle of wet fur on the tip. At least I'd determined the sex. Then it shook its hips at me playfully, and, embarrassed for it, I went back outside to the porch to call Ramsey one last time to see if this was his lost pet or if he was using Kentucky bushmeat for Martian pies.

"Yes, I put out the trap!" Ramsey told me over the phone.

Turned out the owner's name really was "Ramsey." I didn't know if this was a first name, last name, or both, or if he really was from a red planet, but he was understandably offended by my insinuations.

"I treat all animals with kindness!" he said, apparently trying to sound as sketchy as possible.

"This is a serious-looking trap, man," I said. "You ever heard Van Halen's *1984*?" Nothing. "So this little guy is *not* your . . . cat then?"

"There are many strays, yes," he said cryptically, and I caught a bit of an Eastern European accent. Less Martian, more Asian? I could only pinpoint accents when Americans screwed them up in movies, but I was considering how offensive it might be to come out and accuse this guy of eating cats, especially since he already seemed to be way ahead of me.

"Listen, I take care of these animals," he said. "We have a farm in Bullitt County. We have many, many creatures, and they are happy."

"Oh, *Bullet* County, you say? Could you pick a scarier name? Christ, where's this farm exactly? North of Necropolis, just outside of Scream Town?"

"If you can find the cat a home, fine," Ramsey sighed. "But I want my trap back."

"Are you sure you're catching cats? I mean, what's the deal with this trap? How many cats has this monster snared?"

"What do you mean? I've caught many strays. It is a very humane trap."

"You know what? You sound like you love this trap. That's kinda weird. I bet you have a name for this trap, but not for any cats. Am I right?"

"I catch them to save them," he said, losing patience. "My farm is a sanctuary. You act like I'm making them serve time!"

Oh, shit, there was that phrase again. I was already sick of it, but I'd still hear it one more time before the day was over.

"More like you serve them for lunch! Boom!" I laughed,

immediately regretting it. Now the cat was out of the bag, so to speak, and I swear I could feel the phone getting red hot in my hand.

"How dare you . . . "

I hung up on Ramsey and went back down to the basement to watch my new cat thing grunt and wheeze like an ape as it paced the perimeter. No way I was giving that trap back now. I flipped my phone around in my hand, feeling guilty, worried it was going to start vibrating any second. Good thing I'd star-sixty-sevened that shit. Always did. Mostly out of instinct.

Ha! Fuck you, Red Planet, can't catch me. Wait, was it supposed to be star sixty-nine?

"No, star sixty-nine is when you accidentally sweet-talk into your receiver upside down," I told the beast. "Get it?"

It blinked again at the sound of my voice, seemingly affectionately, and I watched my new cat thing for a couple hours down there, listening to its howling slowly morph into happier, grunt-like vocalizations. It wandered back into its cage eventually, moving low like a gut-shot dog, then it just licked the frozen food, content. I grabbed the handle to spin the cage around, and its back paws gripped the bars under it like a little convict. It seemed to have thumbs?

Grandpa always said that the only thing worse than a cat with thumbs was a shark with thumbs, and never pick either one up hitchhiking.

I looked at its tiny hands, realizing that even with the gate open, even if I shook it like a toy at the bottom of a Cracker Jack box, it wouldn't come back out any time soon. So I sat with my back to the cold wall, and I thought about what Angie was gonna say that night when she got home. I must have dozed off because it was dark when I opened my eyes.

I didn't realize it then, but at that very moment, while I was killing time curled up in the corner of that dank basement, Angie was dying.

Or maybe she was still being abducted. The timeline is a

bit fuzzy because the Louisville Police Department still hadn't had the requisite thirty years of thumb-twiddling and nose-picking for the case to solve itself. All anyone knew for sure was that she was probably distracted by our phone calls as she walked down the street that day. So the only thing there was no denying, the one thing everyone, including myself, would later agree on 100% without question, was that I was the one to blame.

III

RED CAR SYNDROME

I GOT THE teaching job at Elizabethtown Community and Technical College because it was the first thing I applied for when we moved down here. Angie was in the doctorate program at U of L, studying the emergence of Junior High Schools in Kentucky, before she got into that weird prison stuff, and I was closed-captioning reality shows in Pittsburgh in my first of many nerve-wracking, dead-end careers. Her work seemed more important than mine, so I quit my thankless task of filling in the blanks between clever fakery and utter bullshit with the closest textual approximation, and I followed her South instead. She'd told me about her dissertation project any time we were in a car for long periods of time, so I got a double earful during that long-distance phase. I tended to creep up the volume on the radio when I heard too many words I didn't understand, and I'd regret that later. But then again, I regret everything. But I do remember she was fascinated by Zimbardo's original Stanford Prison Experiment, just like everyone else who's ever heard about it. One day, she asked if I was ready for a "big twist," then went on to say she'd uncovered proof that Zimbardo's fake prison was populated with real prisoners after all, only they were pretending to be the guards, and this is why they were so violent. She was also onto something very strange that she'd discovered going on in a town called Brickwood, Ohio, which was real close to the Kentucky border (according to the internet, not any Kentuckians). I knew her obsessions had a lot to do with her brother, a former prison guard who was killed on duty when she was just a kid.

"Brickwood? Man, babies have to be born with blue collars in a town with a rugged name like that!" I joked.

"You mean iron deficiencies?" She nodded. "Babies born with blue-hued necks due to malnutrition in a real thing."

"You're the worst."

"We're all the worst, and I'll tell you why . . . " Then she dove back into her impenetrable thesis with the impossible title while my knee goosed the knob on the Journey power ballad "Stone in Love." I'd never understood the title of that song, either. She'd have called that an irony deficiency.

Brickwood was going to be our next road trip, once we saved up some more cash from my captioning job. She'd been there without me at least three times already, but she wanted us to make a little vacation out of it. And once we both got to Kentucky, and I had started teaching, she'd explain her research for hours on our new deck, planning the final investigative trip to Ohio with her head half in a bottle of wine, and I'd sit out there playing with a toy helicopter we'd gotten as a gag gift for our wedding. Sometimes I resented her drinking, since I never touched the stuff, guessing that eight drunk uncles in my family tree meant that alcohol was probably a time bomb for me. Maybe not a gateway to full-blown addiction, or the kind of ridiculous brawls I used to enjoy watching during family reunions where one uncle would hip-toss another through the charcoal grill, but I was convinced a couple beers would be a gateway to being an asshole in public, the kind of guy who was five seconds late on his jokes. Or worse, five seconds early. And any loss of control and I was convinced I'd be discovered as the fraud I was, with no place in academia or Angie's life. Angie said this was called Imposter Syndrome, but my personality meant that labeling one of my Top Ten Fears had the opposite effect of burying it.

So maybe there was some resentment when it came to her research, a defensiveness due to not understanding what the hell she was talking about. Sometimes I'd pick up her dissertation, but I could never bring myself to read it. I did help her gather up loose papers and pack them into her vintage Trapper Keeper, though, the one with Sonic the Hedgehog on the front. On the back was the actual cover of an 1823 all-girls high school "Memory Book" slipped into the plastic. This was a prize find from her Ohio research, one of those primeval scrapbooks that eventually morphed into the yearbooks we're familiar with today. As Angie explained, the fact that a student made something that reminds us of a yearbook is "proof that it was a recognizable genre by that point." And we were a recognizable couple. She even had random people sign the inside of her Trapper Keeper, too, to maintain the illusion. But mostly she just scribbled notes in there, or questions to herself like: "Do I still love him?"

Did she really talk about an invisible prison? I honestly couldn't remember if this was a metaphor or something stranger. It seems impossible now that something like that didn't grab my attention by the throat, but it's hard to recall when I first started realizing the implications of everything around me leading up to her death. Even though her dissertation was some heady shit, I *do* know I heard an "invisible prison" mentioned at one point. How would anybody forget that combination of words? I probably wrote it off as one of those insufferably cutesy thesis titles. So how could I know she'd been talking about a real, live, invisible friggin' prison? It's no excuse, but when I first got to Kentucky, I was busy teaching college freshmen commas and interrobangs and periods for the first time, *teaching* for the first time, period, and that had a lot to do with my indifference.

Not that I was a terrible teacher. Before they brought me

in at ECTC full-time, they gave me a trial run with five comp classes, so I was immediately off and running, cooking with meat, kicking back with a ragtag army of English 101 students, and also grading at least a hundred-and-twenty-five papers a month for low wages. All this effort for a school where the most important theoretical work we did was a social experiment they called The Graffitocalypse Project, a dumb fundraiser where local Elizabethtown kids scribbled colored chalk drawings on the sidewalks to draw attention to various humanitarian causes. It was mostly to get rid of all the colored chalk our Arts & Humanities Division had accumulated in our storage closet. They liked to pretend they were a real college, and that was hard with all the crayon drawings and cotton-ball snowmen along the hallway walls. When I got there, they'd just switched to dry-erase boards campus wide, so this renovation meant kids were much more likely to scrawl rude portraits of their teachers, since black marker was less alien to them than a dusty piece of chalk, and therefore much more likely to inspire amateur artists. It was rare that kids carried chalk on them past the Great Depression, so those old green blackboards were rarely sullied by any wannabe Picassos. But Magic Markers were everywhere, and permanent markers, which meant walking into a lot of surprise portraits of my raccoon-like beard and close-shorn, prison-ready noggin. In my teacher evaluations, one of the kids said I looked like a "cholo." Another said I looked like a "biker who listened to Journey." Little bastard was half right. Maybe two-thirds right. I owned the *Vision Quest* soundtrack on tape, and I may have ridden a unicycle more than once.

But there's this trick to getting rid of permanent marker on a dry-erase board that none of the kids knew about. You just outline over it with an erasable one and *presto!* The permanent one comes right off with it, no joke. This was very handy when I'd get a "Mr. James" and an arrow pointing at some snarling, pointy-headed, double-dicked hellbeast every morning.

Inspired by my students' unprompted handiwork, I finally participated in their yearly Graffitocalypse, as part of my crucial "external service" promotional requirement, but I couldn't help but draw the same bullshit monster I'd been doodling since Junior High. It was this one-eyed critter, sort of a reptile, but also sort of a cricket? Probably more cat that cricket, as some requisite whiskers and divided eyes were always added as comfort food after the fact. And I later realized that this cricket/cat combo was not entirely unlike the drawings my students would eventually do of me, which gave me that ol' existential "chicken or the egg" crisis as I'd stare for hours at my students' passive-aggressive anthropomorphic but insectoid felines, brainstorming how to use this unsolicited artwork to fill the internal service requirement for my job, and also wondering if the name of this duty implied surgery. Because I was ready to try, with or without anesthesia.

Nobody was trying to Save the Crickets at the fundraisers, though. There was a lot of head-scratching as people walked over my Graffitocalypse drawing, smearing it with their tennis shoes. In fact, most people in E-town had a deep-seated, irrational hatred for crickets, as well as outsiders, and for good reason. The two previous summers, farmers in the nearby counties had been dealing with a massive locust problem right out of the Book of Revelation. The next year, we guessed we'd probably be drawing chalk outlines of the Four Horsemen instead, or the nine of us Arts & Humanities professors who still showed up for stuff like that. So that would be 36 horsemen? I shoulda taught math.

But Graffitocalypse was always a big hit, and in a weird way, it validated my terrible job. Right up until those kids got into a fist fight over a chalk drawing of the Confederate flag. My colleagues were disappointed I broke it up so fast, and one of the tough guys from the automotive school muttered the strangest insult on our way to our cars.

"People hit people, Dave. And other people write about it."

Huh?

But I was too busy separating feral children to explain to this guy that even though I'd never punched anybody in the face in Kentucky, at this point in the story anyway, I *had* done this in every town I'd previously lived. Who'd have guessed this carried so much weight down South. I should have put it on my CV and I would have skipped the probationary period and sailed right into that Associate Professor slot.

Okay, maybe I haven't punched someone in the face in every single town I've lived in, but definitely in every state. Top that! Of course, I'd only lived in three other states up to that point—Ohio, Michigan, and Pennsylvania. I should have figured heading down South was a sure-fire recipe for more of the nonsense I was trying to leave behind. But it was weird. The more likely the locals were to start brawling, the less likely it occurred to me to join in. Maybe there was a mysterious formula at play that I wasn't aware of. Humidity combined with residual stress levels from a decade of cubicle work? But because she moved to Louisville six months before I could get down there, I'd started remembering my old captioning job through rose-colored glasses, or at least rose-color fighting glasses? I missed that horrible job, you see, and, in some ways, the toughest six months when we were forced to make do with a long-distance version of our relationship.

And Cube Land was sweaty for the wrong reasons, as I mostly spent time transcribing tons of true-crime stuff, like *The First 48* (unfortunately *not* a prequel to the Nick Nolte/Eddie Murphy masterpiece, and "Another movie without a realistic prison!" Angie would complain). Telling her over the phone about all the murders I was transcribing seemed interesting and important, like I was actually playing detective. This made any fist fights I'd get into on the weekend while I was still alone in Pittsburgh seem like the most natural thing in the world. Beatings were just part of the beat! And I told myself it didn't matter, that once I got down there to Kentucky and started teaching, I would automatically become respectable, just like her.

Another thing I remember about those phone calls was how quickly I was realizing that Louisville, Kentucky, was actually the murder capital of the world. Forget the imaginary Santa Carla in *The Lost Boys*. Louisville was genuinely dangerous. No, I know what you're thinking, and this was not a case of "Red Car Syndrome" or whatever they call it, where you caption a crime show with a red car, and then you start seeing red cars everywhere. Although a variation of that did happen when we hit Kentucky. But down there they called that affliction "Confederate Flag Syndrome" instead.

No, this is absolutely true about Louisville, at least according to the high-water mark of crime shows, *Forensic Files*, a show with the most soothing, easy-to-caption narration of all time, a show my co-workers and I used to fight over. It was the perfect length: 20 minutes long without commercials. So I could work on three times as many programs in a day, which was how we got our Beats by Dre headphones bonuses. And this show knew how to get shit done! It got in. It got out. Crime solved. None of that "Ten Years Later" bullshit on the screen like in *Cold Case Files*. It made you fantasize you really were on those investigations, and it kept you paranoid about your neighbors or your wife on every drive home.

One night, I captioned five of those shows in a row, always where some young woman was murdered while out jogging or just walking and minding her own business, or checking the mail not ten feet away, many of them distracted by the cell phones pressed to their heads, with the jealous husbands or boyfriends or whoever on the other line checking up. So, yeah, I got so paranoid that I would make Angie call me every time she left her house down there in Killer Kentucky. Me stuck up there in Pittsburgh, starting to flip out in spite of the obvious fact that this was *exactly* what I shouldn't be doing, and that she would, of course, be on the phone with me because of my paranoid phone calls and not aware of her surroundings and maybe walk into traffic or worse . . .

This, as you now know, is what they call a self-fulfilling prophecy.

But back then, not checking up on her seemed impossible. Not after doing five episodes of *Forensic Files*. Not after watching local cops bungle the investigation and give terrible, incoherent interviews, not after I transcribed interviews with loved ones left behind who, if they'd have just done one thing different, could have altered the course of events that day so they didn't end with a young woman reduced to a couple charred teeth fragments in some psycho's burn barrel.

I can say it now without hesitation. Closed-captioning crime shows drove me so insane with worry that, even if they're not responsible for my wife's death, they're definitely responsible for me punching people in the face in Pittsburgh. In another three months, I could have moved to Louisville and finally broke the streak. But that previous punch was an unrelated incident. Well, there was a red car involved, and an ex-girlfriend, and some cattails. But it's a totally different story really. I was a different person. I doubt it will come up later at all.

But five years in Kentucky, around all these Confederate flags and good ol' boys, and I never threw a single punch? Impossible. So I was as amazed as the weekend warrior from the automotive school when he shamed me in that parking lot, to be honest. But, you know what, I *did* get fired from ECTC over Confederate flags, so maybe that counts too. This was months after Graffitocalypse and the previous flag incident, which would be quite a coincidence if flag incidents weren't as common as mosquitoes in Derby Town USA.

Got a minute to hear how my teaching career finally came crashing down? There's just a ton of silent driving at the beginning of my road trip, anyway.

Okay, this particular fiasco happened in class, where we were putting on a play as part of our Emergency Sensitivity Training, after the Provost counted nineteen (!) rebel flags scrawled in chalk on campus sidewalks. Three were those goofy "Don't Tread On Me" jobs, and, sure, one of the nineteen might have been a Union Jack, but do *not* give the little dipshits credit for pairing their beloved Stars and Bars knock-offs with their British inspiration because, in all likelihood, they couldn't tell what they were looking at on their dad's sweat-stained shredded baseball caps anyway. But this play I got fired for, my "One-Act Dramatic Work Detailing Confederate Flags and Misdirected Anger," presented by the students of Dave's English 101: Writing Good Arguments, went something like this:

Two boys are standing in front of a mirror (actually the word "mirror" is written on the dry-erase board next to a winged-and-horned sketch of myself). One of the boys is depressed. T-shirts are strewn everywhere.

"What's the matter, Billy!" asks "Joey," a 45-year-old nontraditional student who talked enough in class for the rest of them put together.

"I just want to wear my favorite shirt, Joey, but I can't!" says "Billy," the kid sitting next to the kid who always wore a rebel flag to class and seems as annoyed with this as myself (he wrote most of this dialogue, but that didn't carry any weight with my Division Chair, the Provost, and the President, at what they called my "Come to Jesus" meeting when they asked for my resignation).

"What shirt is that?" asks Joey.

"The one with the kitten on it," says Billy.

"Why can't you wear it?"

"Because there are a ton of people out there who wear this exact same shirt and say horrible racist stuff all the time. But this kitten represents cute stuff and, like, freedom. What's that got to do with racism?"

"Ya got me, Billy. You make a good case, so maybe those guys are confused. But a lot of horrible people sure love that kitten. I Googled 'kitten' once, and holy shit you're outnumbered! And a lot of crimes against humanity were committed in the name of that particular kitten, so maybe you shouldn't wear it? I sure wouldn't want to wear a shirt like that if so many people think that kitten means something else. Don't you have any other shirts? Holy fuck you've got 50 other kitten shirts here, which is weird enough! How about this one . . . "

"Argh! It makes me so mad."

"Who are you mad at!"

"I'm mad at you!"

"Why me, dude!"

"Because you don't understand what my kitten means!"

Curtain. Well, we didn't have a curtain, so I just had five students drop the blinds at the same time to make the room a little darker. It was no Homer, sure, but applause filled the halls, and the sneaky English Department Coordinator, who was always slinking outside my door listening for a reason to bounce my ass out, clicked "stop" on her digital recorder and sealed my fate. I can't prove any of this, but I sort of put it all together later. And I'm pretty sure she owned a Confederate hat of her own, just to be cute, just to be a scamp. She was one of those. You know how these days people are a little smarter about that stuff and preface things by saying "This is gonna sound racist how I'm gonna say, 'This is gonna sound racist,' but . . . "? Yeah, that was her.

I also got kind of lit at a work party at one point and started saying how stupid it looked, and how if you're gonna be a "rebel" how about a design that doesn't look like you're sucking royal cocks. "Meet Union Jack's little cousin, Union Jerk-off!" I may have yelled. Not the best idea in Kentucky, but I wanted to continue to indulge in the irony that I was too old and set in my ways to ever change my feelings about the Confederate flag. And it gave me something interesting to talk to Angie about when we got home. She called all this flag stuff "semiotic situations."

Hold on. Hard truth time. That stuff about the play was slightly exaggerated, and I know that was mighty white of me, but red flags are important later, mostly how I never used to notice them, and the *real* reason I was fired may or may not have been for having our classes perform racially charged versions of *Three Little Pigs*. There's still some debate about which performance got me canned. But that one was all Angie's fault. And, if something had to be the last straw, wouldn't a story about the *Three Little Pigs* make the most sense? I got the idea from her dissertation. Well, from *not* reading her dissertation when I had the chance and I was just staring into Sonic the Hedgehog's eyes on the back cover of the folder like some numb nut, until all his shiny gold rings morphed into infinity signs. Semiotic situation indeed!

Most of that doesn't matter, but it was always a great topic of conversation for us, and about the only time her descriptions of her dissertation were crystal clear. There was this formula down south, she'd say. Racial tension plus escalation times denial equals a demand for law enforcement accountability. Ergo body cameras. Something like that. The seething anger in that town that radiated off our TV every night (as well as from our students' essays) was so hot you could probably roast marshmallows a foot from the screen. But the real point buried in all this is a bit simpler, and it's one we already know:

All these problems were because of me. And this legacy would continue. I wasn't a good teacher, and an even worse closed-captioner, and I paid lip service to a partnership. But those mistakes were nothing compared to the new levels of incompetence I would soon bring to my imaginary detective career.

***

When I first put the thing in the car, it finally stopped chattering, and even came out of the cage for a bit to explore the back seats and sniff the windows. I guess it thought of the car as its new cage, because it would be the better part of a year before it even touched the ground again. No joke. The cat thing would end up living more comfortably than me in that Rabbit, just like all the happy summer spiders that would rappel down from the sun visors and freak Angie out. And although the cat thing still maintained the mystery regarding its identity, it allowed a bit of domestication nonetheless, even if I wasn't quite ready to fully acclimate to the idea of "it" being a "him" (which still seemed too intimate, at least for the first fifty miles or so). But it had everything it could ever want in there: litter box, food, water dish, and a magical fuzzy world of floor mats just under its feet that hummed and purred and rocked it to sleep some nights as effectively as any mother. My car wasn't too much bigger than the cage anyway, so it honestly seemed content to exist in this box within a box for as long as I was there next to it. I could even leave the windows open, and it would show no inclination to escape. Maybe it was the nature of how I found it? Maybe it was used to incarceration? Or maybe our glorious first day on the road, when it licked my hands clean of the anemic blood of terrible street musicians, still lingered in the pleasure centers of its brain. We both subsisted on the memory of such nourishment for quite some time.

So our new home was a 1980 Volkswagen Rabbit, first-generation, three-door hatchback version. Diesel. So hollow it felt like you were bouncing around a coconut. It was red now, but it used to be yellow, and allegedly "white" before that. The red paint job looked dusty and bad, but it was cheap, and anything was better than a white car, even if, statistically, red cars got pulled over far more often. They say you start seeing red cars everywhere once you own one (or if one cuts you off), but that's nothing compared to the white cars. I'd never even thought about owning a white car before my stepdad offered to help with the down payment on a new ride when my green Cavalier's transmission took a shit on all those Pittsburgh hills. And since he was financing, he insisted I go white. Because they "hide dirt" or something. I'd always heard that black cars did that, but he said, "Nope, my granddad was half Apache, and he said black cars show dirt the worst." All this sounded way too racially charged for me, and sometimes I thought he was trying to compete with my real dad, and a childhood growing up with a genuine Native-American next door. But mostly I think he was just resentful of his role as a reluctant member of our lingering support group of angry men left behind by my mother. But paint jobs aside, my stepdad was always doubly horrified by the unassuming size of the green Chevy ("You look like George Jetson in that thing!"), so the color turned out to be the least of my worries. With all his bluster, I was afraid bringing him along to a used-car lot would mean I'd drive out in an aircraft carrier, blazing white, of course. But something about the Rabbit spoke to both of us, and I was relieved to drive it off the lot without him.

After one day, it looked dirty as fuck. My stepdad was disgusted. He said my car looked like something an elephant would use to wipe its ass, and he forever prohibited me from parking it in his driveway. Which sounds totally like a fable, right? An elephant using a rabbit to wipe its ass? Then some sort of lesson learned? Either way, the moral is always bet on the black car whenever possible.

So here I was, all these years later, driving outta town in a white supremacist Rabbit turned redskin, with a pointy-headed, round-eared little lab animal, two white circles along its sides, racing stripes on his head. I was already calling it "Purr Machine," even though "Zero" made a lot more sense because it still hadn't meowed or barked in my presence (but primarily because of the perfect circles on its belly). Then I changed the name to "Piss Machine" because it didn't get "car-broken" for the first couple days. Then the "it" changed to "he" for good because one time, when he was trying to spray the speedometer, I saw that nasty wet peen of his poking around until it plugged into the cigarette lighter. I almost had to drive us into oncoming traffic to erase the trauma. But once he was Rabbit-trained, things got easier. I could dump cat litter out at any red light, like some people still emptied their ashtrays, and we both agreed to stop fucking the dashboard.

Approaching the Kentucky line, I checked the messages

on my phone. Angie always paid the bills months in advance, so I'd have service for a while, even without a job (or future).

"You have to come home," the messages all said.

Well, not all of them. Some wanted to know exactly what happened to her. And if I was hiding anything. But I wasn't ready to talk about that yet.

Oddly enough, some of the messages were about an "exit interview," the kind of thing you do after you quit, not after you get fired. I guess the murder of my wife made them feel bad back in Elizabethtown because I didn't think they'd ever talk to me again after I had pushed "send" on my Statement of Teaching Philosophy. Did I already tell you how I got fired? Well, I lied. Actually, it was from bullshitting through an ill-fated promotion process, when Angie helped me come up with stuff that sounded official as hell. But at the same time, as a gag, she'd been secretly typing some *other* stuff I'd been saying, the real stuff. And this was the unfiltered file she emailed to me, giggling, after we were done. And "David James's Actual No Joke Statement of Teaching Philosophy" went something like this:

"I like to teach arguments. Arguing! I think we should argue. I'll fuckin' argue with you right now. I like to take an argument from a rant to a reasonable claim. Eliminate all the dumb shit their parents have told them, particularly their fathers. Have you looked into their dead eyes lately? Their dads are dangerous, and my wife's dad is the worst. So it's my job to shame these little fuckers into reading books. 'You don't read?' I say. 'That's like telling me you don't wipe your own ass. You ever hear the fable of the Elephant and the Rabbit? Don't be like them.' I totally say that shit in class. I am a teaching machine! But I like to force half of them to drop my class, and drop fast. Fewer papers to grade, and the quicker we free up those seats, the better. It takes the pressure off when I'm late. Now promote my ass, thanks, fucknuts!"

We got a good laugh, but I meant every word of it. In fact, I began to think it was a moral obligation to mentally kneecap the little tyrants that surrounded me every day, to hinder their rise to power if I could. I mean, imagine if they were bullshitting their way through med school like I was bullshitting through E-town. It would be our duty to stop them. I even began to wonder, would I cage them all if I could?

But it must have been that self-fulfilling prophecy stuff again, because this was the teaching statement I sent to the promotion committee by mistake.

***

"Where are you going?!"

Me and my newly christened "Racing Stripe Piss Machine" (I'd be back to calling him "Zero" again in ten more miles after he almost choked himself out on the seat belt) were both muttering to ourselves about a mile from the state line when my sister started calling. Erin called a lot, even before all this shit, and though I never answered her calls, it was still twice as many calls as I'd never answer from anybody else. But she knew I was avoiding calls even more than usual, so she'd started texting, adding another question mark and exclamation point every time she re-sent an inquiry. Her previous record was seventy-two, but it already felt like she was on her way to breaking it. This is why my English classes weren't allowed to double up on question marks in their essays. It was more off-putting than an exclamation point. They *were* allowed one interrobang per semester, mostly because I loved those damn things. Plus I figured they should be rewarded for taking the time to copy and paste an obscure punctuation trend from the '70s instead of the usual swipes from Wikipedia. But my sister had found a loophole, with an interrobang tattooed to her shoulder, so those squiggles peppered through those underachieving essays and exasperated text messages would always remind me of her, especially when they *were* her, and surprise a smile out of me.

"Where are you going?!?!?"

Even the most sophisticated phones aren't interrobangenabled, so I turned my clamshell over to hide her messages before the punctuation circled the globe. The last time I'd seen my sister in person was when she drove down to join one of my classes on a field trip to the Kentucky Creation Museum to research non-persuasive arguments. She got us kicked out by climbing into an Early Man exhibit and beating her chest like a gorilla ("Evolution represent!"), but the way she looked at it, the Creation Museum owed her money. See, my sister actually designed the heads of the freaky animatronic cave people that made the museum famous. You know, the fuzzy robots feeding carrots to "pre-sin," and therefore vegetarian, dinosaurs? Erin had been trying to do something with her Chicago School of Art degree and instead found this much more lucrative job making rubber molds for the heads of some clockwork Early Men. She did this for all sorts of museums nationwide, and she told me that in order to keep herself amused, she'd modeled some of them after Orson Welles's own curiously simian skull—specifically the young Orson Welles seen in *Compulsion,* where he played Clarence Darrow, the guy from the original Scopes Monkey Trial, which made perfect sense if you knew her. Sometimes she mixed up those heads with what she called a Spencer Tracy/silverback gorilla hybrid, but she figured these trails of breadcrumbs weren't incriminating enough to get her in trouble because Spencer Tracy's version of the guy in *Inherit the Wind* (the lesser Monkey Trial movie) was named "Henry Drummond" instead of "Clarence Darrow," and actual research was like Kryptonite to a creationist. Of course, I probably shouldn't talk about science or research, since a few minutes of my own anatomical investigations might have revealed what kind of animal Zero was. Maybe I just didn't want to ruin the surprise when Zero finally had something important to say.

But it was still pretty hilarious thinking about how Creationist Kingshit Ken Hamm had no idea he'd paid my sister to plaster the faces of the most famous defenders of evolution onto every goddamn one of his creepy Adam and

Eve automatons. And that whole day at the Creation Museum was a blast. It was probably Kentucky's finest moment. Ours, too. Right up to the end when one of the security guards got on the red phone and had us surrounded. It was just bad timing that our expulsion occurred the same day that a certain right-wing Senator was touring the brand-new, full-scale Noah's Ark exhibit, and we ended up making the local news that evening as we were hustled out of the jungle and through the revolving doors. You'd think that kind of notoriety would have gotten me fired, because our English Department Chair actually believed in goofy shit like that. Okay, maybe that is why I got fired. I know it seems like I'm avoiding the topic, but I also keep bringing it up, don't I? Doesn't that show a willingness to confess? But do you really want to know why I got eighty-sixed from my first teaching gig, handicapping a career before it even got started? Isn't there a better mystery waiting in the wings where someone was killed instead of merely emotionally crippled?

To be honest, I'm sure all of those things had something to do with my unemployment, because it's really hard for me to accept the fact that I was likely canned for something as noble as having my class reenact a variation of the infamous Milgram Experiment, which I also did.

So, yeah, that was probably it. Meaning it was really my wife's fault because I'd heard Angie mention Stanley Milgram's obedience studies during one of her excitable "wine o'clock" dissertation marathons, but I'd misheard her so many times that I got a few key things wrong. And the next day in class, hard pressed for lecture content, we did something called the "Milligrams Experiment" instead, as in "ten milligrams of cinnamon," and I coerced my students to snort some. I didn't realize at the time that the peer pressure inherent in our activity was in the spirit of Milgram's original tests after all, where students gleefully administered electrical shocks to each other as long as an authority figure endorsed it. But I also didn't realize cinnamon could be so traumatic.

Don't fuck with cinnamon, kids! Several students ran into the halls, eyes running, brown smoke billowing from their nostrils like little Smaugs. Someone even pulled a fire alarm.

But if it's starting to sound to you like I'm tossing out excuses as a smokescreen for my own failures, well, you might be onto something. But I was sorry for them all. It was just a lot easier to blame rebel flags and assholes riding dinosaurs and kids snorting cinnamon like dragons (a creature Creationists don't distinguish from dinosaurs by the way) than it was to blame my wife.

She was so sure I couldn't be worthless at both teaching and learning, but I was always surprising her, right until the end.

***

As I drove on, with Zero sniffing at the insect buzz of my phone and watching it hop like popcorn in the passenger's seat creases, I thought about what that surly mailman lady had said about cats only meowing for human beings. Unprovoked, this damned thing chattered like a monkey, and watching him watch the phone, his head was low like most felines, but I'd yet to hear anything resembling a meow, or, at the very least, a reasonable question. Like where were we going? I was starting to resent the lack of trust.

So I unsnapped the Trapper Keeper, trying to ignore her question on the inside cover (*"Do you still love him?"* Wait, didn't that say "I" before?), and I rifled through page after page of Angie's dissertation with it balanced on my steering wheel, probably not the safest way to drive. Even without a cat thing chasing after the intoxicating rattle of important papers. But I was on a mission. I didn't know how much time I'd have to aimlessly drive around this country until I found some satisfying way to punish myself, or anyone else, for the death of my wife.

As we drove, I searched the text for any mention of the Invisible Prison. The bulk of it was Angie's thesis, cleverly titled *Walls, Of (Dis)course and the Panopti-Con: The Problems of*

Self-Discipline in the 19th Century Extracurriculum, a.k.a. The Man-opticon, and in her opening chapters, she argued that the urge for voluntary self-confinement by some students was inevitable, and maybe not without its benefits. She wrote, "Even outside institutional barriers, they will recreate their own walls, of course, walls of internment, walls of discourse, walls, walls, and more walls . . . "

Whenever we talked about her book around the house, we just called it *Walls*.

Hold on. Self-confinement of students? What the what?

The translation of all this heady material, as well as the return of her voice on the page, would probably be pretty rough going in normal circumstances. But my concentration also had to contend with fresh memories of her on our back deck saying exactly these sorts of provocative claims, squeezing the last of the box wine out like it was toothpaste, explaining out loud with those big green eyes of hers how kids in some mysterious Midwestern school might be locking each other up for fun. I couldn't believe I never asked her if this was something kids used to do, or if it was something they were doing now. But coherent memories were even harder to decipher than her prose at eighty miles an hour.

Over the years, I had skimmed her dissertation once or twice, even nodded along with some degree of confidence, but I'd promised her I'd really *read it* read it one day. So this was the day I was going to read it. I mean, she'd read every word I ever asked her to, even if it was something I'd pissed in the snow, but I'd put off her life's work every chance I got, even as I watched her interest in my own words, urine or otherwise, begin to slowly drift away.

I'd be lying if I said some part of me wasn't relieved I'd never had to complete this homework. And I didn't think it was fair to call this a broken promise if she died before I could have gotten around to it. But maybe because I was technically off the hook, I decided that reading my wife's dissertation and understanding everything it contained would be the thing I'd do before I did another thing in this world. Then I'd complete her research. And I'd find that town with the library she loved, Brickwood, Ohio. We'd do it all.

I drove on. And when one of those earnest Indigo Girls songs she loved so much came on the radio, I turned it up until it crackled, just like her driver's-seat singing would crack after a couple beers. I looked at the last hills of Kentucky I was leaving behind, vowing never to return, but still desperate for one last glimpse of a goldenrod, the state flower. It was late in the season for that kinda thing, but there were other landmarks. Like the roadside crosses, which were always in bloom.

A crucifix is a perennial, I thought. Angie would have laughed at that, back when she still loved me. She used to steal a kiss every time we passed one.

IV

CAPTAIN MUSHFAKE AND THE BODY CAM CRUCIFIXIONS

ALL MY LIFE, I've been convinced that describing your dream was the most torturous experience for all involved. Otherwise I'd tell you all about my nightmare with the aquariums and the lizards I forget to feed and all those tails hanging out of each other's mouths. But no one wants to hear that shit, and for good reason. So I've vowed to leave out the dream sequences. That means if someone explodes into insects mid-punch and then fist-fucks a motorcycle, or if I'm miraculously getting the upper hand and the fight sounds more like a movie than real life, feel free to ignore everything that preceded it. I just don't want to start lying yet, since things get weird enough without any embellishment. And dreams are always lies.

But the only thing worse than describing a dream is describing a fight.

So this is exactly how the crazy road trip started, with the first leg of my exodus being, predictably enough, a soothingly regular, unswerving route. Certainly more linear than the journey ended up. Unfortunately, dead-ends always had the comfort of being the logical conclusion to any straight line.

I was rolling toward Brickwood, somewhere between

Cincinnati and Chilo, according to Angie's notes. It was hot for October, and the sun was threatening to come back before I could get up to speed and cool Zero and myself down, but I was stuck in some construction and trying in vain to pass a red Chevy C10 pickup with a dirty white top that was rattling in front of me like an empty boxcar. For miles, I worked to put Kentucky behind me, veering to avoid blown-out chunks of tire tread, thinking, *Goddamn, is that more exploded wheels than you normally see on the road?*

But as I got closer to this pickup, before the eyes in its rearview mirror noticed my car weaving back here trying to peek past them, I watched some guy in the truck bed toss out a beer can, quickly followed by strip after strip of jagged black rubber. He stopped throwing junk when we got bunched up real close by a gaggle of orange barrels, and we just sat there a minute. This guy bouncing in the bed was what we used to call in the Midwest a "stunted man," one of those smallish, white-trash dudes who never grew much bigger than a teenager, even at 50 years old. They were wiry with the muscles they built from fast-talking and bullshitting all their lives, deep creases around their mouths from sucking off strong authority figures, arms streaked with shitty tattoos, beards struggling to grow along their jaw lines, forever riding bikes or truck beds or motorcycle sidecars. He crouched there with his back against the window of the cab, glaring at me as he re-lit a cigarette, and it started to feel like I'd busted these guys doing something they shouldn't.

Totally out of character, I was nipping tequila from a flask, the same tequila that was still stewing in there from an ill-advised wedding toast years ago. Remember, I wasn't a drinker because of the eight drunk uncles, and I was even less of a "drink away your sorrows" kinda drinker, but I'd found the flask tucked down deep in my duck pocket so I figured "fuck it." I'd seen this post-tragedy strategy in movies, and this seemed like a good time as any to try. But when I was at my cousin's wedding last fall, my uncle (who'd just gotten bounced for his joke about the bridesmaids, and me along with him for laughing) gave me the flask and explained which alcohol was the best to drink while driving (I hadn't asked). Apparently, it was a myth that vodka didn't make your breath stink. Yes, vodka can be flavorless and odorless, but anything with alcohol will make you smell like bathroom garbage. But what supposedly *did* work was chomping on charcoal between swigs, and my uncle gave me a black smile to prove it. Turned out, I had a bag of charcoal under the seat that we'd never used up on our summer cookouts, so a couple red lights back, I started chomping. And it tasted terrible. Turned my tongue to ink. But I was so miserable it barely bothered me. Not much worse than the gasoline swigs of tequila, and this was as close as this widower was gonna get to wearing black. Also, I needed a vice, and my slick new black lizard tongue suited my repeatedly-broken nose, a feature my wife called my "thrice-baked potato." My nose looked better broken, however, in spite of it impeding my sense of taste, in food or movies. I never had much taste in anything else.

Traffic started moving again, and I hoped we'd find another red light soon so I could pass the pickup, maybe lean out to ask the hard questions. And I had a lot of questions. I mean, what if those tire strips I'd been seeing since I got my license weren't from 18-wheeler blowouts? But now that I thought about it while I limped along at five miles an hour, I couldn't remember seeing a truck tire ever actually *pop*. Not once. The opposite of the road skunks you always smelled but never saw. But then again, I did see dead dogs on the highway all the time, and I never noticed any mutts actually getting smoked either. Maybe stunted men were responsible for dumping all the dead dogs in the world, too? "There are worse jobs," they'd shrug. Then, after asking for money, "Hey, you like this tattoo? It's a bald eagle hatching the White House like a turd!"

Eventually, we slowed down enough for me to stretch my head out the window and hold their attention. But I'd already overthought everything leading up to the confrontation, so my questions made little sense to them.

"Hey, man, are you throwing dead dogs out on the roads, too?" I asked. "Or do you just collect all the skunks?"

He stared at me long enough for us both to feel stupid, then he bounced his cigarette butt off my hood with a splash of sparks. I brought my head back inside. A road sign screamed, "Chilo! Stay for our Yurts!"

What the fuck?

Another fifty orange barrels, and time was slowing even more. We were down to about two miles an hour tops. In a daze, I mistook the red glow of some emergency lights on the horizon for the sunrise. Another in a series of disappointments.

Once we were finally up on the accident, I realized by the halfhearted efforts of everyone involved that it must have been a bad one. It might seem like a contradiction, but first responders only moved slow when someone was dead. And since we'd already been whittled down to one-lane traffic, this accident meant we were all stopped cold now. I swear I even saw my odometer flutter backwards a mile. So I slammed more tequila, popped a corner of charcoal briquette, then got out to stretch my legs, leaving Zero to investigate the gas and the brake pedals in my absence.

The guy in the back of the C10 saw me step out and immediately hopped down and around and scurried into the cab with his buddy, either to duck my questions or to scrounge for another butt. So I walked past them to see how close I could get to the crash, maybe treat myself to something else unhealthy, maybe coax them out of the truck, maybe distract from my situation before I got to the state line and hit rock bottom all over again.

I'd be lying again if I said I wasn't dreaming about still being in Kentucky and regretting that vow I'd made to Angie about never punching anyone in the face in the Keystone State. But dreams weren't allowed. Vows either. I know what you're thinking. I'd already punched a bunch of idiots back in that alley, but beating up buskers didn't count, as they could barely be considered human. So I figured this might be my last chance to break that final promise, like she always knew I would.

Up on the accident site, it did not disappoint. It was more death all right, but it didn't involve me. I looked at the body, thinking:

That's the only time they leave you in the road like that, laid to bed forever across a bright yellow line while a dozen people mill around, trying not to stare. At least they're thoughtful enough to tuck you in with a heavy blanket!

She wasn't tucked in very well, though, because I could still see it was a young girl in an orange jumpsuit who was sprawled out on the asphalt. Judging by the length of the comet streaks of gore leading up to her tennis shoes, she'd been run over by something big. Not just clipped, but ground down. The fleece blanket (or "calamity comfort object," as one of my nursing students once called it in a term paper about the incompetence of most paramedics) was still mostly folded, and draped across her torso diagonal, haphazard like she'd just been in a beauty pageant, or lost one. But I could see there was no car crash at all really, at least no metal strewn around, besides the emergency vehicles. It was only the girl and her blanket on the road while time stood still. I glanced around for more details, saw some tire tracks but no tread, then spotted a big black garbage bag on the edge of the ditch. I peered off into the distance and I counted even more black bags all up and down the horizon. I realized I'd been driving past these garbage bags all day. But like the black-rubber tire chunks, the black bags were something I'd gotten used to seeing and filtered out, I guessed, like all the random road hazards and shadowy bullshit that was the natural fauna of any American highway.

In fact, you could line every road in this country with all sorts of horrible, mangled Sleeping Beauties like this one, and nothing would seem out of place for commuters, if they noticed it at all. Something about the sides of the roads were fair game for death, refuse, and ruin, and it seemed like even the Fifth Circle of Hell could break loose and dance for hours in those ditches before anyone turned their heads.

Wasn't that the circle with all the angry sinners? No, they were mostly just gurgling in the water in Circle Five. So more like the Seventh Circle, the one with the poets who get turned into trees and pissed on by dogs. Yes, that's it. One more lap around to make it count . . .

There has always been a comforting Americana, side-of-the-road vibe to the Seventh Circle of Hell.

I decided this was why I'd always been so obsessed over those rubber strips. Because they were in the *middle* of the road. This made them a legitimate problem. Drive long enough and people get understandably protective of their lanes. But *along* the road? You could have as much black rubber and as many dead dogs and wailing poets turned to shrubs fucking beneath giant billboards to warn you of impending damnation that they could pile up and touch the sky and then light it all up with a torch and nobody would notice unless the fire showed up in their rearview.

I looked back to the road behind my Rabbit to see if any cars were starting to stack up in the bottleneck. I was so close to the state line that I could smell it, like a concentrated essence of eleven million greasy bike chains and upper lips.

It was either too late or too early in this town for traffic outside of shitbags and solipsistic road-trippers, so I crept closer to the body to push my bad luck. I could see the girl more clearly now, the long, blonde hair, not unlike Angie's, flared out over the road like she was soaking up rays in a swimming pool and had just kicked away from the side and would never ever sink. I stopped moving forward, suddenly uninterested. I remembered when we'd first moved to the sweltering Bluegrass State, and Angie chopped off all her long blonde hair (me, I just went one notch closer on my clippers), then coiled her severed yellow horse tail up in a manilla envelope marked "Locks of Love," which somehow ended up pinned to an empty doorway in our home like a macabre mistletoe. That caused some confusion at parties.

I saw a cop noticing me for the first time and starting his purposeful March of the Authoritative Asshole straight towards me. I leaned against a mile marker and tried to look like I belonged there with the rest of the litter.

"What do you think you're doing there, boy?" the cop asked, barely containing his anger at a civilian showing interest in a scene that any living being would find riveting.

"Legs cramped up, man. Had to get out and stand up a second."

He just stared at me, mirrored glasses mercifully up and balancing on his head to make him have to blink, which was throwing him off his game.

"Nobody's going anywhere right now, you know?" I offered, always pushing a little. I couldn't help it.

"No, I mean what the hell do you think you're doing *there*?" He reached past me and slapped the mile marker next to us with the heel of his hand. I saw it wasn't a mile marker at all. It was another one of those roadside crosses, a homemade monument to mark the spot where a loved one died. *Truly the* least *someone could do!* I may have seen it for what it was a bit sooner, but the arm of the cross was loose and swinging. Of course, I probably should have realized mile markers didn't normally have teddy bears duct-taped to the bottom. I jumped back and straightened the smaller piece of wood to give it a powerful "The power of Christ compels you!" intersection again, and now I could read the name carved into the crucifix.

"Christy Briggs?" I read to the cop. "Check it out, 'Christy!' Like 'Jesus Christy'? Now what are the chances of that?"

"What do you mean?" the cop asked, and he put his hand over his heart. Well, near his heart, and I instantly recognized this move from the Three Stooges on my porch and knew he wasn't just covering his badge. He was getting ready to do something shitty and, hopefully, anonymous, but his badge number was still clearly visible etched into silver, peering out over his thumb. Number Five. I wasn't there yet, but I imagined Brickwood, Ohio, being so small they'd have a single-digit police force.

But he changed his mind about something, and his hand came down. Sunglasses, too, meaning any chance to have an actual conversation about the accident was probably gone.

"You know, like, 'Key-rice-tee'?" I went on. "Christy on the cross? Get it! Never mind."

"Get back in your car. And shitcan the attitude."

I smiled. He had no way to know this, but he'd just reminded me that, even if I loved it when people used the word "shitcan" as a verb (and I truly do), I was still holding out hope that I'd see an actual can of shit on the side of the road some day. Meaning it was probably time to get going.

"So, was she picking up trash or what?" I asked, not walking away yet. Push. Push. "Community service or whatever?"

The cop was almost up my nose after that question, conclusively proving the validity of my uncle's charcoal-munching cover-up once and for all. But I just kept thinking about miles of ditches, all filled with shitcans. Ditches just made more sense that way. I must have used that word a lot because my only friend in the English Department, a space cadet with the impossibly good-natured last name of "Goodfellow," once wrote this riddle on my inter-office birthday card:

"If your students can prove 'shitcan' is a verb, then my dog has proven 'pussy-foot' to be a noun."

"What's it to you, boy?" the cop grunted, snapping me out of it.

"The orange jumpsuit? The trash bags? Did someone swerve and hit her?"

"Go. Back to your car. Right now."

"Great! Thanks for your help, Number Five!" I said, backing up. "Since you got things under control, why don't you scrape her the fuck off the road so we can all be on our way? Or you guys wanna stand around another six years?"

I couldn't see his eyes behind the glasses, but his eyebrows and nostrils told me he was as surprised as I was by my outburst. I switched gears.

"Sorry, sorry, sorry," I said, putting up a hand and grinning. "I thought I knew her, so I walked over. Got my heart beating is all."

"Really? Who did you think she was?" He sounded interested now, like if he'd been a movie version of a cop, he'd be flipping over a fresh page in a tiny notebook. The hint of professionalism took me off guard, so I said the first name that jumped into my mind. He continued to step forward with every one of my steps back.

"Well, I thought it was Christy," I said.

"What?" The sunglasses came up again, eyebrows back down. His nostrils stopped flaring, too, like he was holding his breath.

So many emotions on those detachable features! Officer Potato Head up in this bitch . . .

"Wait here," he said finally, then he marched back into the mob of flashing lights and half-ass activity.

I looked up and down the highway for escape routes, saw my cat thing doing laps across my dashboard and headrests, then I watched the stunted men in the window of the pickup shaking their heads at me and gave them a grin, too. But the cop was back too fast, this time flanked by a man in a suit who had all sorts of tiny notebooks. I guess movies got that part right. He also had two wallets in his hand, one purple plastic, one weary black leather, sagging with the weight of badges and importance like a wise, ancient testicle. He reminded me of the insufferable senior faculty members at my previous job, the "dinosaurs" who refused to sign my letters of support. Or my birthday cards.

"Old balls hate young balls," Goodfellow always said.

"I heard you knew the deceased," the detective asked, somehow sounding both impatient and interested at the same time. A miracle of science, this guy. He clapped his badge shut, and I flinched, still thinking of it as balls.

"What? Who? Her? On the road? I was joking . . . "

He flipped open the purple wallet so I could see the license. It read: "Christy Briggs."

Jesus Christ on a cracker cross . . .

"Whoa, wait a second. So you're saying the girl on the highway, she has the same name . . . as this thing?"

Right as I pointed to the crucifix, another important guy in a suit stomped up and kicked at the base of it a few times to work the stick up and out of the ground. Once loose, he folded up the two pieces of wood, ripped free the teddy bear, then punted the toy into the weeds. It flew far, too, like teddy bears were always made to be punted. I imagined how satisfying it would be to kick a real, live shitcan down the road to the state line.

"There are approximately one hundred 'Briggses' in this town," the detective said. "That part was just a coincidence."

"That's a hell of a coincidence."

"I already said that. And what the hell is wrong with your tongue."

Oh, shit. Detectives doing some detectin'!

"I asked you a question, sir," said the other detective, the one who hadn't asked anything at all. Then the first one jumped back in.

"Did you know the deceased? Do you have some kind of I.D. on you right now?"

"Funny story," I said through my teeth, trying to keep my black tongue in the shadows. "I lost my license back in Kentucky. Not *lost it* lost it, but you know, *lost it.* I'm in the system though, just check my plates."

"Yeah, we did that."

I handed him one of my old driver's licenses, an expired one with a hole punched through the face.

"Get used to that," the detective laughed, fingering the hole. Then, "So, you're still in Kentucky."

Don't I know it, I thought.

The cop and the detective stared at me like they were waiting for me to solve it all, whatever it was, so I started bullshitting and fast-talking my way out of things. And even though I started off with one of those rhetorical topic-shifting "listens" that law enforcement loved like brothers, I felt myself shrinking with every word. I half-expected a long, lost stunted brother to drape an honorary rebel flag over my shoulders.

"Listen, I was only reading the name off the cross, just messing around. I didn't realize that was actually her name. But isn't that the freaky thing here? Doesn't that part interest you? Seriously. Here you have a memorial set up before the person was even killed. That's lunacy."

"Listen, don't get carried away here, sir. She was picking up garbage, yes. And maybe she lingered near this cross and let her guard down because she shared the name. But what I want to know from you is . . . how did you know her?"

"Jesus Christ," I said. "I didn't." I spit towards the crater in the stones where the cross had been.

"Listen! Show some respect!" the cop yelled. Then, cryptically and a bit quieter, "Crosses are everywhere."

I wanted to say, "Listen, how about you show some respect for that adorable fuzzy friend your buddy just kicked for a field goal," but he was walking off, and I was getting nervous and could feel myself treading water in that dangerous limbo where authority figures most certainly didn't want you to say another word, even to answer their questions. But after another few minutes, they'd loaded up the body in an ambulance, and the first cop came back to clear me.

"Listen, I want you to get the fuck out of here," Johnny Five the silver-eyed Supercop said, and I high-tailed it back to my bunny, and me and my not-quite-a-kitty were creeping through construction again before we caught a jackboot.

And he was right. Crosses were everywhere. Okay, maybe

it was the ol' Red Car Syndrome again, but I was seeing miles of those crosses and fluffy martyrs after he said that. Toys and flowers for the women and children killed on the road. Flags for the men. Just cross after cross. Usually first names on them, but some full names, too. Vaguely ethnic? Lot of females near the strip bars, of course, but overall mostly men, the white, stunted kind. And for a dash of color, the names of Dead Presidents sprinkled in between them.

"Stack Washington," "Bonita Jefferson," "Jerry Lee Lincoln," "Terry Lee Lewis," "'Runt' Allen," "Chris Morley," "Leticia Smith," another "Goodfellow," which will always seem like a bullshit name, kinda like "Jimmy 'Loved By' Millions." There was also a "Harlowe Thrombey," a "Kenny Thompson," "Somethingsomething Leonard." I even saw an "Our Beloved Joey," then a mile later, "My Beloved Quarry," and another mile after that, "Our Beloved Billy Charlie . . . " It seemed like hundreds. But the names all sounded fake, like maybe the road crews accidentally busted some crosses and had to mix and match during reassembly.

Have there always been this many?

And between every cross was a teddy bear that died for our sins, surrounded by black rubber shreds and bulging black bags as far as the eye could see.

***

Construction hung me up for so long that the engine got too hot to keep driving so slow. My Rabbit lurched and hopped along, cylinders knocking, and I stopped dreaming of getting back up to highway speeds any time soon. I'd sucked out the last drop of tequila from the flask, and Zero was hungry enough to start snipping at my head. Now that the sun was up, I figured some kind of chicken would satisfy us both. And between all those cock-eyed crosses and the tiny, invisible Kings of Kings getting martyred along the road, I finally found a bar with a real-live chicken painted on it, and it gave me high hopes for food, or at least the safety of a bar of chicken-hearted cowards? Who else puts a chicken on their wall? But as I stepped out, I heard a grown-ass man revving his motorcycle. Or making engine noises with his mouth, which is the same thing. And on the other side of the building was a sign that read, "We Welcome Soldiers and our Boys in Blue!" and I thought:

Wow, way to take a stand against the riff-raff. Is there a sign around back that reads, "We'll Never Turn Away Beloved Heroes"?

I went in anyway, remembering something a terrible teacher told me once in college. She said, "If you spend a day in a town, you can write a book about it. Spend a week and you can write a letter. Spend a year and you can't write jack. Unless Jack's in prison." What?

I'd been driving just a couple hours so far, but even this was starting to make sense. I left the mystery critter in the car, and my hunting jacket with the hidden duck pocket full of weapons, too. This turned out to be a tactical error, but maybe it saved my life.

Inside the bar, I sat down a little dizzy, mouth like the ashtray made of pesos that I was staring at. My lips dodged the black sandpaper of my tongue, and I considered giving up my new charcoal habit. I ordered my food, and the dripping bag of fried chicken came way too quick, and I contemplated making this complaint because of how funny it would sound out loud.

'Scuse me, this chicken came too quick. How about some foreplay next time?

The chicken was tough and stringy, like trying to eat an old man, but the meal gave me plenty to work on instead of cracking jokes. I needed all my concentration to masticate that shit, and I was only on my second finger, or "wing," when I saw who was having lunch right there next to me. My God, it was Johnny Five himself. Sans sunglasses but still in uniform. I dragged my stool and deep-fried octogenarian closer to him.

"Hi!" I said, cracking a barbecued knuckle and hoping it

was from the middle finger. I gave him a good-natured elbow in the shoulder. I'd heard different people grieve in different ways, and I was realizing my special way was a kind of fearlessness combined with already being a prick.

Johnny Five turned to look me over, bloodshot eyes straining like they were propped open with toothpicks. Up close and off the road, with the reflections and light bouncing off the bottles behind the bar, he was a more impressive sight, and I noticed he wasn't just wearing a shiny badge and a lot of black and blue. He was wearing a camera, as I'd anticipated. Of course he was. Even before I saw the cover-ups in action on my porch, Angie had told me all about those cameras, more times than I could count. Just the other day, she'd shown me an article about a test run of body-camera-wearing cops in New Orleans. The idea was to discourage corruption, but there was resistance on all sides.

"Are you recording us . . . " I started to ask, pointing my bone at the tiny one-eyed box pinned to his pocket. I swear I saw it blink.

He spun his bar stool and took a long swig of Coors Light (*nasty!*), then he sighed. He began to talk, and I don't know why, but I'd expected him to sound a little more human? Me catching him out in the wild and all. Impossibly, Number Five was even more of a machine, and he started to short circuit.

"When an individual or party is responsible for willful deception directed at or towards a second individual or party, the former is culpable," he said. "But when such deception is repeated subsequently, the latter is no longer excused of liability."

"What?" I laughed, chicken strings hanging from my teeth. I wished I'd been mid-drink so I could have given him a classic spit-take. His delivery had been hilariously stiff on the road during a crisis, but here in the bar, hypothetically relaxing, he was absolutely mashed potatoes. "Mushfaking" they called it, in prison lingo, and according to Angie's dissertation. In prison, a mushfaker cobbled together contraband out of any available material. But in schools, mostly around lit and discourse types like my wife, they had a much simpler definition. It just meant "faking it." Like I did at my teaching job. Like the kids did in the classrooms. It was like that lawyer-speak you'd hear from cops in court, chronic D students every one of them, as they floundered on the witness stand to describe very simple scenarios, tying their pink, unsullied tongues into knot after embarrassing knot.

I loved all the stuff I was learning lately from my wife's diary slash memory book slash Trapper Keeper, and I felt even worse about never reading it. But now it was some kind of medicine, helping me forget her and remember her all at once. I really can't explain it. Certainly not to a cop.

Mercifully, Captain Mushfake translated his oratory gruel for me.

"Fool me once, shame on me. Fool me twice, shame on . . . "

"Oh, oh, gotcha, right," I said, but what I mean was, "Please stop, dude." I looked back down at the black box and its glassy eye. Possibly, the gaze of this camera was causing him to ramble like a wannabe John Grisham. When I'd first given thought to cameras on police uniforms, I was halfway through *The Big Easy* (the movie, not the town), and I wondered if they'd stop those cops from running red lights when no one was watching, or even better, limit back-of-the-cruiser beatings to one or two a week? But now I was starting to think cameras were the worst thing to happen to these fools since Tasers.

"Do you carry a Taser?" I asked, trying to change the subject.

"You mean a tether? No, I'm not a parole officer."

"A what? No, a *Taser*," I said, then pointed. "So, that's a camera on your shirt, right?"

"Did you know that tethers were originally to reward people?" he said around another gulp.

"Fine. What's a tether?" I asked, giving up.

"You know, an ankle bracelet, a 'LoJack.'"

"Oh, right."

"Originally, they were for the good of the community," he said wistfully. "We would attach them to problem youngsters, then reward them for spending time at the YMCA or various after-school programs instead of running the streets unsupervised. But tethers have lost their meaning."

"Uh huh."

I was convinced everything he was saying was a thinly-disguised soliloquy about the camera, or *for* the camera, or just not being all that careful to sound like he wasn't talking nonstop about fucking cameras. You get me? I blamed all our communication problems on the camera is what I'm saying. But then the bartender brought him another Coors Light and tossed his empty, and as I followed the can's path to the trash it snapped me out of my spiral. There were enough empties in the garbage that I started believing we could be buddies, or at least he was drunk enough to put aside our differences to solve this case together.

"So, officer, what was going on today on the side of the road? With that girl?"

He cleared his throat and got comfortable. I closed my eyes, suddenly sure that, despite all those crappy beers, a straight answer would never come easy from this guy. I was right.

"One time on the beat, an account was related by another deputy in which a parcel of methamphetamine crystals was placed on the roof of an automobile during suspect interaction. The alleged criminal, a real Adam Henry, forthwith headed E.B. from the scene, while the parcel remained on the exterior of his vehicle, which inadvertently distributed said crystals across a three-mile expanse. In a subsequent unrelated incident, six individuals convicted of minor misdemeanors were rendering service to their community in recompense for their crimes by collecting garbage from said highway, when suddenly . . ."

This is worse than a back-seat beating, I thought. The

bartender asked if I needed anything, and I pleaded, "A shotgun?"

"Like I said earlier," Johnny Five went on. "When an individual or party is responsible for willful deception . . . "

"Oh, man. Shut up!"

"Excuse me?" He covered the camera's eye like it was underage and there were titties on the screen.

"It's just . . . I mean, come on! There's got to be easier ways to say things, dude."

"I've told you everything," he said, hand still over the camera. "Don't you understand?"

"Understand what? Everything about what? That a bag of crystal was left on the hood of somebody's car? And that six people picked up just the right amount of petty crimes to receive a community service sentence and clean up the highway? Wait a minute . . . "

A light flashed on the nearby trivia machine. It may as well have been over my head.

"So they pick up rocks and shitcans or whatever, but they also pick up the treasure, too, and they stick the bags on the side of the road to get collected later? 'Cause the guy picking up those bags is in on it? Am I close?"

He said nothing.

"But did you see that? How I did that? There's an easier way to say stuff. Why do you gotta overcomplicate it?"

Johnny Five, more machine than man these days, scratched his robot eye and actually smiled. A couple beers after that, and Johnny stopped talking for a stretch, just sat with me, drinking. I started tuning in to whatever the barflies near the jukebox were yammering about.

" . . . if someone says they're getting their uterus removed, never ask if you can have it . . . "

"Ain't that the truth!"

"Uh . . . "

A couple beers after that, I was wiping the cop's last half-empty Coors Light off the edge of the bar, then standing up to kick the can into the wall with a satisfying explosion of suds. Johnny Five jumped to his feet, but I still had the advantage.

See, cops fight real hard with a camera attached to them, but the camera also makes them fight fair. Big mistake.

***

I promised earlier I would never think of punishing you with a detailed description of a dream. Well, I've since learned you don't dream when you're knocked out, so that won't be a problem. But as far as the fight, here's the highlight reel . . .

First off, he protected the body camera like it was his balls. So I learned early that a punch to this new plastic heart—one dead eye and one red eye—would make him deflate. I suddenly wanted more cameras in this fight immediately.

Lord, give me the strength of six or seven more angles on this brawl. I beseech thee to cover this man from head to toe in lenses so we may document the world's first battle with the future of law enforcement, in God's name I pray, amen . . .

I'd waited for him to drain about eight more beers before I took my first swing because I am a cheap, sucker-punching motherfucker. But attacking a police officer after drinking with him all morning was still a new one to me, and I was shocked how well it was turning out. I'm not too sure if cops work out like they used to, but they must brush their teeth, because I left about a half pound of knuckle bacon on those beautiful, rock-hard incisors of his. And not to ruin the suspense or anything, but that blazing white picket fence of his would remain relatively undisturbed when this was all over.

And he was a freakin' noisy fighter, too. Usually civilians like me are the ones who talk nonstop through a brawl, kinda like McClane in the first *Die Hard,* explaining exactly what we're gonna do and when we're gonna do it . . . to your face! Usually all the talk is so we can magically conjure up all those promises. But something I learned from movies, and movie monsters, is the louder and longer anything screeches, the less likely it is to be scary. Godzilla might have been the exception, back when he was still rubber anyway.

Fuck the American Godzilla! He was never even there! All fire and lies . . .

As I tried to fishhook the cop and cut a thumbnail across his cheek, I reflected on some quality rumbles in monster movies, how Godzilla vs. Ghidorah the Three-Headed Mofo was the best by far. Because, if you think about it, that was a dinosaur against a dragon. Which makes it like Evolution versus Creationism. And that was important.

And I told the cop *all* this while I started choking him.

Hit the pause button. Speaking of East versus West, when I was 7 or 8 years old and I snuck down the stairs to watch *Rollerball*, I was fascinated by "Moonpie's" lowbrow fight lessons and how the Tokyo team would be going for the skillful kill with their spiked gloves and karate chops, but the Houston team aimed their punches for something Moonpie called the "ganglia." See, I believed in Godzilla back then, but I never believed in this ganglia. Was it that mythical G-spot I kept hearing about in my father's porn stash?

But the cop found my G-spot easily enough when he pistoned a punch up from the peanut shells on the concrete floor, and he lit my chin up like a pinball machine. And just like Moonpie warned me back then, "It rings a bell!" In fact, I felt like I was hovering in the air for a good hour, while Johnny Five almost lost another of his solid punches deep inside my own cavernous, charcoal-dusted mush. Then I think he tied my arm into a pretzel, but fortunately I was a soft pretzel like you'd get at the carnival because my arm didn't break. And my spring-loaded fighting glasses soaked up some big shots, flattening on my face, then rebounding back to remain locked on my ears. My brain was definitely swimming, but mercifully not swelling, and probably not dreaming, so I guess I didn't get knocked out after all. Close enough.

Listen, I'm about 6 foot, 200 pounds—pretty unremarkable

before this new generation started shrinking and Stunted Men became the norm—where as Johnny was relatively average-sized, even with all his extra testicles and technology. And, remember, I never drank a lot before this trip. But that day? I'd have to review the tapes, but I can definitely take a punch, especially if I think there's a camera nearby.

At one point while we were both still standing, I looked up and the bartender seemed genuinely excited, and I fantasized I was doing the town a favor by kicking this guy's ass after years of abuse, or years of gibberish.

I'm a goddamn community service, Your Honor! Fifteen minutes of community service served. You're welcome. Now that's the kind of sentences judge should be handing out.

Toward the end, we ended up on the ground like all fights do that aren't in cushy rubber suits or intangible CGI. I was hugging his waist and trying to pick him up like an idiot, and he sent a special delivery of elbows to the invisible target on the back of my head, and I saw his belt and his gizmos and noticed his gun must have shaken loose of his holster. Later, I found out he'd given it to the bartender when he first walked in, just like outta some Western.

I found this out at exactly the moment when the bartender tapped the butt of this revolver against my head to turn out the lights.

***

As I started coming back to Earth, I could hear the cop and the bartender discussing roadside memorials and garbage bags and orange jump suits, and I tried to keep my eyes closed to mentally stockpile as many clues as I could.

"Right next to a highway cross and teddy bear," the cop told him, talking normal all the sudden, without all the Johnny Law bluster. "We thought we had them dead to rights, but all we found in the bag was papers. Custodial trash from the local schools . . . "

Evidence and shit! I thought. I wished I had a tiny notebook to write everything down.

" . . . one time, they cut up a man and left him along the road in fifteen plastic bags . . . "

Are you hearing this, Your Honor?

"Listen. Someone's looking for this guy . . . "

But the barflies around us were talking too loud to catch any more important information, and someone pulled up "Sussudio" on the jukebox. Good luck concentrating through that, am I right? However, I did catch fragments of a conversation about some videogame the bartender had invented. At least, I hope that's what they were talking about.

"So, I finished that Search for Extraterrestrial Life I was tellin' you about."

"Fuck that. First contact would be the end of us all."

"And that is why, for my version, you don't even have to turn on the TV or plug in a controller. You just stare at the screen and pray nothing shows up."

"Perfect. You should call it *Ready, Get S.E.T.I . . . Nope.*"

"You kill me, Johnny . . . "

Then someone had my collar like a handful of puppy scruff, and I was tumbling outside in a heap. I sat up and blinked until I could see my Rabbit again, Zero in the back window, waiting patiently for us to beat our feet and try on one of those new towns everyone was always raving about.

Do they call the gutters behind bars "Shitcan Alley"? Because they should, I thought, patting the rain-slicked tar around me like a friend. *Or maybe it should be "ally" instead.*

As I fumbled with my car keys, I looked down at my knuckles and saw that, despite the pain of the teeth scraping, there was no blood at all. My hands were soaked, but clear, like I was bleeding water. For some reason, this didn't surprise me, like if I ever had my chest X-rayed I'd see my backbone was missing completely, heart like a dripping ziplock and one dead goldfish. Then I noticed something in my other hand, and I got excited again.

I vaguely recalled grabbing for the camera on the cop's bejeweled blue shirt during the scrap, but I'd come up with something else entirely. A souvenir. Proof this cowardly joyride was now more like a responsibility.

I walked past the police cruiser and saw the red light blinking on his dash cam. I hoped his Sergeant got to see the show the next morning at the station and fired his ass.

What's the other word for fired? Shitcanned? Sorry, sounds dumb out loud.

But if our fight didn't get that cop in trouble, there'd at least be some hard questions over coffee and finger-blasting doughnuts when they realized his badge was missing.

***

The engine was knocking louder, so I stopped at a dusty JCPenney visible off the exit ramp to get some oil. And a couple other things. The "J" was sagging, and the "C" was gone, so it was back to just "Penney" after all these years. I enjoyed the symmetry.

I considered flashing my new badge to try for that fabled Thin Blue Line discount, but I forgot all about Johnny Five's shiny I.D. when I discovered not only do they sell plastic and wooden highway memorial crosses in department stores now (complete with a piss squirt of glue to fasten some plastic flowers or something cute and snuggly to follow you into the afterlife), but they were in the goddamn automotive section to boot!

Of course they were.

Some came with stickers to immortalize your own recently deceased loved one. Some had a variety of ready-made names already stamped on them, like those novelty license plates you got at the amusement park.

And they served the same purpose. Proof you'd been on a ride.

***

I let Zero lick the wounds on my face until he was eating more than licking and his eyes started to get scary. Then he curled up on the passenger's-side headrest and twerked his ass around awhile, either trying to keep his balance or getting ready to pounce and finish devouring my head. I was within sight of the city limits when I saw there was another accident. Another orange jump suit smeared on the road, but a male this time, and not stunted at all.

I didn't have to get out of my car to guess that his name would match the memorial cross not more than ten feet from his fractured skull. But I got out anyway.

I'm not saying my detective work was solid gold here. I'm not reminding you that my honorary status as "Indian Police" had gotten a recent promotion to . . . whatever that stolen badge said. But I knew I was onto something. Was Angie following these leads before she died? Was this happening in every town? Whatever *this* was? If we skipped to the end of the story right now, you might be frustrated to learn I never get to verify any of this at all, but so what!

Because there were bigger fish to fry now, deeper rabbit holes to spelunk. And if I wasn't convinced yet, I would be when Johnny Five showed up at this second crime scene like he'd been chasing my Rabbit this whole time.

Come on, man. Like there aren't any crimes to solve where I'm not?

I watched him step out all careful, toe then heel testing the road like a Slinky as he came my way. I saw the black eye spilling out the sides of his sunglasses, and I gingerly tapped the cut between my own. My eyelids burned like fried eggs in this sunlight, and I felt sorry for myself again. Then I realized . . . a cop had a black eye? Holy shit, maybe balance had resumed in this universe. But I was still too pumped up about solving shit to dwell on any of that, and I didn't even give him a chance to tell me to move my car before I was already explaining to him how I'd tied our mystery all together in a big ol' bow. Don't bother thanking me. That's just what partners do!

"Listen, I cracked our fucking case, Johnny. The pickup truck. The garbage bags. The rubber on the road. The crosses. Oh, yeah . . . "

Silence. He was actually listening.

"Okay, remember the bag of meth on the roof of the car you were talking about?"

"Yes."

"Well, what if you misheard that story. Just bear with me a sec. What if they were saying 'a bag of . . . math.'"

"'Mash?'"

"No, no, no. It wasn't a bag of 'meth.' It was a bag of 'math.'"

"What the fuck are you talking about? What are 'math crystals?'"

"No, maybe he said math 'questions.' And maybe math *answers*. See, back in the bar, someone said the bags were custodial trash from the schools. What if they were stealing tests? Compass exams, the SATs, the ACTs, whatever the fuck you need to test out of the developmental math courses at the local community college. What if all the answers were in those bags? Hold on, I have some stats. Let me get my wife's yearbook out of the car . . . "

I was losing him. I patted his badge in my pocket to maintain confidence.

"No way people would be fighting over math questions," he said, looking past me now. "I don't think that's how those tests work . . . "

"The hell they wouldn't fight over that! Think about it. How much do classes go for these days? Two grand? Three grand? Tell me that's not worth a scam. You'd save yourself a shit ton of money, and that's gotta be worth a cover-up, right? Shit, that's worth more than a bag of crank or whatever else these rednecks are cooking, right?"

He put his hand over his heart. Where the badge had been.

"Are you talking to me or the camera?" he asked me. It was the most human one of them had ever seemed.

"What?"

"There's nothing to solve here, asshole. Do us a favor. Try the next town."

"You kicking me out of town?" I asked him, loving the idea. "Is that what's happening?" My question was as sincere as I was able, about 25% less sincere than normal people.

"You kicked yourself out."

"Can I ask you one last question?"

"You just did."

I stared until he spoke again.

"Go ahead."

"Do you think a human being could fit in a guitar case?"

He said nothing. Time ticked away as his cruiser's engine cooled.

"Listen, there were tire tracks but no tread, get it?" I'd lost him, but I didn't care. "The construction slowed down the Stunted Men, see, and they didn't plan on that . . . no time to drop off the tread, so why don't—"

"Stop helping us, Dave."

"Have you been following me?"

His hand moved to hover over his gun. I got back in my car.

***

When my wife started her fellowship year, about a month before her murder, she used to talk endlessly about the Dunning-Kruger Effect. And I only had to hear her bring it up twenty or so times until I realized she was talking about me. From what I understood, this theory meant that, if you're incompetent at anything you're passionate about, you won't know you're incompetent. Because the skills you need to produce a correct answer are exactly the same skills you need to recognize what a correct answer is. She told me this interpretation was completely wrong, but I was pretty sure she'd take all that back if she saw me cracking cases with the cops left and right.

And another thing, I didn't have all the evidence just yet, but I was now convinced that merely driving too long is what created those roadside crosses. A typical eight hours of any car snorting the white lines on the road would logically result in a cross. And crosses beget more crosses, and those beget more crashes, and so on.

I stopped again after I crossed the state line. Then I backed the Rabbit up a bit, kinda like a guy who gets bounced from a bar but keeps tapping his foot barely inside the doorway just to be a punk. Parked on the Kentucky/Ohio border, I popped my trunk and dug around my pile of empty 5W-30s to get my own shiny, new crucifix, price tag still attached where the big nail would be pounded through the teddy bear's feet. Then I planted it as deep as I could in the stones, propping the dead-eyed stuffed animal up against the base. I'd almost bought one with my name on it because who could resist that shit! Instead, I pinned my favorite cop's badge to the bear's ear. Looking at the memorial, I realized it would probably read like a threat when it was discovered, but it was really more like regret, I swear.

And how long would it even be out here? Like all these stores aren't plucking and reselling the damn things anyway.

Engine no longer knocking, I stomped the gas, and the cat thing dodged my feet, eyes dilated and tail huge, and we felt how strong a rabbit could run with its black blood pumping freely again. For miles, I chewed my inky lizard tongue, and I didn't think about my roadside cross stabbed deep down in that ditch, or the badge that adorned it, or ashtrays made of pesos, or pennies over eyeballs, electronic or otherwise.

I thought about bad news. And how it was your responsibility to never react like they expect.

V

73 BAD REACTION SHOTS

ONE OF THE things that was probably gonna be held against me once I stopped driving was how I didn't call anyone to tell them she died. How I just hopped in my car with a stray something or other and hit the road without spreading the cellular infection as required. And I can understand that.

Her funeral would be coming up. That was something I could not face. I'd been dodging funerals most of my life, and people understandably started thinking, "Awww, poor Dave is too weak to face death," and no doubt they'd write off me ducking the ceremony as more proof of this. But that wasn't it at all. The truth is I was too caught up obsessing over other mourners and what I perceived as their inappropriate, sometimes self-serving, displays of public grief. I couldn't get out of a funeral without a scene, or at least a blood-pressure hike. Watching people's reactions to tragedy just made me angrier than I can ever reasonably describe. And after I got old enough to have some friends and relatives really start dying off, I realized with some horror that it was everyone's reaction to my reaction to *their* reaction that was so insufferable. See how horrible that already sounded?

So, yeah, I didn't tell anyone about her death. But I didn't have to. I'd played every possible version of those hypothetical conversations in my head as I drove. I could hear myself trying to sum up the insanity of the past 24 hours filtered through tiny speakers pressed tight against everyone's ears, and it made me want to bash my head open against the steering wheel. Too bad steering wheels are for pussies these days, all rubber and soft like those Fisher-Price dashboards, so even that suicidal daydream was its own sort of cop-out. One steering wheel in particular, from the old Buick Regal my dad used to drive, stuck out in my memory. It was hard and slick, polished like a high-school basketball court, the place where I slipped and broke my nose (the first time), and my sweaty hands would slip right off on any sharp turn.

I wanted to do the right thing, but if I stopped to call anyone right now, instead of refueling my flask and my Rabbit and my fuzzy totem, I'd just have to relive it all, while also somehow making anyone on the receiving end feel better about how my life was destroyed. As I drove, I imagined the trade-offs, where some sorry bastard such as yourself—I mean, myself—play-acted worse than those cops on the witness stand. How bad could it sound?

"This isn't easy for me," you would say while I waited for you to gut me with the news. "Hold on, someone's on the other line." And then you'd take forever to click back, and I'd have already crashed the car in anticipation. Or I wouldn't get to the phone in time, so you'd have to leave me a message, too long, as usual, with your patented brand of suspense accumulated from decades of resisting telephone communication, something like, "I know we haven't talked for a year, but if you call me back, I'll tell you who's dead." Then you'd hum along with a song I couldn't hear and try to get in a dozen belches and some beatboxing before the beep. A seductive voice would tell you my message will be saved in the archives for only three days, and even the computer would sound oddly threatening, so I'd call you back within the hour.

"What's up?"

"Are you sitting down?"

"I'm driving, asshole."

"You could be running."

"Just say it. Who the hell is dead?

"Guess."

And then you'd tell me. I'd think I was fully prepared for this moment, but I won't be.

"How?"

"No one knows. They found her in a guitar case. Shot through the head. I'm no detective, but either she killed herself or someone else did."

"You deduce that all by yourself?"

"What's the difference?"

"What do you mean?"

"I mean, what's the difference? Murder, accident, suicide. She's still dead."

You will think about this hard, until you understand the difference. You won't say it out loud, but you'll realize that if it wasn't suicide, you wouldn't be dwelling on it nearly as much. Out of character, you will fill this silence with some actual sympathy. It will surprise you both, and give you the creeps.

"I'm really sorry, dude."

Then you'll drive a little more and think about those days when you and her used to watch movies together, and how you'd know immediately that it was a bad one and she was gonna fall asleep with her face in the microwave popcorn if the camera kept lingering on the reaction shots. You knew these bad movie moments well, the ones designed to tell the dumbest viewers when to gasp, laugh, or cry (coincidentally, the typical reactions to murder, accident, and suicide, in that order). Picture the scene. An actor did something shocking like, say, pulling his eyes out of his goddamn head. That should say enough to the viewer, right? Well, a bad movie won't be content with this. A bad movie will cut to someone screaming, maybe even shouting out, "Oh, my god! I can't believe this has occurred! Imagine the pain!" This was infinitely worse if the bad movie in question was trying to make you cry.

"Are you sitting down?"

You'll decide that I only asked you to do this because I saw it in a movie. Unless it was the scene where three authority figures came knocking on the door, that's how the phone call always began. The movies always told you that it was the hardest job ever, delivering the news to the wartime widow, but you were too smart for that nonsense. You've noticed that they never have to actually say anything at all, because just like everyone else they've visited, you will always collapse on the stairs before they even speak, before I even speak, sometimes before I even open the door. You've always been convinced those cocksuckers have the easiest job of all time.

But after you soak in the news, you'll start calling other people, all the way down the line of people who care a little less and less, until eventually you will discuss her death with people who need to prove a connection, and a bizarre competition will surface that neither of you will be consciously aware of. It will sound familiar to anyone listening in because you've said it all before, even outside of the worst movie you and her watched together. Which was this one.

First will be your bizarre rush to react the most inappropriately ("I guess she won't be needing that five bucks back!") quickly followed by a scramble to be the most respectful ("I'd drive nine hours to her funeral if I had to.") then you'll start the world's most subtle duel about who really knew her better ("I remember every word of her alligator poem." "No, you mean 'crocodile poem.'") then you will say something about there being nothing you could have done to change things, but you'll be hinting that one extra word in the last sentence between you two would have changed everything that followed ("I almost forced her to miss a plane by not calling her back.") then you will subtly attach meaning to the most insignificant interactions ("I'm the one who named her dog, even if she never realized it.") negated by a hasty downplay of the least significant ones ("She brought me that article on love being a disease, but she probably showed it to everyone.") or the most significant ("She wrote our names on a padlock and sealed our love on a bridge halfway across the globe.") or somewhere in the middle ("Fine, halfway across the country then.") then you will offer up some embarrassing detail, knowing that although no one can prove her feelings for you, you can change your own depending on who's around ("I hesitate to even say this, but I always wanted to sing 'Drops of Jupiter' at karaoke with her watching in the crowd, and, God help me, sing it well.") then you will make it clear your special connection allows you any joke no matter how many crickets are chirping ("Tragedy minus time equals comedy, but this clock ain't workin!") but then you'll make it clear you wouldn't allow anyone to do the same thing ("Imagine her mother in the car with us before you say that stupid shit again.") then you will desperately try to attach yourself a little closer to the tragedy, hoping that there's at least one person left who hasn't heard the news so you can ask if they're sitting down, too ("If you haven't called her crazy dad yet, let me do it.") then you will remove yourself from the drama ("The funeral reception is too far away, and her body won't even be there.") in direct opposite proportion to your relationship with the deceased ("I'd hitchhike if I had to, even though she probably wouldn't remember me.") then you will take advantage of an opportunity to settle old scores ("I'll tell him I don't want to talk about it if that asshole has the bad judgment to want to reminisce.") then you will minimize her best accomplishments ("I think people should be honest and admit that her poems needed work.") or maximize them, depending on your own level of success ("I told her that one day we'd all rent hot-air balloons when we're millionaires, then put some heart-shaped padlocks on a thunderstorm.") then you will, of course, fall back on the ridiculous contest of who-knew-her-best since it was never really decided ("Once, I saw her hold up a line of traffic while she walked down the middle of the road with her headphones on, everyone honking and yelling over her shoulders.") however, you'll never ("I know, that's so *her*, isn't it?) no matter how hard you try ("Actually, it wasn't like her at all.") really declare a winner.

Unless you make sure to get caught with a drink in your mouth so you can spray it everywhere in shock when you hear the bad news, you can always count on your reaction to be unsatisfying. And you can't just fake it and hold some Gatorade in your cheeks and wait for the punchline like they do in the movies. You're talking about that split-second after the fluid washes over your teeth, that instant before your throat flexes to swallow, a moment that's harder to nail than anyone actually realizes. And if you do spit "uncontrollably" all over everything when you hear the news, then maybe, just maybe, you will believe you reacted honestly. But you didn't.

Just understand that an honest reaction to the news of a tragedy has never happened in the history of the human race. That is who we are.

For example, notice up there how many more times you will say "I" instead of "her," or how many times I said "you" instead of "me." This is because the only people who handle tragedy worse than high school kids are college kids, and the only people who handle tragedy worse than college kids are grad school kids. And the only people who handle tragedy worse than those fuckers are everyone else.

***

If you drive long enough, even with a stray creature climbing on your shoulders, the only relationship you can cultivate is hatred for authority figures who claim more than a reasonable share of your road. You will also begin to think of every cop, fireman, even paramedic as the same person, blissfully ignorant of the destructive influence this generalization has had with other relationships in your life. This is mostly because, much like the initial giggling skirmish you had over that theater armrest on your first date . . .

You simply cannot tolerate anyone asking you to move over.

So when you see red lights on the horizon, or in your rearview mirror, your instinct is to call someone and tell them all about it. But in the movies, the hero never bothers to tell anyone what just happened, no matter how strange or remarkable, even though it is the only time a reaction shot would be justified. This is never the case in real life.

Because someone will call you first, and you'll be getting the news about her suicide all over again. And you will imagine hundreds of friends of friends out there fighting over increasingly sophisticated phones to tell you again and again and again.

You will want to take the high road when you answer, but suddenly, even though this caller will be more sincere than the first, and won't play the game nearly as well, your old reflexes will be back before you know it:

First, you'll quiz each other on all the sexual details you've always suspected ("I swear I never fucked her.") minimizing or maximizing in relation to what the other one reveals ("My shit was up against her shit, does that count?") then you'll Monday-morning quarterback the crime scene with a decade of closed-captioning police shows under your belt as a qualification ("I think they need to track down if she got the gun from the same hardware store that she got the padlocks.") then you'll decide that since you're not directly involved, no one should be involved either ("I think that it's not our tragedy to claim because with every death someone else has earned the right to be more upset than you.") then you'll decide no one can grieve unless they've got identification to prove they're her mother, father, brother, or sister by blood ("I honestly don't think a stepbrother should get the first call.") then you'll complain about how families are the only ones who get to know conclusively if it was really the most unlikely suicide of all time ("I know for a fact her parents knew her least of all.") then you will try to make someone feel better, but only because jealousy motivates you to try to dismiss their influence on her last days ("I'm telling you, it's not your fault. She was upset about someone she just met, not you.") then you will try to make sure no one writes about it without changing everything ("If you're gonna put it on your website, I think you should say her cat died recently, not her dog, in order to protect the dog's family.") or else you'll decide that no one can write about it until you have the time to try ("I honestly think posting an online tribute for her relatives to stumble across when they're searching obituaries is the equivalent of crashing a stranger's funeral.") then you will mourn the loss of the most important password you can think of outside of a heist film ("I tried to follow her on Twitter, but she said she was locked until she could log in again, and now those posts will be out of my reach forever.") then you'll swallow your disgust as you compete with people claiming things that can never be verified ("I'm the only one that can access her profile, but I forgot her password and ruined it for everyone, sorry.") then you'll either say it's a god's fault ("I saw thirty people today that deserved to die before her.") or a dog's will ("I know there's a plan because his tail curls when it rains.") then you will try to hint, as tastefully as you can, that by talking to her last or by not talking to her last, you were responsible for her death ("I want you to admit that you're actually proud you made her cry, not just because I am, too.") because no one is allowed to ever admit such a thing out loud even though this behavior is in our garbage DNA.

This second conversation will be what they called during the Cold War a "race to the bottom," but you will fail to recognize it. And you'll struggle to recognize actual guilt under all the layers of bullshit. And you never will. You will only feel guilty about having inappropriate reactions to tragedy, never about the tragedy itself. You may finally understand that for humans this is simply impossible, and always has been.

But the quickest way to gauge how close you were to the deceased?

How eagerly would you use her death to get out of a speeding ticket? That's gotta be rock bottom, and probably the real reason that talking on the phone while driving is now a crime in sixteen states.

***

One last thing. I just want you to know that the worst movie you ever saw was way better than you realized, and it probably would have been fine if it wasn't for all the reaction shots. I know this for a fact. The opening, the ending, and everything in between was just this long chase where the monster was on a rampage and working its way through a school, or a campground, or a trailer park. But all momentum was destroyed when the camera constantly kept cutting to the faces of the teenagers to show them looking horrified, as if you weren't the one who was the most traumatized by how the movie failed on every level.

Your phone will ring, and you'll finally get to tell someone the bad news. But you'll do it wrong right out of the gate. You'll even forget to ask if I'm sitting down, and oh, shit, here we go again! Then you'll confide to me, or I'll confide in you . . .

"You know, just between you and me, I might have fucked her."

But like clockwork, here comes something that no one can prove ("Just kidding, I probably never fucked her.") quickly followed by something else that no one can prove ("He never fucked her either.") then some shady denials ("I swear on my dog's life.") then you'll try to come up with the best theory no one's thought of yet ("I'd kill myself, too, if my dog died.") then you will discount everyone else's conjecture ("I know for a fact that a dog can't affect someone deeply, even if they gave birth to it.") then you'll try to suggest she was thinking of you ("I sent her a text message the day before it happened.") at the same time you suggest your absence drove her to extremes ("I should have answered the cryptic message she sent me.")

then you'll feel the need to demystify her ("You and I both know she wasn't perfect.") in direct proportion with anyone who dares romanticize her ("Remember when she told us about her sister slashing her wrists on Thanksgiving?") by proudly letting your imagination fill in any blanks that her family refuses to ("I'm thinking there is no sister, never was.") then you'll convince others, as you convince yourself, how well you really knew her and how important your friendship was compared to everyone's ("Today I realized she never knew your middle name, just the initials she wrote on a heart-shaped padlock.") then you'll try to set the record straight on something that will only make you feel better ("I hated how she tried to be one of the guys, saying 'bros before hoes' when we didn't include her.") and ignore the awkward silence when you're finally honest enough to get to the real point ("Just one of the guys, my ass. It was clear that she wanted to get with you, not with me.") then you'll try to make light of it since this said more about you than it did about her ("It was actually 'prose before hoes,' and I went home to do my homework that night because she just wanted to stay out longer with you.") then you'll throw out a bit of trivia ("Once she was up before the sun and called to brag about it, but it wasn't dark anymore when we heard her message.") then shame mixed with relief regarding things you'll only admit to yourself ("I'm sort of relieved that now she can't tell anyone I couldn't get it up.") then you'll try to shock the conversation to a close and be disappointed when you can't ("Remember the day all three of us walked through campus and she couldn't take her eyes or ears off you?") so you'll try even harder ("I thought about killing you so that she'd listen to my stories instead.") then you'll project a bad memory of the last time a cop came to your house and searched your face for the right reaction, as if this will explain your behavior since ("They always act like it's hard to knock on those doors, but they love that shit, and don't let them tell you different.") then you'll gratefully acknowledge you'll forever be second place in this competition and try to end it all quickly ("I think no one knew her at all, not just me, I mean, not just *not* me.") then you'll make a surprise connection ("She was the sister I never had.") but you will mock anyone else's similar revelation ("You mean the sister you never fucked?") then you'll want to get off the phone fast when you remember there's one person out there no one's told yet, someone who might still be standing up when they get the bad news.

But you'll never ask yourself why you've never cared if it was suicide, accident, or murder, or which order those three words belonged in, because you'll be too excited about giving someone else the bad news, as if this would free you from its grip. And as you stomp the gas pedal, all you will know with absolution is that, despite what a murderer in the worst movie ever may believe, the embarrassment over things you said to someone when they were alive never dies with them.

This will be your best and last chance to tell someone first. For the first time, you were the closest to her. But she doesn't have a phone. You threw it out of the car when she wouldn't show you who called, or it got knocked out of her hand when you called her, or I called her, and this distracted her long enough to be abducted. See that? They were always right about the fucking phones. They're dangerous. There ought to be a law.

Soon, you will pass more and more cars that look exactly like one you used to own.

You will consider the collisions.

VI

IMPRISONABLE VISIONS

MY GRAD SCHOOL career in Pittsburgh lasted exactly one semester, and even though this was a full year before I met my wife and I was already fucking up my life, it was probably still worth doing. I'm convinced I met her *before* I met her, though, sharing a quick laugh in the middle of the street when a pedal pub she was singing on almost ran me down. But we didn't realize who we were back then, and it took another year before I met Angie for real and found out that was not her. Unless she was just embarrassed about being on a pedal pub. Or maybe when they pedaled fast enough they traveled back in time. Because her mobile party came later, and it lasted forever, and that's a whole other story. But her life had always been infinitely crazier than it looked to me down there on the road.

I could have met Angie ten times actually, all those years I spent orbiting (but never really directly involved with) two separate MFA programs, after a decade plus three years in undergrad that somehow didn't get perpetual schooling out of my system. However, I *did* get painting houses out of my system, the hairs in my nostril singed after three summers of inhaling oil-based paint for tuition money.

But that would have been ten different versions of both

of us back then, each one a little worse than the one that followed.

But I met Miranda before anybody, first in grade school, then in grad school, after we dropped an "E." Get it? Dropped the "E" off "grade"? They're both drugs? Never mind.

It was also the night I met a bunch of other writer wannabes, most of them at a get-to-know-you party on some dilapidated, half-scraped deck in Polish Hill. After a lifetime in Ohio (or "Flatlandia," as Angie called it), everything in Pittsburgh seemed to be on some sorta hill, so it was easy to get lost, and I sat in my car once I finally found the place hours later, feeling too much like a fraud to go up and meet anybody. So I went around back of the house instead, and it turned out the party was outside anyway, and that kinda made things easier. When I was spotted, everyone respectfully said, "Oh, hi there!" Like I'd come around back on purpose instead of getting ready to peek in the windows then run away like a psycho and drop out of school forever. But my new cohort of grad students was cool. Mostly I talked to this one towering goon, a former basketball player turned Elizabethan poet, so tall he confessed to pissing sitting down, so it didn't "go everywhere," he said. I remember saying, "Maybe stop pissing everywhere, dude?" Then thinking, *this guy should end up in a book someday*, but he never did. A man who pissed sitting down would be way too unsympathetic. Especially if it's in a litter box.

Then Miranda came down from the next house up, and that dark skin and black explosion of curls stood out like a brush fire in the dead grass and chipped paint surrounding us, and I followed her around for the rest of the party. When she dropped either ecstasy or a Flintstones chewable vitamin in my beer, I quickly forgot about all the people I was supposed to meet in order to secure that all-important teaching fellowship the following year. So my part-time closed-captioning, a job that was supposed to supplement my income temporarily until grad school money kicked in, ended up full-time when nothing else materialized. And school went from my part-time gig to a no-time gig, while she became my all-time gig.

Our class schedules didn't match, but I knew where Miranda lived. And growing up in the days before the internet, my stalking skills already were fairly well refined. That's what this new generation will never understand. If you liked someone back then, Google wasn't there playing cupid. You had to stalk their ass, no joke. Idling in your car and peering through windows at their workplace wasn't weird at all. So I vowed to run into her again at some point. But first, before the last of my money ran dry, I had to fail out of school in some kind of spectacular fashion so those other assholes would remember me. Or write about me. Either one would do.

There were early signs of trouble in the fiction workshop we shared. Dr. Fiona Something Something, this vaguely French, long-checked-out professor, had us read Mark Twain and Chekhov, then, uh, "draw our future" with Crayola crayons. So I grabbed every shade of red and, like a goddamn psychic, drew myself as an ape caged in the Eiffel Tower, stretching for a fire alarm at the top, which was padlocked, of course. Then I drew about thirty more little monkey me's standing on our shoulders (definitely coulda used an assist from that gangly, basketball-playing poet, but you work with what you got). When we passed all our drawings to the left, I graded the others as they went by ("D," "F," "F," "C minus . . . "), but I did this under my forearm like I was protecting a prison lunch tray, so that people would think Professor Fiona Something Or Other had done the grading instead. And, big surprise, they all blamed Miranda, who'd been sitting right next to me, kinda making me like Tom Sawyer dipping Becky's pigtails in the inkwell. When I worried about ruining her writing career before it started, Miranda said, "Forget it." Then she admitted she'd slipped me a Vitamin E the day we met at the party, just to see how dumb I'd start acting. She said I didn't disappoint.

As a last-ditch attempt to connect with the University of Pittsburgh Creative Writing Program, I sought out Fiona Whoever's novel and almost read the whole damn thing. I stood in the rain skimming it while I waited for the bus home outside the Hogwarts-looking "Cathedral of Learning," after another hard day of Fiona's guided meditation ("Now draw 'Hope.'" "How about 'Nope'!"). I tossed it right in the bus stop trash can. I don't remember the title any more than I remember anyone's last name, but I do know the entire first chapter was describing a chair. That's it. Nine full pages of intricate chair detail and edge-of-my-balls excitement. I decided two things then and there. One, I was finally done with school. And two, if a first chapter described a chair, somebody better be eating the fucking thing by the end.

***

Here's the first big twist. I initially heard about the invisible prison from a kid who served time there, not from my wife or her crazy incarceration research as I'd previously assumed. See, at the time I didn't know what this kid was talking about, any more than I knew what my wife was talking about. I was at Zanzibar (Angie and I had been in Kentucky for about six months), and I was winning at trivia all by myself against teams of eight people or more, answering questions about terrible music and worse television. I was trying not to watch the windows for Angie's lone working headlight to turn the corner, and thinking about her favorite nursery rhyme, "A diller, a dollar, a ten o'clock scholar, what makes you come so soon? You used to come at ten o'clock, and now you come at noon." Never mind that the time doesn't make a lick of sense (like how the fuck is noon sooner than ten o'clock?), but whenever I drove home alone, the added subtext of infidelity always added a clarifying layer to the couplet that I didn't need mixing with my standard overnight cocktails of white-line fever.

So it was during the sports questions—my worst category—that I finally went to piss, and I struck up a conversation with some punk at the urinal. He was urinating with one hand and texting with the other, something I'd been seeing more and more of lately, but I guess I was relieved he wasn't two-handing the phone with his pants around his ankles like a toddler. This I'd seen at least twice. Anyhow, I leaned over to him totally without looking at his penis and said:

"Hey, man, I hope you're cheating on your girlfriend and not this trivia game."

This was pretty hypocritical of me considering my brief fling with '90s Girlfriend, out in the alley behind Keep Louisville Weird on a half-dozen occasions. And he must have thought so, too. He said, "Fuck you, dude," and then I saw that he was on his phone looking up whichever actor had been in two Nick Cave screenplays, which wasn't even a question we'd had. This should have made me less suspicious but now, for no reason, he had me convinced he was definitely cheating at something. Looking up questions that hadn't even been asked yet? And even worse, he didn't know the answer. "Guy Pierce." Come on. So before he could stop pissing, I'd already fantasized three different ways to smoosh his face down onto that urinal cake before he would be able to reach the fire alarm. This would be his future . . .

When I opened my eyes he was at the mirror.

"You serve time before?" he asked me.

"What?" This kid thought I was an ex-con? Was I hugging my "Death Star Cookie" too tight back at the bar? I mean, Zanzibar made a great dessert, scoop of vanilla ice cream covered in that delicious chocolate plastic shell, all melting on a bubbling chocolate-chip cookie in a miniature cast-iron skillet. Good stuff, but was I eating mine with a protective arm again?

"I said, 'Did you serve time?'" Then he smiled, and I could feel the joke coming.

Don't say it.

"Or did you let time serve you?"

I groaned, but when we got back out in the bar, he followed me to my stool, and for some reason, we started talking. I admitted that I'd never been to prison. He hadn't either, in fact. Real prisons, I mean. Not just jails, or overnight coolers, or the invisible after-school fantasy I was soon to learn about.

"But between you and me," I whispered to him. "I kind of wanted to experience prison." This was before everything that would happen in Brickwood and beyond, and, of course, meaning I wanted to visit a prison for real, but I still had some fairly juvenile ideas about a lot of shit back then. Though I had seen every movie on the subject, well, most of the classics anyway. Like *Cool Hand Luke, Caged Heat, Escape from Alcatraz* (spoiler, they didn't escape shit), *The Big Doll House, Papillon, Das Experiment, Kiss of the Spider Woman, Jailbait,* what else . . . Oh, yeah, *Dead Man Walking, The Glass House, Bad Boys* (the white one, not the Bruckheimer shit), *Johnny Cash Live at San Quentin, Deathwatch, Weeds* (a.k.a. *Deathwatch II*), *Undisputed, Con Air, Hellgate, The Concrete Jungle,* come on, what are some more . . . Okay, I even saw *Ghosts . . . of the Civil Dead,* the prison movie with all those dumb ellipses, starring Nick Cave, not Guy Piece, and some actual prisoners. The point is, I had seen every big-shit, mostly-legit movie on pretty much every subject, which is why I spent three hours hiding from Angie in Zanzibar and winning movie-trivia matches single-handed so I could pay for a soggy burger with the twenty-dollar grand-prize gift certificates. Who does that?

But this kid musta saw something special in the way I ate my tater tots, or stood at the urinal with him, something about my lunch-tray safeguarding or my top-of-the-urinal etiquette that signified to him "prison time." It would have taken about a decade of hanging out with me for real for this kid to understand how bad I wanted to get arrested back then. I think I was looking for some structure, and doing head-stand push-ups and looking all intimidating to whoever wandered by my cell didn't sound like such a bad idea. A reachable goal! And, at the time, my firm belief was that watching every single film about incarceration was the same thing. But I guess it wasn't because now I was lying about it. Or lying about lying right now. But who can keep track of these things after you've been *inside*?

" . . . I kind of wanted to experience prison," I confessed. "Until it happened for real."

"Exactly," he said, laughing.

"What's so funny?"

"No, man, nothing. It's just . . . " He looked me over, then pocketed his phone. "You reminded me of somebody is all."

"Somebody in jail?"

He walked back to his trivia team in the corner booth without answering me. I couldn't remember their clever team name, but the whole bar looked real young to me in that moment. They were probably called "Tale of Two Titties" or "Wolf Pussy" or "Senile Felines," a name they claimed was a palindrome, meaning they could put it on a T-shirt and raise an eyebrow in the bathroom mirror. So I headed back to my corner, still trying to earn enough gift certificates to skip the burger and maybe snag my first free pizza. Angie loved pizza so much that she even tolerated breadsticks, the biggest scam perpetrated on the dining public. Once I tried to explain to her that breadsticks were just someone stopping halfway through making a pizza and saying, "Fuck it. Send it on out." But she swore they were delicious. I never said she was perfect.

Hours after trivia was over, it was just the one-handed urinal bandit and me at the bar, splitting the last two slices of Wolf Pussy's pizza, him twelve beers into his evening, which was plenty to really start opening up.

"So did you say you served time?" I asked him. "Or do I remember that wrong?"

"I don't think I said that. But sorta, yeah. You remember me from the joint, huh?"

"Uhhh, right," I said. "So how do you 'sorta' serve time there, Houdini?"

"Have you ever been to the invisible prison, Dave?"

"The what? No," I laughed. "Did I tell you my name? Okay, let me guess, are we in an invisible prison right now?"

"Sure," he said, turning away, and I knew he didn't mean it.

Then I saw Angie's one headlight reflected in the mirror over the bar, and when she bopped in to play some Frogger and some Attack from Mars: We Swear We're Not *Mars Attacks!* pinball, I didn't think about invisible prisons for the rest of the night. For the rest of the year really. But it turned out she'd been thinking about them enough for all of us.

***

I let the phone vibrate on the passenger's seat for about five hundred miles. I'd avoided talking to her family, avoided talking to *my* family, thought maybe I'd talk to my sister in a bit if I talked to anyone. But I never did. I was pulled over twice, the first time by the only female Highway Patrolman I'd ever seen in my life. I was so startled that I wished she'd been on a motorcycle so I could have had the shock of her long hair tumbling from her helmet when she took it off.

"Have you received a citation in the last year?" she asked me.

"Negatory," I said like an asshole.

But something about the cop's voice made everything fade away for a minute, and I started thinking about the Kentucky Derby incident. And Angie. About how her drinking started all over again every time we moved to a new state, no matter how many discussions and debates we had about how it distorted her personality, how it made me, at first, wait patiently for "the real her" to return the next morning, where I would explain that I merely tolerated a drunker version of her temporarily. Luckily the real Angie was worth the wait, and she'd promise to never get that wasted again. But she was reckless when she drank, and there was some incident on a "party bus," whatever that was, where she just said, "I'll tell you all about it one day," and I just assumed she got roofied, or worse, which wasn't much of a surprise considering the bad reputation those buses had back then (even if they weren't nearly as embarrassing as a pedal pub). Once, I saw something in the news about some college kids getting killed on a party bus around that same time, some antique fire truck converted into a hot tub, and I told her all about it. She laughed and said a big red truck was definitely a "big red flag," but her eyes betrayed the intrigue, because that was exactly the sort of thing she'd get drunk on.

All this was a touchy subject, though, because a lot of it had to do with her voice. It got higher the more beers she had, even higher after the third glass of wine. Three *anything*, that was our "limit," a rule necessitated by the Taco Hell dollar menu. If she drank enough, I swear her voice would get so high she had the neighborhood dogs howling. When she was little, her dad told her that her voice got on his nerves, and that was a shitty thing to say to a kid, mostly because it made the issue impenetrable for us. Sad, really, because it was one of the few times her dad made any sense at all, and from what I heard he was never quite there for her after the loss of his son.

But we'd just been getting ready to crash another state, to hit the reset button all over again, as we both landed jobs in San Francisco. Or I should say, she landed the Respectable Assistant Professor gig, and they agreed to hire my sorry ass as a favor. What's got two thumbs and is technically a Trophy Wife? This guy! And that cat I found in the cage. So the celebrations meant the beer and wine were flying again, and all her grad-school bores were back at our house and out on our deck talking academia into the fucking ground. Me inside on the hardwood floor, lying on my back, working the remote control to send a toy helicopter outside to buzz-bomb their beer bottles or throw off the rhythm of their endless pontificating. It never fazed them.

But in the morning, she swore that as soon as we moved again, it would be "no more drinking every night." She said, "You'll love me again, I promise," and that kind of broke my heart. But that's what she'd said in Pittsburgh, before we moved to Louisville. And that's what she said in Minnesota, before we moved back to Pittsburgh. We'd hit a new town, and she'd get comfortable around the newest batch of word-slingers, and that other person would show up, with a voice heading straight up through the stratosphere.

I should acknowledge that it wasn't just her voice that was affected. It was everybody's. Something about PhDs when they got excited about rhetoric made them sound like helium addicts. Maybe it was their own throats trying to choke them out. But when Angie swore it would be "just one beer from now on," I sighed and said, "Thank you," as if those voices didn't swirl out of the first bottle as soon as the cap was popped. It was a trigger for me, I guess, maybe after spending all that time with a pill-snorting addict when I worked at that bookstore in Pittsburgh, or mildly alcoholic '90s Ex-Girlfriend. Did I say that was Kool-Aid colored hair? More like wine coolers. So any signs of substance abuse or indulgence and I'd equate it with dishonesty, even when I was participating. Hell, it got to where I could tell if someone was even *thinking* about alcohol, just by the tenor of their voice when they answered three key questions, as long as the third question was, "Are you drunk?"

At one point, we talked about getting a camera so I could record how she sounded, but that just led to discussions about how she'd certainly act different with the knowledge of a camera's eye, which was some rhetorical sorcery straight out of her dissertation; the body-cameras, law-enforcement, the "Panopticon," and all that shit. But she was right. There was an inherent performance for any camera, which I'd seen first-hand with Johnny Five's star-making turn back at the bar.

The cop was still standing at my window, writing up the ticket, sneaking looks around the Rabbit. She finally returned my license, and I should have been relieved that there was no warrant out yet. As the cop walked off to her Crown Vic, she did say something about my license being "almost" expired, but all I could think about was our last day at the Derby the previous week, when all her high-pitched friends bailed on us at the first sign of a crisis. If our relationship had an expiration date, that probably should have been it.

It was our second Kentucky Derby, an event we'd wanted to attend as many times as possible before we moved again. We'd been to the Churchill Downs racetrack to bet a dollar here, a dollar there (the University of Louisville had a lot of days they sponsored for her classmates to get a bleacher box and pretend to be big-time gamblers), but the two times we tried to hit the actual Derby, it had been raining. See, if you were a student and not some Colonel Sanders mofo with a $500 reserved box or Turf Club membership, you could only stand in the infield, corralled like a show pony. And if it was raining, there were no umbrellas allowed down there because, supposedly, it was a "safety" concern. Maybe they thought snipers would take out a favorite horse. But living in a Red State for five years made me realize these rules had nothing to do with safety. Watching all the poor people in the infield getting soaked was just a perk for the overlords in the box seats. They could give a shit about the race. All those peasants stomping around the mud, deluding themselves that if they wore the big hats they were just like all the moneyed fucks up in the stands? That was the real sport. So twice we sat in my car in the parking lot and watched it rain out the window, Angie's giant crown of flowers she'd worked on tirelessly the night before slowly getting crushed up against the roof of the Rabbit. She tried not to cry, but we knew there was no way we were going to dance in the infield mud puddles like a couple of rubes for our feudal masters, even if her hat was probably big enough to protect a family of five from a tornado.

So the year of the incident, with the sun blazing, we were excited to finally participate for real and cross it off our

Kentucky Bucket List. But Angie was hammered before the bell even rang. I tried so hard to not get mad about this, not ruin our big memory, but when all her friends bailed on us because they saw the day was gonna end with a "carrying a drunk to the car" for a finish line, that's when things really went south. We were lurching back through the tunnel, stuck in a sweaty traffic jam of stinky drunks, me holding Angie up by her triceps, when some hairy, shirtless monster elbowed me for elbowing him, then grunted, "Watch your bitch, bitch!" I could tell from his voice that his beers were in the double-digits, and normally I would have reveled in sucker-punching him right there in the tunnel, away from any authority figures, and letting the crowds stomp over his ribs until his lungs stopped inflating. But then I looked down and saw Angie's feet. She'd lost her shoes at some point while I was dragging her, and her toes were bleeding pretty bad. She didn't feel this at all, even insisted I take my hands off her and let her be. Later at home when she slept it off, I stared at those feet rubbed raw and tried to get my heartbeat to slow down, swearing I was going to end our relationship forever when she woke up. But I didn't. Not because she was crying about her feet, but because I didn't want her to think I couldn't stand the shame of backing down from a fight in that tunnel. Not that she'd remember it or anything. But I would. So that hairy monster saved our marriage, for a little while longer anyway. And I'd probably thank him if I ever saw him again. Just kidding. I still planned on getting back at him one day. He'd be easy to find. He definitely lived in that tunnel.

After Angie's feet healed, we sort of healed, too, and I didn't care about her drinking as much anymore. That argument was a thing of the past, and I began to worry that the lack of conflict didn't mean I was growing to empathize but instead that I was becoming more aloof about our situation, starting to not give a shit what she did one way or the other. I felt like my lack of emotion was signaling the end of us, not the end of arguments, and I told her as much. But

I'd already thrown so many tantrums about her drinking that the prospect of me not caring anymore was something she couldn't comprehend. She saw my hands shaking and held me tight, voice cracking in a way that didn't trigger me at all, "You just have to be on my team, Dave. Even when that team is the *Bad News Bears!*"

She knew I was a sucker for a well-placed movie reference. That was one week ago. And it should have been a happy moment. But the morning she disappeared, I'd said something to her that I wouldn't have believed if they played me back the tape.

"I know you're sick of me. But that's okay. I'm sick of me, too."

She shook her head. But I was never sure which part of it she was denying.

***

I crumpled my speeding ticket as I drove on, cruising with the window down, face cooking in the sun, sometimes smiling in the rearview mirror at the Dreyfuss in *Close Encounters* "50/50 bar" sunburn I was cultivating. A truck flew by almost close enough to nick my sideview. Then the next one, a black F150 with dually flares, was almost close enough to clip my elbow. Trucks everywhere all the sudden, but it wasn't a surprise. As soon as you were south of the Mason-Dixon line, it was like you were exploring the borders of *Grand Theft Auto*, where there were no missions, and the game got lazy and only spawned rickety pick-ups to populate the roads. A couple more miles, and I swear I saw a tow truck . . . towing a tow truck. I wished there would have been a tiny truck in the driver's seat, playing with a toy truck, of course, maybe listening to Drive-By Truckers.

I was only about a hundred miles and three more years of flashbacks when I was pulled over again. A cop in a Silverado this time. And it was another female officer. It was suddenly like I was trapped in one of those all-girl utopian movies, the ones where they pretended it was a "Hell on Earth" situation to be whipped by powerfully-breasted, jackbooted women, even though all the little brats too young to be watching those movies knew better.

"Have you received a citation in the last year?" she asked me.

"Uh . . . how about the last hour?"

"What did you say?"

"I mean, is this a two-for-one special? Can I use a coupon?"

"Tired of getting pulled over yet, sir?" she said, not laughing.

You have no idea, I didn't say. Then she saw Zero chewing on the bars of his cage and took an uncertain step backwards.

"What are you doing with that animal?"

"Is there a law against driving with a cat?"

"That is not a cat," she said. "That's a goddamn badger, and they're illegal to transport."

"You don't say? That's not a badger, though."

"That thing has two black stripes on its head. That is a badger. But what have you done to it . . . "

"That's not two black stripes. It's black with three white stripes . . . "

"Same thing. And still a badger."

"Impossible."

"Sir, do you know what a cat looks like?"

"This is Zero," I said proudly, reaching into the cage and nervously pulling some stray blonde hairs away from his rounded ear. It was likely my wife's hair he'd picked up from crouching on the headrests, and now I was suddenly convinced those hairs would somehow convict me. "*CSI* Effect" and all.

"Say, 'Hi,' Zero! He hasn't meowed yet," I whispered from the side of my mouth, shrugging. "But what are you gonna do, right?"

"A badger is never going to meow."

"Who can say really?"

"The science is settled, sir."

"I like to teach the controversy."

***

I stopped off at a rest stop to throw away more tickets and grab some dinner, maybe see if Zero needed to do anything vile with his body. There was a dog park at the end of a winding walking path, and a duck pond at the end of that, not unlike those very special episodes of *Family Circus* where Billy documented a twisty path to the mailbox like it was a map to the *Treasure of the Sierra Madre* itself. A map to the movie, I mean. Nobody wanted that treasure. Wasn't it just a bunch of sand Bogart was carrying? It's the journey not the reward, know what I'm saying? Anyway, I carried my creature along this overly-intricate trail, hoping that an animal being dragged along and straining to get away from its owner was equivalent to the exercise it would get walking next to me like a normal pet. I vowed to get a leash next time we stopped so I didn't wear out his tail. A lot of personality in that tail, though. Felt like a whole extra friend in the car.

I found a good spot in the shade, and I pulled out the Trapper Keeper to flip through Angie's research some more. Along the side of an otherwise blank sheet of paper, she'd scribbled "Who's the Vice President?" She'd circled it more than once.

What kind of question is that? Who cares?

Then I smiled, remembering how she'd studied for hardcore trivia matches at Zanzibar, back before one of her drinking surges when I insisted on going all by myself. I rifled through some more pages, until I found a bundle of photocopies marked "Restricted Stacks," all with the same signature in the corner:

"Matt Fink."

Now that's *the name of an intriguing new character*, I thought.

At first glance, the pictures seemed pointless, grainy photocopies of class portraits of young women gathered in formation in front of their designated schools. But a couple photos were more recent, showing contemporary teenagers, give or take a decade in either direction, standing spread out in a field, a dozen or so as haphazardly arranged as one of those dull-ass soccer games we could never escape on the airport televisions during our honeymoon flights. *Who watched that shit? How about a nice Strongman Competition before boarding? Golden Gloves? Golden Knuckles? Tonight at 11:00: Globalism Ruins Waiting Rooms . . .*

My heart stuttered a beat and I squinted at the next photo, more kids in the woods, with serious faces, arranged in a pattern I couldn't discern. And in the corner of the photo, in a chaotic scrawl, more like a doctor's script than a script doctor:

"Matt Fink, Archives and Special Collection, Brickwood, Ohio."

Then I saw he'd added a little doodle next to his signature. A tiny heart, with a key hole in the middle. Next to that was, "Thanks, A!"

Come on, his name is really "Fink"? That has gotta *be the name of the villain!* I thought, and my fingernail popped through the photo before I could stop it. *Calm down, dude, you're destroying evidence . . .*

Deep under some old school yearbook receipts, I found a stash of our Paris honeymoon photos she'd tucked away, and I flipped through them fast like I was counting cash. I caught a glimpse of a lock-bridge selfie, and the graffiti-covered padlocks the day we'd secured our own to the fence, and I quickly closed my eyes. I counted the rest of the pictures in my hands, eyes still shut. It was unusual these days to come across physical photographs, and I hadn't realized she'd been printing them out. There was something much less sentimental about the digital photos stockpiling on our computers and phones, but when they're conjured into reality, into paper that could crease, or get warped by the salt of your tears, they were much harder to shake. I was pretty sure the grieving process would be much longer if I ever went through them, so I stuffed them back into the folder and snapped it shut.

When I rubbed my eyes clear, I looked up and saw we were at the duck park. The ducks were fighting over Fritos and whatever other garbage the traveling families of waterheads had thrown at them, but most of them looked healthier than you'd expect a gas-station Frito-eating duck would look. My sister once scolded me about feeding ducks bread, how it results in an awesome-sounding (but in reality absolutely ghastly) condition called "Angel Wing." Don't look it up.

I thought about how feeding them a bullet would probably be less cruel than whatever the purple popsicle-stained imp was throwing into the green, caffeinated water, but I tried to force a smile when some nearby whelp saw me petting Zero and ran over to see what on God's toxic green Earth was in my lap.

"Whoa! Is theeese yoursss?"

"Sure is."

"Is that a groundhog?"

"Yes," I said, not wanting to argue. Or talk.

"You wanna feed the ducks with me, mister?"

"No, I do not," I said, suddenly ready to argue.

Zero was noticing the ducks for the first time and sliding down my leg, clearly wanting to eat or possibly fuck one, and I had to scruff his neck hard and scoop him up. I headed back around the bendy path toward my car. The kid trotted along behind me.

"You sure? You sure? Hey, hey, you sure . . . "

He finally lost patience and threw a sticky handful of snacks at my car in anger as I hopped in to drive away. I rolled up my window and I stabbed the gas pedal a little harder to give him a nice gravel storm, likely his first shower in weeks. Then I rolled down the window to wave to his parents, who were now running up, mouths agape, pointing phones at me like revolvers. I nodded at Zero.

"Yes, I'm sure."

VII

EGG TOOTH

"NO, I DO not want to feed the goddamn ducks," I repeated to Zero as I drove off. "How many times do I have to say this?"

But why would anyone refuse to feed ducks with some apple-cheeked youngster? Who would reject such a "Normal" Rockwell-esque moment of peace and introspection to break up their quest? Me, that's who, and I'll tell you why. Also, this might shed some light on how me and some mystery animal in a trap became so inseparable. Here's a secret. It's more about the cage.

Even though my favorite coat had been specially designed for transporting freshly-blasted drakes, I've only known three ducks in my life up close and personal. Five if you count the two ducks that Angie's dad shotgunned on Christmas Eve so he could dangle the damn things in our face first thing in the morning because that's totally what Santa does. Thanks, New Dad! But as far as real live waterfowl, for some bizarre reason, my sister, my real dad, and myself all ended up with ducks instead of dogs running around our house. It all started back in third grade, in Diamond, Ohio, an overly optimistic name for a coal town. That summer they brought a bunch of eggs into the classroom, and us kids were like "Holy shit!" and forgot everything else we were supposed to be learning until they hatched. I picked an egg with a hole in it, initially because I thought it would never hatch and I'd get an automatic "A" out of sympathy. So when we were all told to carefully write our names on our eggs, I drew a sad monster face instead. But then when something started wiggling around inside that hole, I started hoping it would hatch after all.

I spent every second I could, even recess, near the incubators, waiting to see what would pop out. I went from aloof to hopeful to scared as I started thinking the sad monster I scrawled on the shell might curse the egg to birth something deformed. Did all the kids get eggs? I think so? It seemed like there was one for every kid if they wanted one, but some didn't give a crap, of course, so the teacher took at least five eggs home for herself. She told us that if our parents said it was okay, we could keep the baby ducks as soon as their feet hit the ground. No owner's manual, no warnings on the label. Yeah, it was a different time back then.

To my surprise (and slight disappointment), the broken egg hatched. And because I was leering over it when this happened, the poor little bastard imprinted on me immediately. The other kids weren't eclipsing their eggs quite as obsessively, or maybe their eggs just hatched when they were out on the playground, but I ended up the only instant father in the room. Problem was, after about a day of shivering and orienting itself with the world of a shoebox, this duck wouldn't stop screeching unless it could see me. If I went back to my desk, a steady, rising squawk would drown out the teacher, Miss Circle (an unlikely name, but that body was made of circles all right, high five!). But, seriously, it might have been "Mr. Circle," I mostly just remembered duck stuff.

So, if I ran over to the box, the incessant squeaking would quickly turn to these low, contented chirps and mutterings. Was it somehow messed up because of the hole in the egg? I didn't think so. It looked like any old duck, I guess, after it dried out anyway. Boy or girl, I never solved that mystery, but it had these black circles around its eyes, so I called it "Masko." I lied to the other kids that I drew the circles on its face. Circles everywhere in that classroom. It also had this weird tooth on the outside of its beak that gave me a scare at first, but all the baby ducks had them. Miss Circle explained it was a temporary horn to help them crack the shell and get free of the egg, something Masko never needed because of his hole.

This was the only thing we learned about ducks the whole year.

After all the ducks hatched, it started to get real noisy and pungent in the classroom, and Miss Circle had everyone who'd volunteered for adoption to take them home. I'd never bothered to warn my parents (weeks earlier I'd forged the permission slip like always), but after a raised eyebrow and a sigh in the car when he picked me up, my dad just shook his head and gave in.

The thing is, it's hard to take care of a friggin' duck, especially for a third grader. It's not like a dog, or even a cat. You can't really train a duck to do shit, *except* for shit, which it does about every seven seconds. And this little maniac followed me everywhere, shitting all the way. Sliding and falling all over itself on hardwood floors, scrambling hopelessly at the side of the tub when I was in the shower until one time I finally grabbed it and plopped it in with me, so it could happily paddle around in the suds and fight the swirl of the drain. It even hopped into the toilet once, doing figure-eights and chirping away until my mom pretended to flush it to teach me a lesson. It worked. I never left the seat up again.

With time, Masko grew a bit, feathers turning from yellow to dirty white. Eventually the egg tooth smoothed out, it started to put on some weight, and my brother swore it was sprouting not one but two gnarly peens, which had to be impossible. But it wasn't like we learned a whole lot about their anatomy, or at least we didn't retain it.

I had no idea how to take care of it either. When I let it

outside, it ignored all the games a dog would play, so I guess I treated it a little more like a cat by default. But when water was around, it was more like a toy really. I'd be in the back yard, drawing treasure maps or digging for elusive arrowheads or whatever, and, for a while, it would follow me. Until it saw its first puddle. Holy balls, that was a game changer. Masko loved puddles more than toilets. And this was about the time our neighborhood was flooding every year and had standing water in everyone's basements and around their foundations. So here's my duck frolicking in stagnant insect larvae and bacteria and who knows what else. But isn't that what they'd do in the wild, without the wise, watchful eye of third-grader supervision? This was something I told myself as I watched it paddle around that black water. Now that I'm older, I realize a wild duck wouldn't be swimming near a house. A house is leaking all sorts of deadly stuff, which is exactly what was going on in the miniature swamp of oil-slicked rainbow water that the air-conditioning exhaust and gutters had created next door. Our neighbor's name was Bruce, or "The Big Indian," as my dad called him, and Masko loved The Big Indian Swamp. So, yeah, of course my duck got sick.

And that's right about when things turned bad. You knew this story was too good to be true, right? Well, whose idea was it to give little kids goddamn birds anyway? "Fowl"? Even the name sounds grim.

But whatever ailment it had picked up in that black water hit the legs first, and suddenly its pool-party days were over. I started noticing Masko couldn't follow me as fast anymore. Just got weaker and weaker, falling over, even on carpet where it got the best traction. We all thought it had a broken leg. But then the tail feathers stopped wagging, too. And the wings shriveled and flipped upward, almost like it was making a snow angel. Something was shutting down the power on my duck from the bottom up. And after it stopped walking completely, it ended up back in that very first shoebox that I'd carried home. And now I had to haul that box all over, or else that steady, climbing squawk would drive everyone nuts, just like before, the first weeks it hatched.

So it was me with my hand perpetually hanging in this box to keep it muttering and clucking away, and that's the way we were for a few days. Then it was lying on its side and couldn't flap its angel wings around anymore either. Just the neck and head moving. But it was still eating oatmeal and baby food, and it still seemed aware of everything, so I kept on feeding it until it was finally just a head, barely moving. Then it was dead. I'd tell you that this actually happened on my birthday if I didn't want to minimize the little fucker's struggle. But it did.

The next day, we buried him in the yard, and someone's cat dug him up about an hour later. That was fun. The duck's story was depressing enough without an epilogue where there's this tiny skeleton on our porch like something out of *Titus Andronicus* saying, "Remember me? Do not let your sorrow die. Read the instructions next time, asshole."

***

What about the other ducks in my life? Yeah, it gets better. About ten years later, my sister hit the third grade, and they were still handing out ducks like mad scientists, teachable moments for kids they thought might be too well-adjusted, I guess. Only this time, my sister doubled down with two eggs instead of one. Jesus Christ. Get comfortable for this part. I wasn't around for the hatching, obviously, so I wasn't as emotionally attached to these ducks, and there'd been no imprinting on me this time. Or so I thought. Turned out ducks had imprinted on our whole family.

She named them "Quack" and "Stupid," which just about covers everything you need to know about them. Simple creatures, maybe, but these boys could sure be endearing. And they *were* boys, because even if education in elementary schools hadn't advanced far enough along to warn children about the horrific penises ducks were packing, it had progressed enough for teachers to identify gender. The duck's gender, I mean. Mr. Circle was long gone.

And the ducks won over my dad, something that dozens of the cutest dogs, cats, and children could never do. Quack was especially attached to my father and would nest on his feet whenever he stopped walking. But Stupid didn't seem to acknowledge his surroundings at all. Every minute was his first minute on Earth. They were lots of fun in our above-ground pool, though. And my dad really got into it, eventually building them their own pool out of some old tractor tires. And then he built sort of a kennel, using all the construction supplies my grandpa stored on our property. My dad would go out every morning before work and hose down the tires and the doghouse, then he'd fill up their pool party with fresh water, and they'd sprint on in, gibbering away, happy as hell. Sometimes they'd hide until he put the hose away, thinking it was a snake, which was weird because they'd gone straight from my sister's classroom, to the car, then to our back yard, and I doubt there were any snakes along this journey. But that's a duck for ya. And once the hose was coiled up under the deck, they'd run out of their dog house, slipping and falling over each other in the excitement, then splash around in their truck-tire pool until the sun went down and my dad flipped over the wheel to drain it all over again. You know, people always act like it's so cute that ducks love water so much, but no one says that about fish. Like, "Oh, my fish are so adorable! They would just splash around in that puddle all day if you let them!" No shit.

They were ducks, and that's all they did. Every day, splashing around, sometimes not dying. It's how they rolled.

Anyway, my sister moved out, and my dad inherited the two little idiots, using more lumber scraps to add onto their enclosure until this crazy duck hotel was as high as a man but twice as confusing. If you can picture this, it was like a double-decker dollhouse surrounded by a huge cage, sort of like the ones that separated dangerous inmates from each other in the prison exercise yard. And my dad started taking them to the vet, too, just like real animals, sitting in the waiting room with an upside-down duck hypnotized between his knees, since that was the only way they'd tolerate being held (the result of my sister cradling them like newborns all their lives). The vet told us this was also known as "holding them all wrong." My dad even started giving Quack some daily steroid injections, prescribed by one veterinarian who finally took the ducks and my dad's endless questions about their health seriously. I know what you're thinking, that maybe my dad was there when they hatched for them to be so attached to each other. That maybe my sister forgot her lunch money and he popped his head in the classroom and, in that moment, they accidentally imprinted on him or something. But it wasn't like that. It was more like the ducks were there when my dad hatched.

So, with all this attention to their health, these guys were getting real big, and turning bright white all over, outliving Masko by a long shot. And then the boys started laying eggs, too. Oops, so much for third-grade science! I panicked when I heard we had eggs, worrying we were heading for a swarm of ducks through the neighborhood. But those liquid Daffys couldn't be activated without any real males around, and my dad would just throw them out. If he didn't dispose of them quickly enough, they'd sit on them until they turned rotten. For a while, our garbage cans were getting tipped over every night by something in the neighborhood sniffing out all those rotten eggs. It was happening so often, we thought we had a dog terrorizing our block. But eventually we found out that the ducks were actually tipping over the cans because they wanted their potential spawn back. They'd knock over a trash can, root the eggs out of the bags with their beaks, then roll any unbroken ones across the grass with their faces, all the way back into their crazy kennel. So my dad rigged a latch they couldn't nose open and started locking them into their shelter after dark.

Oh, we tried eating the eggs a few times. Same as chicken eggs, better tasting really. Big, too, like Brontosaurus eggs (this was back when there were still Brontosauruses, and Pluto, and the all-egg Atkins diet). But we stopped when some of the eggs gave me horrible diarrhea. That was my fault though. I must have left one incubating too long under their feathers before I grabbed it. So we had to give up our giant pterodactyl omelets, and dad went back to throwing the eggs away. As soon as the ducks got out to roam in the morning, while he was hosing everything down, they'd waddle over to the trash cans and start that shrill, climbing squawk I knew so well, and my dad had to start throwing the eggs over the back fence for a few days. But then they started flattening themselves down and scurried under the fence into the noxious Big Indian Swamp to look for them. So, as a final solution, my dad had to herd the ducks over to the side of the shed so they could watch him whip the eggs against the wall one by one. This finally seemed to work.

But a couple days later, even with them locked in every night and no more eggs in the trash, they somehow seemed to be knocking the trash cans over again. My dad started watching their towering cage with binoculars to see if they were standing on each other's head, maybe wearing a trench coat and sunglasses and picking the padlock with their egg teeth. He never caught them in the act, but every morning, the cans would be tipped over and rolling around the yard. How many times did I just say "egg"? Egg. There, that's gotta be a dozen.

This mystery was finally solved, or a new one was introduced, in the worst way possible. One morning, my dad found approximately half a bloody duck padlocked in the cage. Something had eaten them. Both of them. Most of them. And the latch was still secure, a classic locked-room mystery. Eventually we put two and two together and realized whatever killed the ducks must have been the same whatever that was tipping over our garbage cans, and everybody felt even worse about blaming the deceased.

It was a dark couple days around our house, and you could see by the way my dad was grinding his teeth that he was planning something. First, he lied to my sister about how they died. Having no time for a good alibi, he claimed they drank the black, poisoned yard water like Masko had, then he quickly buried the evidence out by the fence. Then he dismantled the monstrous duck hotel with the reverence and ceremony of a decommissioned World War II battleship. He burned everything but the tires.

A day later, my dad started sleeping on the deck with a rifle, talking about possible impossible cryptozoological culprits ("Do Bigfeets eat birds? And why not?"), and he waited for the killer to show itself.

There was some collateral damage when my childhood friend (forever shortened to "Jay" after that day) got the shock of his life, which was probably shortened after that day, too. He was walking around our house one night to take a piss while Dad was on mystery-monster duty. As Jesse had just started to unzip, he heard an ominous click-clack, and turned around to find himself staring down a rifle. My dad was sprawled out on our deck, flat on his stomach like a green plastic Army man. Clock radio, potato chips all around him, thumbing the metal "bustin' eggs" tooth on the end of the barrel to keep his target sight clean.

Jesse always had bad luck with my dad, though, so don't feel too sorry for him. One time, Jesse made the mistake of driving by our house too slow to check out the scene after we got toilet-papered real bad by a rival school's football team, and my dad yanked open Jesse's door and dragged him out onto the road while the car was still rolling. He apologized, but Jesse had a slight lip twitch around my dad after that one, always trying a little too hard to be funny when he talked to him. And trying his hardest when he talked to me.

"Hit the bricks, Jay," my dad said from the deck. No time for full names on monster duty, or afterwards.

Eventually the raccoon returned to the scene of its crime.

Or maybe it was a badger. Either way, my dad got the culprit. Well, sort of.

Remember our neighbor who had the drainage ditch with the *Toxic Avenger* water? Bruce, our big Indian? Well, Big Bruce always felt bad about that black-water incident, so when he heard about our latest duck casualties, he put out this big-ass raccoon trap next to his woodpile to catch the killer, exactly the same sort of rehabilitation cage Zero would be discovered in.

Big Bruce was a hunter, always skinning something red and horrible in his back yard in full view of the neighborhood, but to us kids he was also a nice guy who let us cut through his yard to get to the basketball court. And he'd actually cleaned out the stagnant air-conditioning swamp so any new ducks wouldn't be tempted to roll the dice, real good guy. We never got the "Big Indian" thing. He just looked like a regular blue-collar guy to all of us, except maybe for all the bloodstains on his grass. Or maybe because of them.

But one night, after my dad finally wasn't spending every waking minute scoping out the trash cans for clues, the Big Indian stopped by and said he had "someone in custody." We followed him next door, and there locked in the trap was this hissing, glowering raccoon only slightly smaller than a grizzly, and actually the spitting image of my dad with his newly cultivated black-and-gray, length-of-chin beard. A creature that was easily big enough to lift up that huge cage like a blanket and crawl under it. Big Bruce told my dad he didn't kill it because they were my dad's ducks, and he would let him do the honors. So my dad retrieved his rusty—but never trusty—.22 rifle, stood outside the cage, and stared at the raccoon for about five minutes.

Then he went home.

Later, he told me and my brother (but never my sister) that, "Bruce took care of it," whatever that meant. Then he said he was pretty sure it was a muskrat, and not a raccoon, which made for some terrifying hushed conversations where we wondered if it had actually been a cat after all. This confusion over its identity might have helped explain my dad's lack of vengeance, or his guilt about condemning the creature to Bruce's Death Row. But his recent replacement in my life, Angie's dad, my new, gun-toting father-in-law—who thought of me not quite as the son he never had, but more as a piss-poor replacement—of course never met an animal he couldn't kill with impunity.

So that was the last we heard of the duck killer, and we all figured it ended up in a Big Indian sandwich. And duck season in our household was over for good. No one even thought about them again until we heard Bruce killed himself five years later out by that same woodpile. We were all off at college, but we got the story from my dad. Shotgun to the head. And when his sons came by to empty out his house, they told my dad that Bruce had been dealing with cancer, acting like their father's brutal suicide was the most normal thing in the world. Maybe that's why Bruce did everything outside, so the grass could absorb the blood and hide his brains, just like it always did, and his sons would only be tasked with cleaning up material possessions, which only filled the trunks of two cars.

One night, some time after that, my dad confessed to me that he must have ridden the lawnmower past Bruce's headless body at least twice without knowing. Was he sorry he didn't see the body? He said it was his one regret in life. And I wished I could have asked my dad about this once more to find out what he meant, but he died from a heart attack on that lawnmower the following year, which was better than dying on the road we decided.

Sometimes I think that strange confession was just my dad before the ducks talking, one last time.

VIII

FASTEN YOUR MEAT BELTS!

AS SOON AS we hit Brickwood, I decided the best thing to do after those run-ins with the Highway Patrol was to start looking for the DMV. This wasn't just because beautiful lady cops were suddenly popping up to remind me about my expired license (expired life, expired wife . . .), it was also because it felt like the most suspicious thing I could do at that moment, and I was convinced this might help exonerate me. Like the ol' double bluff, where I would say to a judge, "Who, Your Honor, would incriminate himself by messing with new identification when he was supposedly on the lam?" Then I'd start belting out Billy Joel's "Innocent Man." Not a dry eye in the courtroom, since I'd insist my trial be held during allergy season.

This is normal, right? The overpowering urge to be suspicious? I think I showed my first inclinations toward such behavior when my third-grade class was lined up against the fence on a field trip and questioned by a park ranger about who kicked in the front panel on the Coke machine outside the gift shop. I wasn't guilty, and nobody thought I was guilty, but it wasn't for a lack of trying! I just couldn't get my tiny feet through that plastic. So when the ranger was standing in front of me, I tried my damnedest to dart my eyes around, shuffle my feet, chew on my lips, anything to try to get him to *please* pick me, but he walked on down the line, checking all the kids' shoes for red paint chips, like the dipshit version of *Cinderella*. I hoped there'd be a Coke machine at the DMV so I could leave my footprint square in the middle of it.

"Who would leave their prints behind on purpose?" Exactly, Your Honor!

Cruising through the main streets of Brickwood and trying to find a pedestrian to get directions, I saw a missing-cat flyer on a telephone pole. Only this one was a gag. Remember that "lost possum" poster that was all over the internet? Same thing. It read, "Kitty Found! Not Very Friendly." And below the photo of the possum, "I think he might be scared! Not housebroken either!" Then the frowny face. I'd always thought it was a joke, but now, with the cargo I was carrying, I started to see how there might be some confusion. I mean, I've had some issues with animal trauma in my life, but no more or less than any other Midwestern kid surrounded by woods and creek beds. Nevertheless, this thing in my car had to be a cat. No way it was a possum. No way it was a badger, no matter what that cop said. Identifying cats was not part of a police officer's training.

What the hell was a "badger" anyway? There's a lot of cat in a badger's dumb face.

I looked up at Zero in my rearview mirror, and I saw that he was hungry and vying for my attention. He still hadn't meowed yet, but I was good at reading his mind anyway, especially when he was nesting on top of my head.

I circled around town for another dozen miles or so, wearing Zero like a hat, before I finally found some skateboarders who pointed me toward the Brickwood branch of the Ohio Department of Motor Vehicles. I realized I'd passed the skaters a few times without noticing them at all, the level of invisibility street musicians had acquired in my peripherals. Before I'd tried to kill one.

When I pulled into the strip mall parking lot, I tossed out

some of the empty cat-food cans that had accumulated on the floor of my Rabbit, then dumped Zero's shit box in the trash as I held my breath against the stink. I'd grabbed a metric ton of beef jerky inside the last gas station, but it was messing with his digestion, turning his turds into steamy little meteors, like the one the vagrant cracked open in *The Blob*. I figured, cat or no cat, beef jerky would have to do for now, because it felt like my bumblefuck investigation was getting closer to some answers regarding Angie's death, or at least getting closer to some better questions. Luckily, Zero loved it, but we were both paying the price.

My plan was evolving, but it was pretty simple. Get a new license, find the asshole who made all the photocopies for her at the Brickwood library, then maybe try to figure out if this was a cat on my head. I thought about copy machines, how that one was probably covered with her fingerprints. Copy machines were basically modern-day Cupids, the way they wasted everyone's time but simultaneously forced connections and conversations. Worse than water coolers, where something entirely different happened when you were lined up. I myself hated having to battle the urge to fall in love with Angie all over again when I spent a single afternoon at the Louisville Free Public Library watching the light flash across her face as she stood over an ancient, laboring Xerox behemoth. Those machines were warm, and the flash underlit your faces, like you were sharing secrets under the covers, making anything mundane potentially scandalous. And that day, Angie and I were both relieved when her huge pile of photocopies were finished, but for opposite reasons.

Better off letting your girl hang out at a truck stop than a copy machine . . .

I knew this guy in Brickwood must have talked to her about all sorts of stuff in that insanely intimate situation, whether he was the one who drew the heart with the keyhole in her dissertation folder or not. That fucking heart. It was doodled on the inside of the back cover. She might have done it, sure, but I'd known her for seven years, and she didn't strike me as a doodler of hearts. But she wasn't careful about hiding that heart when she was alive, so I hadn't thought anything of it. There was a "Thanks!" written next to it, however, and I'd raised an eyebrow at that. But I never had the chance to bring it up. And now I never would.

***

The DMV was weird. They had a big line of cars idling and waiting for the checkered flag on their driving tests, stacked up next to the entrance and blocking the front door. Maybe this wasn't a design flaw, because as I weaved through the bumpers it seemed like a clever way to incorporate pedestrians into a driver's license exam. That was the only explanation I could think of for why one driver kept waving me on to the door, then lurching forward and waving me back again. I'm not sure what this was teaching anybody, but the teacher seemed pleased by the teenager's braking skills. Also in the line was a car with a personalized plate that read, "SCRUGS," and I spent the remainder of my time navigating this obstacle course imagining Scrugs's final car wreck, and all the heartfelt eulogies and roadside crosses. Inside, things got weirder. At one end of the counter, there were about a half dozen kids all getting what must have been their first license, or first photo ever, judging by how excited they were to primp for it. And at the other end, gloomy faces slumped and frowning as another clerk handed them the laminated, finished product.

I feel ya, kids.

I was the least photogenic person of all time, so I was never surprised how hideous I looked on previous license-renewal days. The only thing that would have surprised me would have been if my new license did not look like some kind of disoriented toad monster.

I got in line and took a number, my registration and social security card at the ready, then stared at a mystery puddle in a nearby seat for way too long. To my right, I watched someone borrow a broken comb from a total stranger before taking off her N95 respirator to groom her remaining tendrils for her photo. I shuddered.

I hope when they call my number it means I go straight into the crematorium.

But I expected my renewal to be quicker than normal, since I'd originally purchased my car in Ohio, way back in undergrad, and, for all those years, never bothered to get it registered in Pittsburgh, let alone Kentucky. My procrastination was finally paying off! Full circle back to the Buckeye State with my Rabbit and my monkey. It was like a fable. More like a doomed TV pilot, *D.J. & the Bear,* tonight at 8:00 on NBC.

My number came up on a screen, and it just meant I remained in line. But when I got to the window, I'd somehow timed my approach to be between songs on whatever '90s mix CD was playing backstage on a boombox, and I locked eyes in this sudden silence with the clerk, an attractive thirty-something with wild black curls. Then "Nothing Compares 2 U" kicked in, I swear. It wasn't Prince's original version, but it would have to do. Angie loved Prince. Our wedding song was an acoustic version of "7," effectively rendered by her sister's arty friends.

"Hello!" I said, way too loud. I breathed deep. Something smelled so good, I could have sworn this place was baking apple pies.

"Hi, there. How can we help you?"

We were both smiling like freaks, although to be fair, they say this is an unconscious reaction whenever someone gets smiled at first. I think chimps do it. Definitely chimps on '80s TV shows like *B.J. & the Bear*. So it was my fault. Plus she'd said, "we." Gross. I thought this was about us.

"We need to get our license renewed," I said, handing over my old one. She took one look and the smile dropped.

"I know," I said. "Hideous, ain't he?"

"We'll do this as fast as possible," she said, smile returning. "As this is clearly an emergency."

"Don't you need an electric bill or something else with my address on it?"

"Nah," she said.

It was all going so smooth, I started to panic. She snatched my Social Security card from my hand and typed my information into the computer, which also should have alarmed me, given my "possible fugitive/at least detain for questioning" status. Instead it gave me a chance to give her and her half-cubicle of knick-knacks and paraphernalia a good, long look, and my panic evaporated. She was beautiful, with that Black-looking-white-girl thing, something that reminded me of my white-looking-Black ex-girlfriend, Miranda. Or was it the other way around? I couldn't remember. Not that it mattered. In five more years, this country would all be mutts like Mir anyway, as indistinguishable as the beast in the back seat of my car, if we were still alive.

Next to her Earth-shaped stress ball, I saw a picture of a Siamese cat and deduced she didn't have a boyfriend. And her name tag was some sort of joke, probably to keep idiots from hitting on her. It read, "Hi, I'm Mad! Stay Behind the Yellow Line!"

Then I felt terrible for wasting my burgeoning detective skills on flirting when my goddamn wife had just been murdered. I suddenly felt like this guilt was written all over my face, and now my smile was gone. I walked over to the blue wall for the picture, and, like always, proceeded to be photographed as I squinted and pondered my absolute worst qualities as a human being. I stood against a wall and counted to a thousand until she motioned me to the other end of the counter for the result. The license camc out as expected. Frog powers, activate!

"Is there a way to change this from 'male' to 'amphibian'?" I asked her, but the curly-haired clerk was no longer behind the counter. I turned around and was surprised to find her standing next to me, no longer tethered to her position of minor authority. She snatched the license from my hand, looked down, then looked up. Down, then up. I looked her over, too. She was much shorter off-stage.

"Did I forget something?" I said, trying to retrieve the license.

"No, I just wanted to see if it was any better than your old one," she said with an apologetic tone.

"Nope, it's always terrible! I could have saved you the time and told you it was gonna be another Frogtown Johnny."

We looked at the picture together, her leaning in. I heard her shoulder pop. It sounded amazing.

"Do you like toads?" I asked her, trying to sound smooth.

"Aw, come on, I've seen worse. But no, you're right, it's pretty bad. Your glasses are a little . . . froggy."

"Nice," I said. "Yeah, every picture comes out like that."

"So, why do you do that to your face?"

"That *is* my face!" I said, wanting to add something about how I'd been pondering my involvement in the death of my wife when the machine clicked and how, you know, that might have screwed up my close-up, Mr. DeMille?

"No, you are different in person."

I stayed on her green eyes longer than I should, and I decided that, fine, I was going to be a terrible person again tonight, but maybe this was the kind of distraction that could somehow keep me on point. Trapped in a car with a possum and only my own thoughts was getting stale. Also, I decided this would go a long way toward acting suspicious, which was my favorite thing in the world. Having a fling with a girl at the DMV and then somehow working in a joke the next morning about it being bad luck to kiss frogs or whatever was now pinballing around my brain. This would be the worst possible thing I could do given the circumstances, and certainly not the actions of an innocent man. Sold.

Angie used to love how all my new driver's licenses were worse than the last. So we saved them all, even with the holes they punched through them, a couple holes right through my face. Those were her favorites, as they reminded her of the commercials with the padlocks standing up to gunfire. She called the miserable, perforated faces in those licenses "DMV Dave," and we joked around imagining hypothetical situations DMV Dave would screw up. "What would DMV Dave do?" she'd ask. She even put "WWDMVDD?" on a T-shirt for me, which sounded like an acronym regarding the dangers of venereal diseases. Perfect!

"I make a great third impression, though." I grinned, and I walked toward the exit with her by my side. "So . . . "

"So . . . what?" she said.

"You want to hang out or something?"

"Huh?"

"I'm sorry, I'm just heading out the door, and you were following me and . . . "

She pointed to a sign above my head. It read:

"*Driving Tests in Progress. Wait For an Attendant to Exit.*"

"Yeah, I'm the attendant."

"Aha. And I'm the idiot."

She rattled a ring of keys in front of my face to rub it in, then unlocked the door to peer outside. The line of cars had thinned, and she nodded for me that it was okay to leave.

"Great third impression, huh?" she asked.

"Yes! And we're halfway there!"

She squinted and gave me a top-to-bottom evaluation. Unlike myself, she'd never look bad squinting.

"Okay, if you want, come back at 6:00 when we close. Get some tacos?" She pointed off into the distance where I assumed these tacos were waiting, but I kept looking at her.

***

At 6:00, Zero and I had all our feet on our dashboard, watching the door of the DMV for the new girl with the crazy curls, both of us nibbling on beef jerky. But somehow she snuck up on us, knocking on the passenger window and sending Zero bolting under my seat.

"Hi," she said as I leaned over and opened the passenger door. She climbed in. "I do appreciate this."

"Appreciate what? The promise of tacos?"

"It smells like you've already been eating some in here, among other things. But, yeah, that, and I needed a ride. One of the students wrecked my car during a test."

"You teach Driver's Ed, too?"

"We all pull triple duty at this branch."

"Gotcha. So let's get those tacos. We're both hungry."

"We?"

See how that feels? I thought.

"Yeah, the royal 'we,' me and my cat." I patted the seat next to my leg. She titled her head to get a look under it, then sat up straight.

"Dude. You have a skunk in your car."

"No, that would be ridiculous."

"It smells like a skunk."

"A lot of things smell like a skunk."

"Yeah, like skunks."

I smiled. She had a point.

"Before we go," she said, shaking her head to change the subject. "Why don't you tell me who I remind you of."

"What?"

"I could see it on your face when you came up to the counter. I remind you of somebody. It's okay, I remind everybody of somebody. I'm a good combination of features. It's a curse."

"Okay, you got me. To be honest, you are a spitting image of an ex-girlfriend."

"Gross. Is there a worse phrase in the world than 'spitting image'?"

"Uh, 'blow your socks off'?"

"Ew. 'Getting the wrong end of the stick' always horrified me," she said.

"Yikes."

"What was her name? Your ex?"

"Mir."

"Mir? Like the Russian space station?"

"No, short for Miranda. Like the warning they give criminals."

"Really," she muttered, suspicious. My mouth must have gotten tripped up on the word "criminal," because I was suddenly sure she was onto me. "Still not as bad as my name, I guess," she decided.

"Which is what?"

"Didn't you see my name tag?"

I shook my head.

"Come on. It's 'Mag'! Short for 'Madeline.'"

"No, way. You're a Magdalene?"

"No, I'm a Madeline."

"So, like 'Mad' for short?"

"No. 'M-A-G.' Are you listening to me or . . . "

"Oh shit! I totally thought your nametag said 'mad.' Like to keep people from fucking with you at the window."

"That, too. Okay, man, let's get going. Drive up to the stop sign, take a left, then a right at the light. It's on your left."

"What is?"

"The tacos."

"Oh, right," I said, still not starting my car. "I'm Dave, by the way."

"It's just curly hair," she said.

"What?"

"The hair. That's what does it. That's why everybody thinks I'm somebody they knew. Any female with black, curly hair is the same in their heads. It's kind of insulting, really."

"No, it's not like that. You act like her, too."

"I doubt it."

She suddenly reached across my throat, and I gasped until I saw when she was doing. She grabbed the shoulder strap with one hand, wiped the foot-long beef jerky wrappers off my lap with the other, then clicked it into place.

"Fasten your meat belts!" Mag laughed. "I've always wanted to say that."

"Why would anybody want to say that?"

"You teach twenty dumb kids a week how to drive safely, and then let me know the things you come up with to entertain yourself. So, are you gonna start this thing or what?"

She reached down and flicked my toy camera keychain with her finger.

"Oh, sorry," I said, turning the ignition. Her fingers stayed down by the ring, skipping the novelty porn camera, thank god, and thumbing through my keys. She stopped on one half the size of the others. It had a heart sticker on the end.

"Is this real?"

"What?" I didn't understand her question at first. "Oh, yeah, it's for a padlock."

"One of those love locks, Romeo?"

"Yep, exactly. Where you hook it to a bridge. How'd you know that?"

"Oh, I know all about them. We have one of those bridges here. Goofy shit like that isn't just France, baby."

My stomach flipped, and I tried to be cool, but my face betrayed it.

"Don't French deviants spray-paint those locks in protests?" she asked. "We do that here on our bridge. Especially if you clip a love lock on a bike rack. But it's good luck if some vandal tags your lock. If you think graffiti is ugly, you aren't very French."

"I'm not very French."

"Good for you. Have you ever *really* looked around Paris? Those are some love-struck weirdos. I swear I saw a heart spray-painted on a dead rat. But if you think that's unsightly, you haven't been to the Louvre, specifically the new Anglo-American exhibit. Now that's insane. George Washington's head is so tiny I thought it was an ad for the Mario Bros. movie!"

"You've seen the Mario Bros. movie?

"No."

"But you've been to France?"

"Not once."

She reminded me of Angie just then, how she'd held court with all the tourists in our hotel foyer, French, Dutch, German, didn't matter who, talking about life, love, all that shit. I joked that terrorists probably unplugged the dynamite and alarm clocks on their chests and went home to reconsider their life choices because of her rhetorical skills.

And though I didn't tell Mag this, we did see a dead rat with spray-paint on it. Pink. The same graffiti that was written across a hundred padlocks. "Rule #7," the graffiti read, whatever that meant. On another corner, we saw a "Rule #14" sprayed-painted across the ferns in a window box, which we assumed was unluckier than the cryptic message on the rat. Was it the French Fight Club? There were dead rats everywhere, too, and more graffiti on them than New York City subway cars. I wished we'd never left. For a couple reasons.

"Is that why you're here? For the lock bridge?" she asked, and I said nothing. "I knew it!"

"Knew what? No, that's not why I'm here. I live here."

"You don't live here. You came back looking for your old padlock on the Bridge O' Love." She feigned retching out her window.

"I did not . . ."

"Admit that bridge is why you're here."

It was now. She was persuasive, too.

So I followed her directions and got our tacos, and we ate them in the car. They were good tacos, from a place called Mondo Burrito. I told her I'd have to remember to come back.

"Yeah, none of that Taco Hell shit," she said, and I was so proud of myself for not bringing up a certain Taco Bell incident from our past, which led to a story about how my wife and I accidentally made a movie once. Don't ask. I only mention it now because I wanted *her* to ask about it. But there wasn't time for any of this fencing. This kind of fencing, anyway.

"Remind me to tell you about a movie I accidentally made once."

"Tell me about a movie you accidentally made once."

"Later," I said, and she rolled her eyes. But I was too busy pretending I wasn't suddenly certain that the same key that opened a padlock on a bridge in Paris would also open a padlock in Ohio. Only I never came with her to Ohio.

After we ate, Mag offered to show me the bridge, and I said "Why not?" Inside, I was saying a whole lot more.

***

"So, let me get this straight. You think your wife is cheating on you with someone in this town?"

"Yes. Kind of. I have a name right here . . . " I pulled out Angie's dissertation, all three hundred pages of it spilling out the sides of the Trapper Keeper like a poorly stacked sandwich. Mag stared at me bumbling with the taco wrappers as I tried not mixing them with page after page of correspondences and clues and antiquated red herrings. Mag slowly reached out to press the pile of papers down against my lap, and I looked up.

"Does she know you're doing this?" she asked.

"No."

Not a lie!

"Are those your notes?"

"No, they're hers. Listen, long story short, there are answers in here, and I need to talk to this guy . . . " I picked up a page stained with Mild Sauce and stabbed at the middle of it with my finger. " . . . this guy right here." Mag grabbed it and looked close at the signature page of a photocopy.

"'Matthew Fink, Archives and Special Collection, Brickwood, Ohio.'"

"That's him." Mild Sauce indeed.

"'Matt Fink?'"

"Yeah, why, you know him?"

"Hold on, you don't know who *Matt Fink* is?"

"What? He's some academic here at the library, someone my wife visited to help with her archival research. I saw his name in her phone once or twice. He makes copies. Big whoop."

She just kept staring at me.

"Matt Fink? Rhymes with 'rat stink?' So what?"

"Dude, Matt Fink is the keyboard player for Prince."

"Shut up."

But she was right. That *was* the name of the keyboard player for Prince. And this wasn't the kind of trivia a couple who had a classic funk-flavored ballad like "7" playing at their wedding should have overlooked. "Matt Fink" *was* the name of the fake doctor guy in the scrubs from the Prince and the Revolution days.

Prince and the French Revolution?

I *knew* I knew this at one point, but I guess I'd forgotten. But maybe that was why it had been so easy to remember when the name started showing up on her phone last year once or twice a week, for a couple months straight. She hadn't bothered to program a clever cat meme for his cell-phone profile, so I didn't think I had anything to worry about. But Angie was a huge Prince fan like me, and she was from Minnesota . . .

"Unh-uh, couldn't be."

"I'm telling you," she said. "He's like a hometown hero around here. Gotta be the same guy."

"You ever heard of the Vice President?" I laughed. I was trying to imagine Prince's keyboard player working as a librarian.

"You mean Aaron Burr?"

"Never mind."

"The Vice President" was another clue I'd found scrawled into the margins of Angie's notes. Usually with a circle and a line through it, something my English 101 class would recognize from my lecture as the archetypical "Fuck that guy!" semiotic situation.

"Matt Fink, huh? That's weird, but it's probably a common name," I said. "I'll bet you money it's just some guy who tells everybody he used to play with Prince, like that guy who went around running up tabs as 'Bootsy Collins.'"

"I don't know. I swear I've seen him in the news once or twice, or maybe it was a car commercial."

"See, that can't be him! It would be a doctor commercial!"

"Slow down," she said, hands up and shaking her head. "So you come down here to confront a guy who's sleeping with your wife , and . . . "

"This just seemed like a good place to start. They were both working on similar projects, talking at all hours. She came down here at least three times, sometimes for the weekend, once for a whole week. I just want to talk to the guy."

"Get a second opinion?"

"Something like that."

"'Do you still love him?'"

Mag was flipping through the pages with me, reading some notes out loud. I thought about Angie's question on the inside of her proto-yearbook. I was suddenly convinced I wasn't the "him," or she was the "you." But, impossibly, not being the subject of a soul-searching question about falling out of love was the worse proposition.

We studied more of her scribblings, rubbing our eyes, a little sleepy from the Mexican food.

"*'Who is the Vice President?'*"

Could be trivia-question prep work, that one. Not the hardest riddle in the world to answer, that one, but sometimes they asked those for the bonus rounds, like who were the last *five* Vice Presidents. That was a little tougher.

Then, just inside that cover, I found the envelope. It was stuck and tucked, hidden deep in the book, immobile from some spit and glue that had been squeezed out when she'd licked the seal. I worried it had nothing important inside. I ran my thumb over the dramatic "Invisible Prison" written carefully on the outside. Precise, almost like calligraphy. I moved on. We also found what looked to be a hand-drawn map of an ancient military campaign, specific battles circled, stained with food, blood, taco sauce? Flipping to the back, I saw that someone named "Zamboni" had written "Hope to meet you at Stanford," and near that a "Party Bus!!!" with at least three exclamation points over the drawing of a fire truck. Then I saw the heart with a keyhole again, this one on the inside of the back cover, right where the binding was beginning to tear, and the big "Thanks!" under it. It was the same handwriting. I looked up at Mag, unable to process anything she had been saying for the past 15 minutes, except the tail end.

" . . . but it sounds like fun." At least she was still smiling.

I was glad she was game, but I was a little scared, too.

What would DMV Dave do? Try to fuck the clerk then eat some flies. Ribbit.

I secretly hoped we'd discover this Fink had been killed days earlier, maybe stuffed into his keyboard case. A keyboard case was way bigger, right? Then I'd know I was hot on the trail of some serious shit. And I was kind of hoping he was the keyboard player for Prince, like for real. Because of course she'd be into this guy. The fucking keyboard player for her favorite artist ever? The Artist Formerly Known As Our Wedding Song? Man, I could marinade in an amazing betrayal like that forever.

And any response I had to such a thing would be considered reasonable. No court could convict me. No jury of Prince fans, anyway.

"We have come to a decision, Your Honor." "And what is your verdict?" "Go crazy."

Inspired by my possible immunity, I decided to turn up the heat with Mag. I pushed through the lettuce and cheddar shavings and the beef jerky strings like they were cattails and wildflowers, and I went in for a kiss. She got to me first.

It's not cheating, I told myself as we flicked our respective buttons and our car seats went back and Zero zipped to the rear to avoid being crushed. *This is the best way to be as suspicious as possible, something a real killer would never do.*

After an hour or so, we were strapped into our respective seats again and on our way to the bridge. I told her we could scope it out like a couple and fake a romantic stroll, see if we could find another lock to fit my key. It sounded less dubious when I said it out loud.

"That's a skunk back there," she said as she buttoned her jeans. "Is it going to be okay in here with the windows up?" Her respect for my animal touched me a bit, even if she was only worried about getting gassed by it. But, come on, where was she getting "skunk"?

"That's a hedgehog," I said, eyeing Zero nesting comfortably in the rubble of taco wrappers. "A hedgehog is an American hero. Skunks are French."

***

On our way to the bridge, we went over our master plan to interrogate this Matt Fink, bullshit artist, graffiti artist, and probable WebMD. In a ridiculous stroke of luck, Mag Googled him and discovered he was playing at some music festival near the Brickwood lock bridge the very next night. We decided to go see the bridge anyway, to nail down our strategy.

"We could pretend to be interviewers from a local music magazine," Mag said. I liked that. Get him alone, then I could shake some answers out of him. Or at least some songs. Then once he admitted to the fling and I lost my temper, or at least pretended to do so, Mag would see what I was made of, and, by proxy, Angie, too, theoretically. And maybe he could tell me who killed her. Or at least how she died, which were, technically, two completely different things, one no more important than the other.

And then maybe I'd find the invisible prison, if it was even a real place. And I'd see if my keys worked there, too.

As we drove, I found my eyes drawn to the ditches along the road, ditches I'd never noticed before.

"Didn't there used to be guard rails here?" I asked her, now driving half as fast.

"No, ditches are like this everywhere. No rail, no nothing. That's the world now. You're on your own."

I tried to look straight ahead, but even the shallowest road-side ditch seemed to drop off into miles of blackness, like an oceanic trench and the promise of sharp teeth and glassy eyes below. I kept both hands on the wheel, foot hovering over the gas, taking deep breaths at the occasional reprieve of an intersection or four-way stop. When I was a kid, I would walk faster and faster along a railroad track without losing my balance, and I had trained myself to do this without looking down, knowing full well I would never do it when it counted, like on the ledge of a building, or the rail of the Eiffel Tower.

When we finally got to the bridge, we couldn't get close. Park rangers had chained off both ends. "Closed at Dusk" the sign said. But it would be easy enough to step over the chains, so I grabbed a flashlight from the trunk. And even though we knew I had little chance of finding anything, especially since I didn't know what I was looking for (a padlock in a haystack?), I was ready to start checking a thousand keyholes anyway, just to keep myself busy. Before we headed for the bridge, I climbed into the back seat to stuff Zero into his cage, just in case we needed a fast getaway. I didn't want to take the chance of having a loose skunk panicking in the car and diving under the gas pedal at a crucial moment. This would turn out to be the only good idea I had that day.

"Have you looked through that whole folder?" Mag said. She was rolling up her passenger window and pointing toward the Sonic the Hedgehog Trapper Keeper on the floor.

"Hell, yeah. That's the heart of it. My wife's college dissertation is where it all begins. And, of course, I read it cover to cover. It's the least I could do."

"No, I mean the other folder."

"Huh?"

I followed her finger and saw that Zero had kicked most of the peanut receipts and stolen birthday cards from out of the homeless squatter's brown mailer, and now all of the bum's bullshit was strewn about the floorboards. She reached in and grabbed a birthday card off the top and opened it wide to fan her face. The card was big, with some cartoon old crone and a tired joke about memory on the outside. Inside there was no name, no age, just these words:

"We all have to make sacrifices."

"Oh, don't worry about that. That's just a bunch of mail some vagrant was stealing from us at our apartment." I snatched the card back and flipped it around to see if there was any more information. "And stealing from other people, too, from the looks of it," I mumbled.

"So you stole it right back," Mag laughed.

"Heck, yeah, I did."

She came around to my side and took my keychain from my hand. She held the toy camera up to her eye and aimed it at the last of the light on the horizon. She stifled a laugh.

"What?" I said, playing dumb.

"Nothing," she said, and she unhooked the camera and put it in her pocket.

"Hey . . . " I started to protest.

"What?"

"Nothing," I said, and I went back to securing the car. Once Zero was wrangled into his cage, I gave her a padlock key off my keychain to double our efforts, and we went looking for matching slots.

The bridge was different than its Paris counterpart; less "little league," but, ironically, more like the Eiffel Tower itself, with tough wrought-iron and weathered, flowery designs between the rails. Locks of all kinds were hooked and clustered along the bottom, and we worked through them for quite some time, reading names in our heads, mocking the earnest romantic sentiments out loud. There weren't nearly as many locks as Paris, but it was still enough to kill a couple of hours, as well as my spine from all the crouching. Eventually, I sat cross-legged in the middle of the bridge with the flashlight between my legs, and Mag plopped down across from me. I shined the beam up under my chin and smiled.

"Tell me a scary story," she laughed.

"I don't have any," I said, clicking off the light. Another lie.

"The hell you don't. We're in the middle of one right now."

I hadn't thought of it that way, so I started talking, trying to be a little more dramatic than usual, which overshot the mark somewhat.

"It's hard to explain, but I'm kind of having a good time. I mean, it's an appalling mission I'm on down here, and I seem to be terrible at this job of looking for answers, but this is the most . . . purposeful I've ever felt in my life?"

"I think I understand what you mean," she said, taken aback a little by the manic tone of my voice. "Actually, no. No, I guess I don't."

"It's not a relief that my marriage is over. I think that happened a long time ago when I wasn't paying attention. But there is some comfort. Realizing you're going to be getting a divorce while you're in the middle of an argument with your wife is very similar to someone deciding they're going to commit suicide in the middle of a normal work day. No, I'm not talking about the kind of attention-craving asshole who takes pills and calls an ambulance before they even start dissolving. I'm talking about someone who decides with complete conviction and certainty that they will be dead by the end of the week. When this thought occurs to them, psychologists tell us that it makes them very happy, and the sun comes out to warm their faces, because suddenly no bills are going to be due, no embarrassments will surprise them again, and all pressure is instantly lifted. This is why doctors tell you not to be as alarmed by the darkening depression of your friends and family as you should be when a smile suddenly cracks through those clouds. Real doctors, I mean. Not Dr. Funkensteins."

"Was it that bad?" She wasn't laughing anymore. "Your marriage?"

"No, it just never clicked. I never clicked. Never clicked with her friends either. They were academics, talking shit into the grave that I had no interest in, and I just never fit in with them. They'd be on our deck throwing around 'problematic' like it was going out of style, and I'd be flying my remote-control helicopter trying to . . . never mind."

"That doesn't sound so bad."

"It wasn't that bad. That's the thing. That's what's bad. But the end was the worst part."

"Not sure I follow, but maybe you can still fix things."

"I'll try!" I said, not stifling the laugh, and she took it as more of a sob and scooted a little closer. She took the flashlight from my hands and turned the beam into my eyes. I figured this meant she wanted me to keep talking.

"Fine, back in high school, I was dating a girl, can't remember her last name, Jenny Something? And I wanted to surprise her with a midnight picnic at this park in our small town. I'd planned ahead by stashing all sorts of stuff in my trunk; blanket, stolen construction cones, even a little orange barrel with a flashing orange light. And I had this cooler with beer and snacks. Back in high school, we went to great lengths to get alone time, you know? But we'd barely popped open a bag of pretzels before a cop shined a light in my face and made us pack it in. Exactly like you're doing right now. So, a month later, I was in court paying for open-container violations, theft of state property, trespassing fines, etc. And she called me afterwards to say, 'You had to pay? Ha ha ha, the judge let me off. She said, "Save your money for books."' I guess she meant for college. But when I was in front of that judge, her eyes burned a hole right through me. And for a second I was sure she was going to ask me the most important question. And then she did."

"Who, the judge?" Mag asked, taking the bait. "What question was that?"

"She goes, 'Before the cops showed up, you two had at least half an hour alone. So why couldn't you get an erection when it mattered most?"

"Oh, my god," Mag said, disgusted, trying not to give me the satisfaction of a laugh.

"No, listen! Jenny Someone told me she never told anyone about this, but she *had* written it down. She showed me, too, and I slapped her diary out of her hand and said, 'It happened to me, goddamn it, not you.' Seriously, leave it up to people that don't buy books for college to keep diaries, am I right? And that's why I couldn't get it up. That diary was probably entered into evidence. Exhibit A."

"More like Exhibit D."

"Nice."

"So, did her diary have a little lock on it? With a little key?"

"How did you guess?" I laughed, hand up to block the beam.

"They all do, you know," she said, taking the light off my face and shining it up and down the love locks decorating the bridge.

"Our night was weird, though, even before that park ranger showed up. I still think Jenny Whoever called them on us when I wasn't looking. I think that she was worried I was gonna do something to her, like pull something weird out of my trunk, weirder than all that construction gear, of course, which probably seemed pretty weird at the time. You didn't earn points for creativity in high school, only for normalcy. She was always suspicious of me, too. All week leading up to that night, she would ask about everything I was doing and who I talked to, all jealous, you know? She had this crazy cat that sniffed candles until his whiskers disappeared and it left him dizzy—remind me to tell you about that some time, it was all confused and bumping into everything until they grew back—and just like that cat, curiosity never once helped Jenny Whatshername or the judge discover anything about me that was in the least bit incriminating. So fuck her and her diary. I never cheated on her, I swear."

"Whoa, I didn't ask, dude."

I saw something flash in the corner of her eye and my heart skipped, anticipating police or park rangers again. I thought about the rest of that story, how I went back to that park long after high school and found our orange construction barrel half buried in the mud, the light still flashing on and off for years, still waiting for us to consummate that night. It was hard to see at first, but I walked up to the reflector and cupped both my hands around it, and there was the faintest pulse of light against my palms. I couldn't be sure if it was some invisible battery still beating or just the setting sun over my shoulder. Either way, I finally got that erection.

I didn't tell her any of this because the glimmer in her eye was another flashlight coming down the bridge, on the opposite side of the water, where we'd parked.

"Look, over there. Is that a ranger or . . ."

A shotgun blast hit the padlocks to my left and lit up half the bridge in a shower of sparks.

Mag was up and running before I could get my legs untangled, and I followed her lead back toward the Rabbit. Another gunshot exploded over our heads, and Mag threw the flashlight into the water. Her distraction worked, and the bobbing light in the distance hesitated, then trained its beam off the bridge and into the dark. We heard a shotgun ratchet to clear its shells.

We jumped the chains and fell all over ourselves getting back into the Rabbit. I noticed a car parked next to us, a filthy red Jeep Cherokee, similar to the car Angie used to drive when I first met her, but older, missing a bumper, a peeling NRA sticker on the window. Then my side mirror was blasted off in another shower of buckshot, and I started the car and floored it away from the bridge, not slowing below 80 until we were confident we weren't being followed.

"What the fuck!" Mag said when we hit the highway and finally caught our breath.

"That was no park ranger. Unless your park rules are more strict than the rest of the country."

"No, that was no ranger. Or the fuzz. Did you recognize that Jeep?"

"No." I paused, not sure. "I don't know." I shook my head clear, checked my remaining two mirrors for anyone in pursuit, then swerved for a well-lit exit ramp. After our hearts slowed to relatively normal, Mag turned to check the back seat.

"Wait a minute . . . " she mumbled, and I craned my neck to see most of the bum junk, all our old mail and peanut wrappers, now missing. Even the taco bags were gone. Zero was still in the cage, eyes blinking, dilated and black. But his door was open.

"How did you do that, Criss Angel?" she asked him, grabbing a handful of remaining mail and piling it into her lap to sort through in the front seat.

"Is the Trapper Keeper still there?" Mag glanced back, then returned to sorting photos.

"Yes, it is. Are these your pictures?"

"What pictures?"

"They were on the back seat. A bunch of pictures. Like mementos."

"Pictures of what?"

"I don't know. The Eiffel Tower? Is it supposed to be that color?"

"Oh, yeah, that must be from our trip," I said, gulping to stay calm.

"Oh, really? So is this her?"

I glanced over, but quickly looked back to the road when I saw Angie's distinct blonde ponytail.

"That is her."

"And is this you?"

"Of course," I answered, not looking this time.

SHE WAS FOUND IN A GUITAR CASE

"Sure doesn't look like you," she said.

I hit the brakes a good 50 feet before the red light, inhaled deep, then looked closely at the photograph in her hand. I looked long enough for the face to fade at least twice, but I still recognized him from the album covers, even without his surgical scrubs.

Motherfucker.

IX

BEATING THE LIVING SHIT

THE ONLY TIME you've ever had a girlfriend cheat on you, as far as you know, was back in Pittsburgh, before you met Angie. You rarely remember her name—Penny Something Or Other—but details don't matter, except that you didn't handle it well, mostly because everybody at the diner where all three of you worked knew something was up way before you did. Nobody likes to find out they're the last to know, and (in many ways) you were no exception. Even fewer people can deal with the discovery that they were the wrong corner of the love triangle all along.

When you first started hearing the rumors, you thought, *how can she do this to me?* How could the girl who rescued an earthworm off the street after a goddamn rainstorm so she could drop it safe in the grass, the girl who was with you before you served your sentence, and was the only one you ever told you did time, the girl who swore she loved you in spite of what you did, or was planning to do . . . how could she get drunk and fuck another guy like it was nothing and think you weren't gonna lose your shit?

To clarify, when you say "served your sentence," you don't want to sound like you're bragging, because it was only about 48 hours behind bars. You had been stalking the two of them when this cop came by and shined her light in your face. She didn't even ask why you were staking out that stretch of condos, or if that was a rubber horse head in your passenger's seat. She just ran your plates, saw the bench warrant for an unpaid ticket, and off you went in plastic cuffs, which were doubly humiliating. But for those glorious two days, you laid there after lights-out and listened to the guy in the next cell wash shirts in his toilet, and you predicted everything that would go down once you were free. You thought of every possibility, every variation of your futures when you would finally hit the gate, and some kind of physical assault was always gonna be among the possibilities. Okay, so it was more like an office door than a gate that you hit, but you didn't care. You did hard time! The door made a *clang!* when it slammed shut, you'd tell everyone. So suck it.

Leading up to and right after this arrest, you knew something had already happened between them by the way they acted all week at Ike's No Wait (a diner you used to call "Ike's? No, wait . . . "). It was you on the dishes, her on the tables, and him between the two of you, frying eggs, but mostly showing off and flipping around food like Tom Cruise in *Cocktail*. You could tell something was up, not by the way he sneaked little looks at her, but by the way he sneaked little looks at you. And you could also tell by the odd quack in her voice as she took orders from customers that she'd been snorting pills with this guy in the storage room. Her voice was suddenly like Dizzy Gillespie's trumpet echoing through that kitchen, but also weirdly content. It should be clear by now that an unrecognizable voice popping up on someone you thought you loved, this will always be a trigger for you. The worst kind of treachery, you thought. Until you discovered more kinds.

So one night after she got back from a party that her friends were way too careful not to invite you to, you confronted Penny Whatsherface. She wouldn't admit anything, so you put her in your car under the guise of going on a lazy Sunday drive, and then you punched down your rearview mirror, another flimsy prop in our fragile existence that must exist solely to be blasted by jealous fists during embarrassing melodramas. Why else would it have exploded so beautifully. Then you stabbed the gas and slammed on the brakes until she was in hysterics. You were giving the steering wheel the ol' snakebite, one of the first things a child learns with their hands, and your bloody grip squeaked on that rubber tighter and tighter until she finally confessed.

So you drove her back to your uncle's, where you'd been staying until you both could get a bigger place, or any place. And you made her pack up her stuffed duck and her pet lizard and get the fuck out of your life. She had this bearded dragon to replace the python you'd raised together. *Bearded dragon.* You used to think that name was hilarious, told her it always reminded you of something nasty. The name was perfect for her. Maybe not as perfect as her "Worm Farm" that she kept out by the trash, though. She should have lived there instead.

After she was gone, you curled up on the floor at your uncle's, hoping he wouldn't come home and ask questions, staring at the ceiling fan and wishing you were back in lockup, maybe for 72 whole hours this time, smiling at thoughts of ceiling fans in cells and hundreds of weapons that could be crafted with the most innocent fan's ornate blades, chains, and wires. You wondered how many men tried hanging themselves from one, and what a surprise that would be for loved ones if they could keep it spinning. Looking around, every object in your shitty basement apartment suddenly seemed potentially lethal, the same way how, in the best cartoons, the other guy on the desert island always looks like a sizzling turkey holding a noose. Yes, he was holding a noose. Look closer.

So you went to your uncle's bathroom, and you got his razor to help you focus. You've always had trouble with your "vision" (all definitions of the word), and you held the blade tightly to find solace in the one instrument that required no imagination to become a weapon. After some hairy eyeballing in the mirror, you shaved your head dry, anticipating your new home would soon be a cage where grooming could be difficult, and you relished every second of the sandpaper burn and the thin rivers of blood that covered the nervous pulse fluttering in your temples.

The last time you were released, your parole officer told you to lay low. Well, okay, it was Ike himself who paid your speeding ticket, not technically an official P.O., but your uncle was between paychecks, and Ike looked and acted the part. The way he forced you right back to work washing dishes, laboring next to your girl and the guy who'd been fucking her? That was ice cold, and right out of a prison movie. Is that how they tested you? To see if you could take it? Assimilate back into society at a moderately stressful dishwashing job? Well, after those two long days in the clink, you failed that shit, miserably. It's tough out there for ex-cons like yourself.

Ike told you that just one indication of remission, any hint at all that you would sleep in and miss another Sunday, for example (their busiest shift), if even a stray cat scratched your arm and you came to him with the mouthful of fur or even its tail in your teeth to prove your story and tried to explain that you couldn't do dishes because you'd bleed all over the suds . . . he said you were going right back to jail. Or at least going home early, without any French Fries. Or, a worse punishment, no Freedom Fries either, which Ike said were "just like real freedom, meaning 'almost never free.'" Ike was the worst.

Ike had nothing to worry about, though. You weren't going to be reckless. But you were going to take the low road, which meant the road right to the short-order cook's condo. Tonight's target, the Egg Man, was this college kid who was a little closer to her age by a couple hours, this little cocksucker who acted like you were his buddy while you all worked to feed strangers all night, this wannabe who wasn't a 48-hour *almost* ex-felon like yourself, but liked to surround himself with shady dudes to act the part, this actual junkie you were pretty sure was using because of that suspicious row of SpongeBob Band-Aids on his arm from his elbow to his wrist. You laughed at all his contradictory explanations for that arm, depending on who asked him, but no one else thought it was funny.

"Allergic to bee stings," he'd say. "Cat scratch fever," he'd say. "Tattoo gone wrong," he'd say. Or your favorite, "Mosquito bites from an audition for a bug spray commercial. They'll be calling any day now . . . any day now . . . "

So when you drove to the short-order cook's home that day, and he opened the door for you like a fool, you caught that skinny arm right on the smirking SpongeBobs, then caught a handful of his neck, too, and you dumped him backwards over his own crooked sofa. Then you beat the living shit out of him right there in front of his stupid dog.

Has there ever been a phrase more baffling yet as appropriate as "the living shit?"

That's what you asked him. And he didn't know the answer. So you started hitting him harder. So hard you got blood on that stupid dog, a shaggy little tumorous thing that was more like a cat with its lack of concern for its master's devastating beating. For some crazy reason, you were furious he didn't have a cat, as well, and you hit him some more.

As you beat on him, feeling him curl and contort and clench under you like a potato bug, you thought of both him and his dog forced to clean themselves, like cats, when you were done. Licking their paws and wiping their heads, licking their paws and wiping their heads. You thought of Penny Whatshernuts doing this, too. You thought of them all giving each other cat baths while you sat in jail and listened to a man wash socks in his toilet but wash his ass in his sink.

Watching his dog hop with delight at every splash of spit and plasma, you felt your heart slow and could almost see straight again. He asked if you would stop hitting him, and he even said "please," and you told him you promised not to hit him anymore if he took one good shot at your face. Just one good punch. "The old college try!" you said. He looked like college material, too. But he just curled up tighter and said, "No, you'll only hit me more."

Correct! You were amazed he knew you so well. Maybe you weren't the odd man out at work after all. You wondered if he'd had time to map out this moment in his brain, just like you did. A lot can happen in 48 hours. Unless it was cops trying to solve a crime. Did you know that, according to the show *48 Hours*, they barely have a 12% success rate? Get a real job, losers, you'd tell your TV. Like washing dishes.

"I loved her," the Egg Man whispered under your fists. But you barely heard him.

You don't want to brag, but the beating you gave the cook was one of the top-five ugliest things you've ever done in your life, even worse than what you would do to some street musicians years later. Way worse than what Johnny Five would one day do to you in that bar. But Johnny was "Part Man, Part Machine, All Cop." And to the cook that night, you would have appeared to be all hands. And he went wherever those hands told him.

There was a point when the cook started softening up, feeling the blows, really *feeling* them, and you could tell he was worried they might never stop. You were, too. He started muttering things like, "Sorry, sorry, sorry," as his mouth swelled to silence him. You asked him how long their fling was going on, if it was during the two days while you were locked up, but he was long past answering. Then you started saying dumb shit like, "Do *you* have a girlfriend I can fuck?" or "What's your cat's name?" or "Why do you only fry eggs?" and "Tell me that stupid dog is really a cat or I'll kill you."

At some point, you dragged him around his condo, which turned out to be a "halfway house," but for real. You held onto his head like it was a bowling ball, told him to give you the grand tour of his place, show you where they'd had sex, show you his models, including his incomplete skeleton of the Sears

Tower, which would eventually be christened "Willis Tower," though, because of you, would never complete construction, and it would always look remarkably like the Eiffel Tower. You even made fun of his movie collection, "*Demolition Man? Boiler Room? The Lion, the Witch and the Wardrobe?* You really needed to buy that one, huh?" But he did have a decent selection of prison films, if only the most obvious ones, of course. Still, you read those aloud with some reverence. "*The Rock, The Great Escape, Lock Up, Lockdown, Brubaker, Midnight Express, The Longest Yard . . .* " But he also had those terrible Stephen King adaptations, like *The Green Mile* and *The Shawshank Redemption*. Man, how you hated those. You knew you were watching some bullshit when prison movies made you feel like you went to church.

You told him all this, too. Yes, you made little sense. And, inevitably, you grabbed that arm with the rainbow of bandages and tore all the SpongeBobs loose to set them free. Then you turned his arm over and held the holes and roadmap of ruined veins up to the light.

"Mosquito bites, my ass," you laughed. "Did you know a mosquito defecates while it feeds? You know why? To make room for your blood. But did you know that if you catch a mosquito on your arm and squeeze the skin around it instead of swat it, that it might explode? This is true. But it takes a commitment. Sometimes you have to squeeze for a couple days."

Then you twisted his arm like you were making balloon animals. You twisted it like the snakebites your brother used to give you until you cried, or the chokehold you practiced on your steering wheel when it lied to you and wouldn't start, and you held his skin up to your face to see if any venom squirted out.

"Would you rather get bit by a snake or a mosquito? Would you rather fuck a man with a mosquito dick or a mosquito with a man's dick? Doesn't matter because they shit while they feed, brother. It only seems like an injection. It only feels like a tiny arrow through a heart, because it takes more than it gives. It pumps and pumps and fills you up with something else. Is that what we run on? It's not blood. Is it the 'Living Shit' we always hear about? Let's see . . . "

One more roundhouse punch in the mouth and your fist snowplowed through his bottom teeth and was halfway into his head before you knew it. Halfway down his throat.

Halfway to Hell.

You thought about halfway houses and petty crimes and how satisfying it could be to become a shitbag who did those sorts of things all the time. Half a house, surrounded by assholes watching reality TV and lights-out for curfew even on the outside. At that moment, you understood how enticing these things could be.

Then, disgusted by both of you, you dropped the face you were holding and surprised yourself by telling the short-order cook you were "sorry, sorry, sorry . . . " and you walked out. The stupid dog trailed behind you, ready to trade loyalty to anyone who could provide blood or meat. *How is that not a cat? What the hell is a cat if not that?*

It might still be following you around, but who could say.

***

Leaving the Egg Man's condo, you came across a deflated deer at the first red light, a carpet of flies and the heat shimmer of gas hovering over the hole that crows opened between its legs. The smell made your eyes water, but you kept your window down to inhale as much as you could to clear your head. It worked wonders.

In the distance, you saw the glow of a sofa burning in the woods, and you shook your head at the shouting and mayhem that surrounded it. It sounded like a fight, but you'd fallen for that before. Nothing worse than people fake fighting or burning couches for no reason. You thought about how you always smelled skunks on the highway, or more likely Skunk Apes, but you never saw one, probably couldn't even describe what a normal skunk looked like. But one thing you knew for certain was how the community-college lackeys next door to your uncle's always sounded like they were gonna fight until you'd get to the window and discover them laughing. You told Penny Whatsherfuck you were gonna lose it for good if you heard one more wannabe act out a fight all loud to his friends just so he could bamboozle some strangers into thinking something was really going down. She never understood why this bothered you so much, when people acted tougher than they were. A psychologist wouldn't even break a sweat with that puzzle.

Something will come down on them one day, you'd pray. *Right on their heads.*

You drove faster and faster, an arthritic fistful of pins, needles, and purple knuckles screwing the wheel tight as you could. You got pulled over like you always do, and when she got to your window, you showed her your bloody hands, and she had you follow her to the emergency room. She wasn't impressed, though. She'd told you that she'd done this twice already that night.

Silent reds and blues were making a path in front of you, and you drove faster than you ever dared before. Twenty miles over the speed limit at least. It was a long day of records. On the way, you licked the blood off your hands. And swallowed. Licked and swallowed. Swallowing it all; salt, hair, a splinter of bone, and something you couldn't recognize. It wasn't that bad, kind of like chewing on a chicken wing long after the meat was gone. But pieces of yourself went down way too easy, and you couldn't stop. You licked and wiped your head, licked and wiped your head. Licked and wiped your head . . .

When you pulled in, you held up your freshly cleaned hands, which confused the cop and the emergency-room staff equally. You shrugged and said you didn't know what she was talking about ("Whose blood?"), then she pointed to a spot you missed near your elbow, and you said, "Oh, that blood! Heck if I know, officer. Bug bite or something. My bed must be infested."

Not a lie.

Revolted, the cop left, and you forgot about her and Penny Youknowwho for fifteen minutes at least. Sixteen minutes. Another record. *More records than a jukebox today.* And when you got back to the house, you took your time getting inside. You stopped to hang from your uncle's curling bar that he'd nailed to the doorjamb, and you listened to your back crack and wondered what she would say when the Egg Man walked into the diner on Monday with a face like a mile of bad road and eyes like undercooked omelets. Then you realized this might be impossible, unless someone hooked him up to jumper cables, because you might have beat his ass straight to Narnia. You thought about how you couldn't be the only ex-con burning his hands red while scrubbing the silverware at that diner and watching some short-order superstar spin his sausages like whiskey bottles for the ladies. How did the SpongeBobs and Egg Men and Mansquitoes of this world make it so far in life without someone pulling their card?

Then you thought about how he let you into his home without a second of hesitation. Did he consider you a friend, never seeing the contradictions of his actions, right up until his end? Pretty bold for someone whose mission in life was to hook up with other people's girlfriends. But between beatings and tours of his love nest's historical landmarks, he gave you a reason why he hadn't stashed a screwdriver nearby, or leaned a baseball bat against the door, or tucked anything at all under a cushion for just such a reckoning.

"I deserve this, man," he said.

Me, too, you almost answered.

Later, when you had a healthy distance from it all, more things about that day came back to you. You remembered his empty promise about not calling the cops. You remembered swearing you'd kill him if you found out she was passed out at that party when their bodies intertwined, and how you held your breath hoping that was the case so you'd have a righteous cause for murder. You remembered making him tell you about the last time he got screwed over by a girl, and the last time someone punched him in the face. You remembered, right before you grabbed the short-order cook's short-of-breath neck to give him your last, best snakebite you'd been saving just for him, making him call her up and say as convincingly as he could, "Don't worry, there's nothing violent going on here. We're just talking." And you remembered checking his mailbox on the way out, thinking you should probably scrape off his name.

In the living room at the halfway house, sometimes referred to as your "uncle's house," there was a local news story where a church set up an Easter egg hunt and hired this man to ride around on a motorcycle dressed in a bunny suit. The adults in the congregation then knocked him out of his saddle and pretended to beat the snot out of him with Whiffle-ball bats to try and show kids what Easter was "really all about," and you turned up the volume to try and increase the thumping of the bats on the rabbit suit. It was nowhere near convincing, so you went outside.

Down in the ditch by a stagnant creek, you searched in vain for a worm to rescue and then wondered if she'd only been saving them to feed her lizards, which wasn't very noble after all. Then you searched for the perfect cattail and settled for one with a big bite gouged in the side, surprised they could attack each other like that when no one was looking. Then you were laughing and remembering what Ike had said about coming to work with cat scratches on your arms, and you took that tail in your teeth to measure your mouth and make sure the mystery assailant wasn't you.

By the time you heard the voices, you had a pile of cattails at your feet. And by the time you heard thc sirens, you were already stuffing them down your shirt, the bristles tearing out painful clumps of your chest hair, leaving a noticeable pattern of bare circles stamped across your pectoral muscles. On one of those phony survivalist shows, they once said this was the best way for a body to keep warm in the wild. They may have meant with a real cat, but no one had ever seen one, so this worked well enough. And you stayed out there in the ditch all night.

In the morning, you saw a car far across the river slowing as it wound its way up the hill, and you stared at it until it started to smoke, its engine finally defeated by the incline. You felt its pain deeply. Then you spent the rest of the day waiting to be found by someone, anyone, trying to decide if staring at a car until its engine blew was coincidence or wasted opportunity. You would later teach community college students in Elizabethtown about this very same misconception, more accurately labeled the "post hoc ergo propter hoc" fallacy, which your students claimed was Latin for, "You're not that cool, dude" or "Scanners Live in Vain" or, your favorite, "Nobody is ever watching when you need them to."

You decided your last happy thoughts as a free man would have to include how you hammered every inch of that short-order cook's head, and the way his left ear stuck out further than the right, and the small noises he made when he'd lost all hope, and the moment when you rolled him over to see his face again and finally smelled him the way he must have smelled to her during the height of his exertion. It was like smelling his insides, smelling his dreams. In many ways, the cook reminded you of your brother, the only other person you'd spent so much time tackling, wresting, or fighting, decades of sweating into each other's noses and mouth. But that was kid's stuff back then, full of snake bites with no venom, fake fighting like the endless thumping and laughter of the neighbors, and you and your brother only ever injured each other within reason, leaving all your legs, and eggs, intact.

Then you realized you knew this man's body more intimately than you ever knew hers.

You thought about his last words to you, which were also your last words to him, "I deserve it," as you scratched,

scratched, scratched at your arms. And just like he had done, you scratched until there was a hole.

The Egg Man totally survived your encounter, though. You didn't have to worry. What's the statute of limitations on manslaughter? The length of a relationship plus half? And even though you were fired from "Ike's? No Wait!" you didn't give two shits about your unemployment status because you'd finally gotten into grad school that very same week. The creative writing program at the University of Pittsburgh. Where you'd meet Angie. And where you'd be normal. And where you'd react to betrayal like you were supposed to. And you'd use your writing workshops to pretend like you'd made all of this stuff up.

Suckers.

X

FORCED PERSPECTIVE

I DROVE MAG to her apartment, and she promised to meet me back at the bridge for the concert. We sat in my Rabbit for a while, talking, with my headlights illuminating a massive web draping the side of the dumpster like a wedding veil. I asked if she had a spider problem, and she laughed and said spiders were never a problem. She said those webs were "tent caterpillars," whatever that was, and I confessed to her about how, when we were little kids, my buddy Jay and I would walk around our neighborhood with a Zippo and a can of WD-40 and torch the trees trying to light any webs on fire. When anyone asked, Jay would say, "Remain calm, ladies, we're The Mothbusters!" And then someone would try to kick our ass. No clue what any of it meant.

"I seriously can't believe we didn't get murdered," I said. "Hashtag 'The Eighties,' I guess?"

"They were probably gypsy moths," Mag said. "Or just more Malacosoma americanums. Major hardwood defoliators. You punks were eco-warriors in the tradition of the Monkey Wrench Gang. Righteous work, that."

I wasn't sure if she was mocking my foggy memories, but I was still beaming with pride when the glow of her snazzy TV-dinner-sized cell phone filled the car. She pulled up the internet to get the details on the show, and she said Mr. Fink would be playing the "Walleye Derp" tomorrow night. Mag explained that this was the other name the locals had for the Walleye *Drop*, sometimes called "Walleye Midnight Madness," Brickwood's offshoot of a New Year's festival in Port Clinton, Ohio, where fishing-tournament trophies were handed out and a gigantic, sparkling fiberglass fish was dropped from a crane, similar to the ceremony in Times Square, plus the fish. Also, this was done a couple times a year and signified nothing at all. And instead of a disco ball announcing the New Year, the fiberglass behemoth would smash open on the ground and dump out hundreds of pounds of Swedish Fish candies, or so we were told. She said it was basically the only time of year when such a legitimately large fish would be properly immortalized in photos in all its massive glory, as well as its actual size (if not its actual environment). And without the help of forced-perspective tomfoolery.

So, in what seemed like a remarkable coincidence, we learned from a Twitter page that was supposedly being maintained by the fiberglass walleye itself that the festival would be spilling candy fishies all over the love-lock bridge. If there wasn't crime-scene tape on it by then. It was virtually everything I'd come to Brickwood to see and do, all in one place, all in one night. Three birds with one bone, or however that saying goes, plus the fish. Mag said most everything in Brickwood was within sight of that bridge, so I shouldn't get *too* excited.

But there was still no sign of any "invisible prison." At least I would soon be able to slam the book shut on this Fink character, I decided. That was the current goal, before I was arrested or dragged back to Louisville for whatever accusations. Or worse, led in shackles into the public exchange of family grief that awaited me.

My rusty car door shrieked when Mag opened it to leave, and I watched her take out a penny and drop it into a cracked seam in the metal next to the passenger's-side window crank. It rattled around inside my car door like a piggy bank, and I laughed, baffled.

"What was that for?"

"So you'd remember to ask me to tell you the story later."

"Not a huge fan of pennies, but okay?" I said, a little worried what yarn she was gonna spin.

"Who doesn't like pennies?" she scoffed.

"Did you know it now costs two pennies to make a penny?"

"So what? Oh, wait, was that your . . . *two cents*."

I nodded my approval at her joke and watched her walk off, proud of myself for not bringing up the other pennies in my past. Still, I was unable to shake the idea that something was wrong, like maybe Mag had called the cops on me, just like Jenny Someone had *probably* called the park ranger on me years earlier on our not-so-secret date, or like Penny Whatchamacallit should have done long before now. I reached across the passenger's seat and shook the door, trying to shake the penny out. Unsuccessful, I slammed the door hard, still unable to shrug off the feeling I couldn't trust this new girl, even as I was drawn to her. I didn't get much sleep in the Rabbit that night. Pumped for this Walleye Derp, I thought about my brother, and the few times we went fishing. I started counting fish, specifically bluegill, but this made me more restless. Zero, too. He did exactly 27 slow figure-eights around the dashboard and the headrests. I know this because I kept track. It was the opposite of counting sheep.

***

Like most American boys, my brother's injuries started in a garage. What begins innocently enough as a refuge from hot summer days and the promise of shade and cool concrete floors, usually ends up an obstacle course of cuts and contusions. And for one of his most dramatic injuries in that garage, we were barely inside it. Half in, half out, which might be all the proof you need that a garage is the most dangerous place on the planet if just the *door* can mess you up. If I get time, I'll tell you about when I tried to help someone cut down the swing door on an airplane hangar with a chainsaw, and how the spring got unsprung and then the spring block exploded, almost cutting me in half. I was in a doorway then, too.

But my brother's garage-door incident started with us getting chased home from the "mudpit," this milky, borderline-stagnant pond where we went fishing for bluegill before, after, sometimes during school. It was filthy, but the only place to fish in Millbury, Ohio. And our grandma had made us a deal, a dollar for anything bigger than our hands. So we'd been pulling them out of the pond for her to fry up for our lunches, when all the sudden these older kids in a jacked-up 4x4 were tearing after us on our bikes. This was the result of one of us making some smartass comment on the bus a few weeks back (hint: it wasn't my brother). They'd slowed down the truck to ask if we'd caught "anything," and we'd gotten so good at it, so it felt like a trick question. And I said as much. In fact, that day alone we'd caught 17 bluegill, maybe 10 of them too small to eat, but they were all crowded in a bucket of pond water until we could make sure. And we were fishing with our fingers, too. I know, *all* fishing is with your fingers, but we just had fishing line tied to our thumbs, near the knuckle and the bottom of the thumbnail, where it didn't start cutting into our skin as fast. On the ends of our lines were some barbed Eagle Claw hooks (this was before the backlash against barbs, before the backlash against anything). They were the bait-holder-style hooks, with thorns up the sides like a rose stem. And we were putting wet balls of Wonder Bread on the hooks, so we didn't have much use for bait-holders, and we mistook those thorns for extra traction on the fish lips anyway. We'd found them in our uncle's garage, a bundle of hooks, each on a foot of line, or less, with little lassoes at the end the perfect size for a thumb. But like I said, it didn't matter what we were using. That pond was shallow and rancid but positively teeming with bluegill. And snapping turtles, who probably caught more bluegill than we did. These were the only two creatures we ever saw at the mudpit, but there wasn't any money in turtles. Our record was 63 bluegill in one day, throwing out line after line and not really aiming. Only 30 were worth eating.

The fish were stuffed in the bucket of pond water when the chase started, all splashing and jockeying for oxygen. I don't remember what I said, or even when we pulled the fishing line off our thumbs, but the next thing I knew, we were flying down the road with a truck weaving and honking behind us. Since I had the shittier bike with no seat, I'd learned to pedal much faster than my brother, and I got to our house first. I skidded into the driveway and glanced back to see my brother taking the last turn onto our street so fast his knees were knocking against his handlebars, his pedals a whirling dervish so dangerous that his sneakers were hovering up and out of the way of the wheel. I dismounted with the grace of an Olympic gymnast and let my bike slam the wall of the garage, leaving a black streak of rubber across the furnace. In a panic, I realized we were home alone, and I started pulling down the garage door as fast as I could. Right then, my brother came flying down our driveway at Mach 3, feet unsuccessfully trying to get back onto the blur of pedals to stop himself and *bang!* The garage door caught him in the top of the head and scraped him off his bike as quick and efficient as a little kid's foot decapitating a dandelion.

His bicycle, now blind, also got one good bite on me, a fender clipping me hard in the shin and slicing off a triangle of meat. My brother was down, I was down, and his bike was running up my chest like a slobbering dog greeting you at the door, its front wheel still spinning in my face. The 4x4 rumbled up to the edge of our driveway, and a greasy-faced teen leaned out to survey this scene of me wrestling a bike and my brother splayed out Christ-like, pre-Easter, in the gravel.

"Oh, shit, he's dead," the kid laughed. Then the truck was

gone with a roar. My brother woke up before the wheels of his bike stopped spinning in my grill, and he ran past me into the house screaming his head off. I don't remember who got in trouble for the crack in the garage door or the dent in the furnace, and nobody noticed the gash in my shin. It should have received a handful of stitches, but everyone was too worried about my brother's possible concussion with a football game coming up on Friday. For days, I dreamed of fishing line pulled tight between my thumbs, strangling that kid from the 4x4 like an assassin with piano wire.

My brother lost the football game, and there's still a scar on my leg. And for about a week, what I thought about most from that day was the smell of that bike tire an inch from my nose and the tiny nipples of rubber on the tread that I'd never noticed before. Then we went back to the mudpit and saw the bucket where we'd left the bluegills to die, tilted on a broken slab of concrete, lifesaving water on all sides, and now a year rarely passes where I don't regret not dumping out those fish. My brother still swears he was the one who pulled the door down on me, but unconsciousness can make you an unreliable narrator as effectively as infidelity.

***

I woke up early, relieved from watching the windows the night before that Mag's apartment didn't seem to be facing the parking lot, and I got out to stretch. I let the Rabbit idle and breathed in the diesel exhaust, which was almost as exhilarating as a morning coffee. Then I emptied Zero's litter box into the dumpster, which had kind of become my litter box, too. Don't worry, I was only pissing in it, thankfully. I was still on my "prison" poop schedule, which was one bowel movement a year until I digested a proper dinner. In the meantime, I fed us both some jerky, then I stared at the picture of my wife and Matt Fink and a purple Eiffel Tower in the background for about a half hour, and I felt the blood in my ears rumbling thick as lava.

It was looking more and more like Angie had been coming

to Brickwood for Fink, for some of that invisible *friction*, not for the invisible prison.

But there were a couple clues that calmed me down some. One, the date on the back of the photograph didn't correspond with either of her Paris trips, certainly not the one she took on her own for her rhet/comp conference years earlier. And two, and most importantly, the Eiffel Tower in the background that was peeking through the thick, jungle-like greenery and blotting out the sun . . .

It was painted purple.

***

I got to the Walleye Derp early. Like so early it was still dark somewhere else in the world, and I was convinced the whole thing was an elaborate prank. It gave me ample time to search in vain for suspicious initials scratched into love locks. Five hours later, people started setting up the porta potties along the river, and about an hour after that, a tent was erected for the band, so I went back to my car to stake out the scene from a safe distance. With the toilets in place, I knew that meant things were really going to happen. I turned my Rabbit to point my headlights at the tent, then flipped through Angie's papers some more, retaining every tenth sentence or so about our nation's incarceration fetish, and Zero and I chewed on either end of our last stick of Cajun-spice beef jerky, sort of like a bush-league *Lady and the Tramp*. Considering Zero's rescue, I guessed this made me the titular "Lady," which made sense, as I was now as homeless as that cartoon Cocker Spaniel.

Still half-asleep and digging around the back seat for more gas-station rations, I chugged a Gatorade that tasted more like a color than a flavor, then finally headed out to piss. Rather than adding to the quickly solidifying litter box in the rear, I made a beeline for the tight formation of chunky blue phone booths, spring-loaded doors already banging as the roadies broke them in. Watching the swelling crowd already queuing up, it felt a lot like the Monty Hall Problem: me trying to avoid the goat, or at least a goatee, as I went door to door and found them already occupied. Finally ducking inside one toward the end, the antiseptic smells of cleaners assaulted my nose, but goddamn if that smell didn't remind me of summer concerts and hooked thumbs in the backs of Angie's blue jeans. I started to unzip my own, then quickly became mesmerized by the voices surrounding me.

Maybe I'd never been in one of these Porta-Johns when there wasn't some noisy concert or festival-type situation, so it's possible I never realized that the little mesh half-windows on either side of my head perfectly projected all the conversations between every toilet right down the line, amplified straight into my ears like I was some insect who stumbled into a soup-can telephone during a conference call. I finished and zipped up fast, but I couldn't help but remain inside, standing stiff as I listened in.

First, I heard someone complaining on his phone about missing the big fish drop the year before. "Never again," he swore. Then came the scary stuff: "But I'm telling you, the guy has two dicks."

"Shit, I wish I had two dicks."

"Naw, two dicks only *seems* like a good idea. The second one is usually messed up somehow, so you have to suck or squeeze the extra dick way harder. To like *draw* that shit out, like a toothpaste tube."

"I don't have to do anything of the sort, bro."

"True story though. I know people who have seen them."

"Does he provide the emergency slide out the bedroom window so you can save time when you're screaming all the way to the parking lot?"

"There's a message buried in there somewhere, man, from your subconscious."

"Yeah, the message is, 'If you have to wring out the other one. Send help!'"

"No, I mean a *message* message like a fable."

So many fables lately . . .

I peeked out through the mesh and saw this conversation must have been happening between two porta potties down the row to my right, judging by the hollow rattles of urine streams in the pans. The echoing voices reminded me of the time Angie and I visited C.O.S.I., the now-defunct science center along the Maumee River in Toledo, and how they had a couple giant plastic satellite dishes about 50 feet apart where you could stand with the curve of the dish behind you and have a secret conversation. Only our conversation turned into an argument, first something about the social responsibility of an artist, then something about how her voice was too shrill, and I was immediately convinced people were somehow listening in. And they were listening in, because by that time we were shouting, and the echoes grew so loud that the whole exchange almost made me pass out, my own voice ricocheting around my skull like it had been cratered out with a trowel. But somewhere at the bottom of this metal bucket of stress and commotion, I swore I heard her confess she no longer loved me.

"Would you rather your girl fucked a guy with two dicks, or if she *had* two dicks?"

"That's like asking if you'd rather fight Mike Tyson or talk like him."

That's a great point.

"Hey, if you had two wieners, you'd never need suspenders."

"Fasten your meat belts!" I shouted before I could stop myself, and the voices ceased. I held my breath to suppress a yawn, and there was only one last ghostly comment.

"I heard he can play his keyboard with either one . . . "

Then came the laughter, and all the doors were banging open now, and I stooped down, heart pounding, mind locked on the most pressing question regarding my missing wife.

Could she have been having an affair with a man with two penises? The game of comparing genital size with former partners is reasonable enough, even expected, but insecure dudes now have to compete with mutations? How many men like this are out there?

I was at least three relationships past any urge to look through other people's phones, but I was suddenly consumed with a compulsion to scan Angie's notes for any evidence of this new . . . wrinkle. Normally, I wouldn't even consider the possibility, but we'd both talked about how "dick pics" were an oddly sanctioned form of flashing these days, even without the added attraction of a two-fold freak show. Was he a caveat, or a whispered fable come to life, about what happens if you Xerox your junk too much? So many questions. I wondered where her phone was right now. In a plastic baggie, most likely, buried in the back of an evidence-room shelf, the only physical proof of the Loch Ness Monster, forever forgotten, which turned out to be "Loch Ness *Monsters*," plural, though the second one took some extra coaxing to breach the surface.

I've heard of this, though. This is a thing. And aren't there a couple types of diphallasparatus *or* diphallia *or whatever it's called? Up-and-down schlongs, or side-by-side? Stalactites or stalagmites! Still a better love story than a duck's penis.*

In that moment, I just needed to see the damn things. Not quite a new mission, but certainly a side quest. Probably a bad idea, but weren't they all? True bravery should always be followed by deep regret.

I was still thoughtfully flicking my zipper when the door to my left banged, and the top of a man's head slid into view behind the screen. He looked out through his mesh, not really seeing me, but I could have recognized those Wayfarers anywhere, even without the album covers on our walls.

It was Matt Fink.

Somewhcre in another portable toilet was the distinctive sound of retching, and it might as well have been me.

"One of those days, huh, buddy?" Matt Fink sighed, and I assumed he was talking to me since he'd have to say "buddies" if he was talking to his dicks. I listened close for any indication of double piss rivers.

"You know it!" I said, forcing levity, staring straight ahead.

"Can I ask you a question?" Matt Fink asked me.

"Sure," I said, cautious. And I swear, this is what he said:

"What do you think about the social responsibility of an artist?"

It seemed impossible he could be asking me this, unless I'd been thinking out loud in my own acrid confessional. Angie had hated my answer, which he now supplied.

"Because I think the artist has no social responsibility."

"Yes! Agree completely." I already liked the guy, even though I knew the fumes in those phone booths could sometimes scramble your brains and turn phone calls into a game of "telephone," which made no sense at all, now that I thought about it. But I found him kinda personable as he was peeing. Not that this was the real Matt Fink. Way too young to be in Prince's band. Maybe a cover band, sure. But something about the confessional aspect of our faces in the shadows of those toilet vents really made me want to open up more than my shorts. I wondered if he was feeling this, too.

Wait, did he say "The Artist" has no social responsibility? As in "Artist" with a capital "A"? As in "Formerly Known As . . . "?

"Can I ask you a question?"

"Sure," he said, sounding more like a priest in a confessional than ever. Thank Christ he didn't follow that up with a "my son."

"Did you fuck my wife?"

The door slammed. I stood on my tiptoes and looked for the top of his head. He was gone. So much for our cover story of interviewing him for a music magazine.

Oh shit, forgot about my big date with the DMV. Mag is gonna be so mad. But I met the guy! New developments in the case, partner. The cat is outta the toilet bag and all that jazz.

I stepped out, and there he was, arms behind his back and cracking his neck side to side. I looked him over in the sunshine. And I have to tell ya, Matt Fink's big reveal in this adventure was amazingly vivid, a great dash of color. Even if I didn't already suspect him of having a fling with my wife, or having two penises, I had a feeling he'd made as memorable a first impression on Angie and he had on me. I stood there scanning him up and down, and in my head I imagined the voice of a movie reviewer commenting on such an impressive supporting character.

"You knew right away this character was going to be important, folks, but Matt Fink really swings for the fences with this role, brandishing a menagerie of impromptu Yoga, subtle emoting, and, the biggest twist yet, unique facial characteristics not seen since The Incredible Melting Man . . . "

He was yawning, and he had this nervous stroke mouth, where only one side of his lips were moving. Though there was no way to put a finger on what else was wrong. He just didn't seem to stand like a normal human. And his reaction to everything, such as meeting a cuckolded widower outside a toilet, was to respond as if someone just told him aliens were real a year after they landed. Also, his head was sort of bent to the side, just a bit, like he was perpetually balancing an invisible phone on his shoulder. But one of the big phones, from the '80s, so that part made sense.

"It's as if he knew one characteristic wasn't going to be enough to make him memorable in such a freak show as Dave's Dumb Road Trip, and I want to be the first to nominate Mr. Matthew Fink for Best Supporting Asshole . . . "

But, like I said, definitely not old enough to be the fake doctor in Prince's band. He also seemed too young to be a real doctor, in real life.

"Sorry, sorry," I said, hands out in peace. "I was talking to another toilet."

"Huh? Oh, right," he said, uninterested, cupping his hands over his shoulder and behind his back. His voice was very much like the movie critic in my head, and I just went with it.

"Are you a real doctor?" I asked, trying to appear as casual as I could while leaning against the "Party Time Portables" and the smiling anthropomorphic toilet stenciled on the door. This question seemed to put him at ease, maybe since anyone asking for a doctor's advice might be sick, or weak, and therefore less of a threat.

"Yes, I am a real doctor. Why?"

This answer amazed me even further, because now I was either dealing with the actual Matt Fink, a.k.a. the fake "doctor" keyboard player from Prince's former band The Revolution, who was pretending to be a doctor out in the real world for some bizarre reason . . . or this was a different "Matt Fink" entirely, who was an actual doctor, pretending to be Prince's old keyboard player, and who was also fucking my wife. Who would you rather have perform an operation?

Mike Tyson.

I looked him up and down, with his throwback '80s style and spiked hair—unfortunate fashions that were already coming back when I first met Angie. I wouldn't say I was having fun, but I was certainly awake now, and he had my full attention. He was also wearing those goofy "FiveFingers" brand foot rubbers, those hideous toes with the shoes on them. I wondered if he got any money from their well-publicized class-action lawsuit. But how could a real doctor be the only person on Earth endorsing a fraudulent company and not demanding money back for stress-fractures to his feet? His feet also seemed remarkably small for a man with two penises. I remained skeptical about everything.

"Are you a *doctor* doctor though? I thought you were in the band."

"I'm playing in the band today, yes. Dr. Fink & the Funkensteins?"

"But you're not that kind of *doctor* doctor," I repeated, but he was done stretching.

"Excuse me," he said and started to walk away. I stopped him with a hand on his chest. Now I had his full attention.

"You want to hear something funny?" I asked softly, vaguely threatening. "Me and my wife used to laugh about how she couldn't wait to bust people for saying 'Not that kind of doctor' when she finally got her PhD. Happened all the time, too, even after we changed our mailing labels."

"I am *that* kind of doctor," he said, looking down at my hand. I couldn't stop staring down either, for a couple reasons.

"So you're a doctor but you're wearing flippers that were in the news for fucking up people's feet?"

"What are you trying to solve here, Dave?"

"Nothing," I lied. *Stop the press, he knows my name? Did I tell him my name?*

Matt Fink sighed again. "If you must know, I've been barefoot most my life. Like those African runners in the Olympics. The stress fractures that affected so many people aren't a factor for me. In fact, it's the very problem with these shoes that makes them beneficial to someone such as myself."

"Uh huh," I said, making a mental note never to get in a foot chase with this double-dicked motherfucker.

"Can I go?" he said, still staring at my hand on his chest. "We need to finish setting up our instruments."

Medical instruments?

But after the confessional, I was still in a spilling-my-guts state of mind. Or spilling someone's guts. At that moment, I thought about telling him all sorts of things. Like how we'd once arranged a threesome but couldn't swing an extra female and settled for my buddy Jay instead, because I'd seen his dumb ass naked dozens of times and figured it wouldn't be an issue. But how that disconcerting moment when we both disappeared inside her had precisely the opposite effect I anticipated. "Spit-roasting" was the vulgar term Jay had used for this experience, but rather than a perverse feeling of power, I felt more like I'd been absorbed, devoured, teetering on being disemboweled or thrust inside-out, rendered negligible. I realized that night that this secret interiority of women's bodies made them infinitely more terrifying than the exposed meat of our own.

Afterwards, I couldn't look at Jay, and sometimes Angie couldn't look at me, but we tried to put it all behind us. Until I found the letters. And a level of detail betraying acts once thought impossible. Or improbable. And the riddle returned. If I had a choice, two men or one man with two . . .

Mike Tyson!

And she'd confessed all of this, that day along the Maumee River, whispering that she'd tried it again, just to make sure. One man, or two men, not that kind of doctor . . . it didn't matter. "It was for my own good!" she screamed into the din of those monstrous metal buckets, and I could hear all of this clearly, even 50 feet apart. Because science was fucking scary.

I took my hand off his chest and stepped back for him to pass, but was shoved aside instead as another roadie crashed into the toilet we were blocking. I watched him go, to see if he'd turn around. When he didn't, I went back to sit on the hood of my car and studied Dr. Fink milling around the stage. Meanwhile, surprising no one, dozens of men jockeyed to get the most deceptive shot of their competition walleye by dangling them high and away on their rods to make them seem bigger. But for some reason, obvious penis jokes from the spectators were in short supply. The giant fiberglass fish rumbled in on a flatbed semi-trailer after that, and it was a little smaller than I expected. But it was impressively ancient. All chipped paint and dead, glassy eyes. It rolled past me, and I saw my yellowed reflection in its gaze, fogged over with years of indifference.

No way they're going to destroy that thing at midnight, I thought, as the crane cranked it up into the sky. Mag had said it was full of candy, and I overheard a couple locals swearing they were going to strap themselves to it and ride it into the ground like a Major Kong on that nuke. It all felt like more lies, but I sat through the entire band rehearsal, and the tunes cheered me up. Maybe it was considered an ugly time for music, but I'd always enjoyed the cheesy '80s stuff. Bright, fluffy, and mostly gibberish, but honest in its idiocy, with little time for irony. Also, it should be noted that, like a pro, Dr. Fink played two keyboards at the same time. Of course he did.

One last time, I remembered that I'd forgotten about Mag, but I hoped to remember to forget her again soon. See, that shit sounded like a '80s song right there.

They dropped the fish after all, but the town was too gutless to let it hit the ground.

Or maybe it's still falling.

***

The car door screeched and rattled as she climbed inside, kicked off her shoes, then put her feet up on my dashboard. The door's protests were quickly becoming her signature sound. She lined her toes up with the footprints she'd left on the windshield from our previous encounter. As I watched her get comfortable, I did a double-take. It's not that I didn't recognize her, but there was something that bugged me. Okay, how can I say this . . .

She's not mad, but also definitely a little mad? Mad like the hatter.

"How was the show?" Mad asked, big grin, like she was trying not to bust out laughing at some inside joke. "You forgot about me, didn't you, Dave?"

"Sorry, I thought you were meeting me there," I bullshitted.

"Nope, you were supposed to pick me up."

"Oh. So, what were you going to tell me about again?" I asked after I breathed her in, a wonderful cocktail of some kind of orange-blossom flavored shampoo combined with the midday's sunshine and sweat trapped in the baby hairs of her arms.

"What are you talking about?"

"You said to remind you to tell me something. Then you put money in my car door."

"I put the money in the door first, actually, but it worked, didn't it?"

"What worked?" I was baffled. Mad sighed, blinking way too long.

"Okay, so, I knew this kid who had this cracked piece of metal on the inside panel of his door, a lot like yours, and it made this little slot that was perfect for change, like pennies or dimes or whatever. It was a great way to save money, basically. And any time he'd stop at a drive-thru or 7-Eleven and get change back, rather than tossing it into the jar to save the orphan cats, he'd drop it into this hole in his door. But eventually, his door starts making jangling sounds, *money* sounds, and rattling real loud when he takes hard turns . . . "

"Then what happened?"

"Nothing. He had a car full of cash. That's it." She shrugged, then reached into her pocket for a handful of change and started feeding the coins into the slot on my door, one after the other, all of them tinkling down to the bottom.

"Wait a second," I said. "Didn't the added weight throw his car off balance?"

"What? Shut up. Why aren't you driving? Mush!" she said, whipping the air.

"I'm just trying to figure out why you're telling me that story, and dumping coins into my car door."

"I don't know. It was fun?" She shrugged, leaning over to steal a kiss. It felt performative, and I ducked it.

"*I Don't Know. It Was Fun?* is what they're gonna title your biography," I said. "After the rest of us are dead."

"Great." She crossed her arms. "Are we going to this show or what?"

I leaned back in my seat and cracked my neck on the headrest, searching my mind for a story from my past that would impress her. But the accident with the chainsaw and the garage-door spring hadn't happened yet. Watching me, she was reaching for her handle to leave, and I panicked. As my brother could have told you from the floor of our garage, halfway in or halfway out of any door was the most dangerous place to reside. I dug deep.

"Do you have a Taco Hell in this town?"

"Sick. No. Why?"

"Because I used to work there. Just kidding. Not really. I sort of put them out of business."

"Out of business how? Did you work there or not?"

"Remind me to tell you that story some time!" I said as I fired up the ignition. Zero finally opened an eye. Mad released her door handle and blew a drip of sweat and a black curl off her nose, smiling, and we both forgot about the concert.

As I drove, I heard her drop her last penny into my car.

***

Back in high school, I picked a fight with this dim-witted asshole everyone called "Squeegee." He got that nickname in third grade when the bus driver caught him writing a bunch of profanity on the windows with his bad breath and knobby fingers. This made him a hero at the time (we were *real* short of heroes), especially when the driver had the principal meet our bus at the curb to parade Squeegee into the building with all the gravity of *Dead Man Walking*. But by the time he got to 9th grade, he was a bully and a monster, and one day Squeegee was taking too long at the water fountain and I said, "You want to practice sucking on something else and give somebody else a turn?" It wasn't my best joke, but at least I'd said it out loud. I usually hesitated cracking wise after my last zinger back at the mudpit caused those kids in the 4x4 to run us down and give my brother a concussion with our garage door. And there was a line of kids at the fountain who heard this joke and start hooting, so ol' Squeegee leaned in and told me to meet him behind the dugout on our baseball diamond at 8:30 that night so he could kick my ass. None of my friends heard Squeegee choose our gladiatorial arena, but word of the fight was spreading, and a lot of guys wanted to help me out. Everyone hated Squeegee. But right before my mouth could form the words to tell everyone to meet at the dugout, I got the bright idea to send all these reinforcements to a nearby church parking lot instead. I wanted to take out Squeegee myself, you see, and I figured I'd be a legend no matter how it went down.

So at approximately 8:37 p.m. Eastern Standard Time, my friends went to church, and Squeegee beat me half to death behind a dugout. And for years afterwards, I never lived this night down, constantly getting wrong directions from my friends every chance they got. But I still felt like my friends were a little impressed by how I rejected their help, even if they'd never admit it. My brother wasn't impressed, however, because he'd followed me to the dugout and watched the entire thrashing from the bleachers.

I didn't feel the side of my face go dead forever while I was getting hit, but I heard it happen. A sound like a molar popping the gristle off the end of a drumstick. This was the sound of my sinuses caving in, but the permanent nerve damage was probably silent. When I asked my brother why he didn't help me out, all he said was, "My seats were too good."

I hated him for a while, but then I'd think about the fish we'd left to die, and how five more bluegill might have been enough for the bucket to tip over on its own, dumping them back into the water. Or five more dollars in change.

Some time after the fight, I was lucky enough to run into Jenny Someone (or maybe it was Penny Someone) while I still had scabs and a purple nose and two black eyes from the surgery on my skull, and this was good for my ego at first. She was initially impressed by my battle scars, so I kept going, talking about the dugout, then my noble prestidigitation to misdirect the mob away from my beating . . . until I saw her tuning me out completely. I could hear myself soldiering on, relating the whole story anyway, going through the motions with a minimum of detail, but all the while thinking about the bowerbirds we'd learned about together, in that weird Australian exhibit at C.O.S.I.

The excitable, high-pitched narration of the video detailed the male of the species building this crazy tunnel of sticks, lined by an even more complicated avenue of rocks, with smaller rocks toward the front, and larger rocks toward the back, which the bowerbird utilized to entice a mate. The narrator explained, in a slight bogan accent, that this was the only creature in the animal kingdom that messed with perspective to trick the female. But what we found most interesting was that this bird seemed to do all this work in order to appear smaller. A bowerbird perpetuated its species and won the day with a show of weakness.

Which is how it should be.

XI

SECOND MOST SUSPICIOUS THING I COULD SAY

NOW THAT'S TWO *dicks!* I thought, proud of myself, but not proud enough to say it out loud.

For the first time in days, I wasn't thinking of my wife's infidelity, or her death (in that order), but instead I was concentrating on my favorite two Louisville police officers who had tracked me down to Mad's parking lot and were now digging through her trash. Somehow, this special attention had reenergized me, even more than the night I'd spent in my car with Mad. Having cops on my trail felt like I was doing something important after all.

I first saw them both kicking around the dumpster where I'd been cleaning out Zero's litter box hours before. It was raining, so I had my car windows up, and they hadn't noticed me yet. Watching them root around like stacks of raccoons disguised in suits, I was momentarily convinced they'd literally sniffed me across state lines to the last place I'd pissed. Hell, I was ready to get my own litter box and stop sharing Zero's, maybe just cover the floorboards of the car in gravel and wood chips.

One of the cops tucked back his necktie and picked up a chicken jerky wrapper. He took a whiff, then sent it on its way into the river of run-off bubbling from the curb to the sewer grate. I decided their names would be "Flotsam and Jetsam," and I wondered how long it would take before I slipped up and said this out loud.

The big one knocked on my window, so I gave him a crack.

"Mr. James, were you at the Walleye Drop today?"

"Derp!"

"That's no answer."

"No, I mean, that's the name."

"How long have you been in town, Mr. James?"

"Since yesterday."

"Did you attend the Port Clinton Walleye Festival?"

"No, I attended the Brickwood, Ohio, Walley Derp. And I tried to get someone to take a trick shot of me pretending to hold the giant fiberglass fish, you know, a forced perspective shot, like when you pretend to fuck the Eiffel Tower? But no one would do it. I think they were disappointed it wasn't full of candy. Or that it didn't explode on impact."

"What are you doing in Ohio, sir?"

"And why aren't you home with your family, sir?"

The questions were coming faster than I could answer, so I picked the easy one.

"Listen, Jetsam, that's none of your goddamn business."

I lasted 27 seconds!

"Step out of the car, Mr. James."

I did what I was told. Not just because of the rash of police brutality nationwide, but also because Angie had confided to me a couple weeks back that her prison research had gotten her an exclusive glimpse into actual police-training videos and how I would be shocked ("Shocked, I tell ya!") to know how many of our recent problems with police shooting unarmed Black men seemed to be the obvious result of outdated but action-packed video clips demonstrating how to approach strange vehicles and expect the worst, mixed with more general, across-the-board misinformation (and racism), all under the guise of what she called an alarming spread of the "Quick Draw McGraw or Be Ready to Die" mentality. So I got out slow.

"Over here, please." Flotsam pointed to the back of their Interceptor, and I saw a couple plastic Ziplocs laid out on the top of their trunk. One of them contained a padlock.

"What's that?" I asked, buying time to think, resisting the urge to run over and grab it.

"Maybe you can tell us," Jetsam said, picking up the baggie and handing it to me. My eyes no doubt betrayed my excitement, so I tried to keep things light.

"Evidence! Awesome. Are you offering me a job in the police department?" I asked as I turned the bag over in my hands, wondering what the rules were about incriminating fingerprints on Ziplocs, rather than the evidence itself, and then deciding a good lawyer could probably make a case about a guilty person trying to steal back something that incriminated them.

"Have you ever seen this padlock before?"

I pretended to study it closer. It had a bullet hole in the body of the lock. Just like Angie's favorite commercial. Even stranger, it had a drawing of two cats on one side and a spider on the other. Which was exactly how we'd autographed the "love lock" we'd left hooked to the Pont des Arts bridge in France.

Three thousand miles away.

"How did you get this?" I asked, almost laughing in disbelief. "Did the French embassy extradite this shit?"

Flotsam took the baggie away, looking me over in revulsion. I decided to shorten their names to "Jet" and "Flo." And "Jet" was clearly the "bad cop" in this scenario.

"This lock was found on a guitar case," he said, and my forced levity dissipated like a smoke ring. We all knew he didn't have to say the next part, but he did it anyway.

"The same guitar case where we found your wife."

***

That's impossible, I thought, not hearing most of what they were saying. I felt like I'd skipped an hour ahead just standing there. A dusty red Jeep Cherokee with tinted windows was rolling through the parking lot, and I watched it over their shoulders as it scouted out the scene. Tinted windows were big in Kentucky, where trends were a good decade behind (even Blockbuster was still open when Angie and I first moved there), but I knew tinted windows were illegal in Ohio. The Jeep idled a moment near the parking lot entrance, then did a U-turn and pulled back out. It was moving slow enough for me to make out the peeling NRA sticker on the back window, and below that another sticker with the old joke, "Not Really Aiming!" Then, below that, written in dust on the Jeep itself, a slightly more timely interpretation of the acronym: "Nuts, Racists, and Assholes!"

I considered telling them about the night before on the bridge, getting shot at from a Jeep like this one, all that pulse-pounding excitement, maybe shift their attention elsewhere. Then the Jeep gunned it down the street and was gone, and, for some reason, I decided not to mention it.

It's my adventure, and they have no business being involved in it. Who needs them?

"Now listen to us, Mr. James. We are considering charging you with . . . "

I changed my mind immediately.

"Hey, did you see that Jeep? That guy shot at me last night!"

"Listen to me . . . "

"No, you listen to me . . . "

Flo reached for my wrist, and I was scared. The black-eyed gaze of a camera lens peered at me from the box on the cop's lapel, and I remembered my encounter with Johnny Five and I realized I was more nervous because of the camera, not in spite of it.

Then Mad was running into the parking lot and stepping between us like a boss.

"What's going on here?" She sounded chipper, but her brow was furrowed deep. I could never do that. It was like patting your head and rubbing your belly at the same time.

At first, Jet refused to acknowledge her.

"Mr. James, do you know someone named 'Jill'?"

"Friend of Jack's?" I laughed, but also sneered. See that? Terrible at it.

"Your wife was supposed to attend a surprise party for this woman, on the very day she went missing."

Angie did say something about a party, but it couldn't have been the day she vanished. I was sure I would have remembered something like that. But back in Louisville, I skipped every party I could, and though I liked her friend Jill Hawthorne well enough, her parties were no exception to my embargo. So it was possible. But . . .

"A witness placed your wife, and possibly Jill Hawthorne, at Papalino's at 9:00 p.m. Another witness claims to have seen her riding in a fire truck through the back roads of Bullit County sometime around midnight."

"A fire truck?" Now I was truly stumped. "Was she in a fire? Did you check the hospitals? Where was all this? After midnight? Your timeline makes no sense. Are you time travelers? Hey, where's a fucking butterfly I can stomp on . . . "

"Calm down, Mr. James," Flo said, but he released my wrist.

"We're still looking into it." Jet blinked extra long to indicate that topic was closed.

I thought about all the partying on Bardstown Road every night, and how the only fire truck we'd ever seen down there was that ridiculous anachronistic nightmare with the flashing lights and the bubblehead drunks splashing and gyrating around in the hot tub in the back. But she'd never ride in that thing. We'd made fun of that rolling nightmare mercilessly. It was always big around St. Paddy's Day. No, she'd never set foot on something so conspicuously idiotic.

Then again, she's been doing a lot of things lately she'd never normally do.

"We would like to show you one more thing, Mr. James."

Flo popped the Interceptor's trunk, and in a flourish produced several more plastic evidence bags; one with a chalk-stained 8-ball, one with a shark's tooth necklace, and one with a large earring. He left one bag in the wheel well of their spare tire. It may have contained Angie's iPhone, but I couldn't be sure. I studied the bag on top, recognizing the earring immediately. Angie had worn those earrings to work the last morning I saw her. Locust-sized ukuleles, or "baby guitars," a gift from the music school when she first began volunteering. I reached out to touch it.

"That's like nine more things," Mad said, stepping in to divide our space again.

"Have you met Flotsam and Jetsam?" I asked her. They had me rattled. No more nicknames. Flotsam took a bag from Jetsam and held the earring bag up in my face.

"We're particularly interested in this. Can you tell us anything about this object?"

"Well, it's Angie's, and she was probably wearing them when . . . the day she was killed."

I tried not to look at Mad, but I didn't need to. I knew she was looking at me. Then she was trying not to look at me. Even though this was the first she was hearing of a murder, it didn't seem to be a deal-breaker. This thought stabilized me somewhat.

"What do you think we'd find if we dusted this tiny guitar for prints?"

"I imagine you'd get a very confusing result," I said, arms crossed, smug as a mug shot. "Also, that is clearly a ukulele."

"And why would we get a very confusing result?"

"Because a month ago, I used those same earrings as a prompt in the fiction-writing class I was teaching. I sent them around a circle, where the ukuleles were fondled by 25 students."

They stared at each other a moment, then turned back to me.

"Why would you do something like that, Mr. James?"

"Because it was the most suspicious thing I could do."

They looked ready to arrest me on the spot, so I clarified.

"I mean it's the most suspicious thing I could say? *'Say,'* I totally meant, 'say.'"

"Good lord," Mad muttered.

They both blinked this time. It looked like they'd blown a fuse. I decided if they blinked real slow at me again I'd make a run for it.

"You're doing great work though, guys," I said. "Keep it up. You'll make detective in no time."

"One last question, Mr. James. Some of your students reported seeing your wife on several occasions. In fact, they say following your wife was part of your class as well."

"Damn right it was. I send my students on many 'people-watching' assignments, which are very common dialogue exercises. You know, 'describe your setting,' 'describe your subjects,' 'describe the conversation,' 'bonus points for describing a lost dog . . . ' That last one caused some controversy, actually, since what made a dog 'lost' turned out to be pretty subjective, and half the class said it was just something in the eyes . . . "

They both wrote this down, as I trailed off, reluctant to add that, unbeknownst to my class, I was 100% having my students spy on my wife. And when they turned in their stories afterward, I'd spend most weekends scouring their adaptations of what they'd seen or overheard during Angie's day for any clues to her indiscretions. Unfortunately, this was exactly the sort of plot a college student would embellish, meaning I'd read a dozen horrific versions of my wife's affair, each more melodramatic than the last. Which was worse than the truth, most days. But my most talented students understood that the more unremarkable they described Angie's day, the more suspicious any reader, not just myself, would find the narrative. And they were right, of course. I, like most married men, could easily wring hidden messages out of the worst fiction if it meant it verified my worst instincts.

With one last narrow look, Flotsam and Jetsam packed up their evidence baggies, and tossed them in the trunk. Flotsam climbed into the Interceptor, as Jetsam handed Mad a business card.

"If you think of anything that could help, give me a call."

They drove out of the parking lot without another word. I took this abrupt end to my impromptu interrogation as a bad sign.

"What the hell?" Mad asked me after they turned out of the lot.

"No clue."

"Really." No question mark. She was inspecting with the same scrutiny as the cops. We'd hooked up in the car the night before, and she must have assumed I'd drive off afterwards. But here I still was. It felt like I was seconds away from her realizing what a mistake a new relationship with me would be. Then she tucked the cop's card into the front pocket of my jeans and gave it an alarming swat, and I recoiled.

"Why don't *you* give him a call," she said.

"Ouch," I grunted.

"Are you sleeping out here again?"

"Maybe."

This must have been the right answer, because she turned and waved for me to follow. I cracked a window for Zero, and trotted to catch up.

She let me use her shower, which was something I certainly needed after living in my car with an unidentifiable animal. I cranked the water up hot, until I could barely stand the scalding spray on my shoulders, then I put my head under the nozzle. Ever since that high school fight with Squeegee, the right side of my face had been a dead zone, a Bermuda triangle from eye, to jaw, then back to the corner of my mouth. Technically it wasn't the beating that killed my cheek forever. It was the compounded nerve damage from the surgery I needed to repair a broken nose and cracked sinus cavity. The doctors had packed my face with gauze, but somehow stuffed it *underneath* my face, like behind the scenes, where smiles and frowns were hurriedly being constructed, just jamming this spool of fibrous dressing up my nose and through the collapsed antrum to reshape the new depression under my eye. Kind of like popping dents out of a fender. A week later, when they pulled the cotton from my nostril, it stretched at least three feet from my body, like a magician's handkerchief trick if those hankies were bloody, and it took four orderlies to hold me down. It was a couple months before I realized I'd lost the feeling on that side of my face, and that my smile was forever crooked so I mostly retired it. I spent the next year or so slapping myself to prove this numbness to friends and family. Then the slapping tapered off, and I graduated to the longest, hottest showers of all time. They were quite extravagant, those showers, but I had to do it. In case anyone was ever looking.

Hands finally off the wall, I found whatever fruity orange shampoo Mad had in the shower that made her mess of black curls smell so good, even through a hole in the plastic and the haze of despair at the DMV. It was Angie's shampoo I was smelling, of course. I brought the bottle up to my nose. White Rain. That Dollar Tree favorite. Angie called it "The White Trash Starter Kit," and she wasn't wrong. But the heart wants what it wants. I stood with the hot water running off my nose, thankful Mad invited me over.

I stepped out of the shower, riding a wave of steam, and I put my old clothes back on. Mad said my attempts to smile looked broken, and this was a big turn-off, but there was something about my eyes she could trust. Or maybe it was the other way around. Like I already explained, there was little feeling left in my face, which made the features more interchangeable in my mind. And any attempt at expressing real emotion, or honestly answering any direct question would be close to indecipherable. But that's who I was, more so now that ever.

She had driver's licenses of men, young but ugly, pinned to the back of her bedroom door, under a sign that read: "Hall of Shame." I asked if she'd dated all those monsters, and she shrugged it off.

"Sort of? I'm in it for the licenses mostly. An embarrassing I.D. is way worse than a regretful dick pic. *Those* are the organs they should be donating."

Mad closed her bedroom door and joked about putting up "Wanted" posters with my face on them. To see who would claim me. I hoped she wouldn't hold her breath. She didn't. And neither did I. Because her shampoo smelled like oranges. And it had a butterfly on the bottle, which made sense further down the timeline, but not here. Eyes closed, Mad breathed me in, and she seemed to revel in breathing in a whiff of herself. When she rubbed some new memories into the stubble on my head, I smiled my broken smile best I could, then I cried a bit and wished I was back under the water where there'd be no evidence of it at all.

***

Growing up, my brother got hurt a lot more than me, or at least that was the outward impression, based on all the attention focused on him instead of myself. He even broke his smile, for Christ's sake, and I was the one blamed. It's true, a lot of the injuries were my fault, and whenever I dwelled on these things, it did seem like I was constantly chipping my brother's teeth, or worse. But it was really only twice, and it was always the same front tooth that got chipped. The first accident involved a Nerf football and an Etch-A-Sketch. Remember those? Two dials, weird silver sand, and an invisible needle that drew on the inside of the glass screen like a Flintstones dinosaur toiling inside a prehistoric television. In case you ever wondered, there are all sorts of things waiting to be discovered when you crack open this amazing toy with your father's hammer. Like it stops working.

So, my brother was lying on the bed playing with this thing over his head, and I casually threw the Nerf football at him (as hard as I could), and the Etch-A-Sketch bashed him full in the mush. After a couple seconds of silent bleeding, he tore screaming down the stairs, lips and mouth gushing blood and drool. I got in big trouble for that one, but less because of the tooth and more because I used the toy to scrawl "Aaaaargh!" on the screen afterwards, trying to convince my parents this was what he wrote on impact.

Accident number two (maybe twelve, whatever). Days after he got his tooth fixed, with all of us kids jealous of his fang-like shard, we were skating on the Big Indian's frozen yard when my brother wiped out trying to skate backwards, busting that same tooth all over again. Remember how I said the nearby "mudpit" sucked? Did you believe me? Imagine how bad it had to be if we preferred skating on frozen lawns.

But now that I think about it, I didn't have much to do with breaking his tooth that second time around, because that day I was too busy at the other end of the neighbor's frozen field, down on my hands and knees with one skate off my foot and gripped tightly in my hand as I chopped away at the ice. I was numb to my sock growing heavier and heavier as it soaked up all the snow and mud around my foot like a magnet. This is because I could see the fish suspended just under the ice, and I needed to hack my way down to it. For some reason, I thought setting it free into the winter air would save it. I was way too old to have come up with such a naïve plan, but I really thought I could flap it around to startle it back to life, then rush it home to the toilet for full rejuvenation. Either way, I was confounded by its predicament. How could a fish freeze in someone's back yard? I had to have it.

It was a crappie—I could see the spots—and I did hew it free with my rusty skate. But at the cost of half the fish's tail and a series of deep gashes across my own wrist. When I got home to show my mom my demolished miracle fish, she shoved me out of the way, the long phone cord wrapped around her neck as she screamed into the receiver at my dad about what I'd done to my brother "this time." I turned to see my brother sitting at the kitchen table with his hockey stick over one shoulder like a soldier, mouth swimming in blood. I walked past him and ran my wrist wounds and the ragged fish tail under the warm faucet and wondered how many creatures lived in our yards. How many fish hid in our high grass all summer and then froze in the winter? See, the yards in our neighborhood were in a constant state of flooding, and you'd have thought we lived in a Vietnam rice paddy instead of a Northwest Ohio suburb, but this field had only been frozen for a week. And it had just snowed the week before that. How could there be fish? I was now convinced if any puddle sat long enough, something would be swimming in there when you looked away.

After the mysterious fish in the field, I didn't feel as guilty about those bluegill we'd left to die in the bucket. And this might have nothing to do with anything, but after that, whenever I put a saucepan under a leak in a ceiling, I had no problem leaving it overnight, but when I dumped it back out, I rarely looked inside.

***

"So I was reading about those love locks of yours last night," Mad said while she was looking out her window for more signs of cops in the trash cans.

"Oh, yeah?" I went over to Zero's cage to let him out to explore her apartment. I'd retrieved him from the car once it seemed dark enough to do so (Mad had insisted), but he showed no interest in her Pier 1 knock-offs or inedible wooden peace lilies.

"Is that thing housebroken. Or just broken?" she asked.

"Hey-ooooo! No, it's cool. He has a litter box in my car."

"Nasty. Never trust a dog that uses a litter box."

"Okay, now you think this is a dog?"

"What the hell is it then?"

I clicked my teeth but still didn't have an answer. Neither did Zero. I could have just declared him something, *anything*, you know, to be done with it, but I wasn't ready to make that kind of commitment.

"It's a . . . Zero?" I explained.

"Anyway, so, I was surfing around online, and it turns out that people in France resell those locks to tourists from all over the world, but you probably suspected that much. But what I thought was most interesting was how they'd take entire *sections* of these lock bridges, strip them clean of padlocks, scrub and sandpaper off any inscriptions, ship them back to the front lines for the *touristas*, then, in the middle of the night, rotate the bridge parts."

"Okay, but what does that have to do with my lock?" I asked her, hunching down to read the iPad over her shoulders. She angled the screen so I could get a better look. I was excited to research stuff with her, and it reminded me of my wife and the look in her eyes when she found an old yearbook at the library. But there was a little something extra in Mad's eyes, a darker energy, probably leftover adrenaline from being shot at, and there was absolutely no way I'd ever think of her as merely a "Mag" again.

"Do you see that bridge?"

"Yes. Love lock city." On the screen was a small, concrete bridge over a river, its sides draped with brilliantly colored padlocks.

"Look closer."

She was right. I leaned over her shoulder, breathed in some black curls like I was huffing gasoline, and noticed the locks weren't different colors after all. Someone had actually spray-painted graffiti across hundreds of them, enveloping the locks in trendy Chinese characters. I guessed this place was somewhere in Asia, judging by the graffiti, the oversized, exotic-looking foliage, and the steamy background.

"Now look at this bridge."

She swiped to another picture, a bridge somewhere in the United States, judging by the obesity, bad lighting, and Confederate flags. But spray-painted across the padlocks, along with the ol' Southern Pride, was the exact same Asian calligraphy.

"Okay, so it's the same vandal."

"Or it's the same section of locks."

"Huh?"

"That's my new theory. Companies realize this love-lock thing is good for the tourist trade, so they buy up entire bridge sections. But now they buy them pre-locked! Why wait for love-struck idiots to fill them up again? No one wants to be the first one to hang a lock, right?"

"I'll buy that. But I still don't understand what that has to do with . . . " I trailed off, thinking.

"Me either," she admitted. "But I had fun."

She turned off her iPad and leaned over to smell my head. Her teeth clicked, and I flinched at her hot breath and tucked my chin against my neck. Such a hypocrite, I know.

"Settle down, freak."

"Sorry. Just suddenly felt like my ear was in mortal danger."

"Don't worry, I already ate dinner."

"Awesome," I said, standing back up.

"Are you thinking about her?"

"If I wasn't thinking about my wife, I'd be a real piece of shit."

Mad got up to walk around, running a finger along Zero's cage. "Some people are good at these kinds of games. Not me. I put the 'lousy' in jealousy."

"Hashtag 'me, too!'"

"Gross. So why are people shooting at you, Dave? Why do you have cops questioning you in my parking lot? Going through my trash? Are you . . . "

"My wife is dead."

Mad's shoulders tensed, but not in shock. She'd heard as much from the cops, but this was me and her all alone, stated cleanly, openly. And with eye contact.

"Did you kill her." No question mark again.

"I'm looking for who did."

"So, what was the deal with those things the police were showing you?"

"They showed me a lock from a bridge in Paris, like I told you. It had a bullet hole in it."

She stared at me, eyes blazing through a curtain of ringlets. So I told her the rest.

"That lock was found on a guitar case. The guitar case she was found in. Murdered."

"Impossible. How small is she? Jesus Christ."

"She was small, but not that small. Like, not a dwarf or anything." I could see it dawning on Mad how the human body would have to be rearranged to be crammed into such a space, and her forehead finally softened.

"And you think Matt Fink did that? Come on, dude . . . "

"No. Maybe, I don't know. He's not the guy. No way he's the guy. But he fucked her."

"How do you know?"

"Because we had every Prince album, up until Prince got too religious. Even on cassette . . . " My voice was getting louder, and I started pacing. Zero's ear went up. " . . . and one of those tapes had an insert that folded out like three fuckin' feet long, and everybody in the Revolution had their own square on these liner notes, okay? So I know exactly what that asshole looks like. And this other asshole, that's not him! I mean he kinda looks like him, kinda looks like a doctor, too, but that's the gag. That is not him . . . "

"Wait, 'that's not him' what? Not the guy who killed your wife or not the guy who was in Prince's band?"

"Both. Neither? End of interview!" I laughed.

"So, why would they be connected?"

I got nothing.

"I still don't understand why you have two cops following you across the country and they don't even ask you if you killed your wife."

"Geez, haven't you ever seen a crime show on TV?" I asked.

"There is no 'TV' anymore."

"Not the point! This is right out of the television playbook! They ask me *related* questions, but never the million-dollar question, at least not yet. Keeps everybody tuned in to the same frequency. Then, when they finally do ask it, I've settled into my role as the bad guy and stopped rehearsing alibis in my head, and then I fuck up. And they got me."

"'They,' huh. See, this was always the problem with TV. Because I can't tell if that was a terrible answer or not."

She went to a window, and now I circled Zero's cage. I strummed it like a guitar, and he swatted at me with a strangely human paw until I stopped.

"Have you ever served time?" Mad asked from behind me.

The *real* million-dollar question. I coughed in surprise at the familiar phrase, but cleared my throat and didn't answer. I was sure anything I said would sound bad, particularly my 48-hour stint behind bars back in Pittsburgh. Okay, not behind bars. Behind *walls*. That counts, too!

Instead I tried my favorite tactic, confession mixed with misdirection, and I told her more about Angie and our marriage and how she drank too much and was two different people, one I tolerated and one I loved, all that cringey shit. I told Mad that Angie was someone I admired but never really met, whatever that meant. Then I admitted she was actually four people, and I swear that brought "Mag" back for a second, a stranger asking me what I was babbling about, and I said I had no idea, head slumped, as if I was frustrated with myself more than anything, and that got her back on board. Then, in the middle of all this needless exposition, Mad admitted she'd been with Matt Fink, "like the rest of the town."

"Am I the only person who didn't bang Matt Fuck?" I said, kicking the cage, then regretting it when Zero shrunk into a corner. Mad did, too.

Maggie and Matt, sitting in a tree . . . I sang in my head, then Mad moved along the wall toward the door, understandably alarmed by my outburst. I wanted to ask her if Fink really had two penises, but my overreaction had screwed up any chance, for now.

"I'm sorry, I'm sorry," I said to both of them, hands up. "This week's been a doozy."

"One question. What do you think I can do?"

"Do you know where he lives?"

"Matt? Yes."

"Can we please go see him? No more undercover concerts, no more Walleye Drops, no reading the tea leaves and the love locks. I just want to ask this guy a couple very simple questions." Of course, I'd already had the chance, when I cornered him outside a row of portable toilets, but I hadn't mentally prepared for that confrontation. Now I was ready. Mad drummed her fingers on the doorjamb. Zero gripped the bars with his paws.

We were all ready.

"Fine," she said. "We can go see him tonight after he gets off work from the hospital."

"The hospital!" I yelled. "No way that fucker is a doctor!" No amount of evidence could convince me otherwise.

Mad was staring, one finger up.

"Try that again."

"Sorry," I said, composing myself. "That would be excellent, Mad. Thank you so much."

"It's 'Mag. I'm not 'Mad.' How am I going to get you to remember that?"

Oh, you're Mad all right. Mad as a badger. Mad as a cat in a hat with a badge . . .

"Copy that."

I didn't tell her that remembering her name was probably impossible. Dates, times, birthdays, how much to tip the pizza guy . . . not a chance.

"Okay, we've got some time," she said, coming back over to collapse on the couch. Zero took her cue, giving us a toothy yawn, then walking in a circle twice before snuggling up with his bushy tail to sleep. "Why don't you tell us a bedtime story, Dave."

"It's not even noon."

"Tell me about that movie you made once."

"Huh? Oh, you really want to hear about that?" I said, excited. "Nah, you don't want to hear about that. Are you gonna judge me? Promise you won't judge me." But I was pumped. I'd always thought I came out of that particular story looking pretty clever, which was rare.

"I promise I won't judge you."

"Then no way," I joked.

"'I promise I won't judge you,' she lied."

"Perfect."

"Great!" She hopped up, grabbing her denim jacket, then the cage. Zero didn't stir. "You can tell me on the way."

"Well, it all started at a Taco Bell drive-thru . . . "

"Barf. I changed my mind."

XII

TACO HELL

OKAY, NO ONE believes we had a real Hollywood movie based on our whirlwind relationship, but it's true. We didn't believe it either at first, but when we finally stumbled onto this flick on cable, the implications of what we'd done started to sink it. It was kind of scary actually. We were sitting there watching . . . what was it called again? *Conformity* or *Obedience* or *Sucker MC* or some such nonsense, I can never remember. *Compliance*! Yes, that's the one. We'd avoided it because too many scenesters to count told us we just *had to* see this thing. So we did, and we decided it wasn't too bad, maybe a little far-fetched. "Crazy how it got out of hand like that," we said. But things got *slippier*. We saw in the opening crawl that it was purportedly based on a "true story." Then the closing credits thanked the city of Pittsburgh. Uh oh. That was enough for us both to turn our heads towards each other real slow.

If you haven't seen the movie, it's about this guy, under the guise of being a police officer, who prank-calls a McDonald's (or maybe MacDaddy's, the sad knockoff) and accuses one of the employees of stealing money from someone's purse so that he can get a manager to strip-search and eventually sexually assault some poor underling due to the overwhelming influence of Big Bad Authority looming on the phone. That's the whole movie. Not quite the Milgram Experiment, but if true, an interesting and skeevy enough incident to fictionalize, with some of that popular white-trash (my bad, "working class") exploitation of fast-food employees by the filmmakers. But when we saw on Wikipedia that the movie wasn't just being cheeky about being "true" (like the batshit crazy/total fabrication *Fargo* had used in its opening credits), we immediately started second-guessing every motivation of the filmmakers, and even the victims of the crime, which was always a fun game. Because people are horrible, right? Including us. But then, while dissecting the movie and watching each others' pupils dilate (the universal signal of affection in the animal kingdom), we suddenly realized . . .

We were the ones who had inspired the film.

Or maybe it didn't happen that fast. Because during the movie, I just kept saying stuff like, "Ha ha, we called a fast-food joint to fuck with them once. Glad it didn't get as nutty as this!" And the film itself was this low-budget, artsy affair, mostly consisting of dramatic close-ups of bad hand-acting and lovingly filmed burgers and Freedom Fries. You know, whatever they could do to make fast food seem "sad but noble." But after Angie found details of this real crime online, and after we both went down the list of phone calls to various fast food places during this supposed prank-calling crime spree, we started sweating. Then we noticed the location of the first phone call, "Taco Bell, Moon Township, Pennsylvania," smack dab where we used to live, and I gave Angie a kiss right there on the spot. But her hand blocked most of it.

See, a couple years back, I had made a phone call that went a little south, but it was a righteous cause, goddamnit! And it was her idea really, if you want to point fingers. What's the statute of limitations on crank calls anyway? But what if they change lives? What if they affect the results of an actual

Presidential election and alter the course of history itself? Just playin'.

***

All I wanted was a taco. Like, almost as bad as Mike Muir wanted his Pepsi. And the last three times I asked Angie, my spanking-new partner-in-crime at the time (hey, that rhymes) to please *please* pick me up some drive-thru tacos on her way home from work, something wild happened where I ended up not getting any. Tacos, that is. It got to be a running joke in our apartment, me standing there looking down at my pathetically empty, no-taco hands. There was always a reason; fights, fires, even firefights! But mostly simple confusion over store hours. It should have been so simple since the Taco Hell was right next to where she was working nights, after her first-year PhD funding at the University of Louisville fell through, delaying our exodus from Steeltown.

So the night of the Presidential debates, back at the tail end of two-thousand-whatever, when there was no *way* that one motherfucker was getting elected, my unofficial farewell party to Pittsburgh, Pennsylvania was no exception to my taco-free streak of bad luck. So, if anyone's still listening, here's the play-by-play of how it really went down, to set the record straight:

The evening starts out innocent enough. Angie and I are having Jay and Dee over, childhood friends. Though he is insisting on being called "Jesse" again by then in a desperate bid to reinvent himself, they both represent the last remnants of my youth, as well as the last splinter faction of our old University of Pittsburgh crew, and they've come to say goodbye, watch the debates, maybe engage in some grab-ass and thumb wrestling later. I figure if we drink a Busch beer every time our no-*way*-he'll-be Commander-in-Thief fumbles and fucks up English like it's his second language (miraculously, this was both before and after a dim "W" cast a Bat-signal-like shadow of stupidity over our nation), which likely caused an entire generation to speak with tortured drunk-uncle metaphors and stuttering sentence fragments, we will be well on our way to being drunk enough to not care who actually wins. Or how badly his infectious grammar-cide affects us. With fragments, I mean. The worst. Just. Don't.

An hour passes with me and Jesse bored and confused at all the pre-debate interviews and the premature Sunday evening quarterbacking from the talking heads.

"Have you noticed how mediocrity typically leads to punditry?" Jesse opines, and I flick him in the balls. We wait and wait for Angie and Dee to get back with the tacos, eyes getting heavier, desperate for some grease in our bellies to soak up the alcohol and extend our evening. The girls are on taco duty since Angie works next to one, like I said, but Dee *lives* by Taco Hell, so we're hoping they take this mission very seriously. Hopes are sky high is what I'm saying, in spite of how nervous our Never-Future President is looking. At this point, it's been years since my first half-dozen undergraduate Taco Hell run-ins, so I'm almost ready to think of the joint as just another place to get food, and maybe no one gets hurt this time? But this Taco Hell is already different. It has burned down once before, or so we'd heard. I'd driven up there one night, thinking my luck would change and secure an illusive taco, maybe that mythical burrito, but instead I saw flames reaching up all the way to lick the tip-top of the (not offensive at all) stereotypical Mexican-church-looking steeple. Back then I thought, "Well, at least there's no more suspense?" But then in the morning, the place was fine. Opened back up like nothing had happened. No smoking rubble, no grizzled firefighters coughing and shuffling through the smoke. But I think all fire trucks had been converted into "party buses" by then anyway. State law. Still, not a mark on the stucco! Just business as usual. Everyone already called it "Taco Hell," but now there was a reason. Maybe fast food was fireproof.

It should also be noted that this place was, for some reason, considered in Pittsburgh to be a vaguely healthy alternative to the "other" drive-thru fare, maybe because you're able to get four different food groups into your hands in the least amount of time? Or at least four different colors. And didn't some sting operation prove it wasn't really meat in those tacos? Just a fluffed-up protein powder, kinda like dog food? But what was supposed to be some big indictment sounded healthy to Yinzers. And, okay, maybe they weren't as fast as MacDaddy's, or even Burger Queen. But, hey, anything called "Taco Hell" sounds pretty damn fast.

And getting fast food at a drive-thru is always the Great Reminder. Sure Angie is slumming by working at Starfucks or wherever until she finishes her dissertation, but it is certainly nice to keep in mind that our existence will not be permanent. And watching those dead eyes at those sliding windows makes you regret quitting whatever job you just bailed on, or be grateful for the shitty one you have, because, shit, it isn't *that* bad, is it? Look at that sorry motherfucker hesitating to pull back the glass, torn between getting some outside air and having to decipher another stranger and his squawking carload of baby birds. But isn't there something about that window that always makes it real easy for small arguments to escalate out of control?

So when the ladies start running late with the food, I'm already uneasy, both worried that I won't get to eat and that Angie picked up a job application there instead of a taco and now we'll never leave town. So I call up Angie again and ask her to *pleeeeeese* remember to hook me up with some tacos on their way over, just in case she and Dee started tittering in the car and talking smack about us and completely forgot. But there's no answer. I should have known, because now that I have a second to really think about it and stop the hyperbole, in spite of the dozen or so times I've walked through their door or rolled up to the drive-thru window smiling, sweaty balls of money rolling around my hand like Captain Queeg, I don't think I've ever actually *received* a taco from this place. Or anything at all. I'm not kidding. Have I ever eaten Taco Hell in my life? I suddenly have no answer, and it feels like panic.

I don't know why I'm even surprised. Throughout history, drive-thrus have always been a bad idea. Road rage mixed with hunger? Think about it. The honking, the impatient drivers, the garbled instructions, the colorful posters of sizzling food just out of reach? Why not release clouds of bees into the cars to raise the stakes even further? Or raise *actual steaks* above people's heads so they can't reach them. Or, I don't know, put the window up a steep hill surrounded by sprinklers? They already do that, you say? Right. It's a perfect recipe for disaster. Now add a strategically placed camera. Do they want people to burn it down?

Angie, of course, would tell me that drive-thrus were a "fascinating rhetorical situation," especially with the addition of surveillance. She had at least three unfinished essays all about them.

So, sure enough, right on cue a half hour later, in walks the two of them: fists clenched but empty, eyes narrowed, and visibly shaken from some kinda drive-thru trauma. Her story comes out like this, but imagine Angie grabbing a microphone and pacing the stage when she delivers it:

"So get this, we pull up to the speaker to order your stupid food, and the chick inside is having trouble hearing us. So Dee says, 'No, not bean burrito, beeeFFF burrito.' And apparently by exaggerating the letter 'F' like this, and by stalling out your truck again—sorry—and then having trouble getting it started, Dee sends this bitch into a downward spiral of madness. We pull up to pay, and she takes the money—Mexican girl, cute purple braids by the way—might be one of my students—then fires off all mad, 'By the way, don't you *ever* get smart with me again . . . '"

Time out from her story while I explain the strange hiring practices of these franchises. They always hire hot, young Mexican girls such as yourselves. If that's what you are. Is this strategy racist, a gimmick, or just equal-opportunity employment? Who am I to judge? But Angie did write a seminar paper on all this, just like you knew she would, and I will admit, those incredibly ornate fingernails seem to make them work even faster. So I'm told! Not that I've ever gotten the correct order from one of them at the drive-thru, or any order. I'm so fucking hungry. Oh, yeah, Angie's still talking:

" . . . and I'm like, 'What did you just say?' And she's like, 'You heard me.' And I'm like, 'I'm afraid I didn't.' And I'm wondering if it's the expectation of an invisible camera, or if I always talk like this, and she just slams the window shut and walks over to another employee to rant 'n' rave about us, waving her arms all around like she's being attacked by bees . . . "

"Bees!" I say "I knew it!"

"Knew what?"

"Nothing. Just my stomach growling." I'm smiling, but mostly because I'm familiar with this role we fall back on sometimes, sort of a comforting regression to "rust belt redneck" stereotypes, the kind of people who are happiest when complaining about fast-food altercations. We're most susceptible when we're limping through college, like now. Angie says this sort of backsliding is a defense mechanism called "code switching," but even more closely connected to that ol' standby, The Imposter Syndrome, something that always sounds terrifying as fuck, but the more it comes up, the more I become convinced it's the ultimate humblebrag.

"Can I finish?" she says. "Okay, so, it's taking way too long with the food. And Dee decides to ask for the money back because now she's thinking someone's going to do something to it . . . "

Dee jumps in.

"Yeah, I figured someone was gonna spit in the 'beeeFFFF' burrito. Or worse!"

Burrito? What is that? Sigh. It sounds delicious, doesn't it? I will never see one in my lifetime, so I'm sure glad I didn't try for their even more unattainable "Choco Taco" dessert (more like *desert* item, am I right?). Oh, my Christ, I'd eat a hundred of those bad boys no matter who spit on them. Anyway, Dee's taking over the story now, and she's legit white trash, an actual garbage person, so get ready:

" . . . so the crazy *scrunt,* Kim—now we can see this bitch's name tag says 'Kim'—she throws the money at me and snarls, actually fucking snarls, like she's not even a human female, 'You're so lucky I'm in here or I'd come out there and kick your motherfuckin' ass.' So now we're getting loud, too, and some other employee comes over to calm down Crazy Kim, but she just shoves this guy up into the air, bonking his head off the heat lamp, because now she's got that 'In Case of Emergency Break Glass' super retard strength, and she yells out, 'Don't tell me to relax, I'm the shift supervisor!' By this time, everyone is swearing, and Crazy Kim the Crisis Actor is making these moves like she is seriously going to come outside and attack our car."

"My car," I say.

Jesse looks up at this.

"Actually it's your brother's truck, and I made the down payment."

"How is that important?" I ask him. "Just let her finish. Maybe at the end of the story, there's food."

" . . . so our Angie starts pulling away, loudly declaring that she's gonna call the 1-800 number on the window. You know, the one that asks how smooth the transaction went? Right under the one that says 'Always hiring'? Anyway, this bug-nutty twat yells out, 'Go ahead, I don't give a shit! They're not going to fucking fire me!' And Angie shouts a final, 'What the hell is your problem?' And Crazy Kim answers back, 'Your mother!' who *is* kind of a problem, to be fair . . . "

Angie laughs, then jumps back in.

"And if she's talking to me, that's even more *ridiculous,* since my mother is at home watching Court TV at this same time every day."

"While your dad hunts coyotes with hammers," I add, then lean over and give her a little kiss on the cheek and she shrugs.

"We don't choose our family, Dave," Angie says, and she kisses me back.

"Who has the hammers?" Jesse asks, but we ignore him.

"So, yeah, that was pretty much it," Angie says. "The debate ended with hard stares right out of those crappy westerns you're always making us watch. And after two or three stalls in your truck to ruin my dramatic exit, we were off. So, yeah, sorry, babe. No food."

"Why me," I sniff.

"Hey, we tried!"

"No, that's funny. It's a good story," I admit. "It's almost worth it."

"You know what I hate?" Angie says, pushing away from me. "When you say 'That's funny' instead of just laughing. You sound like an asshole when you do that. What made you this way?"

Before I can answer, Dee starts excitedly telling the story all over again, mostly just to Jesse this time because, even since his Casio G-Shock stopped, he's been a little slow on the "uptick." It gets a little better the second time around, though, as they start adding extra flavor, extra hot sauce, you could say, even some extra steak sauce, then raising those stakes and sprinkling in some more insulting details about their nemesis's appearance. And by three and a half revisions, Kim's purple braids are not "cute" anymore, more like "glued down with peanut butter and hamburgers." Which makes no sense because it's Taco Hell, and they don't even use real burger. But this is back when Angie talked a lot more trash about other females, particularly after such a juicy rhetorical situation like a drive-thru with its own body camera. And this is right before fifth-wave feminism really sunk in around our household.

But now I'm getting all worked up right along with them. Partly because, in my head, I'm picturing Angie or Dee stalling my truck over and over and looking sheepish on their way out, and partly from being on the verge of fainting from malnutrition and lack of taco love. And I'd be lying if I said there isn't something about how Angie acts when Dee is around that's a little horrifying. Her voice gets a little . . . animated. More like "anime." Not that Dee isn't cool in a lot of ways. I mean, she's *real.* But she's like an earlier version of Angie, pre-college, who, though perfectly charming and acceptable in normal circumstances, is someone I could never fall in love with.

Looking around the room, everyone and everything looks like a giant taco to me now. Even the Nope-Nope-Nope President. Remember that old *Looney Tunes* cartoon with the guy imagining his buddy on the desert island as a huge steaming chicken? It's just like that but everybody's a taco. And there's no island. And there's three tacos instead of one. And there's no steam, as most fast food requires reactivation via microwave or it reverts to its natural inert state, which is faux-burger, industrial plastic pellets, or SeaMonkey dust. So forget everything I said. They look nothing like that cartoon, but I'm dying. And now I got a dilemma. If it was a *guy* that was threatening people at some drive-thru, instead of Crazy Kim, the Purple People Eater, I could just go over there and be all chivalrous, and maybe he'd say the wrong thing and I could pull the little bastard out of the window by his head, his crooked but carefully arranged oversized baseball cap with the fake purple dreadlocks glued on for a gag falling slow-motion to the pavement. But no, here we have this girl-on-girl madness. And we're already 15 minutes into the Presidential throat-clearing and wet sneezes that signal the true beginning of the debates.

But Angie has an idea. She's leaning on the tower of her overdue psychology books, one hand thoughtfully flipping the corner of a shelf-worn dust cover, and she looks kind of scary. But her plan is intoxicating the way she explains it to us.

Reservations aside, me and Jesse soak in her scheme a second, then start rubbing our hands in diabolical circles and get working on Plan A. Or, should I say, Plan "Egg." Angie's proposal involves us taking two raw eggs (I know, kinda weak, but that's all that was in the fridge, though we do get the big ones, almost like duck eggs, for nostalgia purposes) and then me and Jesse pelting Angie and Dee's archrival when she slides open the window to take our money. "But we need to think of a way to do this so that we can still get a goddamn taco," I say, and they all jump down my throat. So I force myself to stop worrying about my stomach and think about the greater good of mankind.

We get to work, and Jesse taps the TV, saying, "'I think a good gift for the president would be a chocolate revolver. And since he's real busy, you'd have to run up to him fast to give it to him.'"

"What are you talking about?"

"Sorry." He puts Jack Handey's *Deep Thoughts* back down on my stack of overdue library books, smaller than Angie's in every regard. Even though it's a tiny joke book, no more than fifty pages (and half are pictures), I'll still be at war with Taco Hell before I ever finish it.

So kicking our plan in high gear, I plop two eggs in a plastic bag, grab my keys, and we're getting ready to roll, but then I start to think about collateral damage again because Angie's in my ear about it. And it should be noted that the phrases "greater good" and "collateral damage" are at that very moment being volleyed back and forth on our TV screen between the Not My President! and a two-thousand-year-old Green Party candidate. That and some talk of "compliance" to certain treaties? Oh, and something wacky called "the very real threat of World War III." But the egg toss is the issue at hand. Angie is saying we have to consider innocent bystanders, and she asks, "What if Kim is no longer manning the drive-thru after all the excitement earlier?" and Jesse's agreeing, "She's right. What if we bean some poor waterhead who's just working there one day a week for extra beer money?"

We chew on this a minute, then Angie has me call up the Taco Hell real quick to do some recon. Later I'll understand that this phone call was Angie's entire master plan. Because a telephone was more than enough ammo to do the job. The *huevos* in our hands were just props. To get me into character. She's a born director.

A bored teen answers, and I do what Angie tells me to. I inquire who's working the drive-thru tonight, claiming "Someone forgot my darn food!" And when an irritable female voice gets on, sighing before she speaks, I know it's just gotta be Crazy Kim.

"I cannot say I have to respect the person who is not me . . . " our Dumpster Fire "Send Halp!" President says, and for once he's making sense. I clear my throat to ask Kim all stern:

"Am I speaking to the manager? Yes? Okay, did you or one of your employees just have an altercation with two girls about ten minutes ago?"

Keep in mind, this is before the "Karen," "Becky," or "Chad" memes sweep the nation, so, come to think of it, we probably started those, too. But Crazy Kim isn't having it.

"Listen, that is n-n-n-not what happened, sir . . . " She's stammering. Maybe because of the raspy authoritarian tenor of my voice (due to starvation more than anything), but she's going into this alternate reality version of events where she's just this victim who wants nothing more than to happily take money and hand out tacos, Diablo Sauce, life, love, and happiness forever. I'm confused about something in her tone, though, how it doesn't fit with Angie and Dee's play-by-play. And then something starts to dawn on me. All her "sirs," stuttering, rapid-fire explanations, and defensive over-enunciation? Is Crazy Kim running for office? Because she could be on our TV right now.

Wait, no, now I get it. But Angie's already got it, and she's nodding at me to keep going. This dunce thinks I'm calling from that 1-800 number they were talking about. It's true. Kim believes I'm actually some sort of authority figure. Holy balls. I clear my throat louder, and now I'm suddenly working for Taco Hell, and shit gets kinda strange.

"Well, I heard that you were physically threatening customers and swearing and . . ."

"That's n-n-n-not what happened, sir. They were causing trouble, and I was just reacting and . . ."

"Well, I'm afraid I must be privy to different facts than you are." Privy?! Who even am I, right? Now I'm just trying to imitate every dressing down I've received from a boss, but I'm also quoting our Alternate-Worst-Timeline-Ever President almost word for word as he denies ever saying Arctic wildlife "was an eminent threat to global warming." This isn't where Angie first teaches me about "mushfaking," by the way, but she could have. She was always teaching me something. And Kim is on the ropes. So when she whispers the $50,000 (a year plus benefits) question in my ear, I don't even hesitate.

"Who is this?" Kim asks.

"Your District Manager."

Okay, it feels a bit like a demotion after the Presidency, but I figure the jig is up anyway. I wait for her to say "fuck off" and the phone to go *click!* because she's gotta know who her DM is, right? Wrong.

"Listen, sir, they were making fun of me at the drive-thru, and I can't believe that I would get in trouble over this when it's just my word against hers and . . ."

"Well, it's not just your word against hers because (pay attention, I'm really proud of how fast I pull this next rabbit out of my ass) there was a vehicle behind them and someone from that car also called the 1-800 number to complain about your behavior."

I should mention here that I, her District Manager, am wearing a homemade "I Fucked Your Martyr" T-shirt with the sleeves cut off, twirling two eggs in a baggie, and trying to stifle the three giggling goofballs leaning in to listen.

"Hey, they started it!" She's scared now, folding faster than Superman on laundry day.

"So you were threatening and cursing at customers

because you thought they were being rude to you? That is simply unacceptable. Why do you think you can just . . . "

"They started harassing me first, sir! It's not fair I should get in trouble for this and . . . "

"Okay." Big, authoritative sigh. "When is your next day off?"

"Tomorrow."

"Ask her to come in," Angie whispers.

"Yes, I'm going to need you to come in so that we can sit down and talk about this and figure out what should be done."

"Oh, no. It is not fair I should have to come in on my only day off when I already rearranged my schedule once this week because it's my only day off and it's just not fair that I would be the one to . . . " And blah blah blah. Dee whispers in my other ear:

"This bitch is big on 'not fair'."

And now I'm holding out the phone in disbelief. I don't know what's funnier, the fact that she really thinks I'm her District Manager, or the fact that I, totally her fuckin' boss now, can't get her to come in on her day off, even to save her job. Where's the work ethic? On the television, the (can't even say it) "President" holds a hand tight to his gristle-y, tomato-red earlobe, and a camera zoom reveals an earpiece no one knew he had buried in that swirl of piss-stained cotton candy. Angie would have been all about this debate-rigging technology, but she misses it. But Jesse catches it.

"Are they giving him the questions or the answers?!" Jesse really wants to know, the girls are ignoring him. However, I can't help but squeeze the phone painfully close to my own head. And after another minute of "not fairs" from Crazy Kim, I finally give up and switch tactics:

"When do you work next?"

"Sunday. I open."

"Okay, don't worry about opening the store because . . . "

Time out. This is where some people who work in middle management start getting that disapproving "You've gone too far" kinda look on their puss. But, hey, I've only been a District Manager for seven minutes, so I'm gonna make some mistakes.

" . . . we're going to take care of that," I go on, reading Angie's cues. "You come in later. I'll meet you there at noon so we can sit down and figure out what we're going to have to do."

"Fine."

Wow. That was a cakewalk. Angie signs "I love you" (or possibly, "We need a worm farm"), while I marvel at how it will always be infinitely easier to convince someone to stay home instead of coming in. It's a lesson we all remember from grade school: better to get suspended for ten days instead of having to stand in the corner for just one.

I hang up, and we're all laughing our asses off, hoping she actually comes in late on Sunday and gets canned. We talk about it a lot, drinking and ignoring the end of the debates even after Jesse turns the TV back on. I do, however, catch one of the candidates saying something self-righteous about "never judge people by . . . " something. We can't hear the rest over all the fake applause.

And that's all I really remember from that day, because I spend most of my night fantasizing about being behind one of those podiums, next to the actual District Manager of Taco Hell, carefully explaining our party's platform with purposeful hand gestures and reassuring nods. I declare, "My fellow Americans, you can never judge people by the color of their dreads. However, you *can* judge people by their favorite books, songs, or movies. You *can* judge people by how fast they yank clothes out from under a sleeping cat. And you can *only* judge people by how rude they are on the phone, or in traffic." Dramatic pause. "Or, of course, at a drive-thru, the unholy bastard combination of both. Thank you and amen."

When Angie and I discuss the whole thing way later, she's convinced Crazy Kim flipped out because of the rhetorical dilemma of "the drive-thru Panopticon." To translate Angie's high-minded theories for you, imagine a phone call where the person you just hung up on suddenly jams their head through your window to get the last word. That would fuck you up, wouldn't it? And if you're more likely to be rude to strangers on a phone (like most people), you sure wouldn't know what the hell to do if their head suddenly popped out of your freezer. Instant confrontation at a drive-thru window is an unexpected, awkward ending to what's basically a garbled, angry phone call between the hungry and the disgruntled. It's not meant to happen, ever. Like time travel. Or a rational debate. Or cameras on cops. Or me ever getting to eat a taco.

To be fair, Kim probably didn't know how to handle this. To translate one of my own lowbrow theories, it's kind of like when you're in traffic and you're yelling at the car next to you for some imagined infraction, then, three miles later, you're both idling at a red light together. Do you look over? You *have* to look over. Which is why I was always prepared for exactly this sort of situation. If someone was glaring at the red light, I'd slowly pull out my winter mittens, sunglasses, and motorcycle helmet (sounds like a lot, I know, but shallow glove boxes have always been the deal-breaker when I buy a car), and I'd stare them down, leaning on the steering wheel of my rusted-out '92 Baja Fajita. Wait, Fiata? Miata, whatever. I blew the transmission on that one, too. You know what? No one ever raced me.

In retrospect, it sucks our debate party was full of such distractions because it was the most people we'd managed to gather around us in months. I suspect this had gotten more difficult because of the upcoming elections and my tendency to drop my pants and press my groin up against the TV whenever the Are You Kidding Me? Leader of the Free World was talking, which was a lot. I kept trying in vain to make Angie understand that the bigger the crowd meant the less likely I was to exclaim, "Hey, look! The President's suckin' my dick again!" A few years ago when I was in Chicago, I'd tried to piss on the biggest, shiniest building I could find that bore his name. Not easy. And now, of course, nearly impossible when the White House lights are on. "Get the camera, honey!" I'd say, penis covering the microphone, TV screen static tickling my balls. "Get a picture and we'll print out some campaign posters! Where's everybody going?"

Okay, jumping ahead to the middle of the story, it's finally Sunday, and I've told everyone who will listen about our taco-free hijinks, actually kinda getting tired of the story and starting to doubt Kim really wouldn't figure out that she'd been bamboozled in 48 hours or less. Wouldn't she just call the District Manager? The real one, I mean, not me. So I'm as shocked as you are by the happy ending to this story.

Remember how Angie is still working at the Starfucks on the corner of Pestilence and False Profits (near the Taco Hell in question)? Well, Sunday afternoon she calls me to say she told her coworkers all about the incident. Her words:

"So, at about 11:00, a couple of the second shifters go across the street to get lunch, then they come back to tell me the good news. Dave. Are you sitting down? There's a big sign taped to the door that says, 'Not "open" until 1:00. "Sorry" for any inconvenience.' Oh my god, dude. I got five witnesses who saw the sign!"

She got a picture of it for me. Scare quotes around all the wrong words. And on our TV a news anchor is explaining that, in spite of the candidate's mysterious earpiece and Ronald MacDaddy wig, polls are predicting Don't Make Me Say His Name won the debate over immigration. Or is it taco trucks? I can't remember. And the price of earpieces and red noses goes up, while Taco Hell's prices forever remain the same, the Dollar Menu as invulnerable as roaches after the bomb.

"*Cyrano de Bergerac-ack-ack . . .*" Angie starts singing, an Edmond Rostand/Billy Joel mash-up that seems to make her very happy. I don't get the joke. Angie still talks about all this for years after. One day, she even says all breathless that I should have told Crazy Kim to blow her brains out. No way she would have done that, though, right? Right?

Postscript. A week later, Dee actually calls the 1-800 number to complain about her customer service issues, this time trying to get some free food out of it, and she's given the phone number of the store manager. This woman then proceeds to tell Dee that she knows all about "the situation" and that "her District Manager is handling it." Whoa, two things. One, of course this begs the question: is she talking about us here? And two, Angie reminds me that "begs the question" doesn't mean "followed by a question." It's something to do with circular reasoning, and my students used to fuck it up as much as me. Usually while explaining that they "could care less" or I "could give a shit."

For real though, what is she talking about when she says "her District Manager is handing it"? Because I ain't handling shit. "It's not fair!" I will tell the reporters. I've got entirely too many responsibilities that come with my new job titles. Like the truck stop that puts too much salt on their omelets, the kid at the gas station who shorts me on change, that convenience store clerk who stares in my soul way too hard, oh, right, and the future murder of my wife. I mean, I'm sorry, but there are just too many other stores in my district that need my attention.

"70 incidents in 30 states" is what it says on Wikipedia. Incidents? The incidents the movie was based on, or total weird phone calls to fast-food joints? But maybe there's a reason for that. Because, sure, maybe they weren't *asking* for it, but maybe they were asking to ask for it. Seriously. A window where you reach out and grab food while you're driving? How do those dinner-and-drink combos not end in blood and tears every day of the week.

One last thing. Remember those two eggs in the Ziploc? As I'm packing up the last of my silverware for the Kentucky move, I notice them on the windowsill, next to the phone charger, behind my dead cactus and leaky squirt gun, still sealed in their bag and fermenting in the sun to (kissing the tips of my finger and thumb) *perfection*. I'd like to tell you I use them to make a Mexican-style omelet. Or that I force myself to eat them on the day of the second-worst election in American history. Or that me and my betrothed go outside and place those eggs at either end of a parking space as she teaches me how to master a stick-shift and parallel parking on a bright summer day without either of us losing our temper and wrecking my truck for the fifth time. I'd like to say that whenever my past and future wife thinks no one is looking, she replaces whatever pizza box I'm sleeping on with something equally comfortable so I don't fall off the sofa like that "tablecloth under the dinner" magic trick gone awry, then she tucks the eggs into my socks. I'd like to say that something meaningful happened to those two eggs, since this story introduced them but forgot about them just as quickly, like eggs hanging over the fireplace that never went off. I'd like to say that they did, indeed, crack someone on the head as the God of Taco Hell intended, instead of just getting dropped into the trash without any ceremony, or debate. But they didn't.

So, long story long, every time I see the dates of that first incident in the police report, I know it was me, which means it was her. And that shit's romantic. I run around telling the world we did this, tell them this is when we fell in love, or at a minimum, knew our love was real, when she saw me for the first time as a white-collar professional. Or at least Assistant to the District Manager. But no one believes us.

"Unrelated!" they say. "Coincidence!" they scoff. "Why are you so excited to be a phone rapist?" someone very reasonably asks. But much like our President To Be (or Not To Be), I have no energy to debate any of this. Somehow even less than the low-energy Vice-Presidential Debates that follow. And I'll have even less energy later, when we'd fast-forward into an uncertain but no less exciting hereafter where I'll be debating the "Vice President" himself outside some prison gate in the Florida Panhandle. Stay tuned!

But for now, it is what it is. The purgatory we chose. But

at least I know what we did. I simply made a phone call at the behest of the love of my life, which turned out to be the equivalent of us dropping a rock in a puddle, or watching the ripples after throwing a key off a famous bridge in Paris. Maybe more like dropping a Choco Taco off the Empire State Building, or a Mexi-Melt off a Twin Tower. And even though she put that drive-thru camera chapter in her dissertation for the world to one day discover, the experiment forever belongs to us. Maybe we'll share it with those kids in *Compliance*, who immediately start molesting each other in the MacDaddy's freezer or whatever when they get off the phone and the 18-year-old District Manager finally shows up. But it's an important early moment in our relationship, as well as in faux-documentary-style filmmaking. And, when it comes down to it, everyone's just jealous we made a movie and they didn't.

Taco Hell burned down again a year later, but it stayed that way this time. And there was nothing about it in the newspapers.

XIII

MAD MAG EATS THE EVIDENCE

"REALLY?"

"Really."

"Swear to God?"

"Swear to God."

"Your story sounds like the most complicated rationalization for working at Taco Bell I've ever heard."

"Well, I *did* kind of work at Taco Hell," I laughed. "District Manager up in this piece!"

"Uh huh," she said, turning to look out the car window again. "Stop trying to make 'Taco Hell' happen."

"You said it first."

One time, right after a particularly brutal rejection from an academic journal, Angie told me that she suspected the biggest lie ever told was that life is not a zero-sum game. Even though people want to think there is enough success and happiness to go around, the reason that you or I were always just the tiniest bit resistant to anybody else's good news was because we suspected they were scooping up a finite amount of prosperity from the bucket we're all forced to share. But a bucket of happiness still sounded like a lot, and, as Angie predicted, I had found myself minimizing the memory of my wife the more time I spent with Mad.

I told myself that this was only to solve the mystery of her death, not to replace her. I needed Mad to take me to Matt Fink's house. And this would be my final task in Brickwood, Ohio. I'd likely never see Mad again.

On our way there, we passed over the bridge where we'd been shot at, and we saw someone had removed most of the padlocks. Only a dozen or so still speckled the rails. I slowed down to investigate, and Mad pressed down on my knee to accelerate past the scene.

"Stop and I'll kill you," she said.

Now that the fence was mostly clear of padlocks, I could see through it and down to the water below. Diamonds of light flashed and danced, the glimmer of what had to be thousands of discarded love locks lining the bottom of the river. I realized they must not be swapping fences here in the U.S. like they did overseas. They were just dumping them straight into the water to start over. This made sense. It's much easier to start over than people know.

"Stop and you'll what?" I laughed.

"Ha ha, no, I don't mean *kill you* kill you. Just, you know, kill you."

"Okay, but 'kill you' doesn't have any other meaning."

She considered this, then tried to distract me with more tales of musician mutations.

"Did you know the guitarist in Slipknot was born with six fingers on his hand?" she asked. "He would have been the most amazing musician of all time if they hadn't cut them off."

"They cut *all* of his fingers off? That explains some shit."

"Shut up."

"So this is when you tell me Matt Fink is the greatest keyboarder of all time because of his two penises, right?"

"No," she said. "But it's sorta related! Today in the shower, I was thinking, if the Six-Fingered Man from *The Princess Bride* was the Robert Mitchum character in *Night of the Hunter* instead, you know what the tattoos on his knuckles would have read?

"What?"

She punched me in the side of the mouth, not hard but much faster than I thought possible.

"'Glove' and 'Hate.'"

"Where's the ejector seat?"

She laughed at this, and I rubbed the side of my mouth and watched as she dropped a handful of pennies into my car door. *We're still doing that?* I thought.

"Turn here."

I took the next corner kind of hard, to try and regain some control, but Mad just held the dashboard and laughed.

"Whoa there, horsey!" she said, then pretended to play the length of the dash like a piano. "Hey, what do you call that move where a pianist runs a finger down all the keys like *whooooooosh!*"

"I can't remember," I said. "No, I do know this. It rhymes with 'foreshadow.' Like 'Allessandro'?"

"You mean a 'moussandro'?" she said, cocking a thumb back at Zero.

"What's that?"

She started smacking her hands rapid fire down near my steering wheel.

"It means to run a cartoon cat up and down the piano keys trying to smash an irrepressible mouse that was previously introduced to the piano's labyrinthine interior. According to the Oxford English Unabridged."

"See also 'Tomissimo' and 'Jerrissimo'?"

"Stop joking around, Dave. Before we die, just think about what I said."

"Said about what?"

"How a man with six fingers would hate gloves!"

"You're losing me, navigator."

"Straight for the next nine miles."

She was finally quiet, and we drove and drove. At some point, I told her about the ant farm I'd bought on a whim, thinking this time it would last more than three months, even though the lifespan of the harvester ant was right there on the side of the box. I told her my story about putting a strange ant in the ant farm, and how the rest of them bit and stung the shit out of each other until I was wigging out. So I won't go through it again. But I told that story one more time so maybe she could understand how it haunted me. Even though I never cared that much about ants, or farms. When I was a kid, I'd even come up with this horrible game, involving pencils and a shoe box. And some matches. And an ant. No way I was gonna tell her about that. But when we got the ant farm home, Angie called that clear plastic tomb with its lime-green plantation façade an "Invisible Prison." I didn't notice this at the time, but I'm sure she said those words. Before I started hearing those words from strangers.

Mad had Angie's notes and her Trapper Keeper again, holding a bold signature in the inside corner up to the light.

"'Zimbardo.' Do you know who that is?" Mad asked.

"You mean 'Zamboni'?" I asked. "Yeah, he invented the Zamboni."

"No, this says Zimbardo. Look at the size of this autograph. It's like he was signing the Constitution. 'Zimbardo,' sounds so familiar . . . "

"Look him up."

She played on her phone a second, then saw something that made her gasp.

"What?"

Without answering, she reached over to pull my leg up to ease it off the gas. I started to complain, but her eyes were serious. I eased the Rabbit over into the stones.

"What did you find?"

"'Phillip G. Zimbardo.' He's that professor famous for the goddamn Stanford Prison Experiment. Remember that terrifying Nazi shit from back in the '70s?"

"Didn't they debunk that whole thing?" I said, but I was lost in thought. Things were making a strange sort of sense. Just not out loud.

"According to this, he's also the biggest investor in some new body camera technology that's being required by most police departments nationwide." Mad was shaking her head, swiping at her screen. "He is the *Vice President* of the company that invented them, 'Opti-Cop' it's called. Says here he started down the road of investing in the private sector because of, get this, 'the pressure in academia for external funding.' Mean anything to you?"

I gripped the steering wheel and gave it another snake bite as I thought about the name of her dissertation and this new information.

Who is the Vice President?

"Unless this signature is his brother's? Maybe it's 'Gil T. Zimbardo' we're dealing with? Apparently, ol' 'Guilty' is a county judge somewhere in Pennsylvania. But whoever signed your wife's yearbook didn't use his first name. Or maybe none of this means nothin'." Mad sighed, flicking something off her screen in disgust.

I squeezed the wheel until it squeaked. It all sounded so *important*. I wanted to remain in that zone, the excitement of almost solving something without ever actually doing it.

"So, do you know him or what?"

"Who? The brother. No, it's gotta be the other guy. The V.P."

"Who's the V.P.?"

I asked another question rather than answer hers.

"Do you think a human being could fit into a guitar case?"

"Not unless they were liquefied."

I put the Rabbit into gear and slid back into traffic, satisfied I'd gathered enough clues to delay making any sense out of them.

***

I crashed through Matt Fink's front door so fast he made no move to stop me. The photograph I'd discovered of him and my wife was committed to memory, right down to the angle of light on their faces. So, as if I'd lived there for years, I was able to walk straight to the window in the back of his apartment that framed the afternoon sun. I stood in the sunbeam, spun on my heels, and found myself looking up at a bookshelf along the opposite wall covered with Mr. Fink's impressive array of healthy succulents. And nested within the leaves was a tiny pink Arc de Triomphe, an emerald-green Big Ben replica set to the wrong time, a Pyraminx toy painted gold, and a travel-size puzzle depicting The Great Wall of China, still unopened. I relaxed slightly. One thing about Angie that usually surprised people was her distaste for puzzles, and she routinely stole a single piece from any puzzle she found, even pillaging them on store shelves, all in the hopes of helping others hate them, too.

Then I saw the purple Eiffel Tower.

Recovering from the surprise intrusion, Matt Fink followed me into this room, and his shoulders grew rigid and his head lost a bit of that submissive tilt I'd noticed when I first burst in. I reached up to touch his souvenirs and he drew in a breath. I could understand that. I hated when people touched my movie collection, smearing greasy thumbprints on the discs, breathing all over the little windows on my videotapes. Then I thought about fingerprints on my wife, and I was nose-to-nose with him pretty quick.

"Where did you get this Eiffel Tower, Fink?"

"A friend gave it to me."

"Not in Paris?"

"What? No." He almost laughed.

I thought about Angie and I standing over the river, and a joke she'd made that day.

Don't jump, Dave. That would be "in Seine!" Get it?

"Show me your passport."

He studied my face, rightly considering me unhinged, and continued to follow my orders. He pulled a tall travel guide titled *Spectacular Australia* off his shelf, then opened the book to reveal travel documentation tucked between the pages. I felt like the Russians in Eastwood's *Firefox* as I snatched the tiny book away. *"Papers, please!"* I thought, accent and all.

His passport had stamps for practically every country, and I started thinking he really was in Prince's band again, touring the world in his scrubs. No Paris, though. Lucky fuck. I turned the travel guide over, then back again.

"Why isn't there a stamp for Australia?"

"I just keep my passport in the place I want to visit next."

"Uh huh."

I put the Australia book back on the shelf and pushed around his greenery to see what else he was hiding. Tucked behind his plants were ant farms. Ant farms of all shapes and sizes, including the new space-age ones with the glowing blue gel. I'd heard about those. They had this goo, which was all the food and water ants would ever need, and it made up their whole world, right there under their feet. It would be like living in a house made of meat. Or a car made of kitty litter. I shook one of his blue farms, and it was nothing but bodies. I guessed that any ant serving time in such a Willy Wonka-type situation, where they could munch on the tunnels as they dug them, would have their life expectancy cut in half. Just like the kids who toured the chocolate factory, come to think of it.

He had a lot of maps, too. Store-bought, gas-station maps. None of them hand-drawn like Angie's mystery map. I unfolded an Ohio map and saw several bridges highlighted. Then I found a map of Paris and held it up to the light, imagining it leading the way straight to the special padlock we'd left on the fence. This map had lines highlighted, as well. Not quite a pathway, more like checkmarks, or spots someone had crossed off, then moved on. Then, on a blank panel, a hurriedly sketched map of somewhere else.

"Give me that back, please?" he said, trying to retrieve it. "*The Poor State of Our State Bridges.*"

"What's this all about?" I asked him.

"None of your business," he said, that first-impression voice from outside the toilets in full effect now.

"This homemade map of yours looks exactly like a trip I took once. A walk over a bridge in Paris. Who drew this?"

"It's a map of the disintegrating bridge conditions in the United States," Matt said, catching a corner of the map to pull it from my hands. "It's a perk from my job at the library archives. Sometimes I get to keep disintegrating books about disintegrating bridges. I ask you again, what is this all about?"

He was starting to recognize me from his concert, but I could see in his face that he must have lots of conversations outside random Porta-Potties because he hadn't quite placed me yet.

"But who drew the map on the back?"

"There is no map on the back of the map!" he yelled. "Are you talking about that? Those are creases, from folding it up wrong."

"Uh huh."

I walked to his kitchen.

"Where are you going?" he asked, then he watched as I stuffed his passport into the rubber maw of the sink, then I flicked on his garbage disposal.

"Why?" He was more confused than ever. I flicked the switch again, and the grinding stopped. I motioned toward the hole.

"Like you said. It's the place you're gonna visit next."

"I don't get it."

I thought that would be a lot more intimidating, so I walked to his bedroom. Fink followed, with Mad trailing behind him. I was surprised by how passive she was being, but it also looked like she was waiting for an opportunity to say something soon, depending on how out of hand shit got. If he'd noticed her yet, he gave no indication. Inside the bedroom, Matt had two keyboard cases leaning up against the wall. I brushed past them to check his dresser. I don't know what I was expecting, but all his underwear looked normal.

Next to the dresser was a guitar case. There was no lock on the clasp. I clenched a fist, and Mad stepped between us, looking from him to me and back again. I realized she was holding Zero in his cage. "Are we almost done here?" she asked us.

"Who is this guy, Mag? Did you bring him here?"

"Yeah, he said he wanted to ask you something."

"Who's 'Mag'?" I asked them, and Matt noticed the cage.

"Why does that cat have a circle on its belly? My god, what is it eating . . . "

I had my hands on his throat and his back up against the wall before Mad could stop me.

"How do you know there's a circle on his adorable fuzzy belly? Angie never saw this animal. And how do you know it's a cat?"

I can't lie, I was kind of excited someone else thought Zero was a cat.

Matt Fink pulled my hand off his collar, and I let him. He stepped past me, straightening his shirt.

"Fink, did you know Angie James? I was her husband."

His face slumped as if he'd aged a thousand years. Then he ran.

***

He didn't make it far. I dove through his kitchen door to head him off, and I cornered him when he tripped over a crack in his driveway and tumbled into the fender of my Rabbit.

"I guess you forgot your map!"

He got up, brushed himself off, and circled my car, trying to stay on the opposite side.

"You know her!" I shouted, following him around for another lap. He stared at me over the roof, eyes bleary, glancing around for help.

"Yes, yes, I know her."

"I just want to talk to you, doc . . . " The wind blew the map up over my face, so I pinned it under my Rabbit's windshield wipers and held out both hands. "Just relax. Did you know she was murdered?"

"What? Oh no. I'm so sorry . . . " He backed away from

the car, eyes still darting. I wasn't sure if he'd really heard what I said, and then his legs buckled from under him and he sat down hard in the wet grass. He was weeping. I walked over and sat next to him.

"Why are you sorry?"

"I love her," he whispered.

"You mean you 'loved' her."

He looked at me with a surprising amount of fight in his face, and I was suddenly convinced he had nothing to do with her death. If I'd had more time to consider the moment, I'd have realized how ridiculous it was that the goalposts had moved so smoothly from me being relieved he hadn't murdered her, to me not caring if he'd fucked her. I didn't know if the feeling would last, but sitting in the damp lawn together, water soaking our pants and the birds chirping, I felt a curious kinship, and I was tempted to comfort him somehow. So I found myself babbling about Angie's life with me, and our honeymoon in Paris, how we saw cage after cage of birds for sale and how the birds would get beak to beak through those bars with the birds in the other cages, and how I told her this reminded me of the movie *Colors,* when the Bloods and the Crips were kept in different cells and they climbed the bars, itching to get at each other, and Angie reminded me that, when it came to birds, they were trying equally as hard to get through those bars, but for opposite reasons. I told him how she took pictures of those bird cages for her prison research, and how angry I was that she'd fallen asleep while watching *Colors*, and how I hated it when she got so tired after she drank, and I could always see it in her eyes and hear it in her voice, dilated and pinched like insects. I told him how I'd seen the wine in her eyes the last morning she was alive, and how it made me slow to answer her final phone call.

He listened to me, and I was so surprised that we were reaching some kind of understanding that I pulled the blackjack from the duck pocket of my hunting jacket, and I began to beat him with it.

"Hey!" Mad yelled from a thousand miles away.

I avoided his head since I didn't want any more of the trouble that came with cracking a skull. I stuck to the meatier parts of his arms and legs, just enough to keep him curled up. I think I broke a couple of his long fingers. Doctor fingers? Piano-playing fingers. *Moussandro*-playing fingers! And I wondered if this meant he'd never operate again. Or play two synthesizers at the same time. Losing his keyboard skills would be a worse tragedy, though. Homewrecker or not, *Purple Rain* was nothing but perfect songs.

Somehow we ended up back in the house, and just like the time with Jenny Someone and her cattails, it was another tour of where they may have had sex, ending not at his bed, but at his television/VCR combo. He wouldn't provide details between the blows, and this made me angrier, but as he crawled away, I started to root through his movie collection. Old habits, I guess. It was almost a reenactment, and just like that short-order cook, I beat the living shit out of Matt Fink, until he stopped using his movie trailer voice, until his head abandoned that curious guilt-ridden tilt on his shoulder, until I was satisfied he hadn't done anything wrong, or at a minimum, anything to deserve what I was doing to him now. And I swear I must have beaten some newfound resilience into his face, maybe some of my own unearned swagger, smoothing out all his tics and beating him closer to something resembling myself until there was something malleable under my fists I could work with. I was tempted to keep hitting him until he needed a real doctor, or at least a real musician to write a song to remember him by, if only to solve the mystery of this guy for good. I stopped just short of this when I noticed all his movies.

Nothing but prison movies, like the other guy.

Most were DVDs and Blu-rays, but some were videotapes, too; *Undisputed, The Big House, Women in Cages, Chained Heat, Caged Heat!* (apparently everyone was assigned *Caged Heat*), *Hot Cages, Girl Cage, Women in Heated Cages?* Stacked with the movies was a creased pulp paperback named

Brickhouse with sweaty female convicts grinding on its cover, a typical lesbian-panic romp from the '70s, which I pocketed.

What the fuck. Wait a minute. Is that . . .

I stood a videotape back up to read the title. It was *The Longest Yard* . . . the remake with Adam Sandler.

Oh, you piece of shit.

I grabbed the back of Matt Fink's mullet and pulled his face up and away from his knees he was hiding behind. I hauled back, powering up for a death blow from my blackjack, and Mad caught my arm mid-swing, eyes ablaze, thank Christ.

"He doesn't deserve this," she said.

She was right. He deserved something *slightly* better than this. It was a distinction worth considering. Especially after what he said next.

"That's not my movie!" he wheezed, and I let his head fall back down to burrow into his thighs.

"Whose prison movies are these?"

Prison movies everywhere. Too much of a coincidence.

"They're my roommate's. We're in his room."

"Whose room?"

"Angie and I were just friends," Matt Fink sobbed. "She was dating my roommate."

"Who the fuck is your roommate?" I stood up straight, hands on my head to keep my voice calm. I cleared my throat. "Hey, Matt, where might I find your roommate, buddy?"

"He moved to Florida a week ago. Left most of his stuff." A ball of blood shot from his nose.

"Florida?" I looked at Mad. She just shrugged. "And what's in Florida?"

I'd only been there once, saw half a movie, wrestled an alligator. Don't ask.

"Mad?" I asked again.

"I don't know. Fuckin' pill-poppers, for one!" she said, sitting down, rubbing her wrist. "They're the biggest import."

"What's in Florida, doc?" I nudged him gently with my toe, but he saw my foot was serious.

"Prisons. Work."

"Huh?"

"Otto is a prison guard."

***

We were up off the floor, breathing easier, huddled around a computer.

It turned out that Matt and "Otto," the mysterious roommate who wanted to be a prison guard instead of a cop when he grew up, had shared an old desktop Dell. We didn't need to figure out a password, which took some of the fun out of it.

Maybe Matt and Otto shared everything.

His homepage was a website for the Florida Department of Corrections. A banner across the top read: "Trust, Respect, Accountability, Integrity, Leadership, Horse Sense." Below that was a search bar to look up the names of offenders. And below that was the "Inmate Release Information Database." There was a mugshot and a flashing ad in the corner, a reward for tracking down an escaped convict. Luckily, it wasn't DMV Dave.

"Have you seen me?" the pop-up asked as it rotated through more photos. They just kept coming. It seemed like this was a lot of prisoners on the loose.

"Who are these guys?" I mostly asked myself. Matt held his bruised and broken hands close to his chest, but managed to shake his head.

"Gang members by the look." Mad frowned. "See those stupid 'tears of a clown' tattoos?"

"Why was your roommate on this website?" I asked Matt.

"I told you. He worked for a prison. He worked on that website, anyway."

"I thought you said he was a guard."

"He said he was moving to Florida to be a guard. Maybe he guards their computers. I have no idea."

"Cute. So, how did Angie hook up with this shitbag?"

"I don't know. I guess I wasn't enough for her."

I stepped away from the screen and reached back to put an arm around Matt's shoulder. I wasn't sure what my hands were going to do when they got there, so it was just as much of a surprise for me when I went for the hug instead of the chokehold.

He let me hold him a minute. It was honestly sort of touching.

"Maybe it was the Florence Nightingale Effect," Matt said in my ear. "We didn't deserve her."

"But you do deserve each other," Mad muttered.

"Angie was no nurse," I said, removing my arm, embarrassed.

"I know, but Otto, he had heart problems. He was wearing a heart monitor the whole week she was here visiting him."

"How do you know this?" It all sounded like bullshit.

"Because I helped attach it."

"Nah, you're not that kind of doctor," I laughed, straightening his blood-stained collar for him. He ducked under my grasp and opened the desk drawer. He held up a chart, clipboard and everything.

"See? Look. I hooked him up. Literally. Then Otto had to drink Gatorade before his endoscopy, after which he puked two gallons of water all over our bathroom. Angie was here for that. He pulled up his shirt to show off the wires and electrodes all over his body."

"Any cameras?"

"What?"

Johnny Five. More machine than man, I laughed to myself. *If Otto had some decent abs under those wires, the story might make some sense.*

A new banner caught our eye as it scrolled across the screen, flashing between the words "absconder" and "absconded." Below that was a pop-up advertisement for dog adoptions. Angie had all the statistics regarding ex-cons as dog owners. I had no proof of it, but I was convinced the dumbest motherfuckers in the country loved their dogs over anything. Always swearing their dogs were smiling. "I Heart Dogs" license plates. I looked over at Zero. Try "hearting" a mystery, assholes. I never understood the connection. I guess it was because they're in a cage, the dog's in a cage . . . I imagined the Amazon targeted ads: "Customers who enjoyed prison . . . also enjoyed dogs!"

Grabbing the heart-monitor chart from Matt, I scanned the dates along the side. August 6th to August 11th. It matched the dates she'd visited Brickwood to make photocopies at the library archive.

Was she really visiting a prison guard and not *not-Prince's keyboardist?*

I checked the other numbers, and though I was also no doctor, I was pretty sure the way the numbers spiked for his irregular heartbeats that he was going to die very soon. But even stranger were the dates of these spikes. The ones that matched the day Angie disappeared.

Someone had put a checkmark on his EKG reading on the day the cops came to my door. There was a surge of some kind. It was as if this stranger, and probably suspect, had been walking around with his own personal lie detector. No, more like an emotion detector. Had this "Otto" received the bad news of Angie's death over the phone and it got his heart racing? Was he actually in Louisville and did the deed? The hours matched precisely with the time she was telling me about Zero stuck behind Mars. I brought the chart up closer. In the column marked "Event," someone had written, "Bird flew in window."

Bullshit.

"Please don't do that!"

I turned to see Mad shaking one of Matt's ant farms like an Etch-A-Sketch, and I almost had a stroke.

"There's only one ant left!" she laughed. "It is truly an 'ant' farm, isn't it?"

She was scary sometimes, but it did feel like she was back in my corner.

"Please don't. His name is Silverweed. You'll drown him."

"*Her* name is Silverweed, you mean," Mad said. "All these ant farms and you don't know a whole lot about ants. They're all female. Do you know more about medicine? Maybe you should get a worm farm."

"What do you know about worm farms?" My heart was having its own event.

"Nothing," Matt said unconvincingly.

Angie's worm phase at our home had been a disappointment all around. I'd expected something much more "Fulci," I guess, like worms all boiling over each other and making squishy, chirpy sounds every time I opened the lid of the compost bin. Like in *Zombi 2*, or *City of the Living Dead*. Why were those worms making so much noise? This reality wasn't nearly as exciting, like watching a movie called *Box o' Dirt*. Or *Egg Shell Party*. And eventually our worm farm turned into a mold farm, and she chucked the whole mess in the trash.

"How about you? You into worm farms, Mad? It's like having a box of dirt for a pet."

"Sounds great, but, no, sorry. I did have a box of ashes for a pet once." She turned away, and Matt gave her a little more room. I studied them both, trying to figure out the nature of their relationship. Then Mad was back on the ant farm, shaking it a little harder.

"Aw, that's sad," she said. "Look how the ants all huddled together when they died."

"No," Matt said. "That's just how the final ant piled up all the bodies."

"Oh! Good!" Mad said sarcastically. She put it back on the shelf.

Bird flew in window.

Suddenly I was sure this was a euphemism, like every spike of the strap-on heart monitor indicated a time when someone had sex. I stepped over to Matt, pushing his back to the wall. I needed to make sure he was telling the truth about whose bad heart was being monitored. I untucked his shirt and yanked it up to his chin.

"Hey!"

I checked his torso. He was much furrier than I expected, but I didn't see any bald patches in the thick pelt covering his chest or abdomen where electrodes could have been nested, then torn free. I let him pull his shirt back down.

"Sorry. Just making sure you aren't wearing a wire."

Mad laughed.

"You liked that one?" I asked her. I was very proud of it.

"Yeah, but it's all downhill from here," she said.

"What's this Otto's job again?" I asked. "Did you meet him, Mad? He's not the Vice President of anything, is he?"

"Vice President of prisons?" Mad laughed. "Pretty sure that title belongs to the Birdman of Alcatraz. By the way, how come nobody has that movie?"

"It's the *Worm*man of Alcatraz, duh," I said. Matt was sitting in the corner of the room, so I plopped down next to him, hand on his shoulder. It was our new thing.

"Did you love her?" I asked.

"I loved her," he said, and he sounded different this time, but a half hour with me will do that to a person. He stood back up, flushed pink and bloody as a newborn baby, truly a new man, and I looked him over, I mean *really* looked him over, for the first time. His spiky black hair was hilariously outdated, and this, combined with his obvious physical weaknesses, and the way he dressed all '80s with that "wearing your girlfriend's shirt" thing all the punks had back then . . . all these things should have convinced me that she was right about his claim to fame, that he was, for real, Prince's keyboard player. But looking the part had the opposite effect. It made little sense in that moment, but unless I could prove he used to play for Prince, or had two penises, whichever came first, I suddenly was convinced of his innocence regarding all other matters, including Angie's death.

And all of this, combined with the beating and Mad shaking up his ant farm, meant that we'd broken him down, then built him back up. We'd all come to an understanding. I could see it in his face. He hated me, but he was in love, just like I was, and he was going to see this through to the end. He was weak, sure, but I had made him angry (and made Mad crazy), and maybe it would all come in handy.

We were in this together.

***

I sat in my car with my new crew. Matt was in the back seat with Zero, who was sniffing at his bloody nose as he sniffed him right back. Mad was up front with me, clicking through the slides of naked men on my toy camera keychain.

Squad goals!

"Hey, anyone want a free idea for a song? Or even a movie?" I asked them. Matt avoided my eyes in the rearview mirror for now, but that wouldn't last. He was reminding me more and more of my brother by the minute. There was almost an equivalent amount of injuries I'd inflicted on both. Almost. There was time to catch up.

"No," he said, bloody nose still wrinkled. "What's that fucking smell?"

"I wish I could say 'you'll get used to it.'" Mad sighed without turning around.

"Someone should make a movie about Deke Thornton's ill-fated *Greasy Bunch*, you know, the B-squad gang with L.Q. Jones and Strother Martin, bumbling around and chasing the heroes in *The Wild Bunch*."

"That's us," Mad said. "I am feeling pretty damn greasy. You're lucky I have some vacation days for this misadventure."

"I can't believe you work at the DMV," I said.

"I'm undercover," Mad said, clicking the camera faster. "Every license I laminate, I check the box marked 'organ donor.' No one even looks. What a waste of food, you know?"

"Bullshit," I said, then I got out my new license and

flipped it over. "What the fuck! Why did you do that? Are you looking for some new eyes?"

"Nope. Ears."

"Well, you don't want any part of me," I said.

"Except the Greasy Bunch were the only ones in that movie who lived," Matt mumbled from the back, a good minute late on his comeback. I turned around, getting ready to mock him, and Mad dangled the toy camera in front of my face.

"Hey, do you know what's on here?"

"No," I lied. "It's not a kaleidoscope? That's from my bum stash!"

"Talking about the Greasy Bunch . . . "

She passed the toy back to Matt, who was trying to keep Zero off of him as he stuffed his duffel bag of clothes under the seat. He clicked through a couple images, then gasped, then laughed.

"Give me that . . . " I reached back to grab it, then held it up to my eye and hit the button. It was pornography all right. Specifically, hairy, naked men with oiled-up schlongs.

"Uhhhhhh . . . " I said.

"It's a clue! Let's go!" Mad laughed, kicking off her shoes, and I started the car.

"Got any music?" she asked.

"I sure don't."

"I'll keep my eye out," she said. "You know, it used to be you'd find mixtapes all over the street, and you'd say, 'Cool, someone made this for their boyfriend,' then you'd find a CD full of MP3s and think, 'Neat, someone shared every single album they grew up on.' Now you can find a whole device with a thousand songs and be like, 'Oh, shit, someone dropped their brain!'"

Something flapped on the windshield in front of us, making us jump. It was the map, still pinned down by a wiper. I reached out and around to bring it into the car, then I stopped.

"What are you doing?"

I popped open the glove box for my teacher stash of Magic Markers, and I started tracing the lines of the map pressed against the outside of the glass. It had been folded up by someone who'd never successfully folded up a map in her life. Meaning Angie. And I drew over every crease and wrinkle. When I recapped the marker, I'd outlined a pathway, divided neatly by the winding crack of the windshield. Then I plucked the map loose from the wipers and stuffed it into the glove box.

"What the hell is that?" Mad asked, pointing at the crack with a dirty toe.

"That's where we're going," I said, then pointed at the glove box. "And that's where we've been. You know, I think she folded it that way for a reason. It's a message. Whenever we didn't have a pen, she folded things, to remember stuff."

"Who does that?"

"Last year, we made a list of all the jobs we were going to apply for when she got her doctorate, all over a big road map of Southern California. Every crease cut through a potential interview."

"I don't get it," she said.

"It's not really for you to get? But, okay . . . " I tapped the crack. "See those furrows in the glass? Now see the crack that runs through them? Where is that going?"

"Either Loch Ness or Florida," Mad said.

"Exactly. So we're going to Florida."

"You would."

"Hey, does this thing bark?" Matt said from the back.

***

Once, I had a dream of being lost in a maze, my fingers and toes made entirely of black olives. I tried to make a fist, to punch my way out, only to watch my hand crumble against the stone wall. I told Angie about this when we woke up, and she reminded me of my promise to never describe a dream to her again, or a fist fight. Then she said my dream reminded her of an experiment she was researching that involved rats and rewards and how scientists suspected they could navigate their mazes much quicker than most people ever suspected. The rats only slowed down for the treats, she said, and they didn't go over the tops of the dividers because the experiment would be over, meaning the rewards would be over. So they played the game the scientists wanted and never tried to solve anything. She explained that, of all the scientific breakthroughs known to man, this was the most important lesson human beings would ever learn. From rats.

"Remember, if you go through a maze just once, you'll dream of being inside it," she said to me that morning. "But if you go through a maze twice, you'll dream of ways to escape it."

***

Me and my troop (more like troupe) were two hours gone from Brickwood, headlong down Interstate 75 and tickling the edge of the Carolinas. It was dark, and everyone was tired, which made it easy to pretend we were some family on vacation. Mad felt like the dad.

For miles, I thought Matt had fallen asleep. He was sprawled out in the back seat with his legs up on Zero's cage, Angie's papers covering his face. When a sharp turn dislodged them and revealed his haunted eyes to me in the rearview mirror, I asked him, "Oh no, did you stay up all night reading Foucault?"

"I'm totally a prison, bro," he whispered.

"Welcome to the party, pal!" Mad laughed. She always seemed less sleepy than Matt, Zero, or myself. She reached back to grab Angie's stuff from Matt and dig through it some more.

"Searching the research of the research of the research . . ." she was mumbling, then she stopped. "Hey, what's this?"

She'd uncovered the heap of newspaper clippings in depths of the Trapper Keeper and was holding up an article. I knew it was going to be a certain Florida kid's face, even before the next streetlight lit up our interior. "Troublemaker Sentenced Today" the headline read, and there were two photos accompanying it: a hard-scrabble Black teenager, and a close-up of an alligator clamped around someone's ankle. Though the positioning clearly implied this was the teen's ankle, the skin peeking out of the tennis shoe was conspicuously pale. If Mad had flipped the article over, she would have seen the note Angie had made on the back regarding "the troubled history of newspapers dehumanizing Black children by pairing imagery of them with wildlife."

"What's this?" Mad asked. She must have heard me holding my breath.

"I said not to ask. Long story. I'll get to it eventually."

"You never said that, but I'm on the edge of my seat," Mad said, patting the vinyl between her knees. "At all times!"

Mad put aside the pile of newspaper clippings. And to help keep everyone awake, she began to read aloud from Angie's thick dissertation, the heavy-duty nucleus of the folder where everyone's attention usually ended up. There was something in Mad's voice, sounding more and more like Angie with every mile. Her narration had Matt's head, and my own, tilted at full attention. Zero was either purring or snoring.

Then she found the letter.

It was tucked inside some over-incarceration stats, and I hadn't gotten that far yet. But when Mad shook it open and read it to us, my wife's words rode her vocal cords like they'd never left them.

"'I am not going to respond to your points in any kind of systematic manner, and for this I apologize,'" Mad recited. "'I tried doing that once before, and it felt too much like writing a term paper. You know how that is. I couldn't finish without lapsing into interminable equivocations. So I am writing this in a hotel room in Brickwood, Ohio, after a splash of wine, and on these trips I tend to be more reflective and emotional than normal. And when I'm not researching, I tend to veer into inappropriate shit myself. So here it goes. I just finished reading Junot Diaz's *This is How You Lose Her.* Did you ever read him? It's hard to remember right now, but something gave me extra incentive to bring a book on this trip. At the end, he wrote 'The half-life of love is forever,' and reading that line felt like being punched in the stomach. Have you memorized my birthday yet . . .'"

I closed my eyes as if struck. I'd always had a problem remembering Angie's birthday. I was kind of like the guy in *Memento*, except only regarding birthdays. For her present one year, Angie considered making me tattoo her birth date backwards onto my chest.

I balanced my glasses on the stubble on my head and rubbed the itch out of my eyes, and the road came back into focus. I thought of what my passengers must be thinking, hoping it was easier to filter Angie's words through as many ears as possible. I remembered when I had self-imposed deadlines and couldn't think of anything to write for creative-writing workshops I attended, and how I'd take the words from any private correspondence I could find and place them in the mouths of less than fully realized fictional characters. My classmates tore my stories apart, citing Nic Pizzolatto's recent successes with his *True Detective* pastiche as proof of a more slippery line between plagiarism, creative nonfiction, and outright betrayal. But I could never make that kind of theft work for me. *True Defective, that's me!*

Mad, however, stole these words like they'd always been her own.

"' . . . this fist in my gut is turning me inside out, empty and airless. It's true that I don't know how to get close to someone and then stay put. It's disorienting. I know it's hard for the people who have tried to love me, but it's worse for me. Because I'm stuck with it. So I'm sorry. I'm sorry for leaving you with that wondering . . .'" Mad hesitated on the last line, just for a moment. "' . . . but I've been seeing someone else now for almost a year.'"

I slammed on the brakes, and the Rabbit hop-skipped half

in the ditch, the weight of the pennies in the passenger's-side door almost rolling us over. When the car stopped, I was still processing the fact that the last line could still go either way, that it could be addressed to me or to her fling. So I didn't quite hear the sound of the page ripping free, and I'm not sure when I realized Mad was eating the answer I needed. When I turned, she was chewing the paper like bubblegum, smiling as she swallowed, traditionally a good quality in a woman. Ben Franklin said that, not me. Still, I could have killed her.

"Why?" I croaked.

"I don't know," she said, considering this. "To make this my story, too?"

"Are you kidding me?" I closed my eyes as I asked the next question. "Just answer this. Before you ate the last words of my dead wife, did you read everything she said?"

"Yes."

Matt's seat creaked as he sat forward, understandably curious.

"And?"

"And it's our secret now. Me and hers."

"Who was that letter to?" I grabbed for the pile of papers in her lap, and she hunched to protect them.

"Back off, Dave."

"Was that letter for me to find, or . . . "

"I'm not telling you. Not right now anyway."

"Why the fuck not!"

"Drive."

I punched the windshield in frustration. Then punched it again and saw the spider web of cracks radiate from my fist to cover the roadmap I'd drawn for us. Another punch, and the crack turned, curled, went past our destination, almost but not quite touching the coastline. Finally, the fog in my brain cleared, and I looked at the new lines I'd created. There were dozens of destinations now, and I was suddenly sure we'd find the way to them all. I had no reason to believe it, but I was sure one of those fractures in the glass would lead me to the invisible prison, whatever, or wherever, that turned out to be, and by proxy lead me to her.

"Don't worry," Mad said as I started driving again. "I read it before I ate it. It's up here now." She tapped her temple, then her stomach. "And down here."

"I can't believe you just did that."

"You're stuck with me now, Dave. And you know what? Now I know you won't ever kill me. If that's something you're capable of. And this jury is still out."

I thought about the cruelty of her eating Angie's last words for a few more miles, but then I convinced myself I could get the information at some point. I thought of Mad as an Etch-A-Sketch combined with an ant farm, and decided I could shake it out of her if I had to. Then work those dials to build her back up again. I'd done it before. I'd done worse. Hell, I'd done worse earlier that day. I looked for Matt's eyes in the rearview mirror, and watched him duck my line of sight and pretend to fuss over Zero in his cage. He pulled out a thin bone and sniffed it.

"This isn't a chicken," he said.

"Maybe it's what the chicken ate," I said impatiently, and he dropped it to the floorboard. I turned to Mad. "How about you don't eat anything else."

"I'll let you know when I get hungry." She smiled.

"You're fuckin' nuts."

"Nope, just a little mad sometimes."

That was the moment I realized she was right. I was stuck with her now. Stuck with three mystery creatures, right up to the end credits, where, if you were patient enough, you could finally read the names to find out who everyone really was all along. Even if it spoiled the illusion. Which should be required by law.

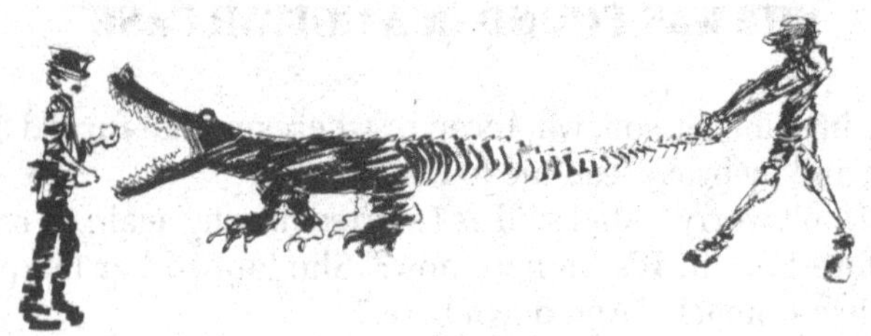

XIV

IS THAT MY SANDWICH IN THERE?

THREE TIMES IN my life, I've ruined a movie. It doesn't happen often, because I take movies real serious, but you should try it sometime. Imagine you're in a theater—let's say you're watching *Jaws 3-D*—and someone walks up to that stage area in front of the screen (like those idiots who act out the entirety of *The Rocky Horror Picture Show*). Now imagine they're waving their hands to interrupt the action and make an announcement about shark-tooth necklaces they're selling on Etsy. Would you buy one? That's what I thought.

The first time I ruined a movie was while watching *Jurassic Park* with my friend Holly, after I'd spent the day helping her move into her new apartment at Cornell. She'd just showed me the crazy house where Carl Sagan lived (you can only see the door at road level since the rest of the compound is on the side of a mountain), and what a real campus looked like, compared to the University of Toledo where I was trapped at the time. Her flashy dorm had a piano in the lobby for students to, you know, just play the piano, like this was no big deal. So, all hyped up for some dinosaurs (and me wanting to get away from that piano), we headed downtown to catch a flick, and we quickly realized the volume was set so low it was like the T. Rex was friggin' whispering. Feeling bad about how shitty my own college was, I wanted to do something to impress her, so I got up and found the projection booth on my first try, this closet with a wall full of space-age controls, and I turned what had to be a volume knob, and . . . wrecked the movie for everybody. It was a pivotal scene, so turning off the film was about the worst thing I could have done to that crowd, right up there with cranking up the temperature twenty degrees, or turning half the lights on. Luckily, I missed the knob that released the bees.

The second movie I ruined upped the ante considerably. It was also my first experience with the enigma that was "Florida." I was watching one of those heavy, holiday-season, Oscar-bait crime dramas. Can't remember the name. *Mystic Pizza*? And this flick was emoting for all it was worth up, holding its bleeding heart out to the crowd in two trembling hands, and the packed crowd was eating it up with their Jujyfruits. We wouldn't even have gone to see a movie at all, but me and Jesse had missed the plane that would have taken us home from a friend's wedding in Gainesville, so we had four hours to kill. The Florida wedding turned out mostly stressful, with the Bridezilla furious because I'd left the groom's contact lenses in the hotel. She actually shoved me into an umbrella stand at the reception and hissed, "He couldn't see me on my wedding day, asshole!" I apologized but wondered how I got saddled with such a responsibility. I mean, have we met? Also, it was weird what my friends valued when it came to relationships. A nearsighted groom wouldn't be confused who he was marrying, right? Then again, I'd always been amazed by what most people considered romantic (or even reasonable) behavior. Like picture a perfect candlelit dinner, two people curling up by the fireplace for a drink, followed by slow, sensual lovemaking on a bearskin rug. Then the dude goes into the bathroom to wash his dick in her sink. And this is considered normal. Does that make sense? Well, it doesn't matter because that's the night he proposed. All of this ended up in my toast to the happy couple.

So with three hours to go, we walked into a cinema next door to the airport, basically *in* the airport (a great money-making location that took advantage of weary layovers like ours), and we asked for two tickets to "the longest piece of shit they had." At first, Jesse tried hiding in the bar, but I dragged him reluctantly away from the local news, which turned out to be better than the movie. Florida's news was crazy as fuck. They had "gator alerts" at the top of the hour instead of weather reports.

I barely remembered this film since we only saw a third of it before I ruined it, but I do know it was a murder mystery. It all went down during this scene where a frantic father was trying to break through a protective line of police to see if his daughter is the corpse inside an old bear pit in an abandoned zoo. The hard-ass, method-actor dad was fighting with cops and screaming over and over, "Is that my daughter in there?! Is that *my daughter* in there?!" And there was this pileup of about 625 uniformed officers restraining him in this massive dog pile as he screamed in anguish at the sky, and the camera soared above the scene, and the music swelled and then . . .

Jesse leaned over to me and whispered, serious as hell:

"You know what would make this scene very different emotionally? What if the dad was screaming, 'Is that my sandwich in there?' instead?"

I stared at him a minute, then blew snot out my nose trying to stifle a laugh. His comment didn't make much sense, and "Is that my pizza in there?" would have at least fit the title, and, sure, it probably wasn't *that* funny, but both of us started snickering uncontrollably. We could actually feel the anger of the crowd rising around us like a tsunami.

If you ever decide to share your perfectly hilarious comment with an auditorium full of strangers, you'll quickly realize no one wants to hear it. No one. No matter how clever you surely were in that moment. Like I said earlier, there are few venues in the world where an outburst is less welcome than a movie theater. Think of it as church with arm rests, zealots tonguing Twizzlers instead of faking the lyrics to hymns.

But after some hateful glares and a "Shhh!" or two, we got ourselves under control. And we were doing fine, until the movie came to the scene where the father has to identify his daughter's body in the morgue. They pulled back the sheet, and her face was twisted forever in a grimace of pain and lost innocence, and the devastated father muttered:

"Yes. That's my daughter."

And right then, Jesse and I looked at each other, both knowing we were thinking the exact same thing. We'd heard the distraught father say, clear as day, solemn as a sermon:

"Yes. That's my sandwich."

We both lost it, braying laughter that later made my stomach feel like I'd done a thousand sit-ups. Angry moviegoers tisk-tisked and stomped out the door to demand our ejection, and we were still convulsing even as flashlight-wielding security manhandled us out the door up near the stage. The explosion of sunlight blasting onto those furious faces in the seats was well worth it.

I still think they got lucky. Who knows what would have happened if we'd made it to the inevitable autopsy, where the medical examiner cut a perfect diagonal through the center of that sandwich, a division any coroner, or restaurant owner, will tell you maximizes exposure of the contents. This is also when the movie would reveal the girl had been six weeks pregnant, a shock for audience, daddy, and baby daddy alike. And if we'd made it that far into the movie, I might have shit myself holding in the giggles.

Bounced outside the building, we dusted ourselves off in the Florida sunshine and discovered our plane was delayed again. So we tried to eat up more of the clock by heading to the beach we'd somehow avoided during our stay. We decided it would be fun to shake sand out of our asses and into their gloved hands when the TSA grabbed our balls to corral us through their security theater of X-rays and microwaves.

We never saw the kid follow us out.

***

Shuffling down the street with the anvil of Florida rays hammering our shoulders, we could smell the ocean but still couldn't see it, and we came across a crowd surrounding an alligator that had apparently wandered into a supermarket parking lot. Near the mob, I noticed an old biddy, way too old to be wearing cowboy boots and a mini-skirt, and I walked over to hear what was up.

"Dunno," the biddy said. "It must have walked a mile inland. Maybe it smelled the deli counter."

"Does this happen a lot?"

"Three times a day!" the biddy declared, pointing at the sky, as about twenty bracelets clanked down her arm to her elbows. Jesse and I looked at each other, and she laughed. "Just kidding, suckers! Twice a day tops." There was a distinct Russian accent when this biddy was at her giddiest. "Stick around, though! They'll be by to shoot it any second."

"They're gonna kill it?!" Jesse was horrified.

"Hard pass," I said.

"Of course they're gonna kill it. How do you think they make our boots!" she said, punctuating this by tapping her heel on the asphalt. I chewed on my bottom lip and checked my watch, and Jesse looked up at the harsh sky, dreaming of the safety of Ohio soil and a reasonable amount of shade. Then we shared a glance and a shrug.

Five minutes later, Jesse was trying to drag an angry gator by the tail, the toothy top half of the primeval beast whiplashing around his feet, and I was screaming for a taxi.

The cab was for me, not for Jesse and the gator, because I was going to leave both of them behind. I knew we were in over our heads. On our trip, it had been so hot that we'd hung out inside a hotel, a church, a reception hall, a movie theater, and various airports, but the first time we'd finally ventured outside for any amount of time, we'd only made it a block before our vacation had gone all Florida on our asses.

That's when the knuckles found my jaw and I was suddenly looking straight up in the air, wondering what happened. When my vision cleared, I saw the local who was wielding such a heavy right hook. A wiry little bastard, his gleaming chocolate skin cut with muscle, cherry-red fists as balled up as his forehead. He grabbed my neck and I truly thought he was going to climb up my shirt and hit me again. Then, nose to nose and him breathing in my face, I smelled it and finally figured it out.

Popcorn.

He'd come from the movie. This little fucker had actually followed us six blocks, livid that we'd disrupted his slice of *Mystic Pizza*, just to punch me in the grill. He stood there on his tip-toes, defiant, promising more of the same. He was a little guy, and he was skinny, but his veins were out, and he clearly had a righteous cause. Sort of like Jesse trying to save the alligator. But I didn't want any part of it. I turned to my friend still fighting the 200-pound lizard.

"Trade ya?"

Jesse looked down at the hissing, snapping reptilian between his legs, then back at the kid.

"No way!" Jesse said, trying to drag it again, sweat pouring off his nose in an unbroken stream. That's when the gator locked its jaws onto his ankle, and Jesse screamed. He sat down hard, frantically trying to kick himself loose as blood seeped through the stripes of his tube sock. I would have laughed if I didn't have my hands full with a native Floridian. I tried to grab the kid and calm him down, but he'd lost his shirt at some point and was as slippery as a bar of soap. And he was punching me at will. And this little kid *bit*, just like the gator. I watched him gnawing on a mouthful of my triceps and thought:

His mouth is gonna brand me for the rest of my life. I'm gonna have to tell everyone at every party all about how some punk weighing a buck o' five kicked my ass in Florida.

So I grabbed his face like a bowling ball, thumb in deep for the fish hook, middle finger catching a nostril, and I flipped him on his back. The old biddy grunted her approval, and I caught a glimpse of her perched on a speed bump with her boot off, painting her toenails, every so often cheering for myself or the gator. Honestly, she made me fight harder.

But both Jesse and I were losing interest in the battle. It reminded me of a fight Jesse and I got into after graduation. It started in the living room, went through a cheap card table, down his narrow hallway, knocking Jesse's framed Springsteen albums right off his wall, which was no great loss. I mean, I guess I understood why he took down *Born to Ruin* after I got a marker and corrected it to *Born to Ruin*. But a framed copy of *The River*? *Lucky Town*? Come on, dude.

The melee finally ended up all the way in his bathroom, where Jesse's thick skull cracked open the PVC trap under his sink and splashed hairballs and sour water everywhere. He needed six stitches, but his mom found her engagement ring, so it wasn't all bad news.

We mapped it all out later. That fight lasted thirty feet.

This one lasted a thousand and one.

***

Three things. Don't tug on Superman's cape. Don't shit into the wind. Don't try to drag an alligator back to the ocean by its tail. And don't fuck with someone's movie in Florida.

No bullshit, all four of us made it to the beach still brawling. The sun was going down, and I could barely see through the sand and sweat and blood, but I got lucky when we all hit the dunes and I caught the kid's head on one of those dog-crap baggie dispensers. I had the upper hand for the split-second I needed it, and I used my weight to steamroller him and sit on his arms.

"What the hell, kid?" I had time to ask between sucking wind.

"That was my sister in there," he said.

Sandwich.

But I still don't know what he meant by that. That was his sister in the movie? Or was that movie a true story? No way. Then Jesse had another theory. He said that when people are poor, they will attack you in the theater, even shoot your ass for interrupting, because for them a movie might be a one-time event. If you can't afford to come back, that means what's on the screen is as fleeting as life. He had a point. I'd been in fights over way less than that.

Jesse's alligator had calmed down and seemed to be going into some sort of shutdown, some eerie slo-mo post-Cambrian extinction. Jesse was actually petting it while its teeth were still locked onto his ankle and its tail made sleepy sand angels in the breakers. I wondered how he'd get through the X-ray machine attached to a dinosaur, then figured if anyone could, it was him.

This was his life now. More gator than machine than man. All cop? All stop.

"Surf and turf!" the biddy shouted nonsensically, and that's about the time we were flooded with blue uniforms and foul aftershave. I gave some trouble to a chubby cop in a crew cut, but the local kid seemed to tangle the rest of them up single-handed. He was definitely a scrapper. At some point, a zookeeper took a shot at the gator on Jesse's ankle with a tranquilizer gun, and the tourists got memorable photos of everything. On the news the next day, the zookeeper swore he'd been aiming for the alligator, and claimed he was sorry a local African-American boy took the dart square in his back (precisely between the thumb and first finger of a cop's swollen hand), but "maybe he shouldn't have snuck into that movie theater?"

A mob was cheering, possibly chanting, but I saw nothing but blue and red lights. Then the chubby cop's Taser barbs started popping and discouraging the rubberneckers, and the crackle of electricity drowned the crash of the ocean in my ears. Even the old biddy and her fresh red toenails scattered, and, without my booster, I suddenly wanted to catch that plane home more than anything.

To be honest, I couldn't believe the dart took the kid down. I don't want to dehumanize him here, but I'd fully expected a juvenile as dogged as himself to catch it in his teeth, chew it up, then swallow it like popcorn. I described this boy to Angie when Jesse and I got back, and she immediately pulled a blurry photo out of her Leaning Tower of Papers and stuck it in my face. It was another snapshot of kids in the woods, all about ten feet apart, circling a nondescript cardboard box in the brush. She asked if anyone looked familiar. I said, "Maybe that's him in the corner of the picture, down on one knee?" I asked where it was, and Angie said the kids were serving time and changed the subject. She was always doing shit like that. But I was never sure if it was the kid who had attacked me, because if he *was* serving time, the kid in the photo seemed to be enjoying it.

Later that night, Jesse and I sat on a curb under the streetlights, answering the same questions from authority figures fairly consistently, but never to anyone's satisfaction. We watched the Keystone Cops and paramedics work on Jesse's ankle, then turn their attention to the spectators who had returned. I heard one tattooed and shirtless asshole refer to the kid as a "Skunk Ape," which I assumed was a racial slur, then realized he was convinced we'd battled a genuine cryptozoological phenomenon, and lived to tell the tale. "It may have been an adolescent, but on special occasions, they come to town to see movies just like anybody else," he told a reporter who had long since turned off his camera. I tried to wave down the news crew and set the record straight, to explain that everyone should take movies seriously, but they dodged me easier than I'd dodged that kid, and the chubby cop with the crewcut asked if I liked getting Tased. I said I could grow to enjoy it. Then I asked if that's what had happened to his hair.

When we were finally free to go, we stuck around. I was convinced they were going to load the comatose gator into the ambulance and leave the boy facedown in the sand. Jesse made the opposite bet. You can probably guess who won.

***

Jesse and I collapsed into the hard, unforgiving seats of our red-eye, knees spread out and bodies slumped as low as the stewardess would allow, needles of sand painfully working their way into the rivers of cuts on our jaw lines, chins, and elbows. We both thought about our encounters with the indigenous population, and Jesse had a particularly hard time shaking the thought that the gator was on its way to being carved into someone's boots. He seemed to be in denial about the human target of those tranquilizers, but that kid was all I could think about. I was convinced that fucking with someone's movie was what had really stopped the boy's heart, and I watched Florida shrink and vanish into the sticky haze below and vowed never to return.

At 35,000 feet, we shared some headphones to save a dollar and watched an old prison movie called *Brick House*. It was terrible, maybe the worst of them all, and it would have been easy to make fun of. But everyone was watching it. And we didn't say a word.

Some day I'll tell you about the third movie I ruined, if I haven't already. I considered going back and revising this story, to make everyone come out a little better. If only there was more time. I mean less time. Anyway, there was never any need. The Sunshine State ended up finishing us all.

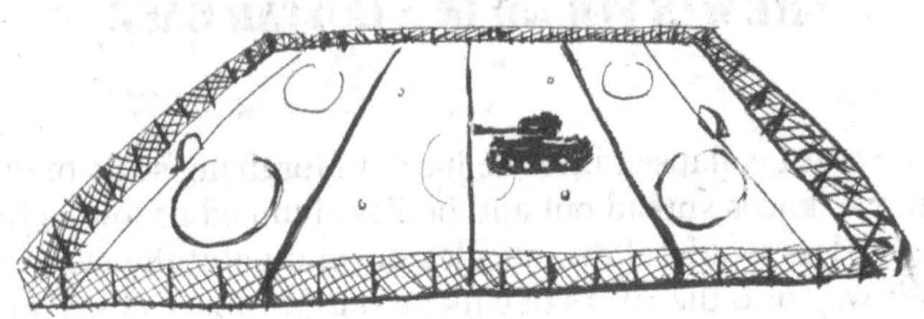

XV

VIETNAM BUG HOCKEY

WHEN WE STOPPED for gas, Mad swapped seats with Matt and curled up next to Zero, and then they both slept for a hundred miles. In the passenger's seat, Matt took his turn rifling through Angie's Trapper Keeper, and I made a mental note of the pages he was stopping to study, wondering if he'd seen them before. And over the better part of an hour, I slowly turned down the radio knob with my knee until it was off. He didn't notice until the click. The sun was coming up, and he looked to the horizon, bloodshot eyes clearing.

"How far are we?"

"Almost all the way. Find anything?"

I could feel him staring at the side of my face for longer than necessary, then he went back to the pages. "Nothing," he said. "Found some stuff I copied for her. Did you see this?"

He held up the sealed envelope I had marked "Invisible Prison."

"Yeah, don't open that. I'm not ready for that yet. And neither are you."

But I couldn't imagine opening it, or ever being ready to prove I'd wasted my time.

"What about this?" He held up the map I'd found early

on, the stained, hand-drawn diagram of what I took for some forgotten military skirmish.

"Yeah, what is that? Napoleon's last stand?"

"It kind of looks like Waterloo, doesn't it? But that's mostly because Waterloo essentially looked like a hockey game."

"What looked like what?" I was lost.

"Our favorite sport. The true National Pastime."

I looked him over good, remembering the feel of his body retreating as I battered on it. He was different now, bolder. At least brave enough to use "our" when referring to himself and my late wife. Maybe he was ready to give up some new information without another beating. So many beatings on this road trip. I hoped they weren't over.

"Tell me, Matt. What did you and Angie talk about when she came to your library?"

"Not a lot. She was a hard worker."

"Uh-huh, but you're telling me she hooked up with your roommate . . . a prison guard with a heart condition. Was she your friend or not?" He caught me glaring.

"Yes, she was my friend. You can't make that many photocopies without becoming close."

"Right. What sport?"

"This sport," Matt said, holding up the military map again.

"Am I supposed to guess? Don't tell me. You were both in Desert Storm."

"No, Vietnam," he said, deadly serious. "We were in that library for ten hours a day some days, and we had to find games to play while the copier hummed. And this was one of them. We called it 'Vietnam Bug Hockey.' It was a game we created. Together."

"Bullshit," Mad murmured from the back. "That's an old game. We played it as kids."

"Oh, boy," I said, mostly to myself, reaching forward and scratching the crack I'd punched in the windshield. It was growing, spreading out to all corners of the glass now, reminding me of the crack the kitchen staff bashed into Sutherland's windshield in *Invasion of the Body Snatchers* (the second adaptation, not the first one, or the third one, or the inevitable reboot, the one with the scream). I looked at Matt and thought about screaming, then even more about "adaptation."

"You ever see *Invasion of the Body Snatchers*, Matt? Donald Sutherland played a Mental Health Department representative, and he finds rat turds in the restaurant's soup and was gonna shut them down, so they vandalized his car."

"Don't you mean 'Health Department'?"

"Either way, you end up on poop patrol. My point is, nobody likes getting bad news."

He put the papers down and closed his eyes to get some sleep. I fiddled with the vents to blow the steam off my glasses and to distract myself from punching the windshield anymore and changing our course yet again.

***

To the left of the highway above the tree line, the dark orange glow of a fire was blazing somewhere nearby. When it was close enough to make nostrils flare and wake everybody up to resume their vaguely nervous upright positions, I rolled up my window to keep from coughing.

On our long honeymoon walk through the French countryside, my wife and I had discovered a similar pyre of swirling black smoke. It was a "gorse fire," the *sapeurs-pompiers* explained through their gas masks, something they called a "fire-climax" plant, a remarkable organism that encouraged its own destruction. It had given Angie something to obsess over on our trip, even though she'd promised not to crack any books or computer screens until we got back stateside. That night in the hotel, she told me that the fire recurrence period in such foliage was every ten years. This was known as a "catastrophic climax," and the seeds actually opened during the fire cycle, then began to grow right there in the middle of their own scorched earth. It was the most romantic thing I'd ever heard.

***

When I first got my driver's license, the open road sort of blew my mind, so I expected this trip to have an even more profound effect on my brain wrinkles, maybe shake loose those deep memories buried in the folds of the gray matter. But all this drive time had really taught me was that on the tenth listen, Billy Ocean's "Get Outta My Dreams, Get Into My Car" sounded like it should be sung at gunpoint, and Sheryl Crow spent an inordinate amount of time describing what Billy was doing at the bar. Those two songs were apparently every DJ's favorite. And if there was one thing that every town had in common, it was shit DJs, also named Billy.

No, seriously, there's a moment in "All I Wanna Do" when you're convinced that the rest of the song, or your life, whichever comes first, is going to be nothing but Sheryl Crow talking about everything Billy is doing, and everything he will ever do. "Down to his *thick fingers*"? Yikes! This is more terrifying than thinking hitchhiker killer Billy Ocean got his name because he was born at the bottom of the deep blue sea. *Gurgle gurgle.*

But even if we all came from the water, we certainly felt more at home on the road. And those drives were some of my best memories, no matter what was bubbling from the speakers. Like the summer Angie and I rented a van to check out the East Coast, and the vehicle came with satellite radio and all those new-fangled specialty stations. During this mini-vacation, the satellite station was running some kind of "road trip station" special (or maybe it was just a scheme to suck in wannabe tourists like ourselves), and we debated this bargain. "Aren't all car radio stations 'road trip stations' by definition?" she asked me. "I mean, you're definitely *driving*. Unless you're in a parked car in your garage. And, in that case, it should be a limited-time 'suicide station.'" She was always making good points like that.

The other thing we discovered during our trial marriage, er, I mean satellite radio trial, was stand-up comedy. After we logged about 30 hours of snippets on those channels, one thing that became clear was that stand-up had recently entered its postmodern phase, because around two-thirds of those comedians would stop and comment on how weird their joke just was, how they delivered it, how it was received, etc. It reminded me of novels about writers and the lack of sincerity in most fiction (as well as most relationships), and had somewhat of the same effect as we cruised along, the landscape alternating between lush and Martian, real and imaginary, a cascade of strange mountains marbled like muscles, and Angie always making a point to tell me why this was interesting.

***

After we stopped for gas and snacks, to break up the miles, I put aside my pride and asked Matt to explain this unusual "sport" he played with my wife, and he was excited to tell me and Mad all about it. He said it was actually mostly *his* game, just to be clear, a game he used to play with the other kids on his street when he was a boy, and one of them first named it "Bug Hockey." Originally it was a game to play with ants, which fascinated Angie the most, although Matt preferred collecting spiders in his jars when he was a boy. He said his dad told him spiders weren't "bugs" at all, then killed one in front of him, but he was never sure what that was supposed to accomplish. It did make him respect spiders more and his father less. Matt said that Angie had inspired this new variation on the game when a research dead-end one afternoon had led her down a rabbit hole of the history of the "Zamboni," and hockey rinks in general. But the original game from his childhood was much more brutal . . .

Matt said this all almost too fast to follow, and I hid the rest of the 5-hour Energy shots.

"First you take a soldier . . . " Matt began.

"A soldier ant?" I said. "I thought you said they were spiders?"

"No, they're soldiers. They're in 'Nam, remember!"

"Brutal."

"We'd play the game in the neighbor kid's overgrown garage, crouched down over a split in the concrete where Triffid-sized weeds were pushing through as you watched, one almost tickling the ceiling! The neighbor kid's dad had to park his corvette on the lawn, the weeds were so damn thick. Your Angie was fascinated by the genesis of the game, see, and how it evolved, so I'll tell you like I told her. You start with the map. You still got the map I drew? That goes on the bottom of the shoebox. You need that. That's clutch. I told her how this all started, how this other neighbor kid—Shawn Whatwherewhen —had a shoebox with the diagram of a little hockey rink drawn on the bottom: face-off circle, the crease, red lines, blue lines, everything. It was a skate box, come to think of it, not a shoe box. I remember the 'Vaughan Gear' logo was in the center of the bottom—I remember that real well—and that definitely completed the illusion of the theater."

"Don't you mean 'arena'?"

"No, listen, a *theater*, like a war theater? This is how you weed out the toughest ants."

I wanted to correct him again and say "spiders," but he was in some nostalgia zone, and it was too easy to imagine my wife listening to him tell this story the exact same way, warmed by the sickly glow of the copy machine. He was rambling like I did after too many Cokes, or Angie after too much wine, and I guess I felt close to them both in that moment. So I let him go on.

"So to play, we needed the 'theater,' and a pencil, and a book of matches. For now, like I said—was I talking about then or now? Doesn't matter. The game is always evolving. There are always more wars. But rule number one is, if the ant touches one of the four face-off dots, then you use the machine gun. And the machine gun is a pencil. You just stab, rapid-fire . . . " He jabbed the air, thankfully not making machine gun noises with his mouth. " . . . until the ant moves off the dot, or you stab the shit out of it, or both! The pencil will be used for many weapons in your invisible arsenal."

Invisible Army, invisible arsenal . . .

"Rule number two. If the ant crawls across the red line, then you use the flamethrower. The pencil is the flamethrower. You take the tip of the pencil and, starting at one end of the theater, draw a fast zig-zag across that line, fast and hard. A little like a heartbeat actually!"

"Like a heartbeat on a heart monitor?" I said.

"No, no," Matt laughed, nervous. "More like a Richter scale. Anyhow, rule number three is, if the soldier marches across one of the blue lines and makes the mistake of stopping, then it's time to radio in the tanks! Beep beep. Vrrrrrroooom." This time he did make the noise with his mouth, and I wondered how Angie reacted to the embarrassing "Jones from *Police Academy*" sound effects. "Guess what the tank is?" he asked.

"The pencil is the tank!" Mad and I said at the same time.

"Exactly, so you drop the pencil on its side so that it's resting about a finger's length from the soldier, then you roll it. Just once. Real quick with your palm. Just one roll to grind up the soldier if you can."

"I'm guessing when the 'tank' shows up, the game is usually over."

"Kinda."

"And Angie played this game with you. While waiting for copies." I had doubts.

"There were *tons* of ants in that library, at least down in the basement where the Xerox machine was."

I remembered a couple times when I'd tried to call her when she was out of town at Matt Fink's Mysterious Library and Arcade Emporium, and it's true that it was impossible to reach her when she was making her copies. So that part of his story checked out. But I sure didn't like the idea of them crouched down over a shoebox and killing ants together. It was as if they were retroactively creating a childhood memory to share. And, of course, it was rumored this guy had two penises. Let's not forget that. Though I wasn't sure when I'd be able to bring it up, if ever.

"Rule number four," Matt went on. "If the bug touches any of the four face-off circles in the corners, then you throw a grenade."

"Let me guess . . . "

"Yep, the pencil is the grenade! You pound at the bug with the eraser end of the pencil, and you keep pounding until the bug exits the circle. *Bloosh!* The chances of this are always slim. But Angie usually let them go after that."

"I believe it," I lied. Yesterday was the kind of day where I'd believe anything, but those days were over.

"Rule number five. If the spider crosses into the 'icing' zone, this means it hits the trip-wires. So you tear out the eraser and hit it with the raw metal ring on the end. We had to be careful doing this so that the eraser could be stuffed back into the ring again. Grenades were too scarce to be wasting."

Rule number five made me flinch. Angie used to tongue pencil ends where her erasers were worn away, absentmindedly leaving circular indents on her taste buds while she typed, and the circles would be on her tongue all day. Sorta like when Angie had me unclog our tub, and I tried a shortcut with a toilet plunger, and on my first plunge, it popped loose and I cracked the top of my hand against the metal mouth of the faucet and left a deep, cookie-cutter wound down to the bone. It took forever to heal, and the scar was way more interesting than that story. But this scar looked exactly like one of Angie's tongue circles, stamped on my fist forever. So I guess I'm glad it happened.

"Rule number six. If the ant or spider or convict or whoever your soldier is touches the dot dead-center in those four face-off circles, you can use the napalm. And this is where the matches come in. Just light one and drop it. *Whoosh!* You got one shot, though. And one little match isn't quite the opening credits of *Apocalypse Now*, but it does the job."

I sang, *"Ants trying to run from their destruction, I know you didn't even care . . ."*

Matt smiled and rolled down the window to let in some of the smoke from the nearby fire. His nostrils enlarged alarmingly wide.

"But come on," I said. "Who are you kidding? No way you were dropping matches into a shoebox in the basement of a library archive."

"Correct. We rarely used actual 'napalm.' There's no smoking in the building, so I usually just said 'whoosh!' Rule number seven! If you warrior is crawling in the center circle, I mean if any leg or claw or fang or antenna or *anything* touches that Vaughn logo, you call in the air strike. I mean the *President* calls in the air strike. 'All mighty, All mighty,' that's the codename. And if this happens, after you said those magic words, you light all the matches in the matchbox and toss it in the box. *Boom*. We never did this either, of course!"

"Of course."

"I know it sounds like all the rules means a dead ant after three seconds and the end of the game, but the air strike was *definitely* the end of the game. But there was a rule number eight, believe it or not, although we rarely got there. That rule is, if your tiny little enlisted man stops and doesn't move for more than a minute, the use of nuclear weapons is authorized. Also known as your foot. Oh, yeah, and rule number nine? If any trooper makes it into either goal—small squares cut into the bottom of the box where the hockey nets would be positioned—that veteran is considered 'home safe.' And then you have to let the little serviceman go . . ."

"Soldier ants are female, dummy," Mad said from the back.

". . . let the little servicewoman go. Or put it in a jar. Or the library microwave. Wherever. But it couldn't really leave because there was a serious ant problem in that basement. Angie and I, we usually picked up the box and raised the whole combat theater over our heads and spun it round and round. Relocated those veterans somewhere."

"There's no rule number ten?" I asked.

"You already know that one."

"I do?"

"Rule number ten. If at any time during the game you feel the servicewoman has cheated death one too many times, like if you think there is no logical reason that it would not be dead in this situation, you can bring down the Knuckles of God."

I liked the sound of that one. I searched Matt's face for recent evidence of God's knuckles. There was plenty. I made him a believer!

"That one happened a lot. Or you could bring in the Foot of God, I guess, whatever you preferred. But Angie preferred to called her shoe her 'Zamboni.' Either way, it wiped the arena clean! I loved the knuckles when we were kids. We couldn't wait to punch the bottom of that goddamn box, punch like we were straddling someone in a fight with everybody watching." Matt faded off for a second, breathing in the smoke, then he rolled up his window. "Later, we came up with a rule number eleven, because we remembered the name of the game was 'hockey' and we hadn't incorporated any skates! So the skate became 'helicopter blades,' and rule number eleven got kind of complicated. It was hard enough keeping Shawn from bringing out the God Knuckles as soon as any creature hit the bottom of the box, so imagine him when fuckin' skates were introduced. But what we realized back then was that the bugs rarely left the box anyway, if you wanted to be honest. Even if they won. Even if we felt bad and turned it over and tried to shake them out. They hung onto the box throughout it all. At first I was disgusted by this, but now I realize I'd probably do the same thing. Just to keep the game going, you know?"

Matt looked at me, his mouth nursing his fat lip like a nipple, and I wanted to hit him again.

"Bring on the knuckles, right, Dave?"

"You know it."

Billy Ocean was back on the radio.

"Get out of your skin . . . and into my jar . . ."

I checked the rearview mirror. Eyes rolling, Mad huffed steam on her window and then wrote 'Help' with her finger.

***

A few more miles, and my wife's papers were strewn everywhere. The car's total consumption was up to about 25-hours of energy, and theories were ricocheting around the interior. Matt was arguing with Mad, sometimes with Mag, too, something about the existence of "any crimes," or maybe it was "any rhymes," and I found myself on the outside of the conversation for the first time. It was a relief for the moment. Earlier, Mad had checked the folds Angie had made in her map and saw they lined up perfectly with the "Bug Hockey" diagram and decided this probably meant something, but wasn't sure she cared. Maybe her heart wasn't in it anymore, but hitchhiking wasn't an option with all the creepy black garbage bags lining the highway.

"How can that be meaningless?" Matt asked Mad. "If we're on a journey that just happens to be equal to the safest path for a soldier ant to take through a war zone?"

"So?"

"And Dave here mapped this same path onto our windshield."

"So?"

"With my fist!" I added. It still stung.

"So?"

"So it just makes me feel a little safer."

"That's called Stockholm Syndrome!" I offered, wondering what they called Stockholm syndrome in reverse. Because that's what I had going on. I assumed it would be closely related to King Midas in Reverse Syndrome, where everything gold turns to shit.

"It's called Lima Syndrome by the way," Mad said.

"What is?"

"Stockholm Syndrome in reverse."

"Did I say all that out loud?"

"Everything about you is 'out loud,'" she said, pocketing her phone.

"Man, I sure wish the internet didn't exist. Because now I'll never consider that subject again," I said, thinking about Angie's father stuck in the web and wishing Greg could say the same.

"Well, if you feel safe, that's the important thing!" Mad said, getting back on topic, and Matt's arm snaked around the seat and snatched the sealed envelope from her lap. Zero retreated to pace the rear window.

"I'm opening this," he said.

Mad slapped him upside the head and grabbed it back.

"No, *I'm* opening it."

"Please, don't," I said, rejoining the debate. "Those words will be the last thing she said to me before her murder."

"No, I ate that, remember?" Mad laughed.

"I'm not kidding. What if this is a suicide note? Or worse, if the words are meaningless."

"How is that worse?!" Mad asked, slapping me in the back of the head. It seemed harder than Matt's. I stopped the car fast enough to bounce it up on two wheels again.

"What if it's nothing?" I asked them.

"That's exactly why you need to open it."

"No, no, listen to me. What if it is *nothing*?" I looked at Mad, then Matt. They finally seemed to get it.

"Then we'll make it something," she promised.

I felt so close to them in that moment that my eyes watered a bit, though it could have been the smoke. Mad ripped it open.

"Fine. Open the envelope!" I said, all dramatic, even though it was already happening.

It was a single piece of notebook paper. Mad angled it away from me slightly, but I could still see Angie's distinctly tight but ornate penmanship.

"What does it say?" I asked.

"Well . . . " Mad took a deep breath. "What we got here is

a detailed list of 'The Rules for Fake Prisoners and Guards in Phillip G. Zimbardo's 1971 Stanford Prison Experiment,' whatever that is."

"Don't you mean 'Zamboni?'" Matt asked.

"Shut the fuck up."

We sat silent for a moment.

"Yeah, she was into that stuff," I said finally. Then I blew a kiss to Zero in my rearview mirror. He was pawing at the steam on the back window, making his own maps. "Someone help him out. I think his litter box is full."

"We're literally in this shit together now!" Mad announced.

"Meow just once, goddamn it," I said to the mirror as we all drove on.

XVI

GRAFFITOCALYPSE

"DON'T YOU GUYS have jobs?"

We were sitting around a picnic table at a rest stop. Hours of silence and double-yellow-line delirium had forced us to pull over and stretch our brains. Zero sat in his cage, blinking lazily at the open door, no urge to explore, and I blinked back, sympathetic. Matt and Mad shared a glance, confused by my question.

"Hey, didn't you kidnap us, Dave?"

"Allegedly."

"We totally thought you had a gun."

"I never threatened anybody with a gun."

"I could have sworn I saw a gun," Matt said, gingerly picking dried blood from his lip.

"Nope, no gun."

"Then what's that huge bulge in the back of your coat?"

I leaned forward and patted the duck pocket along my lower back, then unsnapped one of the flaps. Mad held her breath.

"You want some of those fists you were talking about earlier?" I asked Matt, who looked ready to run. "Here, try these on for size."

I stood up and emptied the contents of the duck pocket

onto the picnic table in front of them. A diverse variety of vintage weapons tumbled out.

"Whoa!"

Matt grabbed the blackjack and rapped it against his knee, and Mad modeled my "Indian Police" badge for us. Then they both spent a good half hour giving everything a test drive. Matt settled on the brass knuckles that read "L.O.V.E.," passing on the Civil War beard comb I'd forgotten was in there. Mad took that, and promptly got it tangled in her thick curls. No one chose the homemade dagger, its craggy handle wound in crumbling string.

I left them to my devices so I could fill the slow-leaking back tires of the Rabbit. I'd had tire problems for years, stopping for air when I'd notice a sag, but never replacing them. And never mind the "penny test." There was less tread left on them than on a toddler's first tennis shoe. So, after my wheels were back to their recommended PSI, I brought out Zero so he could sniff around the grass while we ate ice cream and cooled off. Mad opted for the weird pink crunch bar, Matt had a frozen Snickers, and I was all about the generic ice-cream sandwich. Why mess with perfection? Matt went back to twirling the blackjack like a cop as he snacked, and Mad and I spread out loose pages of Angie's yearbook on the picnic table. As I watched Matt master my weapon, I saw that one of his front incisors was marbled gray and yellow. Dead.

Did I kill that tooth? I wondered. I honestly couldn't remember. I'd hit more people in the past week than I had all through high school. And this was '80s high school, when assault was still considered a normal, sanctioned event. Maybe some lip service about breaking it up, but fights usually proceeded until their conclusion, a lot like hockey actually. Real hockey, not the bullshit with the bugs.

"Try not to jizz all over the evidence," I said to Matt, as ice cream dribbled over his thumb. "How'd you get that egg tooth by the way?"

He curled his lip and covered it with his tongue. "I don't

know . . . " he said, voice fading as he sucked the pain away. I didn't push for an answer.

On the car radio behind us, Captain Kirk was covering The Cramps, and in the process relating to me some very specific instructions: a "garbage man" wanted me to beat something with a stick, and beat it until it was thick. It sounded like the worst recipe ever, but looking at Matt and his dead tooth, I understood these lyrics completely. Stockholm Syndrome was in full effect with this nut now, and I started to worry if it would be hard to get rid of him when the journey was over.

"Did you know there are now rich people who pay big money to eat prison dinners?" Mad said around a mouthful of pink crumbs, tapping a handwritten note with her elbow.

"That doesn't surprise me at all," I said.

"What do you make of this?" She spun a Polaroid towards me on the table. It showed some burly dudes in sleeveless denim and leather jackets, their trucker caps pulled low and their bandanas pulled high so not a single face was visible. They were huddled in a circle and flexing. Someone had circled one of the tattooed biceps in red pen.

"What is that? Oh shit, is that an upside-down guitar?"

"No, I think it's a jackhammer? Yeah, no, that's a jackhammer."

"Great! It's all starting to make sense," Matt said.

"Sarcasm!" Mad said. "I recognize that!"

"Why is this in there?" Matt said, holding up a sprung rat trap as if by the tail.

"It's a Trapper Keeper," Mad said. "It's where she keeps her traps."

"Yeah, get your head out of your ass, Fink."

"Hey!"

We all looked up just then to see a highway worker in a red jumpsuit pointing toward the bushes with his trash picker claw.

"Is that your goddamn groundhog?"

"Groundhog . . ." I pondered. *Fascinating*. Every new animal designation applied to Zero had me newly convinced as soon as I heard it.

"Those little sumbitches tear up the grass," the man said, motioning at the rest stop's mostly dead landscaping. We stared at him until he wandered off, dragging his black bag and shaking his head.

"Does that mean Zero can take his turn driving?" asked Matt. "You know, like in the Bill Murray movie?"

"That was about roaming buffalos, not groundhogs, stupid." I gathered up Zero to put him back in the car, laughing because no one would be touching the steering wheel except me. At least not Matt. I didn't want to wake up in the middle of a mutiny, idling at a police station. I kicked the tires to check my slow leaks and also reassure my new crew of my competence, then went back to the picnic table to reorganize Angie's papers for the tenth time.

"You're a professional mechanic, I see," Mad giggled.

"Can you fix a car?" I asked her. "No? That's what I thought."

"My manhood doesn't depend on it," she said.

"Okay, can you make a wristwatch with your penis? Matt, I'm not talking to you."

"Puke."

"You know, I'd rather have flat tires than no horn," Matt said as he shuffled some prison blueprints on the picnic table to make more room. "I probably honk at nine people a day."

"Honk at them for what?" I asked.

"I have a list of about ten reasons for why I honk at people. Let's see, if you don't use your turn signal, you get a honk. If you use your turn signal at the last possible second, honk. If you use your turn signal only after I honk, you get another honk. If you're walking and have a stupid look on your face, you get a honk. If you drive an off-road vehicle with no dirt on it, honk city, baby . . . oh, yeah, if you remind me of the guy who tried to choke me after that concert in 1995, honk honk . . ."

"Okay, now you're making shit up."

". . . if you try to turn left next to the veterinarian's office where it clearly says 'No Left Turn,' honk. If you do everything right but have your windows down when I go by and you're listening to Sinéad O'Connor, honk. If you're a police officer and I'm hidden by other cars, I cannot wait to honk."

"You should be careful," Mad said. "I knew someone once who punched his horn so many times that his airbag went off. Luckily, it was full of popcorn. Just kidding, Dave, it was full of spiders. Don't try it."

I slinked away from them slightly, thinking about the half-dozen times I punched down my own rearview mirror as a teenager, forced to comb my hair in the reflection of a Loverboy CD on the way to school. Or my more recent adventures in rearview mirror enhanced interrogation, like when I had to beat Penny Whatever's last name out of it.

I went back to the Rabbit to let the engine run so the radio didn't kill the battery. It was just talk radio now anyway, questions from callers about how important the honey bees really were. I turned everything off.

"You guys about ready to get back on the road?" I called over to them.

"Nope. Have you seen this?"

Mad was waving a page labeled "Clearwater, Florida" next to an amateurish drawing of a Native-American headdress. I added this town to my own mental map, the map toward the back of my brain with the stick pins and red string and newspaper clippings draped along the curve of my skull and tickling my gray matter like party favors.

So many maps on this trip. But maps beget maps beget maps . . .

"And how about all these other numbers?" Mad said, flapping another page. "The money spent on body cameras nationwide? It's like millions. Or billions."

"Well, is it a million or a billion?" Matt asked.

"Doesn't matter."

"Yes, it freaking matters," he said. "The difference between those two numbers is more than the difference between a million and zero."

"So what?" I said. I was sort of annoyed how they were more invested in the mystery than myself.

What was that Groucho Marx quote about not wanting to be in a club that would have you as a member, but especially if one of the members has two *members (get it?), and especially if you kidnapped all the members, including one who still remains in a cage?*

"You're right," Mad said, picking up her stick to scrape off the last of the congealed ice cream with her teeth. "To us, it doesn't matter."

I watched her, remembering how she lied about thinking I had a gun, and I was convinced she had her own agenda now, maybe something about putting herself in Angie's shoes or . . .

Then it hit me. She was pretending to solve her own murder. How fun would that be? Now I was jealous of both of them.

"So we've all looked at all the bridge pics, right?" She tapped the stick against her teeth.

"Yes," I lied.

"And that bridge does look a smidge like the bridge around here," Mad added. "Except for the water. It's a lot clearer in this photo. Look at that sparkle. Like diamonds."

"What?" I took it from her to study the glimmer of the waves of the Seine. "No, that's something else, something in the water. We both saw this when we were there. I remember it. Something glittering, glistening, like a thousand twinkling objects on the river bottom, winking at us and catching the sunlight. Sounds crazy, I know, but I *think* they were keys."

"You know what?" Matt took the photo from me. "These look like something else. Have you ever seen a tip-up?"

"What's a tip-up?" Mad asked.

"It's how everybody fishes back in Minnesota," Matt said.

I couldn't help but think that's where Prince was from, and now would forever remain. It was a nice touch.

"It's a pretty cowardly way to fish actually, one step from dynamite. You just set a hook over an ice hole on this spring-loaded piece of wood, and when it lands a fish, the red flag pops up, which you can see from a half mile away. Weak, I know. But it's also easier psychologically, if you're morally opposed to the whole fishing thing. Like those Jewish Rube Goldberg machines to make sure you're technically not making a phone call on the Sabbath, while you're making a phone call on the Sabbath, just in case God was watching. Myself, I was always shocked but relieved when I found half a fish floating in the hole the next morning."

"Why? The poor thing was hanging on a hook for 24 hours," Mad said. "It was probably begging something to eat its ass."

"I don't know. Something about how that simple mechanism took the responsibility of a creature's death out of my hands."

"Like the Milgram Experiment!" I said.

"In a way," he agreed, vaguely impressed.

"Yeah, not at all," Mad said, not impressed at all.

I sat back down and checked our evidence pile. I pulled out *Brickhouse*, the pulp paperback I'd swiped from Fink's roommate, "Otto."

Otto? 'Like Auto Parts' . . .

I scratched at its busted spine, then thumbed it for any provocative flip cartoons. I found someone had flagged the pages for typos. Every error had been circled, underlined, and tagged. A lot of glitches back in the trash lit heyday, I decided.

"You haven't looked too close at the rest of these photos, have you, Dave?" Mad said.

"I took the fucking things," I told her, losing patience. I threw the book back through the open window of my car.

"And you never wondered why all the graffiti reads 'Rule #7'?"

***

This is the answer to everything, I decided, all three of our heads so close they were almost touching. We were a triangle of concentration hovering over the photographs, the sweet taste of ice cream long gone and our collective breath turning sour. It wasn't the padlocks at all. It was the graffiti spray-painted *over* the locks. The vandalism all over Paris, all over its copycat bridges in Ohio, this was the key. I mean it *wasn't* the keys. Just listen! The big secret message was always way simpler. Simple numbers. Not even equations. My composition class could have told me all about it. Logos, bitches.

"Rule #7," was spray-painted everywhere, neon and pink graffiti tags sprinkled all through the background of our honeymoon photos. But you had to be at a distance to see this, not just pulling selfies at the lock bridge. Not just back in the States browsing your adorable pictures. For all to be revealed, it had to be years later, head clouded by pain and confusion, a maximum of two feet above a spread of photographs, sweat dripping off your nose. Like a real detective.

"To scrub the paint off these locks would be next to impossible," Mad whispered.

"Exactly," I said. "But by removing these sections of the bridges and recycling them, or by spreading misinformation about the vandalism of national landmarks or some bullshit safety infractions, *or* by sending this scrap metal back to the furnace or dumping it into the river or by scattering used locks all over the world to resell to smitten tourists anywhere, they were effectively sending the message through the shredder with no hope of anyone reconstructing the words."

"Wait, what message?" Matt said.

I didn't answer him, worried he could destroy the momentum of our investigation by pinning us down to admit this discovery potentially meant nothing. Instead, I thought about my truncated teaching career, and the trick my Arts & Sciences Division Chair taught me for removing permanent ink from the dry-erase board. You wrote over it with erasable ink. That was it. It took some concentration to trace over it exactly, and you had to commit to repeating in your head whatever nasty message the student had left for you as you did this. But the solution was easier than I thought possible. I wondered how hard it would be to spray-paint over a world of graffiti, then remove the world, and if anybody tried it.

"Hold on . . ." My hand darted for the list from the envelope. We had Rule #7 right in front of us. It was a rule we already knew, and it had nothing to do with ants or hockey.

***

According to Philip G. Zimbardo's own records, as well as Angie's extensive research, everyone who role-played at his simulated prison—which was constructed in an innocuous campus building with lines on the floor to represent incarceration instead of the imposing concrete and steel or the intimidating click of locks and keys—was given a basic list of guidelines. These rules were modified slightly after an initial "script reading" of the scenario worked out (in?) some kinks, but the final list read as follows:

Prisoners must consume three meals a day.

Guards must consume five meals a day.

All meals must be fully consumed.

Mandatory one hour of recreation.

Prisoners are allowed only within the white lines.

Guards are allowed within the yellow lines and white lines.

If any lines become obscured, rules 6 and 7 will be enforced to the best of the subjects' abilities.

Prisoners will only speak when spoken to.

Guards will keep their sunglasses on at all times.

Prisoners cannot touch a guard under any circumstances.

Violence from a prisoner to a guard will require a commensurate level of violence.

Violence between prisoners will be overlooked, unless there is a violation of rule 11.

If a guard or prisoner breaks any rule, the experiment is over.

Written below the grainy photocopy of these rules was Angie's flowery but disciplined handwriting, asking first some questions:

"Not all were students? Were students actually guards? And guards actually prisoners?" Then some extended conjecture: "The possibility of a final unwritten rule could conceivably be this—if anyone is released from the mock prison due to a rule violation, and if the experiment is declared 'over,' student reimbursement would be rescinded. However, all 'community service' exemptions could also be revoked for non-students and original real-life sentences would be served in full."

"I saw a 'Rule #14' once, someone spray-painted the unwritten rule in Paris."

"But what's the deal with 'Rule #7' everywhere?"

"In Vietnam Bug Hockey, that means call in the air strike!"

"Shut up. Where are the photographs of those kids again?"

Mad fanned them out, and we studied the kids in the woods, some in a field, one of a crane shot, or possibly a tower shot, of twenty or so figures spread out, milling around on about an acre of land, no rhyme or reason to their formation. Mad read the dates on the timestamps where they were visible and said that one photo was very recent.

"Look at this. Even though styles cycle back every couple of years, this is certainly not from the '70s, not part of the 'Milgram's Salad Days.' They'd be way too young."

"Could the Stanford Experiment still be happening?" Matt asked.

"No way," I said. "That was in 1971. This picture is right now. One of those kids has lights on his shoes for fuck's sake, and I *know* that little fucker . . . "

"Go, Gators!" Mad laughed.

"Wait, isn't that Xenia, Ohio?" Matt asked. "Where they had that tornado?"

"How do you know it's Xenia?"

Matt poked a Polaroid of a road sign that read, "Welcome to Xenia."

"Rumor has it there was a school shooting there," I said.

"No, that was a tornado," Mad said.

"Maybe these kids are standing where the school used to be, you know?" Matt said. "Maybe they're pretending they're in school."

"You mean like staking out where the classrooms used to stand?" She frowned.

"That's what it looks like. Groups of five or six, loitering, facing a single individual . . . "

"But what does that have to do with Rule #7?" I asked. "Why would this message be spray-painted all over the world?"

"Dunno," Mad said. "Maybe this *game* is all over the world. And maybe they don't want the game to end. 'Rule #13, if anyone breaks a rule, the game is over.'"

I stood up and looked to the sky. "Did someone say 'pretending they're in school'?"

"Yeah?" Matt said.

"This could be the 'Invisible Prison' right here in front of us." They looked at each other, and I pounded the picture. "It said, 'Rule #7, if lines become obscured, enforce the other rules to the best of your ability.'"

"So?"

"So?! These kinky little weirdos are pretending they're in jail! But with no lines. No walls. No nothin'."

"And maybe they're waiting for the real game to start," Mad offered.

The gas-station attendant in the red jumpsuit came back out to refill the wiper boxes at the pumps with fluid, and he stopped at our table, angling a thumb at the cage in my car.

"Forget what I said," he mumbled. "That isn't no badger. That's a goddamn raccoon."

"No one said it's a badger," I reminded him.

"That is one-hundred percent a goddamn 'coon that got its head caught in a trap once," he said, pointing with his whole hand now.

I peered into the car and looked Zero up and down. He was cleaning between his thumbs. *Why not. Best explanation I've heard yet.*

***

To shake things up, I let Mad drive us awhile, *Groundhog Day* be damned, but this meant that she talked more than usual. I sat in the back with Zero, not entirely convinced he was a raccoon, but smiling at him with big David Duchovny "I want to believe" energy, while Mad took this opportunity at the wheel to talk about her dreams.

"Where's the ejector seat?" I whispered to the creature.

Dream discussions were normally a violation of driving etiquette, but probably the least of our crimes compared to listening to my extended fight stories (or being on the receiving end of one), and I was too tired to argue. Apparently, Mad's recurring nightmare was very common among her co-workers, where she'd look up from her window at the DMV and see lines of people stretched to infinity. But Mad's variation of this dream was telling. In her version, the lines were all women, all with long drinking straws stretched and looped into other women's purses, and she would watch the straws pulse as they nursed on each other's personal information. So by the time they hit the window, there was a hopeless and terrifying scrambling of identities.

"I'd rather dream I had a peen," she gagged, and Matt adjusted his jeans. Again.

I decided this was probably just an identity-theft dream, like a bouncer's guilt for not checking I.D.s rigorously enough. But I didn't say what I really thought the dream probably meant—something more directly related to her recent insertion into my life, or more specifically Angie's life—so we moved smoothly onto Matt's favorite nightmare instead. His dream was everybody's dream, however, the fear of someone biting off his head. But wouldn't it be heads? I didn't press for clarity, but all I could picture was one of his penises attacking the other while it slept.

Mad drove for miles, and, half-dreaming myself, I heard her explaining to Zero how so many cars were named after beasts. She saw a Chevy Impala and said that was a particularly weird one because cars have stolen that identity completely from the animal, and few people even knew an impala was real.

"And a prey animal to boot," she reminded Zero, wherever he was. "So weird. Bear with me, though, Zero, my day job means I have cars on the brain . . . "

She passed a . . . Ford Mustang? No, maybe it was a Bronco, she said. But the red Dodge Viper surprised her, a car that was "here and gone from the public consciousness faster than the DeLorean." She pointed out an AMC Eagle zipping by at one point, "white with wood paneling along the side, a real throwback!" she laughed. Then the Mercury Cougar, or maybe it was a Ford Thunderbird? And I dreamed a bit about the requisite "Chevy vs. Ford" in-laws on Angie's side of the family and how my new dad would have cared deeply about the distinction.

Speaking of, a Jeep Cherokee passed us at some point, and Mad woke me up by plucking the glasses from my shirt collar and jabbing them painfully against my face to watch it go by. Matt leaned in between us and tried to honk at it, but I grabbed his wrist and shoved him back against Zero's cage. I just couldn't be sure if it was the shotgun-wielding driver who'd tried to kill us back in Brickwood, as it was adorned with tinted windows and a year of dust to boot. Drifting off again, I took off my glasses and told Mad I was disappointed with the lack of red cars these days, that I wouldn't have gotten a red Rabbit if it wasn't gonna multiply. Then I leaned back onto my headrest, content to let her chew on that for a few miles. I remembered when Angie tried to sell an identical

Jeep Cherokee back to her dad, Greg, and how he just came and took it instead, needing the cash to finance his home that was in a perpetual state of renovation. Later, he asked us if we never noticed the secret key he'd left under the Cherokee years ago, in a magnetic key holder inside the wheel well and in the exact same place he was always disappointed to not find those FBI tracking devices that might make all the paranoia worth it. The key holder was streaked with chipped red paint, which must have been the vehicle's original color. When it was still cherry, I was pretty sure the Jeep had belonged to her dead brother, but they never talked about him. But it was hard to be sure. They never talked about him. And now they'd never talk about her . . .

Then I was gone, somewhere else. The passenger's seat was a nice vacation from responsibility. I think I pissed in the litter box at one point, but who could say really.

Eventually, the conversation turned back to me, and it woke me up for good. Mad was insisting I tell her what I did for a living before I became the worst detective in the world.

"Hey, hey . . . hey! You got fired from your teaching job, right?" Mad asked, messing up a rearview mirror that had taken years to align perfectly to make sure Matt and Zero were snoozing again.

"Long story short or long story long? Or the real story, real short?" I asked. She looked like she was regretting asking, so I plowed ahead. "Here's the thing. I get fired a lot. Of my fifty or so jobs, whenever I got excited or gave a shit and applied myself? That's exactly when I'd get noticed and almost immediately get shitcanned. Only when I've laid low have I maintained steady employment. So the *real* reason I got fired from teaching was because some kid in my class was trying to argue that 'cracker' was the worst of the racial slurs. May he rest in peace. I don't remember exactly how I verbally dismantled that boy, but, allegedly, someone in that room said something along the lines of, 'You know what I had for lunch with my chili? Crackers. You know what I didn't have for lunch with my chili? Niggers.' This may have been rhetorically savvy, but, oh, man, a grave error when you're in a classroom with all those iPhones, even in the South. More body cameras than the Secret Policeman's Ball."

"More like the Secret Policeman's *Bawl*."

"What?"

"Huh?"

"That's not what either of you idiots think it is," Mad said. "Also, fuckin' *yikes*. Your last day in class was what my daddy would have called a 'toilet-sized' mistake."

"That means 'big,' right?"

"Pretty sure. The only other things he ever referred to as 'toilet-sized' were meals he couldn't finish."

***

Almost at the Mississippi line, the cell phone I'd mercifully forgotten started blowing up, and I regretted not removing the battery two states ago. My phone I.D.'d the caller as Angie's dad, so I let it go to voicemail. Not ready for that conversation. But once we crossed over into the home of the Delta blues, my curiosity got the better of me. It was Greg, all right, asking about my whereabouts, half-shouting information about Angie's upcoming funeral, provoking me with speculations about my manhood to bait me into calling him back, or at least picking up next time. He was either talking with his car windows down or on his ATV because the wind was deafening, and her dad was skilled enough at provocation even without the added hurricane. At our wedding, he'd worked to provoke my father just as efficiently as me. Greg was a libertarian, you see, meaning he had a confederate flag on his car just to be a scoundrel, and once he found out my dad was a member of The International Brotherhood of Electrical Workers, he started talking anti-union, right there over our strangely inedible wedding cake. Loud enough for everyone to hear, he described the woman coming to inspect the electric work on his cabin as "some cocksucker with a union card," to which my dad said nothing.

My dad wasn't too big on confrontation, unless you killed his ducks, but I could tell this bothered him. Then Greg said, "The only union I care for is the police union, and, of course, the union between our children. Cheers." My dad's jaw flexed at this, but in order to keep the peace, he just stood there concentrating on his rock-hard slice of barely edible cake while Greg continued to figuratively flick his ear. Greg was real good at that. In fact, my ear was turning red from his voicemail at that very moment, and the phone had barely touched it.

Though I hadn't had the chance to join a union yet, I'd already formed some impressions of the working world that were unshakable. One, I had a solid memory of unions providing us groceries as kids when my dad was on strike at the Toledo Edison Power Company. Two, the big jugs of peanut butter that these union guys brought to our house were the shit, the biggest I'd ever seen. And three, after the brawl where my dad and his union buddies tipped over the cars of the guys who'd tried to cross the picket line to take my dad's job for half pay, I discovered that a "scab" was the worst thing in the world. A scab was something that you literally flicked, sometimes from the inside of your ear, and not just figuratively.

I'd been hopeful that our mutual hatred for police, or authority figures, would be the thing to unite me and my new father-in-law, something that should always bring right-wing and left-wing loons together on any topic. But I guess that didn't work when Greg was the authority figure in question. Even though they were so different, I was about five times more likely to talk to New Dad over Old Dad on my phone for exactly this reason. He just kept my blood pumping. And good circulation was healthy. Or, at a minimum, a diuretic. So I gave Greg a call. And I listened to three simulated rings before I hung up. Then I removed the battery so that I wouldn't be tempted again. For about fifty miles, I regretted the detachment, but then I realized a new family was in my red

Rabbit with me, and we could probably replicate a typical heated debate with my father-in-law and his adherence to concern trolling pretty effortlessly. In a car, people are game for anything.

"Okay, I'll be you, and Mad will be him," Matt said. "Ready? 'Hey, New Dad, it's illogical to try explaining the illogicalness of people buying guns in response to gun tragedies, right?'"

"I'd never call him 'New Dad,' but keep going," I said.

"Dave, I feel like you're missing my point when you substitute other words into people's sentences," Mad said.

"What? Are you still doing the thing?"

"Like 'feral rats' instead of 'gun.'"

"I'm confused."

"We're simply talking about the illogicalness of people buying feral rats in response to a feral rat tragedy."

"Okay."

"How about 'confetti.'"

"Feather boa?"

"Dildos?"

"Birthday clowns."

"Facebook stock!"

"So you shouldn't buy more clowns in response to a clown tragedy."

"Yes, there you go, Dave. It's simple economics. When a supply is low or perceived to be low in the future, demand goes up."

"You are giving New Dad too much credit."

" . . . but returning to the earlier game, how about orphanage fires?"

"The illogicalness of people buying orphanage fires in response to orphanage fires is kind of amazing," I admitted.

"Can you see why we write fortune cookie fortunes for a living?" Mad said.

"I'm actually cheating," Matt said. "These are my memories."

"Okay," I said. "I think I'm going for the win. Ready . . . slaves!"

"Crickets."

"Yes, crickets, my boy," Matt said, still trying to be my new dad. The mystery creature hopped into my lap, and I scratched the zero on his belly and thought about my old dad's inability to shoot the raccoon that ate his ducks. It would have been caged just like this thing with the target on its stomach. Did all animals have them?

" . . . still, the emotional response is fear, and one of the many responses to fear is the instinct to protect. So if you, hypothetically and illogically, feared a gun being pointed at you, would you want to point back with a box of cereal? No. Now, you know me to be a strange animal in being an unapologetic gun owner, so if you want a serious conversation about this, I'll be glad to oblige, Dave."

"Stop!"

"This is certainly the place for a serious conversation!" Mad said. "Anyway, buying more edible underwear after hundreds of edible underwear tragedies . . . "

"How about buying the *Footloose* soundtrack when you live in the actual town it's based on?"

"I don't get it."

"Where it's illegal to dance . . . " I added, as I unfolded the map. " . . . which we will be passing through any second now."

"See," Mad said. "That's why I married you!"

"And I'm glad you did, son," Matt said.

I felt oddly content, and I decided their improbable addition to my hopeless quest was a welcome change to a history of minor psychosis and one-sided arguments and the cacophony of mysterious voices whenever I drove alone for too long. And never mind the times I thought people in other cars were talking about me. Driving alone was dangerous for the solipsistic.

Cars are not meant for solitude. That's why there isn't one seat.

A bearded biker gang began passing our car on both sides at that very moment, the deafening noise sending Zero flying, tail sprung.

Okay, motorcycles have one seat. But look how much those losers craved company.

"What does that say on the backs of their jackets?" Mad asked. "'Pantshitters?'"

"Who knows," I said, my eyes locked on a bearded man in mirrored sunglasses to our left. He lingered by my window much longer than necessary, then revved his bike to snake around past us. "Overgrown children, every one of 'em."

When the bikers were gone, I noticed the fly inside the windshield, and I rolled the window down so fast to let it out that Mad took her foot off the gas.

"Don't jump!" Mad said, half sarcastic. Then, "Are you okay, Dave?"

"I'm cool. It's just that six is a crowd."

"Six? Hey, can I ask you something?"

"Anything."

"Have you always been in some kind of a relationship?"

"What does that mean?"

"You just seem kind of needy, dude, that's all."

I considered this, thinking back to the longest I ever lived alone. How I was doing okay on my own until a storm blew up my TV. How, soon after that, whenever any insect took a wrong turn into my apartment, I would get a little . . . attached.

I turned to see the fly still clinging to the glass, but outside now, completely unaffected by the harsh winds of the highway. I tapped my side of the window. I didn't ask anyone else if they could see it. Because I already knew the answer. And now so do you.

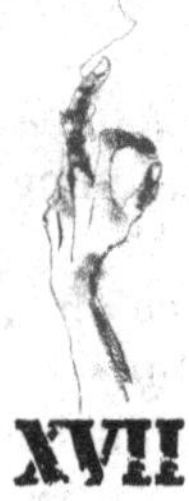

XVII

SHARKS WITH THUMBS

YOU EVER GET *the feeling someone is talking shit about you?*

Like you're right at the end of the movie when the speaker starts popping and you hear that voice. Almost once a week, when you're finally starting to relax around a spider web of power cords and surge protectors, you're reminded you can never trust the wiring in your new apartment. Never move into a new place just because you like seeing a river out your window.

Remember when a nearby lightning strike fried something inside your picture tube and put a freaky green line through the middle of your screen? That green line was there for about six months, mercifully getting smaller and smaller and almost fading away until it was just a glowing yellow smear in the corner of the TV. Like you'd smashed a lightning bug on the glass and never cleaned it up. You don't know if the room has some sort of electric Bermuda Triangle thing going on, but you can't risk any more equipment and that's why you always move fast whenever you hear a speaker snap, crackle, or pop.

So it's another big storm, and you're ready to pull the plug again when suddenly you're hearing two voices from the speaker that aren't part of the movie. You know this because the movie is nearing the end, at the part where everyone should be getting what they deserve, and all you should be hearing is gunfire, one-liners, and big, dumb music. And this whispered conversation is something you'd hear in the middle of a flick, or the beginning, when you're not sure what the characters are really up to and you're supposed to be suspicious of everyone.

The sad thing is he has no idea I hate his guts.

You sit down by the speaker, actually thinking about getting a glass to put between the television and your ear to hear the voices a little better.

Remember the last story he told? Even the goddamn dog was rolling his eyes.

You adjust your legs to get comfortable, hoping the reception lasts a little while. You know the "hearing voices" thing is supposed to make you nervous, but it happens in this building sometimes. A couple years back, when your surround-sound speakers were still working, you picked up some random banter between truckers. It's the bad wiring that does it. Sometimes, you'll suddenly get three more people in the middle of your phone call, and you'll find yourself answering a question about the first time you stuck a finger up someone's ass instead of your grandpa's question about car insurance.

But those fractured conversations lasted a minute at the most, and they were nowhere near as clear as this one. This is like you're holding the tomato cans between two people, but their strings are coming out both your ears.

If that bastard had any idea what people really say about him . . .

Right then, the speaker crackles and the voices are buried under static. You lean in closer and bang your head on the glass. There's a final *POP!* as you yank the cord from the wall. You sit with your back to the TV, feeling the electricity tickle your neck as both you and the equipment power down. You reel in the cord, wrapping it around your knuckles, working to bend the prongs straight. You hold your breath when you plug it back in. Thank Christ it still works. You stare at the green stain in the corner of the picture. It doesn't bother you that it's back. You'd still watch TV if the whole screen was green. Nothing happens in the corners of a movie anyway. A green sunset in a western? The gunfighters wouldn't notice.

00:00:03:57—"Love Without a Life Jacket?"

When you claim there's a long list of things about her that used to drive you nuts, you're not talking about a single sheet of paper, or even a stack of paper with both sides filled out plus illustrations in the margins and a flip cartoon in the corner to reenact the top ten reasons. No, you're talking about the kind of list where you could stand at the top of the stairs and let the pages drop and they'd bounce down the steps and unroll out the door and down the hill and across the street and over the cars until stray dogs are crashing through it like a finish line. And at the top of the list? Surprisingly, it's not how high her voice climbed when she lied or got drunk, or how her fingers ran her keyboard like a concert pianist when she was mad at you. It would be the way she used to sneak into the bathroom to use the phone. It drove you crazy. Well, maybe not *crazy* crazy, but crazy enough to ruin your day. Crazy enough to think about the word "crazy" until it renders the word meaningless. Luckily, that's one thing you don't have to worry about anymore. A new girl, though? Sometimes she will stare right at you, even when she's not on the phone. And she will let you listen to her most embarrassing conversations. And she will never turn the volume down on the receiver in case the caller is saying something you shouldn't hear. She will never press the phone hard against her head, so afraid a secret will sneak out while she's talking, so hard her ear will look like a ripe tomato slice when she finally snaps the phone shut.

The new girl, no, she's got nothing to hide. Probably doesn't even own a phone. She's in the bathroom right now, and you trust her so much you're not even turning down the volume on the TV to listen to her pissing.

Then the toilet flushes once, twice, and chokes on a third attempt. She walks back into the room, then her hand slides down to her hip in a quick motion that would make any gunfighter shake in his boots. Your smile slips when you see her phone drop into her pocket.

"I thought you drowned," you tell her.

00:00:28:09—"Bugs Cannot Use Tools?!"

It's too cold to have a fly on the window, on either side of the glass. There are no leaves on the trees. The birds are long gone. The morning before, you had to dig your car out from under the wake of a snowplow with red fingers. There's nothing alive outside without fur, nothing alive out there smaller than a rat in an overcoat, and you've brought any cats or rats inside with you.

But there it is.

One of those big, blue-eyed garbage flies, crawling around the edges of the glass like it's still summer out there, like there isn't a kid kicking the head off a snowman two houses down. In a daze, you pull the black tape off the window, taking some of the paint with it, knowing it's going to take another hour to seal that window back up. You yank it up with a grunt, cold air freezing the snot in your nose.

It's the first time you've ever seen a fly trying to get in instead of get out.

What the hell do you feed a fly? Usually, you're trying to stop a fly from drinking off the edge of your soda instead of offering it sips of sustenance to keep it kicking. So you stand back and let it ricochet off the walls like a drunk hoping it'll find a soggy cornflake or damp toenail to munch on, watching it circle the room about six more times, increasingly confused by its trajectory, which seems to be a series of frantic figure-eights about a foot from the ceiling. Finally, you grab a stuffed animal, upside down in a corner from three '90s ex-girlfriends ago, and you chase it toward the bathroom. If you're going to have a pet fly, it should be near a bowl, right? You're a pretty clean person, but you figure if there's anything around this place that a fly can eat, it's going to be in there. Hell, cats and dogs get water bowls, don't they? It's settled. You consider writing the name "Spike" on the side of your toilet in one of her leftover lipsticks, right above "Rule #2: Wash Your Hands After Number Two."

00:00:42:31—"You're Gonna Eat What Exactly?"

The next day, your new girl comes over to watch a movie. But halfway through, the speakers start popping again. And while you're screwing with the wires on the back of the box, she sighs and runs to the bathroom, and suddenly you're listening to her urine splashing again even though she's a hundred feet and a closed door away. It's splattering so loud you flinch and wonder is she's squatting over your head. And that's when you remember the fly.

Same old shit, you know? Why do I even come over here?

Her voice is fading, so your crawl over to your book bag and pull out your headphones. Several books tumble onto the ground, but you don't retrieve them. The ones that land face-up are David Weddle's *If They Move, Kill 'Em: The Life and Times of Sam Peckinpah*, Jonathan Lethem's *Motherless Brooklyn*, and R.A. Montgomery's *Choose Your Own Adventure #2: Journey Under the Sea*. You don't have time to imagine the significance of these selections, and you quickly try plugging the headphones directly into the TV. You get zapped with static instead. Like a fool, you sit there, headphones unplugged and dangling, still listening for voices. The headphones are new, the kind that go in your ears instead of over them, sometimes too deep, like you might lose them in your head if you scratch too hard. And sometimes you do. You estimate nineteen pairs of headphones popped through your eardrums and embedded in your brainstem over the years. And just like they always told you would happen when people are talking shit about you, your ears really do start burning.

Okay, I have to go watch the rest of this horrible movie, if he ever gets it to work . . .

You're so excited about hearing someone's voice through unplugged headphones that, at first, you don't care what she's saying. It's not like the truckers you heard through the speakers before. This time you can only hear one side of the conversation. Her voice is a non-stop sigh, like the endless hiss of a tire valve.

Maybe I'll pretend I'm sick. When are you working at the library again? I'll find a way.

Then the toilet flushes, and it's as loud as a cyclone. You grab the sides of the television in case you start spinning around the drain and get sucked on down. You're so wired about this discovery that you're smiling like a maniac when she comes out, struggling to keep your new psychic eavesdropping skills to yourself. But by the time you finish the western, you realize it's not just the headphones.

It was still in there with her.

. . . the first time I've ever seen one trying to get in instead of out . . .

You finally understand that your new power is coming from the fly.

00:01:34:07—"Spiders Are Not Our Friends!"

After she's gone home, you're thinking you should call NASA, or the Air Force, or whatever government office deals with the physical manifestation of metaphors. Or, at the very least, spy on about ten more people you suspect are talking shit about you. You're already making a new mental list, and at the same time considering how you might propose marriage to her, as you go back into your bathroom.

But the fly is dying.

It's cruising slower now, at least. Your eyes follow its sluggish path until it vanishes into a crack in the porcelain box, in the shadows behind the toilet. You panic and shove the clock radio and empty box of tissues onto the floor and take off the lid, shaking your head in disbelief as you look inside.

Impossible, you think.

The fly is caught in a spiderweb, flailing like a drunk trying to navigate beaded curtains at a party. Spiders living in the toilets? Flies living in the snow? You wonder what's next.

Suddenly, you know what to do. You tie the fly outside the bathroom window in the cold. And, just as you hoped, the frigid air seems to revive it. It's moving fast again, but it never gets back to full speed. It's not going to last much longer. You check the clock radio on the bathroom floor to try and estimate how much time the fly has left. Since you never figured out how to set it, the display still flashes a sickly green "12:00 a.m." So now you've got two problems: a new time limit, you can't get everyone into your bathroom to spy on them, and you're not good with math.

Staring at the word "Spike" written in flaked but chic "Ruby Woo" on the curve of your bowl, you decide you should take your fly for a walk. Once, your grandpa told you a story, about when he was a boy and he used to stick flies to his fingers with honey.

"We were bored as heck back then," he said. "Now, don't you think I'm reminiscing just so I can tell you how it built character or any noble nonsense like that, 'cause the only thing playing with flies truly can do is make you wish you had real toys instead."

He also told you about how his flies didn't fly too long because he always smacked them just a little bit too hard to slow them down, sort of like your grandma did to you.

Yours won't last long either, you realize, and you have to move faster. You look around the bathroom, and find some dental floss the second-to-last girl left behind. You have no trouble grabbing the fly out of the air, and it's still sluggish enough to tie a leash around its body without risking a swat to stun it, but the floss is too thick for a knot. You look around and around and around, and finally your eyes stop on the answer, stuck to the side of your toilet all along, something that is underlining your pet fly's new name. You crouch down to get closer. All this time, you thought it was a crack in the porcelain, but it's a long black hair stuck to the moisture on the side of the bowl. You peel it loose and hold it up to the window. Black. Thick. Curly as phone cord. One of hers. You half-expect it to twitch like a severed spider's leg. And even though it's just a hair, even though you haven't cleaned the bathroom since she left, you're amazed to find a piece of her still here. You'd be less surprised to find the five-foot-five layer of skin she'd shed, rustling and drying in a corner, right next to where she'd shed you.

You tie the leash quickly, and the knot comes too easy. You decide this is because you had at least one of your hands buried in her hair for so many years that when a hair is not connected to her head, it still knows your fingers. And even though she was impervious, sometimes you can still get her hair to do what you want.

The fly grabs the hair and starts stroking it with two front legs.

Do these damn things have thumbs? you wonder. *No. If bugs had tiny thumbs, they would have invented the tiny wheel. Or they would hitchhike instead of getting smeared on our windshields.*

You tie the fly to your finger where the skin is still pale from a ring she gave you. Then you put on your headphones still plugged into nothing, the power cord dangling down and tucked into a belt loop. Now you can start your day.

00:01:09:13—"Bringing a Fly to a Fist Fight?!"

You're out the door looking for the sun. It tells you it's time for free doughnuts. The gas station throws out the old ones at exactly 8:00 every day, but you've got to time it just right. The fly tugs on its leash, circling your soap-white ring finger, then resigning to wrap itself around the steering wheel instead. You worry about a sudden turn breaking its leash, so you pull over and carefully unwind the black hair without breaking it, thinking about the old westerns your grandpa used to make you watch, and the way the cowboys made their horses stay put by merely dropping a leather strap across a bush without even tying it up.

Inside the gas station, the new girl behind the counter smiles, and you grab one of each kind of doughnut before the kid can slide them into the trash. He sighs and steps aside, watching you drop them into a bag, then he quickly clears the case. You take longer than usual because you're trying to keep your new fly hand behind your back. You don't know what would be worse: people thinking flies follow you around, or people knowing you keep one on a leash.

When the new girl's counting the cigarettes behind her, you take the fly off your finger and hook it to a bag of peanuts near the register. You don't really tie a knot, but just wind the hair around the peanuts one time, knowing it will stay. Then you run out to pump your gas.

Inside, you can see the girl at the counter talking to the next guy in line, and he throws a thumb toward the pump you're standing at. You quickly pull the headphones from inside your shirt and pop them in to see if this guy is talking shit. Amazingly, he isn't. But she is.

He acts like he's surprised the doughnuts are free even though he was in here last night . . .

Your head down in shame, you go back in to grab your fly. For the first time since you started going to this gas station, the new girl talks to you.

"So are you paying for those peanuts, asshole?"

Next stop is the post office, and you check the stamp machines in the lobby. Just as you hoped, there's a tongue of five three-cent stamps wagging from the slot. You tear them free and put them in your pocket. Ever since the price of stamps increased to such an uneven number, people have been leaving the difference behind. It's not a lot of money, but it helps you stay on the periphery of responsibility. Is also makes you feel like you have a job. And, for some reason, this feels like integrity.

The new girl behind the counter smiles and waves as you leave.

He doesn't have three cents?

What the hell? You scratch your sore ears hard to see if the voice goes away. You scratch even harder. If you could scratch your ears with your foot, you would. You don't understand because the headphones are around your wrist. And the fly isn't anywhere near her. And neither are you. How is this still happening?

You go to the diner. There's a new waitress at the door. Are there new girls behind every counter now? Do they cultivate them back there just out of sight, ten more slowly rising up behind every register at all times, heads not quite clearing the cash drawers, but ready to take over once the previous one is plucked?

The new girl has a pencil shaped like a tiny pool cue. You stare at it, hypnotized, every time she takes your order. You're sure you asked her about it once, but she ignored you. Maybe it wasn't her, but tonight is no different.

"Excuse me," you say. "There is a fly in my soup . . . "

She looks down at the insect buzzing and tugging against its leash on your finger.

" . . . and I think the little bastard just lassoed me."

She wanders away, a miraculous combination of annoyed expressions on her face you didn't think possible. You stop in the restroom on the way out. In the urinal, just above the penile line-of-fire is a PSA sticker that shouts: "You hold in your hand the power to stop a rape!" For a second, you think the sign refers to the fly crawling across your knuckles, and you're ashamed of your new "fly whisperer" status. Even though you're not really aiming, your piss cuts through the urinal puck like a laser, but when you're hurriedly zipping up, one headphone falls from your ear and plops into the yellow water, sinking perfectly between the two halves of the pink cake. You sigh and pull the rest of the wires out of your shirt and toss them all in with it. You wonder if this is what undercover cops feel like when they get made.

Workday almost over, you stop at the garage to get air for your perpetually leaky tires. Your Rabbit will always have this problem, but new tires will never get less expensive. And, when you find the right gas stations, air is free. This garage is one of the only places in town where you don't have to pay fifty cents to fill them up since the guy who owns the place just gives you a knowing smile and the better part of a wave and turns on the compressor, rightfully assuming you're broke. You wave back whole-heartedly, then notice he's training a new girl, and you accidentally bounce your fly off your forehead. He's a bit more lethargic, but otherwise unharmed. You watch the training a second, thinking about how the last time you stopped by, this man smiled wide and agreed with you that "paying for air was flippin' ridiculous."

You get out, tie the fly to the pump, snake the hose, then hit the button.

How fucking low do you gotta be to need free air . . . c'mon.

It's a woman's voice. Over the sound of the compressor, and the jangle of the cash register printing out the day's receipts. You wonder what kind of reception the fly gets, and how you could test this.

I heard of someone stealing dirt once, only that was from a construction site and that shit ain't cheap. But air? Nope. Never heard of anyone stealing air. Pretty sad.

The air pump stops rumbling. Your fly strains on its leash, then curls back to land on a coil of hose to rest.

I have heard of people stealing water, but that was during the war.

You throw the hose. 29 pounds of pressure will have to do. Both in your tires and in your brain.

Honestly, who the hell steals air . . .

You can't contain your rage any longer, and you yell toward the building and watch the shadows in the neighboring garage scatter.

"Well, who the hell *sells* air?!"

A mechanic slides out from under a car and into the sunlight. She stands up and then walks toward you, wiping grease from her fist, blowing sweat off her nose, staring at you like she has your number. She probably does.

00:01:45:22—"Fly Factory Revealed!"

Do you ever not have the feeling someone is talking shit about you?

You end up at the video store to steal some movie inserts. You do this because those throwaway pieces of paper in the old DVDs are great reading. The Blu-Rays are locked down too secure to bother, but grabbing a handful of DVD inserts is like taking out a stack of library books you never have to return. Sure, sometimes you get a paragraph of summary, or some decent production notes, or an interview on them, but this is not what you're looking for. You just enjoy reading the chapter titles. It's a whole movie in ten seconds. The chapter titles on the inserts tell you all you'll ever need to know about hours upon hours of entertainment, and this efficiency seems important today. You grab a random one to get the party going. Okay, maybe not so random. You've read this movie before, and you always anticipate the interrobangs that aren't really there:

Sharks with Guns

"Love on a Lifeboat?"
"Sharks Are Using Tools?!"
"Are You Gonna Eat That?"
"Dolphins Are Not Our Friends!"
"Bringing a Shark to a Gun Fight?!"
"Shark Factory Revealed!"
"Duel to the Deaf?!"
"Quitting the Coast Guard for Good!"

What could you possibly be missing from the story after you read that list? It's all there. The crisis, the love interest, the surprise ending. Didn't someone once say there are really only three stories you can tell? A stranger comes to town. Man goes on a journey. Fool talks to a fly.

You study the box and snicker. It's one of those pre-fab cult movies that are so popular these days, and you scoff. There's no way that shark could hold that chainsaw, you decide. Much less that gun. They would need thumbs to do that.

Now that would be a scary movie, you think. *Grandpa always warned me about them.*

If sharks had thumbs, they could make a phone call. So they wouldn't have to bite anyone. Just show one shark whip out a phone and every asshole in the audience would start screaming. You've seen more far-fetched things in movies lately. Like that time your ex-girlfriend checked her phone underwater in the bath tub so you wouldn't see who called her. You figured she'd ruined it, but the phone worked fine when you blew the bubbles off of it later that night and found out who she was hiding.

You slip some DVD inserts into your sleeves, then you go up to the counter and grab one of those free internet CDs to go with it. This clerk knows you, and you see a strange light flickering in her eyes. You realize she is watching something under the register with the volume turned way down. You wonder when she snuck a TV under there, and suddenly you have to know what movie she's watching. You're convinced it's pornography, or why else would she have the volume down like that? But on the way out, you finally see what it is.

A security monitor.

She was watching you steal those inserts the entire time, and you can see yourself in the corner of her screen, standing by the door, hunched and alone, unbelievably small, looking over your shoulder, then looking over her shoulder, guilty as hell and green as a sunset.

Sitting in the car with your hands on the steering wheel, your heart jumps because your fly is dangling on the hair like a suicide. You turn on the air-conditioning, open all the vents, and hold it in front of the cool air. Luckily, it starts to climb back up its leash like a spider. It's moving slow, but it's alive. You realize that every time you hide the fly, it starts to die.

Sounds like a children's rhyme, doesn't it?

You have to get home. Or get it to the bathroom. Or a restroom. You think about how toilet water is cold even on the hottest day, and, even if you know what's bobbed around in there, it's got to be tempting to swim in that bowl when you're feverish. If you're a bug, of course. You suspect they live in a perpetual state of fever, as it would explain their short life spans.

You drive fast, checking the size of the gas stations as you pass, trying to gauge whether they're big enough for a public restroom. You glance down at the fly and see it slump on the string, swinging from the hair like a pendulum again. You slam on the brakes and make a hard right, but it's the smallest gas station you've ever seen. You ask the third-grade boy behind the counter if they have a restroom. He says no and turns back to counting the candy bars. In desperation, you hold up your hand with the limp fly swinging from your finger.

"My dude, this fly here needs to drink from a toilet or it's going to die."

The kid smiles over a huge piece of gum and stares at you

for 13 . . . 14 . . . 15 seconds. Then he points to the big metal door behind the beer. "It's back there. Hurry up, king."

Unfuckingbelievable. You guess he's seen stranger things than this.

Inside the bathroom, you're assaulted by a stench worse than an outhouse, probably equal to a Porta-Potty, and you cautiously lift the toilet lid. The water is clear as a mountain spring. You carefully lower your hand until the fly's fuzzy head just breaks the surface. You think about the part of the buddy-cop movie, right around the second act, where the drunk detective has to get revived by the more wise-cracking partner, and he gets his face shoved in the toilet bowl. You're much more gentle than that, but you channel the same emotions.

And it works. The fly starts to activate, cranking its legs over its head to clean itself off. You smile proudly. Your fly looks like it's playing a tiny air guitar, even though it would need thumbs to do it well.

"Ears burning?" the clerk asks you on your way out.

You smile. They've been burning for years. Eventually, you'll hear a story about a mythical creature that eats nothing but ears, then leaves behind the rest of the animal unscathed. It snacked on ears like potato chips all day long, leaving a trail of stone-deaf (but alive) barnyard beasts, all through the Dirty South. And when the voices are talking shit again, you'll envy them.

Back in the car, you wonder how many people would believe your concern for this fly.

But I am attached to it, you think, smiling again.

You've never been good with pets. And plants? Forget about it. But this feels like everyone's fly now, and there is the weight of this new responsibility. You imagine yourself in the waiting room at the veterinarian with your drying and dying fly, the only person a kid with a sick hermit crab could mock. You watch it perched on the radio knob, cleaning its wings, and you stab the gas pedal over and over to crank up the A/C.

The car shudders, still in neutral, a slight taste of hot motor oil in the back of your throat, and the sweet chloroform smell of a Freon leak filling your nostrils.

You've spent more time worrying about this fly than all of your exes combined. Even the one who got her appendix out. But she was the worst. You mess with your stereo's settings.

Equalizer, you think. *That's a good word.*

Then you understand something. It only seems like you care about dying flies more than your relationships, but if you were to line them all up against the wall and put a little pencil mark over their heads, you'd find that your feelings about the fly and any "X" were precisely the same. It's not that you think more of a fly. It's just that the more you hear voices when they don't think you're listening, the less you think of human beings.

00:01:58:19—"Your Gears Are Burning?!"

You told a new girl once that you were going to invent a phone that, instead of ringing, released a swarm of bees. You said it would guarantee she would answer the thing every time you needed her. She didn't understand what you were talking about, and thought you meant some special ringtone. So you said, "How about three small bees, just enough to make you swat the air in a panic every single time I called?" She had no answer, and she never answered you again. Later, your uncle will invent an app that plays cupid with strangers on the highway by swapping telephone numbers and license plates, but you won't tell people this story, unless they've had as much to drink as him, because this invention will kill the same number of people as heart disease that year. Which makes sense, you will decide. But you'll be comforted that someone else in your family shares your aversion and obsession with phones calls.

Back at home, you walk out of the bathroom, and she

walks in. You see she is reading that same magazine again, the one with the prescription label with your ex-girlfriend's name on the cover. You told her once how a past girlfriend snorted painkillers off those very same pages, which seems like a worse addiction than drinking, but doesn't feel like it at the time. You think this will make her not want to read it, but instead she folds a page to remember her place. You think about how you tried to get a letter published in that magazine so she'd stumble across it and accidentally listen to you. You also folded pages for her, but you already knew your place.

Did you say "prescription" instead of "subscription" back there? Because that is exactly what you meant.

The speaker starts popping again. *Shit fuck shit* . . . You pull the cords on everything. You hate the wiring in this apartment more than you've hated anyone in your life.

Your wiring destroys everything eventually.

You hear water running in the bathroom sink, and understand that she's going to be in there a while. She does this sometimes, runs the sink so you can't hear. Like you'd really be listening to her pissing, which you've done ten times already. Then you are distracted, and you crawl to your crate of old cassette tapes rotting in the corner. In the box is your first and best pair of headphones, huge scabby, spider-filled poofs from the '80s that cover your entire head. You hesitate to put them on, realizing your headphones are getting bigger as you slide further back down the technology ladder. But once you're holding them in your hands and blowing the dust and insect shells off the foam, you see that they're much older than you thought. They're from the '70s, and they're the only thing left of your mother. When they were new, she came up to you and put them over your small ears, and you were pouting about something, like kids do, so you didn't say anything to her. You didn't even look up to say thanks, but you didn't take them off your ears either. And you've never been able to remember the song she wanted you to hear, or why she wanted you to hear it. Was there something funny in that song? Did the lyrics mean something important to her? Maybe she was predicting your future alone. But you were too busy ignoring her act of kindness for reasons long forgotten. And now you'll never know what song it was because you were sitting there, arms crossed, angry about something stupid, defiantly frowning until the song was over and out of your head forever, and she finally shrugged and walked away. But the strangest thing is, when you think back to it, you could swear you were sitting outside under a tree, crossed legs and crossed arms, when your mother put those big headphones over your ears. But how could the cord have ever reached that far?

The wind blows the dead fly around on its string. Your ring finger is white from lack of circulation, so you unwrap the leash from your skin, waiting for the blood flow to return and paint the white knuckle red again. You're amazed at how strong her hair was, but not surprised.

You hide in the bathroom after she leaves, wondering if it's true that it's the last place the remains of a relationship lingers. But you're no scientist, and even though you have a toy stethoscope stashed in the crate with your headphones, you're not that kind of doctor.

One day soon, you'll decide it's in those heavenly half-empty bottles and the flowery scents of colored soaps where her memory clings. But today it's the hairs around the toilet.

00:02:00:07—"End Credits & Ironic Theme Music!"

The next day, you finally take out the trash. And not a moment too soon, either. You can see a box of sweet-and-sour chicken moving on its own, and suddenly a fly in the wintertime isn't such a miracle anymore, because you can see at least three more green-eyed buzz bombs bouncing around in the bag with their snouts dipping in and out of a month's worth of scraps. Your grandpa used to say that fish would appear in mud puddles if they sat undisturbed long enough, but now you know those were mosquitoes all along.

You recite your favorite line from *Titus Andronicus*, the movie adaptation of the Shakespeare play every ex-girlfriend hated:

"'What dost thou strike at, Marcus, with thy knife?' 'At that that I have killed, my lord, a fly.' 'Out on thee, murderer! Thou killst my heart.'"

The bathroom isn't the last place your girlfriends exist. Now you know it's the garbage, because that's where your children have been hiding, swarming the rotten oranges. You take out the bag, but keep walking past the dumpster, and you throw your headphones into the river before you can change your mind. It's one of those rivers that looks good from a distance, even better from an apartment window, and you're standing next to it and can smell what's been dumped in there for years. You went down there once with her, thinking it was romantic. This was before the fly, but you could hear what she was thinking.

Isn't this the river that caught on fire because of the pollution?

You wonder how your toilet didn't explode from all the cigarettes she flicked in it, and you remember this river is where that little boy swore he saw a shark making a phone call, right before he disappeared from that pay phone forever.

Your headphones bob along, riding the brown waves easily, then something under the water takes a couple nips and finally pulls them down forever. Still, something is flickering just under the surface, millions and millions of somethings . . .

Then there's a new girl standing next to you, and you turn.

"You know what you looked like just then?" she asks. "Like the last scene of a movie. When the sheriff throws away his badge."

"Hold out your hand," you tell her, not really expecting her to do it. And when she uncurls her fingers for you, you fully expect something to fly away.

"What's your name?"

"I go by 'Shell,' short for 'Michelle,' which is my middle name."

"I'm not calling you either of them."

"Then don't."

"I've seen you before, haven't I?"

"I live in your building."

"Do you have problems with your wiring?"

"No," she laughs. "Do you? You sure look like you do. You should get a surge protector. I have three of them."

You stare for seven . . . eight . . . nine seconds. A new record. Then you write your phone number in her hand. Just for laughs, you scribble something else underneath it.

"Sorry, I like drawing flies."

"They are easy to make," she says. "Like a smiley face. You know why everyone draws smiley faces? Because you can recognize it in less than five lines."

You believe her. Then you hear the buzzing again, and you know what it is before she even pulls it out. It's never a fly. She smiles an apology and presses the phone deep into her face, distorting her features, walking away quickly so that you cannot hear.

You walk off in the opposite direction to give her privacy. You think of your phone number and the fly you drew on her skin, and you cup your hand around your ear like a seashell. And even years later, when you're both miles away and her head and her hand are the only things visible above the waves that are smacking your face and filling your nostrils, you still keep your hand cupped over your ear, and you can hear every word of her conversation like she's swimming right next to you. Until you pull her under.

When you make it across the river to the other shore, you remain on all fours, shaking off the water, the music, and the flies, just like a dog. And you forget about her all over again.

Like yesterday and tomorrow, the first girls and the last girls?

They all bleed together.

XVIII

POOP, CRINKLE, SCRATCH, AND ZERO

I WAS IN the driver's seat again, but even though we were in synch on this mission now (our thumbs practically hooked in each other's back pockets), Mad had something else she wanted me to do. She hadn't asked me for *anything* yet, she explained, but she wanted me to take a quick detour and do her this one "teeny tiny little favor" on our way through Huntsville, Alabama, some backwater shithole where she grew up.

"Their DMV is more like a DMZ, Dave," she promised, like this was a good thing.

"What's in Huntsville?"

"We have to stop by an animal clinic. I have to pick up my cat's ashes."

She must have been thinking about her cat from spending so much time in my back seat with Zero, who was more cat than rat these days. Mad told us her cat's name was "Ash," and we'd be picking up "Ash's ashes!" This seemed like a pretty big coincidence, so we were all for it.

"He's named after *The Evil Dead*, not that pussy in *Gone with the Wind*," she clarified. "But mostly I just called him 'Poop.' 'Cause guess what he liked to do!"

Zero liked to carpet-bomb the car, as well, and this was

much worse than normal cat turds, because Zero's feces were oddly human. So instead of the usual ammonia scent you got with a litter box, his "accidents" turned our Rabbit into something like the monkey house at the zoo. A wise man once said, "If you own a cat, you also own a box of shit." Actually, it was Greg who said that, not me, but truer words were never spoken. By him, anyway. What do you call a "bullshit artist" who's actually bad at it?

I was driving slow. I'd always been a notoriously leisurely driver, and it used to drive Angie bonkers. But one thing I've learned is that, when you regularly drive slow, like I do, you can see who's following you. And that's how I knew we had some genuine animals on our tails:

The Eagle passed us first. Then the Viper pursing it, which seemed backwards. Then the Cougar came by again, with the Bronco close behind. Oh, and the Jeep Cherokee with the tinted windows. Weren't some Jeeps called Wranglers? Cowboys and Indians duking it out on the interstate seemed like a terrible idea, but no worse than this mobile zoo. No sign of the Thunderbird, though. There was the Ram, then the Mustang, and then a cute little Beetle, one of the new models with the daisy on the dash (and a daisy in the driver's hair). Then I watched a scary fuckin' Jaguar gaining ground on an Impala, and I felt a little uneasy in something as toothless as a Rabbit. I looked for my caged chimera in my mirror. Zero showed little concern. The real question was, were these the same cars I kept seeing? But I didn't ask it.

A couple miles out of Huntsville, we stopped at Denny's for some breakfast. Mad and Matt got the greasy hangover staples, and I grabbed a miniature box of cereal. When Angie was still with me, I had purchased some generic Rice Krispies on my last trip to the grocery store, and we both laughed when I put the box of "Crisp Rice" on her chest in the morning. She said, "Awesome. Rather than waking up to three fresh-faced elves to brighten my day, I am so excited to gaze into the weary eyes of three grubby rodent coal miners." We'd named the generic mascots "Poop, Crinkle, and Scratch," and I told my crew that this was who we were now. I even got out my Magic Marker and threatened to tattoo our foreheads for our travelling sideshow.

"Not sure about this," Mad said, blocking me with her hand. "Who gets to be Scratch?"

"Much better than calling you two 'M&M,'" I said. "Or Eminem and 'M.'"

"How does that work?

"'Mad and Matt and me'! It really helps to think of us as the same creature. Three beasts rolled up into one. Look how well it worked out for Zero. Now c'mere with that head . . . "

"No way! Eyes on the road, fool." Mad held up a threatening finger and tapped my cereal bowl with her fork.

"You know who you remind me of, Dave?" Matt asked.

"The kid you hated most in high school."

"Yes."

"Great."

"His name was Bob Camelooski, one of those weird animal names. We were friends at first, but he borrowed a lot of junk from me. Drums, guitars . . . he even wanted my keyboard but that's where I drew the line. He took my copy of *The Executioner's Song*, which I know he never read. Have you ever read any 'Normal' Mailer, Dave? That's what I call his early stuff because *The Executioner's Song* was much easier to read than that wacky Egyptian gibbering he scribed later on. Anyhow, Bob beat me up once when I talked to his girlfriend too long at a football game. I was in the band and he was on the team, and he called me a 'faggot' and broke my arm and my nose, almost pounded me as bad as you did! He was wearing a helmet the whole time, which didn't seem fair. Not as bad as when he'd send me pictures of his largest bowel movements. So anyway, years later, I started stalking him for a bit. And one night, looking through his bedroom window, I caught him sucking his own dick."

Here we go, I thought.

"Now, I couldn't figure out whether this was pathetic or embarrassing or just some radical 'learn to love yourself' therapy, but it was certainly horrifying to watch. I tell you what, his throat actually opened like a lizard, kinda like when frat boys shotgun their beers."

"Is that a thing?"

"I'm probably gonna need more information here, but it sounds like you're the creeper in this equation, Matt," Mad said.

"No, you don't get it. He was calling me a 'faggot' but there he was sucking his own dick? What a hypocrite!"

"Called you a 'faggot' for hitting on his girlfriend," Mad laughed. "That's some tenth-level chess."

"I'm not sure sucking your own dick is a gateway drug to homosexuality," I said after some thought. "More like a gateway drug to cannibalism."

"True."

"I have a theory about guys who take pictures of the toilet after a big ol' dump and then send it to someone," I said. "It's just a loophole to sending a dick pic to your bud. Like it's the closest thing your manliness will allow. I mean *their* manliness." There was an awkward silence.

"Well, the '80s were sure a different time. Dudes dressing like chicks. Look at Prince, right? So, I run into Bob years later working the pumps at Speedway, and I tell him, 'You seem like a nice guy now, Bob, even though you don't remember going to high school with me, I used to park outside your house at night and fantasize about killing you.'"

"Still waiting for the point . . . " I lied, stirring around the last three Krispies.

"Then, a couple years after that, I was watching a concert in the park, and here comes Bob's mother. And I know all about her from my hours of watching his house. And I'm off to the side of the stage with my notebook, writing down song ideas, and Bob's mom comes up and says, 'Hi, Matt! Great to see you. You know, you should write a song about high school!

You boys sure had some funny stories, didn't you?' And then she was gone. Later, I realized that she thought all us kids had to be friends, even those jerks who bullied me. And I thought, 'My songs aren't for them! Those were the dullest, most disposable knuckleheads I'd ever known.'"

Matt paused to make sure I saw he was staring at me. "'Get over yourself,' that's what I always wanted to say to him. And that's why I sat in my car outside his house. Not to kill him. Just to say, 'My story is not your story.'"

***

By the time we were back in the car, I was losing patience. Mad gave Zero my leftover milk, and Matt sat up front with me, talking my ear off. After waiting for a train, and then a few more tollbooths, Dr. Matthew "That Kind of Doctor?" Fink was claiming center stage again. He started telling this story about how he did his medical residency in the Navy, of all places, the same year he took the part-time job at the library archives, and how he ran into ol' pillbugging Bob one last time, who'd also enlisted for no discernible reason.

"Who's stalking who!" Mad wanted to know, and Matt went on about Bob borrowing a CD from him, "Prince's *The God Experience*," very hard to find, but his absolute favorite, a detail which muddied the waters even more. Matt said maybe he was dumb for loaning Bob something again, but he figured Bob couldn't hide from him on a boat, of all places.

"Not *The* God *Experience*," I corrected him. "It's called *The* Gold *Experience*."

"Riiiiight. I knew that. Maybe it was a bootleg."

"How long have you been in a Prince cover band, Fink?"

"All musicians are Prince cover bands, Dave," Matt said, and I had to give him that one.

"So a few months passed by, and he never has the album when I stop by his barracks," Matt continued. "And I know he keeps hoping I forget about it, like he hopes I forgot about him kicking my ass. So one night I'm done with my shift early, and I knock on his door. No surprise he's in there because Bob's a typical barracks rat, looking for a lot of 'alone time,' and he gets all self-righteous, denies ever borrowing it! Then he dares me to accuse him of stealing it. And this is the old Bob I knew so well back in high school," Matt said, tapping his temple with his finger. "Then, get this, right before I'm being transferred to a new duty assignment at a real hospital on terra firma, Bob has a very public affair with a CPO's wife who was staying in the barracks while hubby was at some training school. It was all very not so hush-hush. Bob even paid for tickets to visit her in Florida. We're talking over two grand he dropped, all in advance, but he can't give me back my Prince CD? So the day he's leaving for his dream romp, I made sure the CTMC cuckold got a nasty little anonymous letter. And. Shit. Hit. The. Fan . . ."

Mad looked at me like "Who is this guy?" And I gave her a look like, "I know, right?" Matt was suddenly a combination real doctor, Prince fanatic, *and* in the military?

" . . . so the end result? First off, Bob's fantasy vacation is cancelled. The Chief personally drives to Florida to confront Bob and his wife. Bob came back almost immediately, wide-eyed, black-eyed, and frazzled like a rabbit the morning after a week-long moonshine binge. Dumb ass almost gets kicked out of the Navy, too, even got grilled by some NIS goons, but somehow manages to squirm out of it. But his security clearance gets yanked, and he ends up getting rode for everything he even remotely does wrong for the rest of his time by the not-so-happy command that has to deal with his lingering mess."

"Damn, dude," Mad said.

"Did he know it was you, Fredo?"

"Yeah, he found out who wrote the note and gave him the shaft, owing to some eavesdropper with his ear against my door, listening to a friend and me laughing about it in the bunks. He wasn't amused. He busted in and got up in my face and demanded an explanation. So I said, 'Remember that Prince CD you stole, Bob?' He said, 'Yeah, you want it back?' And I said, 'No, you earned it, dude.'"

"Cool story, bro, especially the part about—"

"You *earned* it, dude," Matt said again, looking at me hard, and I gave him a big grin. I wasn't sure if Bob even existed, or if Matt was a soldier or Prince's private physician that accidentally killed him with those designer prescription drugs, but Matt's stories were suddenly sounding like fables without the animals. However, I was optimistic enough to take all of this as a good sign. It was like we were on that ship together, bobbing in our bowl of milk, bonding. Mad sounded like Angie, and now Matt sounded a bit like me. Pretty soon, if I played my cards right, I wouldn't be necessary at all.

***

Even with the battery out of it, and even though I knew it would be impossible, the cell phone in my lap started flashing me like it was wearing a tiny raincoat. The Rabbit's windows were back up as the temperature dropped with every mile, the opposite of what we expected as we headed south. And without the white noise of the highway wind, the phone was a real distraction. I had dozens of calls, maybe a hundred messages. I decided to listen to a few, and I didn't even have to push any buttons to do it. Instead, I searched the vents under my windshield for any dead flies I may have missed. There were plenty. And they still got excellent reception.

If I was gonna be hearing voices again, I figured why not *voicemails*. And the first voicemail I would hear in my head would be from Ramsey, cat-muncher extraordinaire, wanting me to return his cage. I guess I should have hit star sixty-nine after all! The next voicemail would be from a cop, maybe one of those detectives off my porch, probably Flotsam. Or maybe it will be Jetsam. And he would repeat the veiled threats he'd floated by me in the parking lot three states away, and I would find myself unable to concentrate on important new information about my wife's case because something in his voice would remind me of Angie's chapter on "postmodern" police behavior. I was legitimately excited to read that part of her dissertation, since it was born of a conversation after our

Donnie Brasco/Donnie Darko double feature. Angie explained that the "Joe Pistone situation" was a great example of this tragic new law-enforcement vernacular:

"The curious thing about Agent Pistone's Donnie Brasco persona . . . " she'd explained, brushing popcorn from her breastbone and sending the elk-tooth necklace her father had given her spinning, " . . . is here's an FBI agent who sounds like a typical swaggering clown on all his undercover tapes, clearly imitating what he assumes is an Italian Mafioso . . . then a movie is made starring Johnny Depp, who, after studying these same Pistone undercover tapes, does arguably his most clichéd performance of a man imitating a man imitating mafia movies! Then when Joe Pistone—now retired and believing his own hype, eagerly adopting an even *more* exaggerated version of this stereotypical behavior for the rest of his life—is interviewed about the film, he says, 'He nailed my mannerisms perfectly!' Snake eats tail. And garlic burps."

I followed most of this at the time, but I won't be able to follow anything this mumble-mouthed cop would be saying, and my brain would probably delete the message with a belch. *Actually that doesn't sound like her at all. Maybe a little. I think she loved that stupid movie.*

The next voicemail would be from my sister, one of her extra-long ones. Back when I wasn't a fugitive, I used to transcribe her messages, just to keep my closed-captioning skills sharp. And because they were hysterical. So I typed the air above my steering wheel instead:

" . . . so Bernie was last seen riding off into the sunset on a shark, so for the sequel how about we have him land on an island and get buried in the sand so he's preserved until there's a hurricane that blows all the sand away and he's exposed. Then the two guys from the first movie, their cruise ship gets lost—I'm still working on this part—or maybe they're working on a humanitarian program to mend their ways? But their ship runs ashore, and they find Bernie or whatever, and they say, 'Oh, shit, we thought he was on a shark!' And someone walks up and says, 'Hey, guys, who's this?' and Bernie's head turns and then the credits, *Weekend at Bernie's III!* Boom. Then there's some plot bullshit, and Bernie ends up on a ship to Italy somehow, but now he's walking all the time, swinging his arms around—we'll probably forget about the voodoo music in this one, and he just moves around because that's easier—and he goes through customs, and they think he's a monk, so they take him to a monastery, and whenever the monks are arguing about an issue, they'll look to Bernie, and they'll see him wave his arms around but not talking, and they'll say, 'Oh, he's so passionate, but he won't break his vow of silence!' So they make him Pope. And that's my movie. Now please come home, Dave."

It would be tough to think about my sister missing me, even though we always disagreed about each other's love interests, as well as everything else. The last time I got to hang out with her, just a couple weeks after the wedding, we'd gone to see *Black Swan*, and my sister had to sit in the row behind us because she was so late, as usual. And her new boyfriend showed up even later than her and just stayed in the aisle drinking beer. She wanted him to sit, but he just stood there, in our peripheral vision, kinda swaying his hips back and forth, even pulling a second beer from his pocket, cracking it open, just planted there breathing loud and drinking and making dumb observations about the movie to my sister, who kept begging him to just please sit the hell down. Eventually he did, but then he would go "Haw! Haw! Oh, yeah!" whenever there were any nude scenes. The ending finally confused him into silence, and he wandered off.

"Happy Valentine's Day to whoever was that poor bastard's girlfriend!" someone in the theater had shouted. Oh, right, that was my sister. I felt bad because Angie and I got such a laugh out of that night, and sometimes I would forget that my sister and I didn't share every joke, which was probably a good thing in the long run. And a long run was exactly what I was on.

"To save this message in the archive, press seven of your teeth with your tongue."

Not easy, but that's not why I didn't save it. I didn't save it because there was a message from Angie in the archive, and I couldn't risk erasing it, even if I couldn't imagine hearing her voice ever again. That's truly the last place someone exists, you know, saved in the limbo of a voicemail forever.

But when everyone was asleep, I flicked the dead flies into the vent and listened to her voice for real.

***

"So I had a revelation today at the library. Remember how we were talking about police officers 'mushfaking' during trials? Well, sparsely defined on the internet, but we know it as a synonym for 'faking it,' and it's used in a few different scenarios. Something called the 'Word Detective' claims the term originated in early 19th century England to refer to those who sold umbrellas fixed just enough to seem functional, which I love. However, the assumed handiwork soon failed the purchaser, most likely during a downpour. But more recently, the term started to be used as prison slang. Prisoners who creatively make do by using obscure or less useful objects to create practical materials were said to be 'mushfaking.' Morris, 2003. But according to James Gee, the term also refers to a situation in which one is capable of functioning in a scenario or environment where they do not belong because they have acquired enough of the skills and knowledge to appear as if they do. 1996. But as a noun, the term describes a person who is attempting to fit in to an otherwise unfamiliar position. And as a verb? One who is mushfaking is evading the perceptions of those in the dominant position by acting as if they are a member of that culture. So, yeah, I'm sort of excited, and I'd love to further connect the idea Gee cites as originating in prison talk, as something that can be better attributed to women's discourse. Because as we know, women continue to navigate their own prison, meaning a language based in patriarchal standards and restrictions . . . "

There it is again. Listening to her talk about prisons was so soothing, I worried I'd drift into the ditch, but I figured the black bags would just rebound me back into my lane. I thought about how any long road trip was solitary confinement, and maybe I was preventing full immersion into my wife's theories by picking up this menagerie of stragglers. *Nahhhhhh . . .*

" . . . but it was Julia Penelope who theorized the Patriarchal Universe of Discourse Theory, which explains the challenges women are faced with everyday when attempting to utilize language and confrontations that are strictly beneficial to males. She maintains that since the language was developed by men, and for men, there's no way for a woman to access its true meaning or efficient utilization, thus leaving them in a constant state of 'mush-fake' themselves. Which led me to 'engfish,' its bastard cousin, coined in 1964 by Ken Macrorie. So frustrated by what he called his students' 'bloated and pretentious, feel-nothing, say-nothing language, dead as Latin and devoid of rhythms of contemporary speech,' his laments sound eerily like today's police officers on the witness stand. Remember, David, whenever there is the scrutiny of a camera's eye, the fool will attempt to imitate the true expert who testifies before them. What I'm saying is we were absolutely right. We can talk more about it when I get home, but can you imagine the unprecedented communication breakdown for any uneducated police officer if you actually *attached* a recording device to him or her at all times? It's a terrifying prospect, and these body cameras might be the most dangerous thing that's ever happened to law enforcement outside of guns. By the way, we need to get a cat. I'll keep my eyes peeled. Okay, I love you . . ."

I loved you, too.

I thought about how I'd mastered mushfaking and engfishing and bullshitting as soon as I began this fake investigation. How my travelling companions were already becoming well-versed in this, as well. It was all so easy to fall into these roles of fugitives, crime-fighters. Animals in rolling cages, all.

The next time I spotted a teddy bear bound to a mile marker, I snapped my phone in half to stop the voices. Or at least maybe I could slow them down.

***

"So your cat's name was 'Ash'? No bullshit, Mad?"

"Shhh! Yes, my cat's name was 'Ash,' and we are going to retrieve his ashes," Mad whispered. "Ten years ago, this animal clinic called for me to pick up his remains, and I have come to collect. And my name is 'Mag.'"

I pried open the office door with my tire iron.

"Why didn't you ever pick up the ashes?" Matt whispered, voice charged and quivering, adjusting his jeans from all the excitement of committing a felony instead of just crimes against nature. He only used one hand to rearrange whatever hell was nested behind that zipper. As usual, I expected two.

"Shhh. Does it matter? Okay, something about the phone call made me angry. The hesitation of the receptionist telling me, 'Uh, Ash's . . . ashes are ready? Wait . . . ' The cunt was *giggling*. She did manage to say something about how they could store his ashes indefinitely. In a tiny little urn. For only $59.95. All of this happened dangerously close to Ash Wednesday."

"Just like today!" I said.

"Wrong."

"Oh."

Matt grabbed my arm trying not to crack up, and I gave him a reassuring squeeze.

"Listen, numbnuts," she said to us. "I loved that cat, but I could never get through talking about any of this with a straight face either."

"But now you want his ashes," I said.

"Yes!" she said, full volume, and I stopped arguing and did what I was told.

We got in easily enough. It was a duplex, a set-up that

Mad had accurately described to us earlier as a half-office, half-apartment, with the vet living on the top floor all by himself and the offices and clinic facilities on the bottom floor. When I asked her how we could be sure this guy was alone, Mad said he was an old, ruddy-faced drunk, and the nurses did all the work during the day. He only occasionally dragged his ass down the spiral steps to give a random dying animal a hydration shot or two, maybe overcharge for some scientific-sounding special food you could only get from him, then ascend chimp-like back up to his perch. At night, it would only be him, hungover and sawing logs.

She also said there was something in his tortured walk that screamed "solitude" and she doubted he had any friends or family. Myself, I wasn't convinced we'd find her cat's ashes, since the place was so small and any cremation service or incinerator must be off-site, but she swore she saw the little urns on the shelves in his office. This was a decade ago, of course.

But as insane as it all seemed, we found her cat. Possibly. Sort of. Matt and I couldn't see a whole lot of anything in the office once we broke in, and Mad ran right past us and off into the dark. As the two of us lingered, I kicked around at some frazzled cat toys on the tile floor: a mouse missing its tail, and a bird missing its head. I'd seen them before. Back before Angie, Shell and I (or maybe it was me and Miranda?) had rehearsed a relationship at my apartment along the river, trying out a "starter cat" instead of a kid by catsitting for her cousin's orange tabby. We spent fifty bucks on supplies; catnip, stuffed animals, the works. But we never saw it play with any of them. I wondered if fake critters were like fake food, essentially invisible to anything on four legs, due to a lack of blood or heartbeats. At first, Shell and I thought the fake mice and birds were getting batted around somewhat, because they'd turn up under foot in random places all over the apartment. Then, after a couple days, the orange cat vanished, and Shell soon after, and it became clear that my own feet had always been the only thing kicking around the toys.

"Shit!" Matt yelped as Mad came zipping back around the corner with the flashlight app on her phone lighting the way. She had a tiny silver urn in her hand. She showed us two labels across the bottom marked "Ashes" and "Made in China."

"Uhhh," Matt stared to say, and I smacked him hard in the back of the head. My look told him, "Good enough."

"Worm Farm secured!" I shouted. "Let's blow this joint."

"Hold on." Mad brought a framed plaque up into the light of her phone. It was an impression of a cat's front paws. I was tracing the outline of the cat's toes with my finger when Mad's smile dropped.

"What's the matter?" I asked.

"This isn't right."

"What's not right?"

"That paw. That's not his."

"Come on, how can you possibly know that?"

"Because when Ash was dying, he was wailing, and in my rush to put him in the cat carrier, I closed the door on his paw and crushed his foot. The gate on the cage flipped two of his claws completely backwards. He was too far gone to feel it, I hope, but I never told anyone that I drove as fast as I could down here that night so they could put him out of *my* misery. The whole drive, I kept glancing down at those backwards claws, digging my fingernails in my palms out of guilt. Now look at this fucking plaque! I don't see two backwards claws, do you?"

At some point in her story, she'd totally given up whispering for good, so it wasn't too much of a surprise when the footsteps started thumping across the ceiling above us, then down the spiral staircase in the corner of the room that we were noticing for the first time, exactly as she'd described it.

The veterinarian didn't have a flashlight, so he was at the

mercy of the blinding light coming from Mad's phone. We saw his feet first, fuzzy frog slippers not quite covering his heels, and for a second I thought it was the Skunk Ape for real this time. Then we saw the tattered remains of his robe, followed by the less-than-impressive remainder of his large, shambling form. His face sort of looked like a lesser, knock-off brand Baldwin brother, like Stephen or Daniel, or like maybe the Alec Baldwin cloning machine had run out of toner. I imagined him as a former doctor who'd botched a surgery due to being drunk or high, and now he lived out his days in disgrace, toiling in the purgatory of animal care. I know it sounds far-fetched (and I've never had anything to base this on), but as far back as I could remember, I'd been convinced that vets come to work angry because at some point in their past they'd accidentally killed someone under the knife.

"What are you doing here?"

. . . the bargain-basement Baldwin brother barked! Not proud of that sentence.

"Freeze!" Mad yelled, light in his face.

"Yeah, freeze, motherfucker!" I went Full Cop, hand behind my back as I remembered the imaginary gun bulge in my duck jacket that had successfully shanghaied my crew. And Flynn Effect be damned, my gang's original supposition held true. Convinced I was armed, the veterinarian froze at the foot of the stairs.

"Matt, grab some cat food," I said. "The expensive shit. And, Mad, let's get out of here."

"Wait," she said, walking over to the vet. She held the tiny urn up to his face.

"What's in here?" she asked him.

"Ashes."

"Whose ashes?"

"I don't know," he said. "I hope you realize the police have already been called?"

"Lies," she said, but I turned from our hostage and peeked through some nearby blinds with my crowbar. It was still quiet outside, and our Rabbit was idling in the corner of his lot, headlights off so as not to illuminate the hole I'd pried open in the fence.

"What's wrong with your eyes, young lady?" the vet said, leaning closer to Mad's face for a better look. Her skin was burning white in the harsh glow of her phone, but her eyes were glassy, simmering like sauce.

"Don't change the subject," she said, squinting.

"Have you handled animal feces lately?" he asked her, with that "doctor" voice Matt had never managed to master. Then he turned to me. "Or you? Or how about you, son?" Matt said nothing, and he reached for Mad's shoulder. "Or is it possible that your condition has already grown so bad that . . ."

"We travel with a litter box!" Matt offered, and I thumped him in the chest with the crowbar to silence him.

"Wait, do you know her?" I asked the vet.

"No. But it's clear to anyone who takes the time that this girl is dealing with a case of advanced subconjunctival migration of at least a dozen adult worms to her eyes. In the long-term, they may cause blindness. In the short-term, merely insanity."

"Nice try, Dr. Feelbad!"

"But there must be another carrier," the vet sighed, waving at all of us. "As you boys are also most certainly infected."

"He's talking about Zero," I said.

"We're gonna have to start calling him the VPZ," Matt said.

"Who?"

"Very Patient Zero." The vet was right. We suddenly sounded more than a bit insane. "Okay, this was fun, but Patient Zero is patiently waiting in our car, and I don't know how long before he panics and drives off. Now let's get the fuck out of here."

"Patient Zero?" the vet asked, rubbing his own eyes, seemingly terrified at the prospect of such a creature. Then he started to rustle through a nearby shelf, mumbling something about the irrational thought processes of victims of ocular parasites. But he didn't mumble for long, because Mad was opening up the tiny urn and kicking his bare shin to motion him over.

"So, real quick, could these worms affect how we perceive the host?" I asked, finger up. "Is that why they travel to your eyes? So you'll provide the host creature with comfort and . . . "

"Shut up!" Mad said, slapping the counter. "You, get over here. This man is gonna eat some ashes."

"I won't do it," the vet said. "You need your medicine."

"If you don't eat these ashes right now . . . " Mad waited for his full attention. " . . . we will kill you."

"Do it!" I made a threatening motion to the back of my duck pocket again, and the hypothetical gun continued to get things done. The vet sighed and took the urn from her hand.

He was sort of a disappointment really. I mean, if movies are to be believed, every veterinarian on Earth has at least *one* surprise visit from a shooting victim in their lifetime. Some bank robber stumbling in bleeding, followed by grubby emergency surgery peppered with clever jokes about how many legs the vet is used to seeing on his patients. But in real life, vets just hiccupped and scratched their heads after they X-rayed your cat and gave you some pills to unnaturally prolong its life one more week.

And maybe, every so often, deal with a daughter they fucked up.

Because this monster sounded just like her.

He turned the urn over in his hand to buy some time.

"I won't," he said, looking us over. His bloodshot eyes resembled hers, too. And now I was seeing the grey curls, salt-and-pepper where they used to be black. Spitting image really, these Skunk Apes.

"Why not. It shouldn't hurt you. Unless it's pencil lead, like that stuff the Chinese put in babies' milk. It only killed nine babies, but it never killed me, so you should be fine.

"What's happening?" Matt whimpered.

"But if it's *really* my cat's ashes like you say, and if this whole place isn't some scam, you'll be more than fine. You might even live through this."

"Do it," I said, glancing at the windows again, eager to go.

The vet gave Mad a long, sorrowful look, then upended the urn onto his tongue. He gave the swallowing part of it the ol' college try, but blew black dust from his nostrils like a dragon, rivers of snot flowing down his face. This enraged him, and he grabbed for Mad's neck, so I gave him the blackjack to the back of his head, and he went down like a bag of marbles. We all ran out the door.

Matt threw two large bags of expensive anti-hairball, surf-and-turf kibble into the back seat, then dove in on top of it. Mad took a minute with her hands on the dash, breathing deep to regain her composure as I started the Rabbit.

"Thank you for that," she said, and I tore out of there.

"I'm not entirely sure what just happened," I said, watching Matt in the back turning Zero's cage so he could sniff the new food. "Was he saying Zero had rabies? Or Mad had rabies. Do we have worms in our poop or his poop or something?"

"My dad was just trying to rattle us," she said.

"Oh, my god," I said. "Is that really your dad?"

"Don't let him get to you. He's always trying to scare me with stuff like that. Like when I was a kid, and a bat bit me in my sleep, and he said something infected my eyes, maybe my brain. It's hard to remember. Because something of his was always biting me in my sleep."

"That sounds serious," Matt said, moving to the seat behind me.

"In our household, we would wait for rabies results as much as a normal family waited for the morning paper," she said.

"Shit's getting weird," I said. "What meds did he say you're on?"

"Don't worry about it. Hey, what has two thumbs and no rabies?" Mad asked us. "This cat!" she said, and nobody laughed. "No, seriously, that fuckin' cat back there has thumbs. Have you noticed that yet?"

"Cats don't have thumbs," I said unconvincingly. "But sharks do."

Mad untucked her shirt and let the prescription bottles tumble out into her lap.

"Whoa!"

She ignored me, counting everything she'd stolen from the veterinarian clinic's shelves, and I pulled off my glasses to scratch a maddening itch swelling in my tear ducts. The streetlights overwhelmed my vision, and I wondered if the flashes were from my newly diagnosed parasites or just an unseasonal dusting of snow falling from the southern sky.

Pills rattled to my right as she piled them in her hand. I had no idea what medication she'd swiped during her heist, or what effect cat drugs had on a person. But she swallowed half a bottle, and I prayed they wouldn't cure the insanity her father and I saw in her eyes.

***

I was cruising pretty slow, so I wasn't as surprised as they were when the Cougar roared by us again, followed closely by the Bronco. Then the Eagle and the Viper, finally in the correct order that you'd witness such a pursuit in the animal kingdom. And even though it should have been more alarming to get passed by the same cars twice, I was more disturbed that the Cowboys-and-Indians movie I'd predicted hadn't panned out. No Jeeps at all. Cherokees or Wranglers. All animals now, respawning and trading positions to escort us to wherever we finally ended up.

I saw some headlights in my rearview mirror that were winking at me. It was too dark to identify a make or model since there were no streetlights on this section of interstate. So I slowed down until it was right on our ass. Finally, it honked. Yeah, definitely an Impala, but you wouldn't have known unless you heard its pitiful squawk. A true prey animal. But how were these cars breeding? In any case, Volkswagen Rabbits must be the eunuchs of the road, because we were riding in the only one. I remembered a weird line from *Jurassic Park*, back when I screwed up the volume in that theater to impress a girl, ruining the moment for everyone except myself.

"Love . . . finds a way."

"Wait, where's that little gold camera!" I shouted. "I need to check something."

"I can save you some time," Matt laughed, pretending to unzip his pants, and Mad tossed the toy into my lap.

"Don't look at porn while you drive," she said, and I limited my clicks to three nudes.

"You know where this novelty gag camera came from?"

"Yeah, your bum stash. You already told me."

"No. I mean, yeah, it did. But first, that bum must have stolen it from my neighbors."

"How do you know this?" she asked. "And so what?"

"I know this because they were gay. And that shit's rare in Kentucky."

"I highly doubt that."

"I don't get it," Matt said, but I was lost in thought, suddenly convinced that the stash of stolen mail and knickknacks that our squatter had accumulated in the basement right under our noses might contain something important to help crack the case wide open.

"Find the bum stash," I told them. "Go through it." I pulled the mailer from the pile and tore the top with my teeth, upending and shaking the contents all over the car. I saw more of our mail, as well as our gay neighbors' mail, scattered everywhere around us, and I thought about the police that were no doubt crawling all over my apartment at that very moment, combing through our shit, not finding the big, important clue because some crazy bum had swiped everybody's stuff for months. It was pretty funny actually.

"All three of you, get busy!" Zero had little interest in the case, or his new kibble.

But there had to be something in there. I looked at the junk Mad was smearing across her legs. Most envelopes were already gutted of their contents, and others were stuffed with postcards, 7-Eleven receipts, earring backs, peanut shells . . .

Wait, the return address label on one of the envelopes was marked "Mississippi." Mississippi what?

Lovelock, Mississippi.

"Are you seeing this, too?" Mad asked me, holding up the envelope like it was the Golden Ticket. She knew a ridiculous name like that couldn't be a coincidence.

Is that where they make all the locks? I wondered.

"This is important!" I said, jamming at the "Lovelock" sticker with my finger.

"Ow, get off me," Mad said. "Ya think?"

"Isn't Lovelock in Nevada?" Matt asked us. "There's definitely one in Nevada."

"Shut up, Dr. Fuck. How do you know?"

"Because the town is also called 'The Heart of Nevada.'"

"Oh."

"Now say you're sorry."

"Nope."

"There's also a prison there."

"Oh?" I said all casual, but I almost hit the brakes with both feet.

"Yes. Pershing County Lovelock Corrections Center, where the prisoners make little padlocks for pennies in prison credit. Just ask my uncle."

"Holy shit."

"Sounds too good to be true," Mad said.

"I can prove it. Been there lots of times. Some cool little shops. You got Nanny Joe's Vintage Bookstore, some 'precious gems' joint—but it's spelled 'p.r.e.s.i.o.u.s.' on the sign, which has *gotta* be the textbook definition of 'precious'—and, what else, shantytowns and Gypsies everywhere near the highway, and a boatload of padlocks clipped on everything. Oh, yeah, and it's called 'Home of the Mustangs' but that probably doesn't mean anything."

I shook my head, suddenly convinced I'd been there before, or heard of it at least. It was just all too perfect. I tried to slow my frantic heartbeat as Matt went on.

"Go there any time of day and park along US 95 and you'll see all the padlocks stuck to everything that's standing. And there's always a mess of kids trying to pick the locks with random keys. Kids collect them. Which makes about as much sense as everyone sticking them on everything, I guess . . . "

"We did that in Paris," I said dreamily, even though I'd already told them that story. I was lost deep in my worm-ridden memory banks, a couple weeks before Angie's murder, when I'd gotten up early enough to walk with her to school, and a mentally ill woman at the bus stop yelled at me to "Go to jail!" Later, I had to walk past this crazy bitch three more times—with her glaring every step of the way—since I forgot my driver's license at the house and we needed my I.D. to get me on Angie's school's insurance. We laughed about this encounter later, wondering if me walking by her over and over is exactly the kind of thing a crazy lady tries desperately to tell people is happening but nobody believes her. "Why aren't you in jail yet, Dave? Do not pass 'Go.' Do not collect $200," Angie giggled, then she felt bad about it. She was also convinced the crazy lady had screamed, "Go to Hell!" but we couldn't stop talking about what a fascinating command "Go to jail!" was, and how it was missing so many steps. Now I was wondering if the crazy lady had recognized Angie on her way to work the morning she disappeared, then dismissed any and all implications just as quickly.

Parasites be damned, the memory of all these other towns and other jails and crazy ladies was kicking in strong. I found myself wandering places where Angie predicted new private prisons would be popping up, a flood of cheap labor nationwide to make all kinds of worthless souvenirs. She'd written about all these things, I was sure of it. I was convinced they were breaking ground on a new private prison in Lovelock, whichever Lovelock that was. How many little bitty love locks were locking up nothing all throughout the United States of America? Had to be billions. I sped up.

Fuck Florida. We're going to Mississippi.

But we were already in Mississippi. So maybe we'd circle back, after we shook down Otto and verified once and for all if an irregular heartbeat ruined his alibi, and whose irregular heartbeat that was. Mine had finally slowed.

I buttoned up my duck coat against the cold, wondering if Florida would be frozen solid when we got there, which made about as much sense as the surprise ice rink Dante dropped into the First Circle of Hell. Mad let Zero out of his cage, scratching his round ears a bit, and he climbed onto my headrest to lick my neck. Something he hadn't done for miles.

"Have you ever heard him meow?" she asked me.

"What would that even prove?" I snapped, watching him slinking behind my head in the rearview mirror, morphing from raccoon to cat, to badger and bat, then to jackal and all the way back again. He nuzzled harder. I knew that jackals made sounds more human than anything. I never needed to hear that sound to know it was true.

I was used to my ears burning when people talked shit about me, but not so much when a mystery animal nibbled on them. Itching eyes were also fairly new, and I rubbed them until fireworks clouded my vision. I didn't stop until all of the animals in my car were whatever I wanted.

XIX

THE EAR EATER OF JASPER COUNTY

THEY JOKED ABOUT gas-station chicken for dinner again, until I explained that not only was I *not* averse to eating birds every day (even if it's from the same place you bought rubbers and motor oil), but I was becoming quite the gas-station grub connoisseur on our road trip. So when the Kum & Go sign boasted the "Best Fried Chicken in Nine Counties," I probably would have checked it out anyway, even if I hadn't been trying to break up the increasing "everyone is a third wheel" dynamic of our crew and find something fun for us to all do together. We might have been able to make Florida by dusk, but the prospect of this famous chicken, combined with the fact that the flashing light box out in front was also announcing a "Big Foot Problem!" at an "Important Town MEATing 2night!" basically sealed the deal.

"Did you see that?" Mad asked, pointing back toward the road. Matt and I read the sign, then read it again out loud to make sure. Matt shook his head, but smiled until she shot one back. They were getting real cozy since the vet's office. Parasites all like little Cupids 'n' shit.

"You know, sometimes it's tough to get motivated in the summer down South, even to leave your house," Matt said.

"Until you hear about a local town meeting regarding the . . . *Bigfoot Problem*. I know what we're doing for dinner."

"Is this for real?" she asked him. "How do we know we haven't missed it?"

"Well, that's a real, live sign in front of a county store in Jasper County, Mississippi," Matt said. "And last time I checked, 'tonight' still meant tonight."

"Fuck it," I sighed. "Mississippi is obviously desperate to keep me around a little longer. And 'tonight' just means 'dark' around these parts, right?"

"Are we serious?" Mad asked us both. "Don't say 'dead serious'."

"Deadly serious," Matt said.

"Actually that's a very good question," I said to her, trying to side with Mad and score some points. Only I would be dumb enough to sorta/kinda kidnap two strangers to emulate my own failed relationship, and then keep trying to get the girl to like me a little more than him. "How do we *really* know what time a Bigfoot meeting is? That could mean 'every night.'"

"You know, I've heard about these meetings," Matt cautioned us. "They're no joke. And, yeah, this meeting will be going from when it gets dark, to when it gets light. So, yes, 'tonight' means 'tonight.' Sorry, '*two* night.'"

"Stop saying 'tonight'! Jesus Christ," Mad said. Then, "Okay, so we go in early and scope it out, grab some chickens."

I nodded in agreement, now kind of skeptical of the whole thing as I scanned the horizon and calculated only another fifteen minutes until sunset.

"Well, if we're gonna do it, we gotta do it now," I said. "I don't want to crash through the door late at the Bigfoot Party and get shotgunned by some hick." I looked up and down the road, then up into the trees. "So, is there really a *problem* around here? You guys are the locals."

"Locals? Do you remember where I'm from?" Mad laughed, then in her thickest Southern accent, "Bigfoots be like god-danged roaches!"

"Yeah, get out of my garbage cans, ya damn Bigfeets!" Matt shouted. "But, no, seriously, I took a class on this stuff in college. Cryptozoology 101. I learned a lot about Bigfeet, Littlefeets, all the feets. And this knowledge has never been tested. It was almost my major!"

Of course it was.

"Let's do it. But leave Dave's cat in the car."

"Oh, now it's a cat again?" Matt said. "Hey, we need new food for that thing . . . "

"Shush," I told them. We'd been through a handful of states together now, and they still didn't care about where we were going. I was balancing between "sick of them" and "used to them." Today, my eyes and my ears still hurt, so I was leaning back towards "sick."

I opened the door, and the alarming jangle of chimes signaled our arrival.

Inside was like any other gas station slash convenience store, except for the conspicuous rows of heavily armed, camouflaged dudes taping up huge topographical maps and Polaroid pictures onto the foggy glass doors of the beer coolers. A dozen bloodshot eyeballs and cataracts rolled our way, beards working around chewing tobacco and toothpicks. Some guys even had the luxurious toothpicks: thick, colorful, carved like tiny bedposts. They also had a fuck ton of rifles; even thicker, more colorful, and molded like the Terminator's cock. All their guns nervously switched shoulders as they looked us over. One of them might have been slinging a guitar.

"Hi, guys!" Mad said, cheerfully. Then she whispered to us, "I always wanted to go to a town meeting. It's the closest you'll get to living in the world of the *Gilmore Girls*. Redneck reboot, of course."

"Yeah, more like the *Gary Gilmore's Girls*," I whispered back, nodding at the guns.

"I don't get it."

"Me neither."

"He didn't have any daughters."

"That shit was gold."

"Quiet!"

We crept through the intense, hickory-flavored gauntlet of men and found a spot near the snack cakes and overripe fruit baskets and tried to pretend we belonged. I worked on my best "Here to deal with my Bigfoot problem" face, while Matt went off to scrounge some peanuts. They seemed to have forgotten our original intent, and I still craved that chicken, though my appetite was quickly fading. Then I had a terrible thought.

"I had a terrible thought."

"What's that?" Mad asked.

"What if it's a trap."

"A Bigfoot trap! Even better. A big *foot* trap would probably have huge shoes in it."

"No, like maybe this whole thing is to sucker tourists and casuals, like ourselves."

"You kidnapped us, Dave, so we're more like the shady 'locals' in this situation, but, okay, I gotcha," Mad said. "Maybe a bunch of Bigfoots are gonna be at this meeting undercover, wearing trench coats?" She patted my shoulder and didn't wait for an answer. "Don't worry, tough guy. Like you keep pointing out, I'm more of a Southerner than you. I'll protect ya."

"Bigfeet in the house!" Matt shouted as he came back, tearing into a bag of honey-roasted nuts with his teeth.

"Chill out, geez," Mad said, noticing the side-eye from some more hunter types still shoving their way through the doors, overworked chimes clanking more warnings against the glass. "We can't be like obvious rubberneckers in here. We have to act like we have a legitimate Bigfoot issue to deal with. Like, Dave, what was that story you told me? Like don't you have a smashed picnic basket or something weird in your trunk? We could totally say one stepped on our picnic."

"Why would I keep smashed picnics in my trunk?" I asked her, suddenly thinking about the frozen coyote in my father-in-law's trunk, and then remembering the weirdest thing of them all in my own seat, Zero, possibly getting stomped on by a mythical woodland creature. This terrible thought helped me get into character, imagining living in the forest and keeping my litter of cat things safe, and now the Bigfoot situation was suddenly serious. I was getting better at thinking in the hypothetical, so I started getting legitimately angry at these Bigfeets and ready to take up arms against Big Government. Lee Strasberg would have called this "the method." The Rosenbergs would have called this "treason." But I was having fun for once, remembering how mad my wife would get because I never wanted to go anywhere. If she would have organized more fun trips to backwoods gas-station meet-and-greets I would have been fuckin' *in*. Just look at me now, babe.

"Hey!" someone yelled, and everybody turned again, and in walked a goddamn Bigfoot. Well, almost. But I swear even the chimes were spooked silent by the presence of this guy, a mammoth, hairy specimen in a black hunting vest and a hunter green flannel underneath. He stopped near a bubblegum machine and palmed it like a basketball, pointing at us with the handle end of his axe.

"You," he said.

"Me?" I tried that old technique of pointing at myself with my thumb and looking around all confused, as if this has ever in the history of the world, or movies, worked at getting someone off the hook. It was his vest that was throwing me off. Most of the men had camouflage, sure, but also mixed with some other bright color to avoid being a target. But he was all blacks and greens and dark eyes under this black leather baseball cap, and if anyone was actually a Bigfoot in disguise, it was this shadow monster staring into my soul.

"Yeah. You. You drive a Volkswagen Rabbit, buddy?"

. . . *because I just ate it,* I thought, finishing his sentence in my head.

"Yes, sir, I do," I said.

"Well, you left your dog in the car. And that's goddamn animal cruelty. So I smashed your window to give it some air. You're welcome."

The colossal axe man saw someone he knew over by the microwave and strode over for some monster high-fives. This giant moved faster than I would have thought possible, especially down here on our end of the beanstalk where Godzillas and such seemed to exist only in slow-motion. Two smaller hunters leaned on the bubblegum dome in his place, breath fogging the glass where his handprint still lingered.

"I don't have a dog . . . who smashed my—what happened?" I stammered, heading for the door to see what happened. "It's the dead of winter, you fucking rube," I muttered below my breath as I headed out. Matt was still looking for chicken, and Mad was distracted by some handwritten Missing Children posters, so they didn't notice me bailing to check out this unwarranted hole in my car. I felt my blood pressure spiking from their indifference, but I comforted myself with the knowledge that the police could pull the entire town's fingerprints from the bubblegum machine if I didn't survive this shit.

***

Even though Zero was not remotely similar to a dog, and more like something who was pretending to be a cat pretending to be a . . . what now? Are Tasmanian chinchillas a thing? Anyhow, I didn't want him to choose that moment to bolt. Even though he had a name which would make you think he was tailor-made for low temperatures like a freakish Southern cold snap, I didn't want to risk it, and headed for my Rabbit to grab his cage and bring him inside. I saw my car and realized the man mountain wasn't kidding. Glass crystals from the busted window were mixed with a light dusting of snow across my driver's seat. I opened the door and brushed it all out onto the stones, and I was tempted to leave Mad and Matt at the store, just drive off right then and there. The meeting hadn't even started yet, and I'd known them for less than a hundred hours, and now my car was getting fucked up. The hassle was taking the wind out of my sails, I had to admit.

But there was no way I was going to miss a motherfuckin' Bigfoot meeting. And maybe if I hung around long enough, maybe I'd get up the courage to confront the Axe Man about the smashed window "favor," a dramatic face-off with the kind of monster who gripped an axe at the bladed end, but probably still had no trouble chopping down a tree with it, or me.

This shit would impress ol' Maddie Magdalene, even if the rumors were true about Matt having two penises. Top that, Captain Double-Dick!

No, that was definitely a rumor. Car banter would have unmasked that man's pants by now. Maybe we'll try playing Truth or Dare later, though science says any confession in a car is 36% bullshit.

I looked up and down the parking lot, marveling at how fast the Rams and Broncos had multiplied. "Ramchargers"? Horses with horns? Even Zero would laugh at that one. And everything out there was four-wheel-drive, even shit with two wheels. "NRA" stickers on about half of them, too. Union Jacks on the other half, which was weird, it still being the United States and all.

Oh, wait, no, those are Confederate flags! Flying on so many cars you'd think they were delivery boys for Confederate Flag Pizza. One Union Jack by mistake, though. Ha ha, dumb ass!

Back when I was teaching in Kentucky, I wore a Union Jack to work once, and I got fired for it. True story. Not because they thought it was a Confederate flag, but because they thought it was pro-union. Actually, maybe it was a Sex Pistols T-shirt.

Then I saw there were at least three Jeep Cherokees with tinted windows.

I laughed to myself, wondering if Greg was somewhere in there, buried in camo. Moustache, mirrored sunglasses, ball cap . . . he'd blend in as easily as a leopard in Mrs. Robinson's closet. He was a trip, that guy. I remembered the rest of the story Angie told me about Greg selling her old Jeep Cherokee on Craigslist after he repo'd it from her, and how he'd gotten into an endless conversation with someone named "Harry" who'd seen this Jeep but was offering 1,500 bucks to buy a *different* Jeep on his same street. Greg counted five Jeeps on their block alone that night (Jeeps were big in Minnesota), so he explained to Steve that he had no idea if his neighbors were selling their vehicles, and the next email offered 2,800 for a Jeep that was "two Jeeps down from your Jeep." Greg finally went out to count Jeeps instead of sheeps that night, but then thought more about it and decided that price was insane for the Jeep two Jeeps down, and began to haggle prices with the guy just for the hell of it. This went on for days, with no end in sight. It was like a bird getting into a fight with its reflection. Angie joked that Greg and Craigslist sounded like a match made in heaven. "Should change the name to *Gregs*list," she cracked. But I always thought the moral of that story was he never gave up, even when it was stupid shit like that. I wondered how he'd blossom in a real crisis, like the death of his daughter.

When I got back inside, the Mississippi Militia Men were all standing at attention in a half-circle and getting ready for something serious. And on the imaginary stage in the center of this human amphitheater was a beet-faced, well-dressed man in crisp, unsullied hunting gear posted up at the doors of the beer cooler, occasionally running his palms along the maps to smooth them out. He looked even more out of place than us, and the group was clocking him skeptically as he snapped his fingers and cleared his throat to get everyone's attention.

"Thank you, folks, for coming. My name is Henry Honeysuckle, founder of the B.F.G., Bigfoots and Phantasmagorics Gigantology . . ."

"This is amazing!" someone snarfed. It was Matt, wiping

milk from his nose and putting the carton back in the cooler. I walked over near him in case I needed a human shield, setting Zero's cage at our feet.

"'Phantasmagoric' doesn't start with an 'F'," someone near us corrected him, and I was impressed.

Don't let the Union Jacks fool ya!

" . . . and this is our first time in Jasper County," our host went on, undeterred. "We heard about your meeting, and we were hoping you wouldn't mind if we shot some footage for our new limited series, *MANSTERS: Half Man, Half Monster, All Terror*. Could I have a show of hands for anyone who has seen one, heard one, or found droppings of any, uh, 'mansters' 'round here?"

Mansters, I chortled to myself as dozens of arms shot up, half of them high-powered rifles. Henry Honeysuckle took a thick pen from behind a purple, fleshy ear that looked more like a foot, and he tapped the map with it.

"Oh, no," Mad groaned, moving close. "This is one of those stupid reality shows."

"Great!" Henry grinned. "Now, speaking on behalf of the B.F.G., we have discovered through our research that many of these creatures have been sighted along the Mississippi River. So we have reason to believe that this river is being used as a 'highway' by the animals, sort of a 'migration route' of North to South, if you will, 'depending' on the season, or their 'appetite' . . . "

His fingers highlighted random words with air quotes as he traced a path on the map.

" . . . so maybe you men can show me where the majority of your sightings have occurred."

A wide, squat hunter in digital camo from ball cap to boots stepped up, snatching the pen from the host's hand. And before I could make a tired joke about not being able to see the guy—and right about when Matt was processing what Mad said about a reality show—Camo Man jacked Henry Honeysuckle right in the honeysucker with a wild right hook, sending him headfirst through a spinner rack of beef jerky and bright green tortilla chips.

Holy guacamole. We all got low. Zero sniffed the air.

The rack was still spinning, and Henry was still recovering, when the Axe Man, still gripping the blade of his weapon ass-backwards, stomped up next to Camo Man and held the handle under his chin like a microphone. And effectively took over the meeting. He hawked his sinuses clear for what seemed like ten minutes as his eyes scanned the crowd, and I stared at the gleaming axe blade balanced against his seven-point-buck belt buckle, wondering if he held phones upside down all his life, too. Probably no one dared to correct him. Then two men wearing a more reasonable amount of camouflage took a limp Henry Honeysuckle by his arms, kicked the jerky rack out of their way, and dragged him out the door. A wormy little guy in chunky glasses holding a GoPro that no one had noticed until then—presumably a member of the television crew—slunk out after him.

Now that musta been some real camouflage.

"I think someone misunderstood our ad," one of the hunters laughed, slapping the bubblegum machine like his favorite rump roast. Near the register was a bulletin board labeled "Wall of Fame," and I thought of Mad's "Wall of Shame," and threw a thumb at it to make sure she saw it, too. The board was full of photographs, one featuring a mob of hunters gathered around a human shape at their feet. They weren't in the woods, however, but instead smack dab in this very same aisle, the distinct rainbow of candy selections on either side of them.

"Are we gonna hash this out or what?" another one of them wanted to know.

"Lock the door," Axe Man finally said, and I pulled my rat cage a little closer, making myself a little smaller, wishing I could crawl inside with Zero. Zero had lost interest after the punch and was now sleeping like it was his third Bigfoot meeting of the day.

"*Now* it's a reality show," Matt said, eyes expectant, not as nervous as he should be.

"Yeah, this is way better than I coulda hoped," Mad giggled, and I held out my arms and backed us all up against the dessert cooler. Still starving, I looked around for anything chicken-related. Behind the glass under my elbows was a row of evil-looking blackberry snack cakes and a handwritten sign that read, "Edgar Allan Pies." And I could have sworn I felt their chilly, black hearts beating against my spine as the real ruckus started.

***

It took us a minute to figure out what the big argument was about, but eventually we realized these guys were real upset about something and, mercifully, it wasn't us.

"It will not stand, boys!" Axe Man said, giving up his bladed, makeshift mic and letting his namesake clang hard onto the tile floor. A smaller guy in fishing waders stepped up, holding a rawhide chew toy as his own microphone, and the crowd backed up to give him more room to speak. I was convinced this new MC would be handing out dog toys if anyone needed to speak, and I was reminded of the wrinkly, seashell-looking "Fleshlight" they'd passed around in a *Lord of the Fries* porn parody I'd had to caption once.

"I got some pictures to show y'all," MC Chew Toy said as he hitched the suspenders on his comically large rubber pants. He dug deep in both pockets, and I patted my own duck pocket in return, comforted in the feel of my brass knuckles at the ready. But he only fished out another photograph instead of a weapon.

"Robert Loon? Bobby Looooooon!" MC Chew Toy called out, head on a swivel. "Are you here tonight? Why don't you tell us what's going on in this picture, Bobby?"

All three of us glanced at each other, then squinted at the picture, even stepping forward to get a better look. It seemed to show a huge, horned, six-limbed shape lying across a tree stump, hooves high in the air. It resembled a centaur, but with a sheep's body and the scaly torso of a man. One of the horns was cracked at the base, and easily half of the poor beast's face was blown away. A tiny hunter was leaning on his rifle about ten feet behind the damned thing.

"Why, yes, I am," a shaky voice said from middle of the crowd. "And I'll tell ya all about it, men. I was driving down County Road 528144 after work, when, all the sudden, something huge comes up out of the thickets, and it covered both lanes in about three steps. Then it head-butted my car, smashing the grill and sending us both screeching into the ditch. I jumped out, and while it was gnawing my hood ornament like some Big League Chew, I pulled out my scattergun and blew its cursed head off."

"I've heard of this thing," Matt said to us, yanking me back into the dessert cooler, excited to be finally putting his college book learnin' to work. "You know what he's talking about? That has gotta be the famous 'Randy Ram Man of Chesapeake Bay!' But it lives on the East Coast. So, the question is, what's it doing here . . . "

"Quite a story there, Robert," the MC nodded. "But maybe you can tell us why you look to be sitting about five clicks behind this critter when you had the picture taken?"

"Uh, well, I . . . "

"We'll come back to that!" MC said, pulling another picture from his bottomless rubber pocket. "How about Bobby Yupper? Where's the Yoop at tonight?"

"Right here, boss," said the Yoop, holding up a finger.

"He looks like a 'yoop'," Mad said. I agreed, but I couldn't explain why.

"Can you tell us what's happening in this shot?" MC asked, fanning a Polaroid back and forth like he was trying to coax out an image. When it stopped flapping in his hand, we squinted again but could barely discern another hazy behemoth, this monstrous, low-backed reptilian form, but with a man's fleshy arms, and something resembling a humanoid face? Again, a good deal of the visage had been removed with the indelicate assistance of a firearm.

"Fine," the Yoop said wearily. "Well, lemme see. We were camping down by Arkabutla Lake, and suddenly we think we're in a hailstorm, until I start getting a whiff of it. Turned out something is throwing feces at our tent. Now this shit ain't normal size shit, as you can probably figure out by that picture. So I come running out, and here's like this gator, but more like a man-gator, rearing back and hissing, tryin' to get me. So I grab my peppergun and sent its face straight to Hell."

"You sure did, Yoop!" someone agreed.

"Holy shit," Matt said, pinching my bicep hard. "You know what I think that man bagged? That was none other than Mini-Minnehaha, the Microsaurus of McIntosh County! I wrote two papers on that thing. Got a C+ because the teacher was jealous of my—"

"Shut the fuck up," Mad hissed.

"What in the wide, *Wide World of Sports* is a 'Microsaurus'?" I asked him, pulling my arm free.

"Most people took it for an alligator gar," Matt said, authoritative and defiant. "Or maybe they mistook an alligator gar for *it*. In Georgia, there's been gar sightings for years, some almost 20 feet in length, elongated necks, razor-sharp teeth, long, prehensile tails . . . but this thing? It's, like, half dude."

"So did these assholes kill half a dude? Isn't that like half murder?"

"Nutty, ain't it?"

"Are you kids paying attention?" MC asked us, voice booming and taking too many steps toward our sanctuary near Dessert Corner for my comfort. I held up a hand and nodded real fast like, "Yep, we sure are!"

"Keep it down, you guys. We're here to learn," Mad reminded us both, and Matt made a motion like he was locking up his lips and throwing away the key. Bold move, all things considered.

"Good. Now, Bobby, how big would you say this creature was?"

"As you can plainly see in my picture, about the size and color of a John Deere 8000."

"If this bugbear was truly the size of a John Deere, Bobby, then why does your boot look to be as almost as large as a goddamn tractor tire?"

He held the picture over his head, and now we could see the hunter far back behind the creature, pulling the same stunt as the guy in the first photo, but also with one leg absent-mindedly extended to bring his shoe up toward the monster's ruined face.

"I will not answer without a lawyer present." The Yoop picked his teeth in protest. I heard a gun cock.

"Well, I *do* have an answer, Bobby," MC said, getting angrier. "And I'll get to it in a minute . . . " He pulled out another photograph. " . . . now how about Robbie Scruton? Scrute? You gracing us with your presence tonight? Describe your scene, goddamn it."

This picture showed three men, arms crossed and proud, and a huge serpentine mass hanging from a construction crane in the foreground. As a mask, this phantom snake seemed to be sporting what was left of a man's horrified expression over its own, torn free from the skull but remarkably intact.

"Okay, so I come around the corner of the garage, and this snake thing was bent down, see, choking and eating what had to be a dog."

"You're not sure it was a dog?"

"We got lots of dogs. Might be missing one. Who can say?"

"No, I mean, was this thing big enough to eat a dog?"

"Oh, yeah, much bigger. Scaly tail was twice as thick as a Mastiff's ribcage."

"Uh huh. Well, if this tail was larger than an entire mid-size dog, then why is the tail draped across your feet here and looking to me to be about as skinny as a garter snake?"

"Why don't you tell us!" someone shouted in the back,

and there was a murmur of surprise, and a charge moved through the crowd.

"Yeah, what are you trying to say?" another hunter shouted, aligning themselves with Robbie as the agitation grew. Meanwhile, Matt was whispering some shit in my ear about that picture being the first definitive proof of a half-man, half-serpent formerly of Kansas City, Kansas, and partial to quarries, sinkholes, and blasted-out basements stuck mid-renovation.

"Volcano Vince" was its name, he said. Shoulda been "Crater Craig."

Mad shushed him with a flick to the nose. We were much more interested in hearing what MC Chew Toy was getting at and how violent this thing might get. We were witnessing a genuine hometown scandal, and the entire town was armed.

"Now, I know there's stiff competition this year for the trophy," MC said.

Trophy?!

"But an issue has been cropping up over the years that we can't ignore any longer. To put it simply, your feet have betrayed you, boys. And this supposed pictorial proof you have been submitting has clued our judges in to some serious chicanery."

A more threatening undertone rolled through the crowd as MC indulged in a dramatic pause. Some men looked down at the floor, but many ratcheted their weapons, and I visually mapped out two exits and five potential hiding places. But when MC Chew Toy spoke again, the show would be over:

"That's right, soldiers. We are dealing with the forced perspective."

The gas station exploded.

***

When the shouting died down somewhat, and the dust from the ceiling tiles stopped raining down from the bullet holes, we finally understood that this was not a *big* foot meeting after all, but a big*foot* meeting. Just like the sign advertised.

The men had called this gathering to address the rise in forced-perspective photographs being turned in during hunting competitions, and everyone was clearly very upset about this revelation.

The voices were ramping up again, and some of the men were reloading. Mad lashed out at me again to be quiet, actually baring her teeth like a chimp, even though I'd said nothing.

"You keep hissing like that, you're gonna end up dead in a picture. Next to a giant foot," I warned her, and got a quick scratch down my neck in return. I didn't tell her it felt great.

"That is a serious accusation!" a man shouted at MC as he worked the stock of his rifle with both hands like those painful snake bites my brother inflicted on my forearms, something I lovingly passed down to every steering wheel I've ever known to keep his legacy alive. Family!

"You're right, Bob, it is," MC said, stepping forward.

"Is everyone named 'Bob'?" Matt asked, then left the relative safety of the dessert cooler to walk directly into the agitated rabble, palms open and out to them, like Jesus if he was stupid.

"Excuse me, friends," Matt said. "But what about the monsters?"

"What *about* the monsters?" Bob said.

"Your pictures," Matt said, frowning. "I mean, regardless of the photo mischief, so many impossible beasties have been massacred by you men. This seems infinitely more important than cheating."

I would have been more surprised at the ease at which Matt entered the fray. But I'd seen a picture of him posing in front of a tiny purple Eiffel Tower, so I knew he was no stranger to forced perspective shenanigans, and was probably part of the proud history of intimidating upward angles and manipulation on album covers, come to think of it.

"What's your point, boy?"

"My point is that you people have proven the existence of

a half dozen or more creatures that were previously thought to exist only in folklore."

"But the evidence was falsified!" MC said, slapping Matt across the cheek with a Polaroid depicting the murder of yet another fuzzy or fanged oddity.

"I understand that, sir, but that is still a picture of a . . . "

"Doesn't matter," MC said with another slap. "They're too small, and they don't count."

Matt rubbed his face, then sighed. "Oh my fucking god. Never mind."

"Your uncles are cool," I teased Matt when he looked to us for help, and Mad hit me with another, "Shhh!" I leaned over to plot our escape route and see what her deal was, and I was surprised to watch her polish off a Yalobusha Milk Stout and crush the can in her small hand. I'd thought Mad was "shushing" me this whole time, but her hisses had been the sound of all the tops she'd been popping. She was three beers down on the six-pack Matt had smuggled into our corner, so I sat down and slammed two as fast as possible, if only to display my manliness, and also so there'd be no evidence of beer we'd have to pay for. Then I noticed other half-crushed cans in the pile displaying long decals of animal scratches down their sides, and another advertising something else "Monster" related. I hoped the ol' Mad Badger wasn't mixing alcohol and toxic power drinks. She was crazy enough with her fuckin' worms. "Testify!" the labels on one of her beer cans shouted, and I gave up trying to catch her. I was a lightweight when it came to drinking, so I was half in the bag already, and it felt like rocket fuel in my belly. I decided to start cracking my knuckles instead of jokes and was ready to mix it up.

"What's your name, son?" MC asked Matt, hand poised in mid-slap. Axe Man stood behind Matt, looking down at him, caterpillar eyebrow arched.

"Uh . . . Bobert?" Matt said, looking back at us again, hand on his face and shrugging. "The . . . Gargantua slayer?"

"Do say? Well, why don't you have your friends come up

here and join us. And maybe this one can show us what an incredible creature he's got in that cage of his."

Oh no . . .

The shredded bill of Axe Man's cap angled toward me.

"You!" MC shouted, pointing with the Axe Man at Mad, myself, and Zero, huddled on the floor. I slowly slid Zero's cage protectively behind my back.

"Yeah, what did you bring in here for us?" Axe Man grunted.

"Yes, I am here for the trophy!" I proclaimed, and I stood up before I could think of anything better. This did give the hunters pause, and Matt strode over to us to back up my story. He confidently yanked the cage from my grip and held Zero up high. Mad started humming "Circle of Life" and I punched her in the shoulder.

"Gentlemen," Matt said. "Behold! We have captured Balabushka, the Russian Were-Beaver of the Bering Strait! The animal before you has traveled many miles, across that ancient bridge between Russia and Alaska! The very same bridge that brought us all to this land!"

"That shit doesn't connect," Axe Man said.

"True," I said, standing next to Matt and trying to sound spooky. "It doesn't anymore. Ever wonder why?"

Zero peered down from his cage, claws clicking, nervous tongue flicking needle teeth.

"That's a goddamn possum," MC said.

"Were-Beaver, my ass," Axe Man agreed.

"Where beaver? There beaver!" a hunter said, and a bunch of them laughed.

"You want to hear the story or not?" I asked them, and they did. These meetings must have been the highlight of their week, and they loved a good story. So I was fucked.

"Okay," I said, rubbing my hands, eager to emulate what I'd been hearing from them. "So, picture it. Me walking home from a party one night, and here comes this, this *thing* running down the railroad tracks toward me, making train noises . . . "

"Bullshit!" a couple hunters said, moving in closer. "That was a train."

"Or a harmonica!" another one added.

" . . . and, yes, you are correct, this thing actually turned out to be a train! But when I got even closer, I found this here whatever it is, crouched over another, larger animal. And I think it was eating its ears?"

I was trying hard to assimilate. I thought I'd pegged the genre, but I was having trouble disguising the doubt in my voice. But it didn't matter, because at the words "eating" and "ears," the men stopped advancing on us and re-shouldered their guns to share a worried glance. The far end of the mob parted, revealing a "Hall of Fame" poster board of photographs we hadn't seen yet. Scrawled on the photos were words like "Pigzilla" and "Hogzilla" and "Big Fucking Swine!" And all of these pictures portrayed barely-larger-than-normal wild boars in the foreground, with groups of hunters, arms crossed and defiant, waaay off in the background. But, of course, the hunters had their dumb legs thrust out in front of their bodies so that the supposed photographic evidence of school-bus-sized porkers inadvertently proved the existence of Peterbilt-sized work boots instead. But once I got past more of tonight's "double exposures," (*proud of that one*), I noticed something else.

The ears were missing. On the pig monsters, I mean, not the men in the photos. And maybe it was the two beers talking, but this suddenly gave me an idea.

"So, are you missing some ears around these parts, gentlemen?"

"What do you know about ears?" Axe Man said, tipping up his weathered leather.

"I know a lot about ears," I said, waving Mad to start heading for the door, silently mouthing at her the universal mime of "start the car!"

"You better explain yourself, punk, and right now," MC said, and I was excited to discover this ear thing I'd stumbled on must have been a sore spot.

"Fine. I know where those ears went," I lied, my fists and toes curling in anticipation.

"Where?!" It seemed like they all wanted to know.

"We took 'em."

Then I turned to the nearest all-American hunter and threw a punch that would have made a Bigfoot proud, if Bigfeets valued that sorta thing. And there's no way to know for sure because, beside the one I was swinging at, monsters probably didn't exist.

***

We looked up the "Ear Eater" later on Matt's phone, and in the car we all talked about the mysterious monster that had terrorized Jasper County, Mississippi, back in the summer of 1977. Apparently, a series of livestock attacks still haunted this town, maybe not nearly as conspicuous a monstrosity as the handful of supernatural beasts they were routinely blasting, but serious enough to have been immortalized on the internet, and not just on the home page of Henry Honeysuckle's hit television show, *MANSTERS* (which, it should be noted, was just a curiously outdated website, very '90s, all spinning pentagrams and "creepy" autoplay music, but definitely an interesting cumulative effect).

The first reported encounter was by a man named Joseph Dickinson, who found one of his 50-pound hogs wandering around the pen one morning, healthy enough at first glance, but on closer inspection, missing both of its ears. No other extremity had been disturbed, and the hog was relatively unimpressed by its own mutilation, in spite of both ears having been completely severed with knives, scissors, or teeth so sharp they'd sheared them off without so much as a whisper of fur or any sign of jagged lacerations in or around the wounds. Not knowing what to think, Mr. Dickinson cleaned the hog's head best he could, checked the fence line for breaches, then went about his day. But when he corralled the rest of his livestock, he made an even more horrifying discovery: more missing meat from each of his seven cattle, exactly one ear apiece. Mr. Dickinson guessed the creature was developing a predilection and was possibly taste-testing the wooly antennas on his cows until it could find another sow.

The second report, and the first real sighting, came from a Robert Robertson, who owned a small farm about three miles down the road from Mr. Dickinson. The night after the first incident, Mr. Robertson heard his pigs squealing in alarm, and he ran out to find a dark shape hunched over one of his animals, pinning it to the ground while both beasts writhed and thrashed up a storm of dust and blood. But Mr. Robertson had the foresight to bring his biggest "fowling piece" up to the pens with him, freshly loaded with buckshot, and after discharging his weapon in the air, whatever had been molesting his swine's savory satellite dishes quickly thought better of it, and took off in a tornado of hateful screeches and filth. And it took the pig's left ear with it.

The third and final sighting (at least until the infamous Bigfoot Meeting of 2015 where we were in attendance), was documented by Mr. Calvin Martin, of Mary Martin's Dairy. He described finding one of his prized 300-pound sows missing its entire head. And when Mr. Martin came across this gruesome sight, he maintained he witnessed a "largish" shape vault his chest-high perimeter fence surrounding the pigpen and bolt off into the night. Dawn revealed canine-like tracks in the mud, and when a constable's deputy shot a small, feral dog seemingly hot on the trail of the creature, some townspeople hypothesized the attacks were the result of a pack of starving strays. But Mr. Martin swore to his grave that the creature in question was much larger than any mutt, larger than even a German Shepherd, he explained, which was the largest dog he knew of (and an animal he'd always adored in the World War II newsreels he collected). He affirmed to the press that this monster could "jump twice as high as anything on this Earth."

The head of Mr. Martin's 300-pound hog was never

recovered, and local law-enforcement wondered whether the decapitation was the result of the thing growing bolder (or stronger), or whether it was simply harder to remove the ears than the heads from larger, prize-winning specimens. But one thing was certain. It was working its way up the food chain.

All in all, the ill-famed Ear Eater of Jasper County attacked nine different farms in the summer of 1977, leaving only visible paw prints around each crime scene, and was never apprehended. Its whereabouts remained unknown.

Until tonight.

***

Back at the dessert cooler, my punch was the stuff of legends!

Record needle screeches. Pause button clicks. Freeze-frame on my knuckles. When I was a little boy, I had some trouble making a believable fist. Whenever I tried to intimidate the other kids, my thumb would stick out like a hitchhiker, or my fingernails would cut half moons into my sweaty life lines, or my weirdly long pinky would vanish as it cowered under my ring finger. I couldn't bear to look at it, but luckily it was the era of fingerless gloves. Then I graduated to my golden punch extensions, and it was like my fist had swelled in confidence under the suit of armor to fulfill its destiny. But tonight I didn't have time to go for the brass knuckles, and for once, my hand rolled up perfectly without any help, almost like my fingers had never existed, transforming my fist into something solid, like the round knobs of bone that replaced the brains on the coolest of the dinosaurs. And even though you'd think a bushy (but somehow braided) beard like the one draped over the chin of my target would have confused my rapidly approaching fist (like where did his jaw start and my punch begin?), it was like my hand was working with sonar now. I decided it was all the topographical maps on the walls, which had initially only illustrated Pangea, until I punched our planet in its stupid face and my fist sunk deep into every map and the world under them fractured to send the newly created continents pinwheeling to the four corners of the globe.

Ba-plooooooowsh!

I caught him firmly in that ring of bone from the temple to the jaw hinge, the circle that art teachers would typically start you with whenever you attempted to draw the perfect human face. But this face wasn't perfect for long, if it ever was, and my fist lost itself in his surprisingly manicured beard, stretching the five o'clock stubble of the surrounding cheek like the distorted fabric of spacetime surrounding a black hole. Now, I'm not the strongest man in the world, but my punch had something like math or good timing or three beers or a testosterone contact high on its side, and it launched MC Chew Toy a good ten feet in the air, his rawhide microphone trailing him, but failing to follow for long. He flew so high that I fully expected him to have transformed into Criss Angel and give us a "ta-da!" when he came back down. But he never did. His mouth was motorboating so hard from the impact of my fist that it created a kind of impossible momentum, the wind from his lips surrounding him in a vacuum of velocity, like one of those comically doomed, antediluvian flying machines, with some sort of mechanical hiccupping mechanism that no sane person would have wagered could ever get off the ground . . . but somehow ended up proudly airborne after all.

The MC's head took out the plastic arrow pointing to the ATM, then crashed through a closed-circuit camera, the umbilical of wires wrapping a noose around his neck. He came down camo hat first into the impulse buys near the register, the bill of his cap snow-plowing through a combo rack of *Duck Dynasty* lighters, Union Jack truck nuts, and off-label 168-Hour Energy Shots, now in healthy "green" flavor. I swear he tried desperately to catch one of these little bottles in his ruined mouth, maybe thinking it would re-activate him like Popeye's can of spinach. Not his worst idea. Then his shoulders wiped out the Duracell battery bin and sent the "Under 18 No Tobacco!" sign sailing up into the menthol cigarettes, until his limp Pete Rose slide finally stopped with his tongue unrolling like the red carpet to the Oscars to sample the taste of the pennies in the "Feed the Children" charity bucket.

No one believed I threw such a ridiculous, cinematic, positively *picturesque* punch, and later I wished a cop could have been around to record it on his body camera for posterity. I mean, what good are they? But at least I was there as the living witness, photographic evidence be damned! So I was certainly as shocked as anyone when I blinked and MC Chew Toy and I were still nose to nose, and I realized that without any proof no one would ever be convinced that kind of punch could happen in real life. Including yourselves. And so it didn't.

Pap!

He took my Average White Band punch quite easily, then ducked the next one, and then he had me around the neck like I was nothing, breathing Red Man tobacco up my nostrils like my sinuses were a chimney flue.

I heard Matt yell, "Mad, grab the mag!" which sounded even worse out loud, and I followed a clatter of ammo skidding across the tile all the way back to Matt, who had been collared by the towering Axe Man himself. He was yoinked up off his feet as he desperately windmilled his arms and rattled off the names of every cryptid he could remember to try and distract his assailant. But all Matt's flailings had managed to do was to turn Axe Man's leather cap sideways a little, which just made it more stylish.

"Hey, man, you want monsters? I got monsters!" Matt pleaded. "You ever hear of the Spring-Heeled Jackalope? The Donkey Diva of East Texas? What about Bloody Mary? You guys must know about Bloody Mary! Heads up! Skunk Ape incoming!"

Matt pointed to the fish-eye gaze of the theft-deterrent mirror above their heads, and the Axe Man caught himself in the reflection. It worked. Axe Man loosened his grip a bit, and inspired by the return of his airflow, Matt straightened his shirt and doubled down with his schooling, putting a little extra stank on it with his ever-improving Southern drawl.

"You know how every state has a monster? Well, in Indiana, they claim they got 'Bloody Mary,' even though that slumber party bullshit is everywhere! You know the one I mean, where you look in a mirror and say 'Candyman, Candyman' three times or whatever? That's how stupid people are in Indiana, pretending they're a real state 'n' shit. Can't even come up with their own monster! They remind me of the worst sports teams back in high school who would claim us as their 'rival,' like we had nine imaginary rivalries with teams we never heard of . . . naw, fuck that shit! 'Imaginary' does not means it doesn't exist . . . " Some of the men were turning towards him, actively trying to follow his train of thought, but Axe Man interrupted the lecture by grabbing Matt's face like a bowling ball.

"My mama's from Indiana," Axe Man grunted, and Matt slipped backwards on something green and bubbly. MC Chew Toy and myself were still wrestling for his rifle, or maybe it was the chew toy, as I suddenly understood how heavily armed every motherfucker in this place was. The hunters all seemed to remember this at the same time as I did, and a forest of guns came up click-clacking new rounds in their chambers, every eye narrowing to that deadly squint ("not really aiming," my ass). But as luck would have it, the earlier debate of forced perspective photos had soured the country-fried souls of these men, and not every gun was pointed our way. But a few were.

It was worse than a Mexican standoff, more like a New Mexico standoff, which was closer to those crazy Texas weirdos and a lot more dangerous. Gunfire started popping, and camo jackets started giving up their ghosts right there in the gas station. Grown-ass men kicked through the candy bars for the best line of sight, with one veteran even "slicing the pie," as they called it back in Vietnam—or at least that's what Matt said later, explaining this was how vets got the best killing angle, whether they were hiding behind Hostess fruit pies or not. At some point, someone behind the travel-sized

Pringles yelled in an exaggerated Asian accent, "Sorry, Robert, you tiger now!" (wasn't that a Comcast commercial?), and a gunshot blew a huge puff of survival-vest stuffing into the air, sending its cargo under the bargain bin forever. But the resulting gunsmoke and camo fluff was just the smokescreen I needed to get low and away from the center of the melee with my rat cage. But then Axe Man had his arm around my throat, sinking it low into my blood flow, and I thought I was going under, too.

Until I saw Mad. Reflected in the anti-theft mirror like Bloody Mary. Coming down on the Axe Man's back, smooth and deadly. And even before she peeled off his leather baseball cap and sank her teeth into his ear to take it with her, somehow I knew that was exactly what she was going to do. She caught my eye in the mirror, and I grinned back. Why not? You didn't stop at a backwoods gas station for chicken, or even for gas. You stopped there for souvenirs.

***

Okay, I'll admit it. At first, I didn't think she would really do it. With all that talk about ear stealing, I'd been targeting one of Axe Man's mud flaps myself, even before she wrapped her beautiful mouth around the other one, her black curls wrapping around his head to cover up her crime. And, yes, just like you might have guessed, it's *really* hard to rip off an ear with your bare hands. But a mouth works just fine.

Well, hers did anyway! Fuck him though. They probably should have bobbed those pendulous Dumbo ears at birth, like they did to those Schnauzers the Nazis loved so much. These guys probably loved those stupid dogs.

No shirt, no shoes, no service, and no ears or tails allowed . . .

I heard the cartilage crack of her bite, and watched her spit the man's ear into the sky so quickly that he didn't seem to realize what had just happened to him. He didn't even bring up a hand to protect the one he had left. But the next ear came off much harder, at least it came off much *longer*, pulling so much of his head and gristle off with it that I half expected his eyeball to be dangling like an earring from the lobe when it finally snapped loose.

Panicked now, Axe Man made a grab for her, but she was climbing up the snack rack, the expensive snacks, the healthy snacks, the Cadillacs of gas-station snacks. And for good reason. They were the ones with all the nuts, and they were just out of his reach.

It's true what they said, I thought, rubbing my eyes and watching her work. *Not much bigger than a German Shepherd. And she can jump three times as high. Meet my crush, the Ear Eater of Jasper County.*

Everyone had forgotten about Mags The Mad with all the virility dying and flying around, so when she started hopping across their heads, it took way too long for them to realize what was happening, even though she was the reason they were there after all. It was a pleasure to watch her go to town, to go head-to-head on these rubes, biting off an ear and spitting . . . biting off an ear and spitting . . . like they were the useless wet ends of cigars. But the Axe Man wasn't finished. Freshly earless, he was up and yowling, thrashing around the room looking for his assailant, or, preferably, another victim. He grabbed Matt.

I jumped back to my feet, and found Zero's cage where it had slid away in the fray. He was cowering in the corner like a bunny, but unharmed. When he saw me, his head popped up proud, round ears now pointed and stiff as the Spring-Heeled Jackalope (probably). I went after Matt, who was still on the ground, hands over his head, weathering a berserker storm of Axe Man's fists. Then I saw the axe, getting kicked around the brawl by dozens of bloody hiking boots, and I caught it, handle first like you're supposed to. I crawled up to Axe Man and Matt, and I brought it up over my head for the death stroke, but suddenly there was a blinding flash of light, and I bobbled my swing. For a second, I thought it was a gunshot, and I'd wake up in Hell with all the imaginary monsters these men had murdered. Then I saw Axe Man standing up in bewilderment, and Matt Fink holding his phone in his shaking hand, inches from the Axe Man's earless mug.

I wasn't sure if he'd just snapped a picture, but his phone was displaying something very strange, and Axe Man was stepping back, gasping, hands over the new holes Mad had left on his head. Other men stopped fighting and angled in, then looked away, visibly shook. Someone dry-heaved. I tried to imagine what could be on Matt's phone that could have bumped this battle's jukebox so effectively. Then I remembered the rumor. Not the Prince stuff. Miles back I'd decided he couldn't be the guy, then that he must be. Paradoxically, it was the fact that he shared the same spiked mullet with that '80s musician that should have instantly disqualified him. Matt Fink, the Doctor of Funk, was the fake doctor here, not me! So what did I know about biology? Not a lot, but maybe it *was* possible to have two penises.

And if you were the one they were attached to, you'd definitely have a picture of that shit on your phone.

"Is that what I think it is?" Axe Man was shouting because of his ear situation.

"It's the Loch Ness Monster!" someone shouted, and another camera flash went off. Then another. They were taking pictures of pictures this time, trying to immortalize whatever was on Matt's phone.

"My God, there's two of them!"

Between snapshots, I finally saw it.

It wasn't a forced-perspective shot, and it wasn't the Loch Ness Monster either. If I was a religious man, I would have prayed it was something *less* impressive than Nessie, because definitive proof of an extinct aquatic phenomenon wouldn't have caused me to drop my axe mid-swing. I'm not 100% sure what I saw, but it could have been the mythical and no longer mathematically impossible double dick pic selfie. Or maybe it was just Matt flashing a peace sign through his zipper. But that night, if not on my death bed, I would be stuck on the fact that whatever those things were in his blue jeans may have been side-by-side instead of up-and-down. I wasn't sure what this meant, but it seemed important at the time. Maybe because, at the very least, a horizontal alignment made the prospect of threesomes notably less convenient.

Either way! It worked.

Then someone blasted out the indifferent but all-seeing gaze of the shoplifting dome above us all, and the pieces came straight down onto the bubblegum machine, which in turn detonated like a disco ball fucking a piñata, so that pretty much stopped the fight, too.

I looked around the gas station and could have sworn I saw Greg, Angie's father, smoking rifle in his hand. Then sweat stung my eyes, and he was gone by the time I wiped them clear. My fighting glasses were intact, having soaked up the blows like a champ, as always.

"Take your chupacabra and get out of here!" Axe Man howled, and everyone howled back, hands against their ravaged heads. Mad hopped up off some squealing dude's face, ear lobe stretching a good six to nine inches. She let it snap back into his head, and I glanced at my cage. Zero's tiny hands were gripping his portable prison bars again. Poor thing, whatever the hell he was. Unidentifiable, but too small to be scary. His thumbs sure were cute, though. I wondered if he could pull a trigger.

"It is just a cat, people," I lied, backing toward the door. "It's just got some funky ears is all. And now you do, too!"

"Did they say they're 'cat people'?" some earless idiot muttered.

"Never!" Axe Man protested, not hearing or understanding, and he whipped out a camouflaged cell phone and stabbed an unmistakable "911" into the keypad. He held the phone to his head right-side up, like a normal human being this time, instead of the backward-ass Skunk Ape he was. But he forgot about his ear, and he screamed when the phone sunk into the hole.

***

We drove away at about 90 miles per hour, nursing our injuries and munching on some salty snacks, and we talked it all out, like a family should. I still didn't know where we were going, but Florida seemed so much closer now. We'd crossed the Mississippi state line into that little Gulf nub of Alabama, and when were sure no one was following us, I eased up on the gas. Somehow, Mad was still hungry, still winding down from mixing beer and Monster Energy. She found one pork rind left at the bottom of a bag bigger than her head, and she gnawed on it a bit for comfort, then handed it up to me.

"Your trophy, Dave," she said, and I fantasized it was for my legendary punch no one ever saw. But one thing still bothered me.

"How come no one back there cared that they'd proved the existence of a handful of cryptozoological creatures? For real. And all they talk about is their boots."

Mad shrugged. I watched her in the rearview mirror, picking some dried blood from the corner of her mouth like she was fixing her lipstick.

"Think of it like bugs, Dave. They discover hundreds of new insect species every year. No one cares. You know why? 'Cause they're tiny."

"I have another theory," Matt said. I'd forgotten about him again. But not his double-dick pic. "What if those monsters in the pictures were all the same monster?"

"What do you mean?" I asked. "Someone disguised as all of them?"

"No, still monsters. But monsters disguised as other monsters."

"I don't get it," Mad said, ducking down to stretch her legs in the back with Zero. If she didn't get it, I sure as hell didn't get it.

"I'm saying the same monster is everywhere!"

"Yep, it's called the 'Ain't No Monsters' Monster," Mad laughed. "And they don't tell you about it in school."

Matt winced and gingerly tapped his swollen eyebrow in the mirror, then rose up off his passenger's seat. He brushed glass cubes and snow from under his jeans, then rearranged his crotch as I tried not to look. A couple miles back I'd made peace with the answer to the eternal Matt Fink question. At least for now. And if that *was* a picture of two penises on his phone that had stunned an army of grown men into silence, I didn't want to imagine them in the car with us right now, both wrapped around each other like the Rod of Asclepius in his Wranglers. Because I would have to roll us straight the fuck into a ditch.

"So, that was fucked up, huh?" I offered over the cold wind of my broken window.

"Reminded me of an A.A. meeting," Matt said.

"'Hello, my name's Blimpy R. Cheramunk, the Were-Fuck of Waynesboro,'" Mad drawled from behind us. "And I've taken forced perspective shots, too. Now clap."

Matt and I slow-clapped as we were told.

"No, seriously," Mad laughed. "That was one of the names."

I looked back to see if Zero was sleeping, and I saw Matt and Mad holding hands behind the seats.

I drove on until everyone was quiet, then kept driving until everyone was sleeping. I hoped to get pulled over, so I could show the cop Mad's driver's license picture with her giant, forced-perspective tongue sticking out. I drove on until I could convince myself that I'd successfully made my presence unessential to everyone, and that was my plan all along. I drove until I realized that gas-station chicken was nothing to joke about. Then I drove until I closed my own eyes on a straightaway and remembered the hunters' Wall of Fame. I never had to see it again to always know that in the middle of all those camera flashes, someone had taken our picture in that brawl, and, more importantly, taken her picture. Mouth streaked with gore, bright eyes dancing and thick curls rising like cobras as she worked another ear free.

I imagined someone pinning the new Polaroid to the cooler, then covering their maps and the holes where their ears used to be. I opened my eyes and found Mad waiting for me in the rearview mirror, our favorite meeting place. Just like I always suspected with Angie, I was in her story, not the other way around.

Mad was pretending to sleep, so I made a new wish. Then I made a few more. I wished monsters were real. And I wished I was in a photograph with this one, the Ear Eater of Jasper County. And even though it wasn't necessary, I wished I was curled up in the foreground, if only to make her bigger.

XX

NOT REALLY AIMING

I WAS SO rattled from getting my ass kicked by a bunch of hilljack Sasquatches that I drove through at least three states before looking at any signs. Okay, I do remember seeing "Nashville," but it was a totally different Nashville, hundreds of miles from Tennessee, and this got me thinking that searching for clues there was as good as anywhere else. But then I remembered that every corner of anything named "Nashville" was bound to be littered with earnest assholes and guitar cases filled with human remains, strumming for bones instead of coins, hungrier for fame than anyone in the real Nashville, and I decided I didn't need to rub any more blood in my eyes to feed my parasites.

Or to feed the red herrings, I thought, looking around the car at my crew. *Why in the world are you still here . . .*

"I'd bet cash money there's a band in Nashville, Kentucky, at this very moment called The Red Herrings, and they are playing their asses off. Even making eye contact."

No one laughed. "Red Herrings" sounded more like a motorcycle gang, I had to admit.

It was getting kind of ripe in the car, and my beard was real feral, nearing the stage Angie used to refer to as "Itchy the Killer." But no one was talking hotels or motels yet. I didn't want to risk it. Beside avoiding showing I.D. anywhere I could get flagged, just one look at our mystery creature and who knows what kind of pet deposit they'd make us pay. With those thumbs of his, I guessed Zero would trash any hotel room as effectively as a '70s Led Zeppelin. And somehow a hotel seemed too intimate, more intrusive than crammed into the Rabbit. In the car, our lines of division were very clearly defined by now, even when we swapped seats.

Stockholm Syndrome sliding smoothly into Die Hard's *'Helsinki Syndrome' territory.*

I traced my windshield crack with my eyes. I'd been following it as a map as best I could, which made for some surprise dead-ends and U-turns, but we were almost on the "X" now, the broken glass at the end of our journey. It didn't make a lot of sense, and it didn't matter if we'd had to drive in crazy directions to do it. I was like Indiana Jones in the map room, trying to get the sun at a particular angle in order to achieve a particular result. I'd decided that we were on our way, with the sunlight or the moonlight or a streetlight mapping that "X" onto my face, and this meant we were almost there, wherever "there" happened to be. I knew the broken windshield map wouldn't end on a pot of gold, but if there was a bridge anywhere around our destination, that would be more than good enough.

And I needed a bridge sooner than later because, judging by my hostages sneaking all that hand holding, too much time between madcap adventures was dangerous. Besides them bonding, and me on third-wheel status, Mad occasionally tried to lead me back to the topic of the strange fire truck Angie was last seen riding in, a fire engine flying around with no fire in sight (according to the cops anyway). But when I said "Nah, that was just another . . . smokescreen," it caused a convulsive fit of sniggering that we didn't shake for a good thirty miles. We were eating up the miles, but it was seeming less like progress. "Idle hands" and all that.

But in the downtime at toll booths, Mad did make some

headway investigating our eyeball affliction, finding something on the internet about "Loa loa filariasis"? Which sounded a lot like a party. But more like a surprise party deep in the Amazon jungle that you hoped wasn't for you. So rather than relieving our fears, this bit of information off Mad's phone just implanted more bizarre theories about what continent Zero was originally from. And, of course, if we did have his poop worms in our eyes, and if they were actually affecting our behavior, I honestly wasn't sure if I wanted to be cured. The internet, and some reasonably reputable articles, were promising us an unlikely combination of paranoia and fearlessness, which sounded pretty fucking good to me. I decided to endure this new wrinkle, at least for now, and hope it didn't permanently blind us. Erratic as we may have been, and even if we were doing things for the benefit of a parasite that needed as many eyeballs in close proximity to a box full of cat shit as possible, I felt we were living charmed lives on this road trip. Think of all those run-ins back there! We should be dead, caged, in jail, or at least hog-tied to a gas station beer cooler by now. Diagnosis might jinx us. Or at least be a momentum destroyer. Unacceptable.

I looked at Mad, and wondered how long she'd stick around. She was getting real good at research, and reminding me of Angie more and more every mile. It was probably inevitable that, like Angie, she would finally realize that leaving me behind was the easiest thing in the world. But maybe I still needed both of them. All of them. Simply put, if worms in our eyes were forcing us to see things in a different way, until I found just one of the hundred answers I was looking for, regardless if I'd stopped asking reasonable questions, I did not want our current condition to change. For the first time in my life, I couldn't stand to be alone, and I understood why, on a long enough timeline, it could lead to a dangerous inertia.

***

Even though a wise man once claimed any long road trip

might feel like solitary confinement, the actual practice was originally conceived by the Quakers, then adopted by the spectacularly hellish Eastern State Penitentiary in the middle of Philadelphia. In fact, the name "penitentiary" is derived from the process of penitence, or remorse. Alone in your cell, with an alluring view of the Philly skyline, you'd get in touch with the better parts of yourself. That was their hope anyway. And maybe you could stew in your own thoughts (and fluids) long enough to realize the error of your ways and ultimately fly right.

But that was almost never the case. See, no one is meant to interrogate themselves that intently. So long-term segregation had an entirely unexpected result. Almost without exception, it induced paranoia, madness, suicide, even total unresponsiveness. And by 1913, solitary confinement was abandoned all over the world. But the U.S. had invented it. Therefore, just like with bait cars and body cameras and thin blue lines, America decided to stick with it, no matter how problematic it got to be. No quitters! U.S.A.! U.S.A.! We also invented the banjo, which sucks because the movies told us the harmonica was always the musical weapon of choice of the wrongfully incarcerated.

Here's another fun tidbit. Mad said that Angie said that some biologist said that vermin were very popular during confinement experiments because they were cursed with being inherently social animals, just like us. So it's no surprise that the only documented case of a rat spontaneously combusting was during an isolation experiment. The doomed little varmint was separated from its pack for only three weeks, and in the morning, all the scientists found were ashes and a faint black odor, like when a cat's whiskers sniff too close to a candle.

Together, we'd read hundreds of pages of my wife's work in less than a week, storing up so much superfluous information about prisons and punitive actions and suffering in solitude that I was now convinced I could be a "Not That

Kind of Doctor" doctor if I logged only 300 more miles devouring gas-station chickens, ice cream sandwiches, and highway conversations.

It felt so good to be back in school.

***

I had Matt pass me up the litter box, and positioned it between my ankles so I could urinate in the highest corner, where the bottom wasn't peeking through the piss biscuits. I didn't know if an Invisible Prison existed, but I did know that in such a place, you'd likely have to urinate sitting down, something no reputable man should ever do (stop looking at me), *because* of the abundance of space, not in spite of it.

Properly soiled, I handed the box back to Matt, and he smacked the sides to even out the remainder of the sand over the wet spots. Zero was up front with Mad and I, batting around our shoelaces and avoiding the gas and brake pedals like a champ.

What an excellent troupe, I thought. *What would our album cover look like?*

"When's the last time you saw Otto?" I asked Matt when I caught him watching me in the mirror. "Would you even recognize your roommate, doc? Without your stethoscope, I mean." That didn't make much sense, but I didn't care. It felt right.

"Of course I would," Matt said. "I shared an internet browser auto-fill with the man for five years. He was mostly into bestiality porn and pro-cop memes. You don't forget that."

"Ugh. Pro-cop memes . . . " Mad shivered.

"The human race's epitaph will be a misspelled meme," I said, pretending I'd thought of that instead of Angie. "Has he ever served time?" I asked. It was time for Final Jeopardy!

"Good question!" Matt said, but offered nothing in the form of an answer (or a question). It was always a lame way to stall, proving once and for all that this response was still the worst in human history, next to Angie's hated "That's funny," of course.

As if on cue, my phone vibrated between my legs. I tried

to cover it, embarrassed I was still sitting on the damned thing, but the stamp-sized screen was glowing with a photo of Angie pretending to touch the tip of the Eiffel Tower. I flipped it open, and the text message was another picture, a snapshot of a TV screen during a game of *Jeopardy!*, and the clue read as follows: "In this South American country, one body type for women is called 'um corpo de vialo,' meaning shaped like a guitar." Mad was breathing down my neck, likely shocked that it was still working without its battery. She'd get over it. I started to close the phone, but she grabbed it away.

"I got this," she said.

"You got what?"

"The answer is 'Portugal,' or 'Portuguese,' like me."

"Huh?"

"The answer is me." There was a rare sincerity in her voice.

"Didn't you see who sent that?"

"Settle down," Mad said, flinging it back at my crotch. "The cops have her phone now. They're just fucking with you."

But I wasn't so sure. Could Angie be the one fucking with me instead? Just chilling somewhere, watching *Jeopardy!* of all things? She'd always hated the show, especially its idiotic conceit. "They pretend to give you answers in search of questions, but it's such bullshit. Real answers would just be something like 'Blue,' or '366.'"

"How many days in a leap year!" Matt shouted, clapping like a moron. I must have been thinking out loud again.

When is 'Guitarmageddon', Alex?

I considered calling back her phone, but I had to admit to myself that maybe I wasn't really seeking as many answers as I seemed. Prince's "Purple Rain" began playing on the radio, which was quite a trick (and a timely distraction), considering no stations were in range. But when I realized the music was a ringtone, I slowed the car for a serious talk.

"Okay, guys, I'm gonna need you to lose the phones," I said.

Mad was looking at her screen, skeptical. Normally I'd be suspicious and wonder who in her address book she'd assigned the song to. But who *didn't* like "Purple Rain"?

"If any of you got a call from a 'Jesus,' 'Jesse,' 'Jay,' or whatever he's going by now, tell him I'm not here."

Not where?

"Who's that?" Mad asked.

"We went to high school together. Listen, seriously, you need to drop those phones, or stash them somewhere, at least until this is over. And don't take your batteries out or the calls will never stop."

This last statement was baffling enough for them to exchange a glance and begin their cell phone surgeries in earnest.

"You ever notice that when someone gets their service shut off, the old number is immediately taken over by a stranger?" Mad asked us as she fished out her battery. "Why so swiftly? But if you ever have to change your number, the phone company says, 'Sorry, we'll have a new one for you as soon as we can.' How can both be possible?"

I didn't have an answer to this. Their phone batteries were out now, too, and I was thinking about my own power source. I liked to consider myself unique enough, but, even though I was riding in a Rabbit, I was certain that if anyone popped open my back and flicked the springs, they wouldn't find a turbine, or a furnace, or even any Energizer Bunnies. Just some very brightly colored double-A batteries. Meaning, the generic kind. The came-with-the-toy kind. Basic. I thought of my dad's two favorite jokes:

How do you catch a unique rabbit? Unique up on it! How do you catch a tame one? Tame way!

I was driving slow enough to read the roadside crosses, and I finally saw one with "Dave" written on it. I was surprised I hadn't seen more. Then Mad was telling me all about the infamous Dave-to-Girl ratio people were always laughing about in college (except for the Daves) and explaining to me that there were way too many of us in this world. But apparently not along the highway. I wasn't sure if she was getting this from Angie's notes or if it was her own speculation.

I stopped the car. Not caring how much I was tempting fate, I stepped out to stand on my own roadside grave. A 1:1 ratio.

***

There were at least fifteen such makeshift memorials along our stretch of interstate, an area peppered with strip clubs and dive bars and at least one oil refinery that, judging by the gas flare and yellow smoke in the sky, was still in operation. It was easy to imagine a line of cars getting off second-shift, then filing right into these parking lots to get off one more time. And, every so often, maybe after too much warm beer and the confusing friction of some lap dances, crashing and burning away all that repressed energy in one of these roadside ditches. But the overwhelming number of women's names on these crosses, like Diamond, Goldie, and Jewel, made me think these might actually be the strippers who were getting routinely run over out here. Them and poor lonely "Dave."

Wait a minute . . .

I was suddenly thinking back to my brawl in Shitcan Alley with Johnny 5, supercop extraordinaire, and wondering if these memorials were just conspicuous markers for contraband, hiding in plain sight. Diamonds? Gold? Jewels? Are you kidding me? Maybe there was treasure at the end of our broken map after all, buried underneath a hundred wayside teddy bear crucifixions by small-time hoods in red jumpsuits working off their community service,

Or maybe the cultivators of the crosses were working for someone else. Could a local judge steer some road crew parolees to certain spots, then bury something to be picked up later? Or why bury it at all? Just leave a black bag.

Mad and Matt joined me on the side of the road, and I pointed and grunted, lost in thought. They seemed to understand my new plan regardless. They were eager to rip up fake graves, in any case, and they got right to work.

But who is the Vice President? Do they always end up President? There's certainly a precedent . . .

I searched the vanishing point for answers until they stopped digging. They were getting nowhere. The gravel was packed hard next to the road. Even the crosses were barely able to pierce it. But there was no gold, no diamonds, probably no jewels.

Wasn't that the name of Prince's fifth-best album? Or Shakespeare's second-best bed?

I checked their progress. They'd unearthed some shiny shards of broken beer bottles that were cutting up Matt's thumbs as he sifted through them.

"Ow . . . ow . . . ow . . . 'Corona'!" Matt proudly reported as he finished his investigation and started sucking the bloody slice between the heart and head lines of his palm.

"Barf!" Mad said. "You should sanitize your hands."

Matt dropped the shards, and I kicked the "Dave" cross loose, scanning the highway for traffic.

Is this my surprise party?

The cross was new, with my name freshly burned into the wood with a blowtorch or a branding iron. The cement-like soil around it had been recently disturbed, and I nosed around the spot a bit with the toe of my shoe until more dirt and gravel loosened. Kicking harder with my heel, even bigger chunks flew out.

"You guys didn't even try," I said. "Loose earth like this indicates a body has been moved. Haven't you seen a movie in your lives?"

"No way a body was in—"

"Shhh, I have an idea."

"Oh no," Mad said, but they joined the grave robbing anyway, racing around to see who could grab the most crosses.

At least three cop cars cruised by while Mad and Matt

plucked roadside memorials like weeds, and I picked through the packed dirt and rocks underneath them. But not one even slowed down. I guess we looked like we belonged there, which would have been worrisome if we'd thought about it. One cop did seem momentarily interested in what we were doing, but she only acknowledged our investigation with a curt nod of approval, followed by a quick spurt of acceleration.

"Let's get out of here," Mad said after that. "I don't need to get arrested today."

"If they picked us up, I don't think we would be considered 'arrested,'" Matt said between scoops of dirt. "More like rescued."

"Liberated!"

"Extricated!"

But I appreciated my crew's can-do spirit when I threw a curve ball like this at them, but something about Matt's manic energy made me wonder if he was trying to get caught. Get *me* caught.

"All right, wrap it up," I said, clapping some dust and heading back to the Rabbit, rumbling and stewing in its perpetual cloud of intoxicating diesel fumes. "If we get collared, torture is inevitable!" They climbed back in the car, and I threw the stack of crosses we'd harvested into the hatch. Zero hopped up onto the back headrest to investigate the clatter. "Tortured not because of what we know, but because we would be unable to explain our actions."

"Even to ourselves!" Mad said.

"Very true," Matt said, agreeing with one of us. I was never sure which. I watched Mad and Matt giving each other cute looks as they shared some bottled water.

"You know, if someone cut off my ear to get me to talk, I think I'd be okay," I said to them, starting the engine.

"But what if they made you choose?" Mad asked, strapping in next to me. "Like, eye, nose, or ear? Or tongue?"

"I'd almost certainly go with nose because *Chinatown* was a pivotal film," Matt said.

"You would."

"Take my ears," I said. "It's hard to take an ear off, all the way off anyway, not unless you want to spend all day chewing on it. Just ask Mad!" Mad looked at me, confused. "But if that happened to me, like if Mad ate my fuckin' ear, I would just slap a trucker hat over it. Then I could still investigate stuff 'n' shit. It would have to be a funny cap, though, one that said something like 'Whiskey Makes Me Frisky' because this would distract everyone from the blood, me included. The important thing is to remember . . . you can lose an ear, but you can still hear!"

"You should put *that* on a hat." Mad patted my thigh, and my heart tripped over its feet.

I put the Rabbit in gear and noticed a mosquito fluttering and pulsing in the hole where the cigarette lighter used to be. Its proboscis poked expectantly at the coil, powering up for a big finish, no doubt. I wondered whose blood it was carrying.

***

Did you know that when someone is released from prison, after they've served their time and should be able to walk free through those gates, they have one final indignity to endure? One last time, they are shackled, stripped, showered, chained, transported, then finally released. One extra day, in addition to the sentence they have already served, where they're treated as if they are still a prisoner. At first, it may seem as if they're doing this just to fuck with you. But, in fact, maintaining the most dehumanizing of the institution's routines up until the prisoner is literally on the other side of those walls is the most soothing thing in the world to the ex-con.

Were you also aware that studies have shown that those who are most susceptible to psychological damage or pathological responses to solitary confinement are the ones most likely to be put there? They are also the ones most likely to request a return to such conditions.

And here's a handy piece of trivia, in case you're at

Zanzibar and it's neck and neck. Even in the most isolated situations, prisoners almost immediately find a means of nonverbal communication. The "rat line" is one such method, where a piece of cardboard on a string is boomeranged between cells to send messages. This action is a specially acquired skill, like lassoing cattle, and the rat-line method of conveying information has proven almost impossible to master by civilians. Until they are locked in a room.

I learned all of these things from Angie's footnotes. There was more in there than I'd ever be able to process, even if I never stopped driving. For example, do you like movies? Do you like TV? Then you'll love this. Remember the revolutionary scuba equipment designed by James Cameron for his epic, *The Abyss*, where an attempt to make the actors' faces more visible resulted in a new technology adapted by real-world underwater researchers? Well, similarly, the plastic prisons as depicted in HBO's series *Oz*, which showcased its cast in their cells so effectively, were quickly adopted by actual prisons for their transparent security benefits, which moved incarceration one more step closer to Foucault's warnings. So an invisible prison would be the inevitable next step, reflecting the natural evolution of any prisoner who not only was used to the ever-present eye of authority, but who would also crave it. You see what I'm saying here?

Before she disappeared, my wife had been well on her way toward proving that the idea of self-incarceration, and possibly the unpreventable evolution of the invisible prison, wasn't so far-fetched at all.

At the same time, the real definition for Dunning-Kruger Effect continued to fly around the car with Angie's papers. And when I rolled down too many windows and a loose page got stuck to my face, I had a chance to read something about "the more you know, the less you think you know, but the less you know, the more you think you know." Huh? I never knew she spoke Swahili!

One last thing! Current estimates put the total number of people who are now in, or have ever passed through, the US penal system at more than 20 million, stealing the top spot from those over-ambitious Chinese re-education camps and, according to their signage, in a dead heat with McDonald's for total customer service and satisfaction.

But the point of all this is simple. What we don't deserve, we crave, even though it's coming for us anyway.

***

"So, you stole the cage from a restaurant?" Mad asked.

"Yes."

"Who else knows about this?"

"Just me and Angie. And Ramsey. And you freaks."

"Then maybe Ramsey killed your wife. Maybe he was worried he might lose business from the racist cat-eating slander you were spreading."

"Not possible."

"Why not?"

"Because the only one who is responsible for her death is me."

"Oh, no, you'd still be responsible!"

"I mean directly responsible."

Everyone was silent until the rumble of a highway strip shook us out of it.

"Okay, I'm not really saying that. I mean, I just had her on the phone too long, which distracted her enough to be abducted, which led directly to her murder. That's all I'm saying."

"You sound like you don't really believe any of that," Mad said. "But that sure sounds more like an alibi than a confession."

"Yeah, but like an excuse for an alibi, if that's a thing," Matt added.

"I'm lost," I said.

"He means, like less of an admission, but more of an unburdening . . . "

"No, shut up, I mean I'm *lost* lost," I said, wiping the steam from the windshield.

"Now *that's* a confession!"

"Listen to me, assholes. As sure as if I killed her, I killed her."

"Are those words?" Mad asked. "What did those words even mean?"

It didn't matter what they thought. I was convinced. And the Rabbit was slowing down.

"I just think we're on the wrong track," Mad said after another five more miles crept by. She was rubbing her eyes with the heels of her hands like she was stubbing out a pair of cigarettes.

"How about this," I said, eager to bring Angie's dissertation back into it. "Remember the newspaper clipping about those justices who were selling children to that private prison for kickbacks? The Philly 'Kids for Cash' scandal?"

"Of course," Mad said. "I'm the one who read it to you."

"Great. Well, some of those judges got off. Hold on, what was the name in that . . . " I leaned in to tap the cover of the old yearbook tucked next to Mad's seat. "Hey, check out the names of some judges she interviewed in here. Wasn't there a 'Zimbardo,' on the faculty?"

"Judges? No," Mad said after running her finger down some pages. "Wait, there's a 'Zamboni.'"

"Seriously?"

"Yep, she even had a photocopy of his face for a bookmark." She slammed the yearbook shut.

"I remember pulling that up for her on the microfiche," Matt said. "Back in Brickwood."

"Sometimes I forget all about you," I told Matt in the mirror. "I think it's keeping you alive."

"What did you say?"

"What did I say?"

"How can there be a name so close to Zimbardo in any of these materials?" Mad asked, changing the subject. "Way too convenient."

"It's like the ol' double bluff!" I explained. I watched Mad rubbing her eyes again, which made my own eyes itch, and Matt reached up from the back to take the wheel until we stopped. As I ground the itching into a dull but satisfying ache, I thought of the cruel hockey game Angie invented with Matt, and the imaginary "Zamboni" that flattened the insects they imprisoned.

"Are those ducks?" I blinked, hands back on the steering wheel and swerving as the fireworks I'd rubbed into my corneas faded.

"Those are crows, dude."

"I heard they're good luck," Mad said sarcastically.

Another fifty miles, and we were attacking our own eyes again, sometimes with no hands on the wheel at all. Zero watched us, sometimes scratching his ears, which seemed longer every time I looked at him. Eventually, the tingling and burning of our eyeballs grew so severe that we tried to stagger our rubbing sessions, then we realized no one needed to be in control.

***

It was somewhere around the sign that announced "Ohio Welcomes You!" that we realized I'd driven almost 800 miles in the wrong direction. And it was somewhere around the sign that reminded us "Hell is Real!" that we became convinced we were being followed by a half dozen trucks with gun racks lining their cab windows.

"Oh, shit. It's the Bigfoots!" I shouted, curb-stomping the gas pedal and whipping the Rabbit up to a new record of 77 miles per hour. Mad groaned.

"One good thing is," she said without looking. "When they do kill us, they'll take a picture standing ten feet behind our bodies. We'll be giants." Then she glanced back at the pursuers and snorted. "Never mind. It's just the Army."

"Who called the Army?" I laughed crazily.

"Nobody." Mad unbuckled her seat belt and crawled forward to breathe deep on my windshield map. "How are we not in Florida right now?"

“Who’s navigating this boat?” I asked. My eyes were darting, but I was trying to focus on the road ahead. It felt like my ever-shifting vision was sometimes under something else’s control. Then my foot was losing strength, too, and the Rabbit slowed to 50. Then 40. Then 30 . . .

“Zero!” He was slinking between my shoe and the gas pedal, either cleaning his ass or chasing his tail. “Help me out here! Mad! Don’t you teach people how to drive? How are you so useless all the sudden?”

“Is she crying?” Matt asked me. “Are you crying?” he asked her.

“No,” Mad said. “I just have something in my eye. And I think it’s hungry.”

“Fuckin’ hell,” Matt said, slumping back, and I wanted to kiss her or kill her for that one. I vowed to at the next exit, and I scouted for some daylight to my left, then swerved hard to use the cop hole in the divider to make a U-turn. I panicked for a second when I heard something ripping in the back seat, and I tilted my mirror. It was just Zero using his long front claws to shred a Rand McNally atlas of America against my headrest. He worked to detach the Great Lakes with a couple twisting bites, his opposable thumbs gripping each end of Kentucky like a tiny sandwich. He stopped long enough to turn and watch the parade of camouflaged all-terrain vehicles zoom past in the lane we’d just vacated.

At the next gas station, I creaked my weary Rabbit into a spot to see if anyone was still on our tail, watching a baby blue Ford F650 ease into two parking spaces in the front row near us. Then a Jeep Cherokee with tinted windows saddled up next to the Ford, and I slouched a bit in my seat, watching for the driver to step out. The man driving the Jeep exited quickly. He was wearing a camouflage cap and jacket, the required uniform these days. And it was more effective than ever because, combined with my inflamed, watery vision, I had no idea who the guy was. He didn’t move like Greg. But nobody moved like Greg. I waited another minute. The driver of the Ford laid back his seat, presumably to sleep.

"I'll be right back," I told my posse, and I went to check out the Jeep, keeping low to the ground for some reason, with one hand on my head as if I was boarding a helicopter. The passenger door was locked, but I remembered Angie's spare key in the magnetic box stuck to her Jeep's frame, and hoped this Jeep owner might have done something similar.

Sure enough, it must have been a "Jeep thing" because there was a spare key under the vehicle waiting for me. I used it to open the driver's-side door, away from the Ford, then I went straight for the glove box. Inside, I found the requisite stack of weekend warrior Polaroids. Pictured were Hogzillas, Dogzillas, and even some gutted Great Whites hanging from cranes. Always with a bunch of grinning nimrods ten feet behind their kill. Under the photos was a stack of NRA flyers, coupons for lifeboat rations, and the promo codes for everything from bullets to crossbows to baseball caps with massive moose antlers that doubled as beer koozies. Surprisingly, no rubber horse heads. But as a newly minted private eye with superpowered peepers, I was considering sending away for the fedora with the rhinoceros horn to complete my costume when I noticed the map spread out on the passenger's seat.

It was a map of Ohio, with a route outlined in red marker, that was, impossibly, a veritable copy of our windshield-crack map, which led to another mystery inside an enigma tucked under a dead-end: at the end of this red line was an "X," or maybe it was a crucifix, then a final destination that had been circled over and over until it was almost solid. Somewhere in the middle of the Ohio River. That's where this ended. In the water?

No. It was a bridge.

I memorized the map coordinates and went back to the Rabbit. Everyone but Zero had gone in for food. The man in the Jeep came out as I waited, carrying nothing, and he drove off without even titling the bill of his cap in my direction. When Mad and Matt returned from pissing and buying snacks and eye drops and Monster Energies, they were openly holding hands. As if psychic, Mad tossed me a bottle of Tums when she climbed in, and I poured them out on the dashboard like diamonds after a heist. I spread them out until I found a couple of reds.

We got back on the road, first behind the Jeep, then ahead of it, watching the tinted windows roll by behind us. They asked me where I was going, and I said we were going south again, going home, lying to them like I'd lied to my friends when Squeegee beat me halfway to Hades in that little league dugout while my brother watched.

We were close. Close to the bridge I mean. My brother and I, not so much. I couldn't remember the last time I'd talked to him. And my passengers? Hardly knew 'em.

I counted the fireflies dodging the headlights, and I wondered if my brother was invited to Angie's funeral.

When I found another bridge, I feigned excitement. It was a small one-lane bridge over a dried-up creek bed, metal fences on either side. I think a faded sign read: "Ashland." I figured Mad would enjoy that, in honor of her cat (or its remains). But maybe it said "Covington," as in "covet your kidnapper's wife." And Angie would have enjoyed that. But any town or bridge would do. When it came to maps, I wasn't really aiming anymore. Matt and Mad followed me when I stepped out, but I was having a hard time focusing on them. We stretched our legs, rubbed the circulation back into each other's shoulders, and took deep breaths free from the confinement of our seat belts and steamy windows. They were just starting to look to me for answers, more likely for questions. Mad was running her fingers along the love locks on the bridge rails like they were piano keys, coaxing a sad little tune from the metal on metal, and I thought about something she'd said when I was chasing ghost flies in the car. Something about how I'd never really been by myself.

Then I was suddenly leaving them behind in a fishtail of stones and dust. I didn't look back. Neither did Zero. He had headrests to circle. But Mad was right. I needed to be alone or the drive would never end.

***

The real bridge was a couple hours down, where the river was still running. A curved concrete bridge. Spitting image of the one in Paris. I swear a sign said "Licking" and I couldn't imagine that as the name of a town. But something told me I was going to solve something tonight. Anything. I knew the Jeep wasn't far behind, but I felt safe with my mystery animal and my back seat of crosses.

I cracked my neck and put my nose up to my rearview mirror, noting the red rivers crisscrossing the whites of my eyes, and I thought about the male bowerbird one more time. It was still a dead-end in her dissertation, but quickly becoming my favorite part. It was such a beguiling case study. This ridiculous bird and its idiotic tunnel of garbage, lined by an even more complicated avenue of bottle caps and shotgun shells, with the smallest bullshit toward the front, and the biggest bullshit toward the back, a junkyard he utilized to entice what must have been the dumbest soul mate of all time. He was a liar, you see, just screwing around with perspective to trick some chick. But what my wife and I always found most interesting was that the bowerbird busted his ass to appear smaller. It won the day, and the girl, by forever dooming its species with a show of cowardice.

Which is a crime really.

XXI

A VAST COMIC INDIFFERENCE

I WALKED ALONG the bridge, my knuckles drumming the padlocks to get them swinging in anticipation. I heard a car door slam and turned to watch the headlights of the Jeep flicker as a tall shadow rounded the front of the vehicle to intersect my path. His brisk pace, combined with the outline of the rifle bobbing on his back like a huge antenna, convinced me this was the father of my dead wife finally confronting me, and within seconds I was slammed onto my back with his knee in my chest and his beer breath in my nose. Eyes red and black, no whites left at all. Gun slung but already sliding down his shoulder. His camouflage was gone. I figured I had about a minute to talk him out of killing me.

"Hello, Greg," I said from the ground, fingers gripping the slats of the bridge to keep from sliding. "How'd you find me?"

"I showed Angie this spot, Dave. Before she showed it to you. Just like I showed it to her mother, and just like my father showed it to me."

"She never showed me this place, Greg. I threw a dart at a map."

"Then why the hell are you here?"

"Like I said, I threw a fist at a map."

He punched me in the nose, a quick jab that barely drew blood but made my raw eyes water. It helped me focus.

"Are you gonna kill me or what?" Bold question, I know, but I'd learned these head-on delay tactics during my one semester as a psych major and hostage negotiator at the University of Pittsburgh, where Angie and I first fell in love. I was two whole different people then.

"Did you do it?" he asked, eyes softening, fist loosening.

"No, I didn't do it."

"Then why'd you skip town?" The pressure of his knee on my sternum relaxed a bit. "The way you've been acting, you've gone a long way to convince everyone that you've done something wrong."

"I'm not *acting* like anything, Greg," I said, as forceful as I could with half of his weight still constricting my lungs. "Just because I don't grieve like other people . . . "

"Grieve! You're on a road trip with your buddies like this is some fucking joke! The cops got a lotta questions for you, and so do our families, and you're out here on some Midwest tour playing *This Is My Life*?" The rifle strap was down past his elbow now.

I think you mean Your Life, I thought, but I didn't correct him. Instead I tried to come clean.

"You're right. This was her favorite place."

Now the gun was all the way down, the rifle stock in his hand, bloodshot eyes practically glowing with rage. "You just said you'd never been to this bridge before, Dave."

"I know what I said. This is where she was cheating on me."

Wrong answer. He grabbed the collar of my duck coat and yanked it into my Adam's apple.

"Sounds like motive to me," he said, almost spitting the words. "I should blow your fucking head off right now and save the taxpayers the effort." He thumped me back to the ground and looked me over. "You *have* been on a bridge like this before, haven't you? What's going on here?"

I strained to grab the fence behind me, able to pull myself up enough to catch one good, deep breath. Our struggle had rattled more padlocks, and his eyes shifted to the dance of metal. I took the opportunity to crawl out from under his knee and managed a slumped, sitting position. He allowed this, still hypnotized by the Newton's Cradle motion of locks, and I tried to keep him fixated on all that shiny silver and gold rocking back and forth along the guardrail so that he'd forget his gun.

"Is one of those yours?" I asked. "You and your first wife's, I mean."

"Yes."

"Did you throw a key in the water? Like you're supposed to?"

"Can't remember." His eyes were back on me, but now he was smiling. "You don't know what you're talking about, do you? Do you know why you throw the key in the water?"

"For good luck."

"Right, good luck. And did you throw yours in, Dave?"

I said nothing.

"That's what I thought. How's that luck been working out for you?"

***

Even though we had enthusiastically participated in the love lock phenomenon during our honeymoon in Paris, we'd been shocked to learn from Fabio, fabulous full-time hotel concierge and part-time tourist trap snake-oil salesman, that the original idea actually began in Italy, where, statistically, they're not nearly as amorous. Since then, all the romantic bridges with chintzy padlocks may have long since gone worldwide, but no one promoted an impromptu riverside ceremony as hard as the French along the love-struck Seine. One day, after Fabio was done shilling to us in the lobby, I was unable to resist buying a handful of padlocks from him, before my sweaty fellow Americans behind us clamored for the rest of his marked down stash of mangled Eiffel Tower key chains.

One guy got so desperate to buy some bullshit for his wife that he shoved me to the side, and I dropped a ring of padlock keys through the heating vent on the floor. We knew it was all a scam, so we didn't care. Fabio probably got kickbacks from somewhere to push all that junk, and I could respect the hustle. Besides, we'd brought our own locks from the U.S. anyway, with plenty of keys. Before we left, we'd numbered them so they didn't get mixed up, which was doubly ridiculous, especially after Fabio apologized for the key ring I'd lost in the vent and slipped me extra keys for the locks I already bought. That's when we realized everything opened everything. There were maybe three possible key variations, if that.

Despite both of us being pacifists, there was something intoxicating about a certain commercial that seduced her easily enough, when the slow-motion bullet fails to penetrate the lock, and the spokesmodel gives it a tug, then a shrug, then chirps, "Nope, still holds tight!" I wrote off her excitement as the lingering influence of her father (both Angie and the spokemodel). Remember, we still had Greg's "Not Really Aiming" stickers on the toolbox he'd given us as a wedding gift, which wouldn't come off no matter how much I picked at them—a perpetually embarrassing hitchhiker on so many father-in-law hand-me-downs throughout the new era of school shootings, movie-theater massacres, and open-carry Bazooka Joes. Which is probably how Greg was able to cross three state lines strapped and nursing a flask.

Never mind the driver with his rifle barrel hanging out his window, officer. He's just searching for my frequency.

So I knew that after the honeymoon we'd have more locks than we'd know what to do with. But, of course, at the time, I didn't know there was a bridge in Ohio that was a carbon copy of our bridge in Paris, and more bridges everywhere exactly like every stupid bridge all over the world. With the same keys opening everything. And I sure as shit didn't know she'd be walking down one of these bridges, holding hands with someone else. Whether it was a librarian, musician, medical oddity, or prison guard. It was all the same to me. Meaning it wasn't me.

But when she brought them home, it was just adorable. So what, my wife had a thing for padlocks. My one semester of psychiatry and volunteering at a Suicide Hotline told me it must give her comfort to collect them, even if they were hooked to nothing, even if she was hooked to no one. And smuggling American-made, bulletproof padlocks for a bridge in Paris with our initials and our hearts scribbled on the sides of those bad boys? That shit *had* to be true love, man. Maybe to her those locks meant forever.

Her father was right, though. I jinxed us by never throwing our key in the river. The ritual demanded it. Fabio made it very clear that you threw the key in right after you clicked it shut. But Angie and I were leaving locks everywhere, so we were bound to forget. And after Angie and I had dutifully snapped our final memento onto that bridge at the Passerelle des Arts, when it came to tossing that final skeleton key, we were distracted by some unusual movement in the brown water below—bright, strobe-like flashes that we first took for other discarded keys, but later became convinced were the reflections of shifting and organic orbs. Wide and deep, but not just any aquatic globular organ. These were huge eyes where there shouldn't be eyes, and not moving like eyes should move, at least not like the eyes they taught us about in school. Okay, maybe a little like the eyes they tried to teach us about at the Kentucky Creation Museum when we'd go there as a gag. But only if you believed the posters on their Dino-Ramas that insisted plants were "sinners without souls" then maybe you'd buy their hoary old "the eye gave Darwin the 'cold shoulder'" argument. Or was it a "cold shudder"? Who cares. Angie and I had gone back to the Creation Museum again and again, always hoping to get kicked out. We thought of it as renewing our vows. The last time we got bounced was when she rode a Triceratops with a saddle clearly marked "Ages 8 and Up," or it might have been when we were smooching in front of Noah's Ark and blocking the ramp for the unicorns.

So these flashes of light in the water shouldn't have been so much of a shock, as we'd heard the Seine was polluted with all sorts of formerly shiny things. Tens of thousands of pieces of cheap, oxidizing junk hurled into the depths by the smitten masses. That couldn't be good for any ecosystem, and I figured any life it could sustain would be malformed, squinting at best. But these were massive, hypnotic eyes, and throwing a key at them in that moment didn't just seem wrong, but almost sinful, as soulless as a Creationist's salad. Not just the shame of littering in a foreign land, but some deeper, unspoken violation. It was hard to explain, and we never mentioned it later, but I told her it was almost as if I'd had this incredible urge to swim the key down there and hand the damn thing over, respectfully, ceremonially, like presenting someone with a symbolic key to a city that didn't really unlock anything, one that you'd never be allowed to enter. Throwing anything into the river seemed like a mistake after such visions.

But we shook off all these weird impulses for good when, moments later, some gypsy moths tried to scam us with their stand-by "lost wedding ring at our feet" trick, plucking it from near my shoe with the worst slight-of-hand ever and grinning while asking me, "Is theeese yoursss?" So I ended up just taking our key home in my pocket, and, eventually, it probably found a home on my tiny Eiffel Tower keychain with the rest of them, and I never thought about it again.

Lies! Actually, I may have swallowed that key once or twice, but it always came back.

***

"Gimme 'em."

The father of my dead wife was holding me at gunpoint, so I handed my keychain over. Worried about Zero still locked in the Rabbit, I noticed that he only *sorta* had me at gunpoint.

The rifle was laying across his forearm, the stock resting near his shoulder. I wasn't exactly looking down the barrel or anything. But the night was still early, and that's the kind of thing that happened at the climax, not while the bad guy is still talking. Whether the bad guy was me or him, though? That was still anybody's guess.

I expected him to throw my keys into the Ohio River, or the Mississippi River, or the River Styx, or whatever the hell river this was, but he needed to tell me his story first, the true story of the padlocks, or the real story of the two rivers, but definitely his favorite story of how we were all connected in ridiculous ways. He started with his father, when he was stationed in Paris during World War II, visiting the bridge at the Passerelle des Arts, the same bridge Angie and I were drawn to on our honeymoon. But somehow that bridge was this bridge. And Greg was there, too. Even though he was in Vietnam. Not playing Vietnam Bug Hockey but playing real hockey, and with real guns. Okay, that didn't sound right, but he'd just lost his daughter, and I'd just lost my wife, so we both tried to keep up best we could.

"My father stood on this bridge in Paris," Greg said. "And rather than the tens of thousands that adorn it tonight, it only had a handful of these padlocks clamped along its rails, locking down *important* things. Not just symbolic. And we both stood here listening to the water splashing below, and he said he kissed a French nurse, right where you're sitting, a woman who was not Angie's grandmother, though he met my mother here, too, down there in the water, the same water where I met her mother. But that night we only pretended to throw in the key, as it was just a rehearsal for the real thing. See that date stamped in the cornerstone? 1903? That's somebody's birthday—"

"Every day is somebody's birthday! But who did what now? Who stood on this bridge?"

"Don't interrupt me, Dave," he said, finger not quite on the trigger yet, but straining to tickle it. "I'm talking about me, and my dad. Everyone's dads . . ."

I'd met Angie's grandfather, Harry, before his death, a great old guy with a flair for turning old satellite dishes into giant lawn-art butterflies, and someone who could always calm Greg down with a squeeze of the shoulder. Speaking of shoulders, her grandpa had gnarly World War II tattoos on both of his: long turned green, one of the American flag, and one of his wife's name in bold *A-Team* font. The poor quality of a veteran's tattoo always insured its authenticity, so I'd never mock one out loud, especially not with his son's gun in my face, but I did make the mistake of ribbing her grandpa about his once.

"I like my women how I like my coffee, Harry," I joked, playfully punching his shoulder. "With my name misspelled on their arm!"

But he'd never been to a Starbucks before, let alone had his name mangled on the side of a cup. Even worse, Angie's grandma's name *was* nearly misspelled on his skin, with "Peggy" looking a lot like "Leggy." But that may have been on purpose. It was a different time.

Seeing my thoughts wandering, Greg gave me a sharp rifle barrel crack to the cheekbone, then pumped up the volume on his story.

"Do you want to hear this or what?"

"Yes, please continue."

"So, back in Paris, while he disarmed the booby traps under these bridges, my father discovered that at the bottom of every river is a locked box," Greg explained. "Well, to us it's a box, but it's actually more like the *idea* of a box. So it needs the idea of a key. And something in every river has been searching for those keys for longer than my father's father's, or anyone's father's father, has ever stood on this bridge in Paris, 4,000 miles away, which is every bridge. And he was lucky to have this bridge under his feet, because being stationed in Paris after World War II meant that he'd saved these bridges in the nick of time. Did you know that Hitler prepared fifty Paris bridges for demolition, wiring up more than the Allies ever did, and this wasn't due to any battle strategy. It was because they wanted to bury something, Bury it forever. Like some kinda secret."

"But what about *this* river? The Ohio River?"

"You aren't listening to me!" he said, hand squeaking on the rifle stock, making this the first time I ever saw someone besides my brother give a gun a snake bite. "Any main street crossing any main river on this planet is one and the same! And you might think throwing all these little tin keys down there year after year may have bought us some more time, maybe even whipped up a little confusion to keep those boxes shut. But whatever lives underneath us is worming its way through every key as we speak. Trying them in every lock. Slipping and sliding all over the river bed, curling and turning anything shiny over and around in its . . . "

"Don't say 'tentacles,'" I said. "Or were you going to say 'testicles'?"

I couldn't help myself. You've heard of "suicide by cop"? This was "suicide by quip".

"No, no, no," he said, weirdly sincere and drunker than I thought. "People always get that confused. They're not tentacles. They're just fingers. Regular fingers. And regular arms. But with like fifty elbows each."

I thought about telling him how these crappy keys worked in everything, but instead I was remembering this kid in grade school who swore he had knuckles on his penis, even though everyone was pretty sure there was something else going on down there that a quick trip to the clinic would cure. Thinking about ol' Knuckle Dick, I tried not to laugh. Laughing at the wrong things is what got me here. So I thought about Matt Fink and his penile deformity instead, and that helped.

"Have you ever heard of the Inverted World Theory?" he asked me.

Oh no, I thought. *Only about every time we saw you over the holidays. Get ready, kids! It's* Conspiracy Hour *with Crazy Greg!*

I may have said that last part out loud because Greg turned his back on me, unsure if he should continue. But I should have known he was just getting started (insert Al Pacino *Scent of a Woman* voice). Greg was balls deep into kooky internet machinations, and his all-time favorite phrases were "Government's known about it for years!" and "Let Buzz Aldrin try that shit on *me!*" which caught on after Astronaut Aldrin famously blasted a moon-landing denier in the face because, you see, Greg was always frustrated the conspiracy nut hadn't properly armed himself before the confrontation. "Armed himself with *facts*, of course. Not a rifle. Though that could have helped, too," Greg would lecture us.

But the real problem was Angie's dad discovering the bottomless World Wide Web way too late in life, an especially dangerous time to teach an old dog new tricks, which, contrary to popular belief, was extremely easy to do. Greg immersed himself in dubious hypotheses, as well as that beloved "devil's advocate" style of most father figures, which turned out to be quite a liability when it came to unverifiable internet insanity. I'd heard parts of this particular theory last Christmas when we were all vacationing in South Carolina. And, to be honest, in that part of the country, he'd sounded relatively sane. But on the plane ride back, I realized how crazy it all was, all that babble about some motherfucker named Sneed and machines with names that sounded like they were straight out of that gooey Lovecraft movie where you hit a giant tuning fork and *blorch!* a curious scholong erupts from your forehead and starts sniffing around, and it turns out we've all been surrounded by nasty little eels at all times but we just couldn't see them. But in this case, it turned out we were all upside down. That's the thing. Greg had that same thirst for knowledge Angie did. "Like father like daughter" and all that jazz. But he was quenching that thirst with the wrong Kool-Aid, which always tastes so damn good. Then chasing that Kool-Aid with whiskey, and then chasing the wrong rabbits down the wrong holes, if you really want some mixed metaphors with your mixed drinks.

Greg wheeled back around, rubbing his own Marine Corps tattoo on his forearm thoughtfully, face like a man possessed, meaning it looked like he was gonna throw up.

No, that's the wrong word. This was more insidious, not quite a possession, but more like an infiltration. An *occupation,* in both senses of the word. For centuries, this planet had grown complacent with every type of possession, which is why we never learned to deal with anything like him, or his kind. And we should have learned to deal with them. Like it was our job.

***

While bored at work watching the custodial staff clean the radio telescopes, sometime during the brutal winter of 1964, Russian astronomer Nikolai Kardashev first came up with the idea of categorizing far-future civilizations. He posited a "Type 3" civilization would be all about controlling an entire galaxy, which I'm pretty sure was the plot of *Men in Black*. "Type 1," however, wasn't just wild speculation (or a surprisingly enjoyable sci-fi satire with a talking dog). It was within reach. It was a true global civilization, which could be secured with worldwide internet technology. And we did just that. But at what cost? Because on a timeline relative to the development of the human race, this was precisely the machine we always knew would destroy us the second it was switched on.

"Did you enjoy serving, Greg?" I asked him, staring at his forearm tattoo. I'd known my father-in-law long enough to understand these kinds of questions rattled him, but he also found them irresistible, and that would buy me more time.

"What the hell do you know about serving?" he said. "You haven't served anywhere, or anyone. You don't know shit about what's important, Dave. It's all a joke to you. I've known this about you since day one."

This angered me, so my next words were risky.

"Actually, I think war movies have taught me a lot about the military. Tell me, did you guys do all your 'chaotic crisis scream' training every day, or just Wednesdays?"

One big step back, and he was grabbing me by the throat, but he let me keep breathing. Then he reconsidered, and I yanked his grip free to gasp for air, his old-man fingernails slicing my collarbone. He jumped up to raise the rifle, ready to whack my head with the barrel again, and he hauled back, almost in slow-motion, which was scarier. I held up my hands.

"Okay, okay," I said. "I joke around as a defense mechanism, Greg. It's pathetic, I know. Like bombardier beetles and that laughing gas shooting out their ass while they're being devoured. Gallows humor, man! It's the only way I can deal with any of this."

"Gallows humor is reserved for those facing the gallows," Greg said, sliding the barrel of the gun down my cheek.

"That's exactly what I'm saying."

"No, you're not. It's crystal clear to me, and everyone else in your life, that you've been taking things too lightly, even before she died." The gun slipped a bit, and he looked uncertain again. "So for now, listen to me. While you're still alive, I feel the need to teach you . . . "

He had my full attention with that, but then he started throwing around his Inverted World Theory again, and I mentally mapped out escape routes.

They all involved the water.

I watched his mouth closely as he talked. This goofy theory had always been his favorite, and it rolled off his tongue easier than the "Illumi-naughty" stories he forwarded from those stupid chain-letter emails (that was his second-favorite theory, something about reptile porn?), but it was just some nonsense about how the Earth was hollow, and we all lived inside it, and the sun was a ball only like 600 miles across. However—and this was the best part—when you moved toward the center of the void in Greg's swirling planetary stomach ache, the distance became exponential, and "that's where the infinite slept." Or maybe he said "that's where the infinite stepped." Either way! Sure, this theory sounds pretty dumb out loud. But one aspect interested me. The stuff about the incredible shrinking critters.

" . . . and if *distance* is exponential," Greg went on, "then the size of creatures will be distorted. So what we perceive as freshwater fish and frogs and crawdads are simply monsters. Not space monsters, but *space* monsters, get me? They just look tiny to us up here where we're standing . . . "

I loved this idea, that the pet lizards I'd neglected in my formative years had been potential world destroyers in their previous life, a complete reversal of the "crocodiles in the sewers" myth. It eased the guilt.

" . . . so there is a level of infinity, but it doesn't involve holes at the North Pole, and it doesn't involve the vast, deepest ocean. No, the infinite involves the cracks in the surface, the ones filled with water. So anywhere there is a river, you have a pathway to forever. And that's what this bridge is."

"But this part of the Ohio River is only twenty feet deep, tops. The Seine, too, if you still think you're in France right now."

"Doesn't matter! Aren't you listening? This is a different kind of deep. That's what I'm telling you—you jump in and sometimes you get flushed through to the other side. Because these rivers are cracks in the façade, and all cracks are connected, Dave. Just like the leg bone is connected to your brain bone, the Mississippi is connected to the Amazon. And the Mekong is connected to the Nile. And the Danube is connected to the Thames. And, yeah, laugh all you want, asshole, but the Ohio is connected to the Seine, which is where we are standing."

"Yeah, we're not in France. I'm also not laughing."

"Boy, you don't have to laugh out loud for me to know that there's something unsettling about your attitude in the face of knowledge. And, most importantly, in the face of the loss you have suffered. And you *will* suffer."

He wasn't really aiming, but his fingertip was testing the

resistance of the trigger, contemplating, so I tried to keep the balls in the air, still resisting the maddening itch of my eyes.

"Okay, but if this river is a crack that goes through the Earth and, what, pops out the other side? Wouldn't it be a river in China, not Paris?"

"Does a river look straight to you, boy!"

Good point, you crazy fuck. Hadn't thought of that.

But I had thought about his theories more than I'd like to admit, like the one he presented over Easter dinner with the monotone of a seminar paper (if academic conferences let you conduct panels with piles of carefully arranged candy animals). He'd used chocolate rabbits and marshmallow peeps to explain to everyone that any and all creatures you find in a river were actually from . . . "somewhere else." This was the great secret of the cosmos, he told me in hushed tones, very solemn, as a chocolate rabbit melted around his fingers. He asked if we'd ever wondered why monsters were always drawn to resemble our more innocuous friends, like the adorable fish and the frogs of our planet.

"Because fish and frogs are behemoths," he'd said. "And vice versa."

"You mean the frogs are the fish?" I'd grabbed for the bunny ears.

"What? No. Maybe sometimes a big frog gets out and runs amok, but all the hoaxes and Yetis out there help disguise them real good."

And by the time Easter dinner and the chocolate rabbit was fully consumed, he'd almost convinced me. Well, maybe not, but Angie and I thought it was all so funny. Back then anyway.

It wasn't funny now.

"You know what, Dave?" he said, finally aiming at the center of my chest. "Even if you didn't kill my daughter, I've come to make sure the last thing you do is toss that key like you were supposed to. Or maybe I'm here just to force you to give a shit about death, hers or yours."

How did he know I didn't throw the key in the water? I thought. Greg was looking around, as nervous as I'd ever seen him, seemingly stone sober now. Then he took a step back and stood up tall, straightening his windbreaker, looking me over like he'd just noticed me again.

"Pay attention to me now. By throwing the key, you're making a promise, to something besides me. On the drive down, I may have sworn to do one or two things to you, if it was the last thing we do. Well, the last thing *you'd* do, but we'll see. Because we are—"

"We are in this together? Is that what you're saying?" I asked cheerfully, still reaching into my bag of tricks from my single semester of *Psych*. Terrible show. I got a C minus.

He didn't answer me, instead checking the shadows for witnesses, or something worse.

***

According to *Wackopedia*—the conspiracy theory hub of a (slightly) more respectable open-collaboration reference site, and, more importantly, my father-in-law's home away from home—Cyrus Sneed, a mild-mannered chiropractor from upstate New Jersey, first proposed his controversial Concave Inverted Earth Theory in 1969, also referring to this head-scratcher as "Cellular Cosmixology." Sneed and his devoted "Oneness Cult" conducted many experiments on the beaches of Florida (of course it was Florida), mostly equations drawn in the sand with seaweed, and eventually shifted their studies to the many rivers and inlets (before they finally started writing on paper). Sneed's followers claimed to have verified the concavity of our planet with some shifty math and with the help of his specialized "Rezonator," a tool which sounded like something out of that pervy Stuart Gordon movie, but more closely resembled the *Ghostbusters* P.K.E. meter (a movie prop that had been recycled in several science-fiction films, such as *They Live* and, the even more frighteningly prescient *Suburban Commando*). This flashy Hollywood toy "proved" conclusively, at least on one basement YouTube video, that not only were we, in effect, crawling around the inside of the Earth, like insects in the proverbial discarded soda can, but also that there was a rapidly escalating increase in distance as you headed toward the center void in any sphere, including our planet. You could travel miles just by dipping a toe into the silt of any marginally deep water source where you couldn't see the bottom. This included the toilet. Proving that last part took *all* the math.

But Greg was in love with any calculation that confused people enough to prove nothing, and he would point to the horizon and ask why it was curved, once correcting me over a campfire, where he always reveled in the dancing shadows distorting his mouth: "If we were living on the inside of the Earth's curvature right now, everything would be perceived the same as if we were on the outside of it." We'd all laughed at first, but things took a turn as he and the internet grew older. Once, at Angie's insistence, Greg and I waded into a creek in Minnesota to fly-fish for "brookies" and chalk up our mandatory *A River Runs Through It* moment, and he immediately remarked on how quickly we were sinking into the muck.

"This riverbed is rock," he said. "This shouldn't be happening."

"That's just dirt, man."

"No. Keep moving or we'll end up in Australia."

He lied when he said he was joking. Me, I only joked when I said I was lying. And I don't know what the fuck that means either, but I always suspected I had reverse daddy issues.

***

Every time I tasked my students to read an epistolary book, like *Dracula* or *Frankenstein* or (big mistake) *The Whisperer in the Darkness*, they would complain, "No way someone just stood there and wrote those letters!" Also, there was no way someone just stood there and read someone *reading* those letters, which means there's definitely no way someone stood there while a saga like Greg's was being told.

Unless it was at gunpoint.

" . . . the eyes aren't really eyes, or testicles . . . " Greg was saying, wiping single-malt sweat and tears from his face with his tattoo.

Oh, boy, here we go . . .

" . . . so if you want to picture what's really down there, imagine falling asleep underwater while staring at 'Dogs Playing Poker,' those bulbous bodies with a bit of mud shark and a man o' war thrown in for good measure . . . "

"Can totally see it. Happened to me in college. Every dorm had that painting."

" . . . the deep electric dreams . . . sometimes impossible arms can be seen when water levels are low enough on both sides. Often mistaken for various entities, like I said, but altogether worse. Or better. But no worse than poker players. Every poker biography should be called *Rich Kid Junkie Dresses like Magician*. But it's not magic. It's real. That's what I mean . . . "

"What the hell are you jabbering about, Greg?" He was looking through me, and now I was convinced that, just as it had done to so many fathers these days, the internet had actually driven him insane. Then driven him straight to me.

"No. The question is, what in God's name did you do to my daughter?" he said, briefly cogent as he took the barrel off my heart and pressed it hard into my temple. "No, that's next . . . that's next," he seemed to remind himself, easing up again. "What's important right now is the key. Throw it, like you should have done years ago."

"You're losing me, man."

"What even are you, boy? Your wife is killed on her way to work, left like garbage on the side of the road, somehow drowned in her car with no body of water in sight? No one knows what happened, but you skip out. Skip town. Skip the funeral! So you tell me, what are you?"

"That's not a real question," I said. *That's a great question,* I thought. *But I dealt with her loss the only way I knew how, and I hated me worse than any of them could. Maybe that's what I should have told . . . wait a minute . . . drowned in her car?*

"Who said she drowned, Greg?"

"I'm asking the questions."

"Who said she drowned in her car?"

"You said that."

"Did you mean drowned in a *'guitar'*?"

"Answer me!"

"Fuck it, fine. I skipped town for the same reason you skipped town. Because we can't deal with not knowing."

This seemed to unnerve him, and his eyes overflowed.

"Why do you think the Eiffel Tower was never finished?" he asked me, openly weeping now, squeezing my souvenir keychain like a rose stem until his hand bled. "You ever look at that architectural abortion? Covering it with a million golden locks would be an improvement."

Golden locks. Great, now I'm picturing the Eiffel Tower with hair.

"Look at these fastened here. Sometimes you'll see a bike lock, and then a bunch more little locks on *that* lock, like an addition on a house. You two could have had a house, a castle, a tower. But the Eiffel Tower is *not* a tower. It's a bridge of iron, set on its end, and a direct pathway to God. If you can lock it down . . ."

"We could have had a house, yep. Enough with the locks, New Dad . . ."

"Listen!" his voice echoed like a thunderclap. "Every one of these locks represents a new family, the promise of a child, forever marked by an exchange between inverted rivers, a fraction of something larger to come. You have denied our family a chance to be part of this . . ." His mouth moved as he mumbled some arithmetic. " . . . a lock weighs 300g and with 1000 locks on one section of railing, so that's the weight of about four adults. How strong is this bridge? How strong are you?"

"Your point!" I yelled at the sky, exasperated.

"The point is our footing is unsound, and everyone governing our infrastructure knows this. Yet one glorious day something will finally envelop every bridge on this backwards planet."

"You should have never gone near a computer, Greg."

Boom! His gun went off, barrel recoiling up into the night sky, and my sarcasm flew away with it. My fighting glasses shattered and rocketed off my face, and I collapsed. A trickle of blood lined my eye, and I could feel the parasites scatter to every corner of my tiny globes. I rubbed my head looking for a devastating injury, simultaneously scanning my childhood databanks of multiplication tables and first kisses and fist fights to make sure he hadn't blown off a chunk of my memories. Then I felt the narrow gash on the top of my skull, relieved I couldn't feel brain, but not knowing what it would feel like if I did.

My ears were ringing like church bells, one eardrum most likely ruptured, so I'm still not sure I heard him correctly when he told me that he killed her.

***

"She broke the chain. My son was supposed to keep the chain going, but he didn't live long enough. Three generations did it right, but you two fucked it up. Doomed the minute you walked away with the key."

He was dangerous, yes, but one unexpected side effect of the internet was becoming a bit of a con artist, and suddenly I wasn't convinced Greg killed my wife—his daughter, and our one dreadful but authentic connection. But he wanted me to think this, and I needed to understand why. Was he protecting someone? Combined with his impulse to dominate me, as usual, maybe his grief had driven him back to the edge of the cliff. Maybe he couldn't deal with the loss compounded with my perceived indifference. But I'd snapped easily enough, so who was I to judge?

Or maybe I was just wrong, like I was about everything else in my life.

I stood back up, hand on my wounded head, and he let me lurch around the bridge. He followed me, explaining the Myth of a Golden Age in America, how they were always broke growing up in Duluth, how they even lived in Pittsburgh for a stint, and in desperation he tried his hand at beekeeping, until he lost his boy, then his entire business, to the prison that came to their town, and now everyone he knew was broke, and the bees were dead, and a different age was coming, one built on infinite river beds lined with novelty keys and honeymoon boners . . .

Did he say 'beekeeping'?

"What was your son's name?" I asked him to buy my concussion some precious seconds. Angie had mentioned him so rarely that I'd honestly forgotten.

"Greg Junior," Greg said.

"Oh, right," I said, realizing why I'd never bothered to file it away, but my ears were positively screaming from all his exposition, and, even without my fighting glasses, my eyes were hopelessly blurry from the worms. So I may have missed some of his confession, but there was something to do with endless coupling on postnuptial bridges, and how the locks cursed your future child, ensured there would be no reproduction as this union is forever committed to a search for the key to release it from the burden of the honeycomb that was the human race.

Or something.

You know, internet shit.

He was almost pleading with me, explaining that if he could throw it in for us, maybe their bloodline could be saved. And even though he was already gripping my Eiffel Tower in his bloody fist, I knew he wanted me to prove him wrong, to jump in and find his father's key, then come up with it in my teeth 4,000 miles away. This was just one too many keys to keep track of.

See, this was the real reason I'd gotten fired back in Kentucky. I was never able to teach anyone how to make an effective argument, let alone engage in one myself.

I took a righteous swing for his jaw, and he brought the ass end of his rifle down on my forehead and almost knocked me out for good. Murky but still conscious, I watched him cock the bolt action again, but I knew our time was up even before he spoke words that were ice cold but terrifyingly sincere.

"We all had to make sacrifices."

***

It was hard to see due to the burst blood vessels and the resurgence of microbial traffic in my vision, but I knew from all the clicking that he was unlocking every padlock on the bridge. One by one, using any key hanging off my Eiffel Tower because, just as I'd always suspected, it didn't matter. Any key worked on any lock. When he finished his first handful of locks, he let them splash into the river, and I could feel the bridge creaking beneath my feet, wood screaming as if something terrible was going to happen. And something rose up in me right along with it. All I knew was that he couldn't be allowed to do . . . whatever he was doing. So I threw a slightly better punch this time, not trying to be like a guy in a movie, but like the guy in the movie who was training the guy *playing* the guy in the movie. I wagered he would throw the best punch money could buy.

"Aim for an imaginary space behind his head," this stunt guy would say. "Like if his head was a globe, and his eyes were the United States, you would be punching Russia."

So I punched the shit out of Russia, but it had been a long fuckin' day, so it was still more like a slap, and my fingers were also trying to grab the gun at the last second. However, a desperate clusterfuck of fantasy and flailing limbs was more than enough to send anyone off balance.

"You're gonna show me something!" My father-in-law howled as he tumbled back against the rail, steadying himself with the rifle, then cocking it again. "Even if that means I take the blame . . ."

I stopped, dropped, and rolled, and his gun went off

again, and the bullet plowed through a line of love locks next to my wrist. Cheap metal shards rained down onto the slats of the bridge like chrome confetti. *So much for the commercial,* I thought.

Another gunshot sucked the air from my lungs, slug whistling past my ear and detonating dozens more locks. I tried to run, pitching forward, then back, marveling at a bridge that wasn't architecturally beholden to the considerable dead heft of a thousand padlocks now suddenly tilting beneath our feet as if our duel was shifting ballast. These invisible waves dumped us onto our backs as we toppled together into a swaying lamp post. The copper base bowed against the weight and tangle of our bodies, and when it swung us around over the water, we both went for each other's throats.

Then came an impact flash of another punch exploding between us, and Greg's face seemed to come apart and reassemble from the force of the blow.

I didn't do that.

I followed the trajectory of the savage uppercut back down to its source, and I was suddenly reading the magnificent golden letters "L-O-V-E" spread across Matt's gleaming knuckles. My knuckles. Our knuckles. It was a goddamn reunion. The three of us, together again, Mad, Matt, and myself, all on our knees, all wrestling for Greg's rifle. Somehow, Matt was the lucky winner, and he came up with the gun in his hands and a big ol' grin. He pulled back his jacket to reveal my rusty "Indian Police" badge pinned to his flannel. But he didn't tell Greg he was under arrest, thank god.

Reeling from the brass knuckles, Greg ran, blood pouring from both sides of his mouth and leaving a trail behind him. I was tempted to throw down a Zippo and see if it ignited like a fuse. Matt patted me on the back, proud of his intervention. He dropped the knuckles to my feet and shouldered the rifle and helped me up. In the process of wearily climbing up his body and wrapping an arm around his shoulder, the buttons popped off his shirt.

That's when I saw the ample hair on his chest again, and the way the fight had shifted his body's terrain, exposing the circles of bare skin marking his torso. Naked patches of angry flesh where the hair had been ripped free. Exactly the sorts of crop circles you got when they removed the electrodes for a heart monitor. I looked at my rescuer. Matt Fink's head tilt was back in force, and his posture returned to taking on that canine submissiveness, like when we first met outside the toilet confessional. This was the guilt I was reading in his body language back then, tics and mannerisms he'd managed to shed on our extensive road trip, a disguise he'd worn for miles. But now he was back, the fake doctor turned fake musician who had wronged me. And though this would have been the perfect moment to yank down his pants and see if he had a second penis once and for all, I didn't do it. I was past all that. Blame my newfound maturity.

So I seized the opportunity, seized the day, you might say, and I grabbed the still blazing end of the copper lamp post and bent the base once, twice, and tore it free with a final heave. Then I brought it down hard on Matt Fink's head, transforming his skull into its own concave planet, an inverted world with infected eyes rolling backwards in their sockets. And, due to my father-in-law's teachings, I knew that he would perceive everything exactly the same looking inside his own skull as he would looking out.

Okay, I was lying when I said I didn't pull down his pants. No man could resist! So it was no surprise when I worked his corduroys down his hips to find two extra eyes gazing back at me. To add insult to injury, they were aligned up-and-down, not side-by-side, making him officially the worst possible configuration.

"I knew it!" I said, but those two dicks won our staring contest. "You guys should be cops," I said, intimidated, and I shoved Matt's body away, not waiting for the splash.

Just then, a camera flash turned the bridge into a negative overexposure, and I stood up, dropping the shattered lamp.

It was Mad, with only the novelty camera from my basement between her thumb and forefinger. I couldn't understand how I'd been blinded by the toy, but I had no doubt Matt's double penis was somehow now immortalized in its viewfinder. Or me, suddenly naked with a dumb look on my face, burned into a tiny plastic slide. I moved toward her, and, not really aiming, she clicked the gag camera again. The second flash caused the parasites in my eyes to scatter, and I shielded my face with my arm. When colors returned to swim laps around my vision again, I looked up and down the bridge for Mad. I had so much to say to her, but during the fight I'd forgotten she was there. Just as I'd forgotten to ask her what ever drew her to me to begin with. Then I remembered.

It was my terrible license photos. DMV Dave and true monster energy. And she got my picture for her Hall of Shame after all. Only Matt was the organ donor. Frog powers, deactivate.

"Super barf . . . " I heard someone scoff from below. But if she had ever been there, Mad was gone for good now. So was Matt. So was the rifle. The buckling of the bridge had ceased, and I leaned over the bronze palisade, tempting the points of the railing with my throat. The busted Eiffel Tower keychain jangled in my hand. My fighting glasses were somewhere in the river, and with my injuries and astigmatism (Zero's parasites being the cherry on top, of course), it should have been impossible for me to see much of anything. But I could still count almost a hundred burning eyes down below, all watching me survey the situation. I tried counting them, but I kept ending up on an odd number, which was more horrifying than their judgmental stare, because you never found odd-numbered eyeballs in nature.

Just as my own eyes were failing, I heard the sounds of footsteps bounding towards me. But I didn't have to focus to know whoever it was would be headless, and not really aiming. Someone cocked and fired in quick succession. Maybe it was Mad. Maybe it was Mag. Maybe it was Greg. Or maybe

Zero was finally putting those thumbs to use. But regardless of the assassin's identity, my unknowable subterranean audience, otherwise known as the first true global civilization, watched all of this from the water as the last muzzle flash chased me over the edge and into oblivion. I dove toward the eyes, pleading for a respite. But the only one who blinked at my execution was me.

***

In a river, you'll want to swim close, but also try to stay underneath her, remaining deep, and you will follow the memory of her as long as you can hold your breath. You'll still be delusional enough to believe you could do both at once.

You'll be down there as long as you're able, then you'll stay down there some more. Like a shark with thumbs, you consider hitchhiking along the trail of her scent, the last place her memory will remain, and it will stain the water like an oil spill. These black curls of fuel will ride a surface tension that you'll never be able to break, never be able to burn, and, in desperation, you will send the last of your bubbles up her way, for her to swallow if she needs. But she won't. The bubbles will contain excuses, apologies, declarations of love and forgiveness, and she'll know this. And most will pop before they reach her lips. One bubble will contain all your stories that meant nothing to anyone but you, and it will be the first to dissipate in her currents. Your hands will grasp the water in vain where this bubble used to be, for any trace of the story it once contained. And as you slip into unconsciousness, you will know the bubble will not be missed, much like yourself, because it held another pointless digression, detailing the story of the third time you ruined a movie for someone, which was every time. So it won't count for anything, much like your life.

XXII

MOVIES FOR MILKWEED

THE ONLY THING worse than describing a fight is describing a dream.

So I would never do that to you. But do I think there should be a loophole where it is permissible, as long as you keep it as short as your fight stories, and also if you preface it by promising you won't suddenly wake up and the dream never happened? Maybe. Because with me, it's always exactly the opposite. Meaning I'm constantly waking up and realizing the craziness is real. So most of this happened. I mean, *everything* happened. But this dream about milkweed and the first movie ever made definitely happened.

The dream starts out years ago at my first apartment, before it became our first apartment. The parking lot in front used to be sunk into the ground about five feet on all sides, so it looks a bit like a huge community pool, maybe a bit more like the biggest cell in a TV dinner tray, the one that always holds the meat. The inclines on the sides are gradual and only noticeable during the winter, when the tray fills with snow and slush and you need a little extra gas to clear the entrance and hit the road. New residents spin their tires on the slopes for a couple days until they figure out the only way to get out is to keep a routine, maintain that speed.

You'd think this obstacle would make me late for work, and, yes, during the dream, I always have to dig myself out or give the car another running start to get up the hill. However, these inclines are the only reason I ever make it to work at all, because they encourage my legs to start running right before I reach my car, if only for about two or three steps.

And I keep that momentum. Until the day she moves in.

***

In film class, we learned that the first movie ever made was really just a blurry, black-and-white series of images that showed a horse running. For the first time, human eyes were able to observe that, between gallops, every one of a horse's legs were off the ground simultaneously. This was also true of people, which the teacher proved in the *second* movie ever made, a short clip of a man running. The third movie ever made, bizarrely enough, was a disturbing snuff film about electrocuting an elephant. Look it up! It didn't mean much of anything to me. But every movie made after the elephant execution involved a car chase, where wheels left the road constantly.

But what I learned from the first two films was that running was fundamentally the act of throwing your body weight and catching it, if only for a split second. Throwing and catching yourself, over and over, something my brother could actually do with a football, basketball, or baseball when, impatient with my lack of athleticism, he would play every position at the same time and catch all his own passes. Then he would give me a snake bite on my arm. Did I mention my brother was a yellow anaconda?

But in my dream, this brief but significant sensation of flight is the one thing that gives me a sense of urgency. A jog of one, two, three steps tops, stimulates me enough to navigate the traffic and the red lights to get to work and slide behind an all-important imaginary cash register with some purpose. How pathetic is that? I am, in effect, flying to my car, eager to do menial labor for low pay, even in my recurring fantasies.

I did figure this out, twenty-eight jobs, three assumed names, and nine different parking lots too late in life to really have an impact on my trajectory. But the dreams are a reversion. Back to the days when I would worry that I'm late. And I'm always late in the dream. Until I move into the apartment. Then I'm late, but only after decades of being on time. It's not supposed to make sense. But when I buy the shovel? That's the worst. I always buy the shovel. And this makes me precisely nine minutes late.

At first, I blame invisible landscapers and the smoothing out and subsequent slow death of the small hill along the slopes of the TV dinner, the one thing that has me flying to work like a racehorse and soaring untethered to the ground for approximately 3.9 seconds every night. I know that doesn't sound like much, but it's only 58.8 seconds shorter than the Wright Brothers' famous first flight.

But now she's there. And she's slowing me down. Even worse than the shovel. Because once she moves in, she's always in front of me, just one or two short steps ahead on every path, walking briskly enough that I can never pass. And she wastes even more of my time turning around, or slowing down, as if she's trying to catch me sneaking up on her. I want to yell that she's making me late for work, making me late for life, and that I need to run for at least three steps to lift up off the ground, that I will die without any momentum. But my tongue doesn't work, and it takes way too long to explain. Sort of like this dream.

Then suddenly it's a day later, and I'm heading back to the hardware store, payment swinging heavy in my hand, as nervous as I used to be when I stole pornography from my father.

***

Once upon a time, I ruined a movie, and it still haunts me to this day. I would go on to ruin many movies during my vast but haphazard experience as a theatergoer, but it was true what they said. You always remembered your first.

It was the summer of '75 in Diamond, Ohio, a few miles outside of Akron. Technically, it was our first hometown, before the more permanent relocation to Toledo, but it never felt like it. Our one lonely movie theater, called The Exalted (dumb name, sure, but still a better love story than *The Majestic*), had come up with an interesting promotional gimmick. They were letting children pay for their movie tickets in milkweed. The government was sponsoring a program to collect the plant fibres to make parachutes, but it was really just a sneaky recruiting tool for cannon fodder, similar to those rousing military ads they'd shoehorn in between the trailers, right after the dancing candy bar warned a captive audience at gunpoint to turn off their cell phones, which were the size of drive-in speakers back then. Milkweed was rampant in our town, but such uses weren't so well-known. The little goth kid taking tickets would tell anyone who would listen (and with some real zeal) that milkweed had been used throughout history to cure snakebites, and diarrhea, and even new mothers drank it, "thus the name!" And though it wasn't as hardy as Ohio's other invasive plant, gorse (meaning it didn't come back to life after it got burned like that one did), it was arguably much handier. According to the Omaha Tribe of Nebraska, as well as Franklin the Darkling who worked at The Exalted every Sunday, it expelled tapeworms and other parasites, even, on occasion, flushing away microorganism infestations of the sclera, when prescribed as eye drops. Yes, this was a lot to lay on the customers, but everybody got a kick out of Franklin.

Anyhow, someone somewhere must have figured out that any young whelp who made the effort to harvest milkweed from along the roadside just to pay for a movie ticket would likely be living a life hopeless enough to find the prospect of patrolling hateful glares in a foreign land rewarding.

"They're recruiting all the 'side orphans,'" my dad explained. "You know, those orphans in a movie that aren't really part of the regular shenanigans, just orbiting the scenes and lingering in the corners of the screen? Faces all dirty and clutching a broken toy? Side orphans." I understood completely. He was talking about the kind of kid who ran up and down the theater aisle making sputtering airplane noises with an oddly alluring piece of floor garbage when his dad took him to see *The Deer Hunter*, all the while wondering what happened to the "fun" movies his mom used to pick. Maybe you haven't noticed those kids, but I can tell you this with certainty: after they're running those aisles, someone always takes the floor garbage away.

But what better way to let young boys and girls start fulfilling the modest dreams they never knew they had than by making parachutes? These kids didn't even dream about electrocuting elephants or (gasp!) going to work! My dad figured that next summer, The Exalted would announce that a few gallons of bullfrogs could be used to make ammunition. So bring those buckets, Charlie Buckets! He whapped me on the back and said, "Even one cup of snails can be ground up to make a mile of tank treads, so let's all do our part," but this may have been sarcastic.

The theater handed out empty extra-large popcorn tubs for weeks so that kids could collect their milkweed. They turned it in right where Franklin tore their tickets. And the pile of plucked milkweed grew. It grew without growing. It took me three visits for it to click that this nutty barter system was really happening, because when I first noticed the pyramid of empty tubs, I'd just assumed it was some kind of popcorn-eating contest. Or Franklin's overly-creative display for *Day of the Triffids*, which was the matinee I was there to see, and also a "Midnight Movie" all-time favorite in Diamond, due to its inherent hopelessness.

But on that third trip, when I laughed at some kids desperately clutching their buckets of milkweed, and then "accidentally" cut in line in front of them, no less than three boys and five girls went for my throat. I handled them reasonably well, but while I caught my breath and surveyed the dusty clearing where they landed, sprawled between a broken crane game and the unmanned refreshments counter, more children somehow materialized. They were always there, but it was like when you stare at a dying lawn long enough and suddenly dozens of paper wasps become visible. They dropped their buckets of milkweed and came for me, fists and teeth clenched, all hopped up on Monster Energy, filthy faces as flushed as the red sunset on the original four-sheet for *Apocalypse Now*, which hung proudly in The Exalted's vestibule, the very movie they were there to see. I think one of those brats tore it down when I chucked him off my shoulder and through the doors. The poster had hung unmolested for twenty years, until I made the mistake of starting some shit with those side orphans.

Later, when similar run-ins at movie theaters continued to plague me, I tried to remind myself that grubby children got real mad about these sorts of things. Because, to them, movies were not something you could watch again, remember? You'd think I'd have learned by now that these things happening on the screen were bona fide miracles if some broke-ass street urchin could only see them once. And when that movie was in exchange for a bucket of weeds, impossibly that would have made it seem even more important. Like a job. Or like something that might never happen again in their inauspicious lifetimes. "But don't shed a tear for jackanapes!" no one has ever said. Honestly, they were just mad I made them miss the previews.

But I get it now. I slowed them down. I made them late.

***

So now it's way later in my dream, after the parking lot is filled in. And she's gone. A busybody retiree on the ground floor of my apartment building looks over her glasses at me and asks why I no longer have a spring in my step. I try to explain that it's only the landscape around our building that has changed. But she just stares at me out her window, face framed between lush hanging ferns, and silently sips her coffee at this. Then she starts blowing bubbles through her tiny straw. She says my mother once told her to "always watch the bubbles so you know which way is up" but "never blow bubbles in your milk." Fortunately, my mother never breastfed us, then vanished from our lives when I was lucky number 13, which was extra lucky for me because my brain was fully cooked by then and her loss had no effect on me whatsoever.

"What do you remember about your mother?" the old woman doesn't ask me.

"She was always trying to teach us that being clever was way more important than being smart," I don't tell her.

"You mean being kind."

"Yes, definitely. She also said being clever is more important than being kind."

"So, are you going to move with that sense of urgency ever again?" the old woman really asks me this time, and I tell her I can prove I'm still running, still flying, and I dig through a pile of old photographs to find one that the busybody took herself, when she was watching me from her window, her tight, gray curls, once black, cutting hieroglyphics through the fog of her breath on the glass as she leaned forward to get her shot. But I can't find it.

Then her window is suddenly below ground level, peeking around one of those drainage boxes people sometimes fill with flowers, and she's down there doing laundry and taking more pictures, which seems much too dangerous with all the exposed wiring. When I peer through the window, the sparking tangle of wire is up to her chest, and she swims through them as they grip then loosen around her limbs, doing laps from the window back to the washing machine.

And she stays down there, continuing to fling that basement window open near my feet, trying to scare me when I get home from work. I fall for it every time. That final afternoon, she decides to record my trek from the parking lot to the building. She's making a movie, she says. And the pictures in her series will prove I'm no longer running to my car. But she's so low to the ground in her basement window that the angle of her first photo and the sunken parking lot reveal only my head, floating in a sea of grass and asphalt.

When I look at the photo later, there's a girl in the picture with me. A new girl. And just like the first movie ever made, her legs don't touch the ground. But now my head is swapped with a horse's head, its joyous and jutting rubber teeth stretched across the void underneath where my face used to be. Buried somewhere and imprinted on a reel of film, my own latex grin would be pulled tight to the point of breaking over the ghost of the horse's foaming snout.

The forced perspective of the picture makes me a third her size, so I put it on my refrigerator, pinning it with magnetic haikus I never use for poems. Today someone has spelled out lyrics from Nick Cave's song "Wings off Flies."

"She loves me . . . she loves me not . . . she loves me . . . "

I circle the girl's feet on the photo, put it in an envelope, and I slide it under the busybody's door. She never acknowledges this evidence, and her two ferns are moved to her kitchen window, around the corner of the building that faces the highway, and they wilt under the exhaust of endless traffic.

I try to recreate the photo from memory, but I can't. I'm terrified of a girl who doesn't touch the ground. Even more frightened of the face of the old woman at the window near my feet. There aren't supposed to be heads on the ground, I tell myself. Even horses' heads. I wonder if heads should always be buried instead.

Here the dream jumps forward, a decade and nine hundred pairs of shoes later, and I've worn the trail back down again. And every time I bury her head, or my own, every blade of grass stands up straight and green. But this has nothing to do with us. It's the milkweed seeds I've been dropping on my way to work, when no one is looking, which is always. And with these weeds, there's finally enough of an incline to get back my momentum. Until the landscapers leveled it off again. And, like always, the path fills in, and we sprout back up, as straight as any goddamn flower. The milkweed seeds work, it seems, just not like the military advertised.

The next time I have the dream, she's moving back into the building, and I know it's her because she always carries the same number of boxes. Nineteen hundred and three. The year of the Wright Brothers' first flight. She hands me her guitar case and asks me to help carry her bed inside. And then I'm walking behind her, and she's slowing me down again. And soon I'm stopping at the hardware store. This is our dance, and I grow used to it.

I don't need to buy a new shovel every night, but I do. I pay for them with a guitar case of milkweed. Then I wake up in my car, and she is still gone. Because my car is underwater.

***

When Angie disappeared in Louisville, before she drowned in her car or was shot in the head or asphyxiated in a guitar case on the side of the road, she made her last phone call from an alley. She asked me to rescue a cat trapped in a cage, and it *had* to be a cat, because she could hear it. And everyone knows what a cat sounds like. But my momentum was long gone, and when I went to rescue a cat, who was doing time instead of serving it, I walked to the alley instead of running. Both feet never left the ground. And I got there too late to save anyone, even when I broke down the door.

The animal in the cage had been dead for some time. Long decayed, it was more bones than fur. In this state, I couldn't understand how it could have been crying for help less than an hour before. But the only thing I saved that day was a cage, which I will carry with me forever.

The thing about cat skeletons is they're hard to identify. Their framework is like too many other animals. The same way a human fetus tries on a series of costumes before it settles on being a regular baby. If you zoom in on an embryo, first it's a fish, then it's a frog, then it's fowl, then it's a monkey, then it's a man. So when the baby Angie was carrying died inside of her, it could have been anything really, and that gave me comfort. Because if I knew what it really was, I certainly wouldn't be driving around the country with it rotting in my car.

To put it another way, I'm not that kind of doctor, but I do know one thing. Cruising around town crying with a dead cat in a cage can't be good for the eyes.

***

You ride a rabbit underwater, below the bridges, and you allow hundreds of hands to hold you down, feeling your lungs fill past capacity. Through the swirls of alluvium and slime, you can see them, Angie and Shell and Jenny and all the rest, holding hands. Holding too many hands to count. They seem naked at first, until you realize it's just thin cerements clinging to their bodies like seaweed. In the prism of sunlight piercing the waves, you map out navels and nostrils, ears then breasts, your eyes conjuring X's over each extremity. When they swim close, you hold the first nipple they offer in your teeth, not quite pinching it through the second skin of their shrouds, but giving it a gentle, respectful tug.

Somehow, this works, and a hundred hands turn a hundred keys, and the river bottom releases you as you ride a multitude of rabbits and warm bodies you know more intimately than your own. You ride them back to the surface, and there, on the shore, blonde hairs turn black, red hairs turn brown, and straight hairs curl in the blistering sunlight, mercifully wrapping her many faces in defiance of your gaze. Then gusts of wind catch her endless, whiplashing mane, stripping her hair of flowers, then stripping her flowers of petals, and she turns to follow the pull of the tempest to walk away from you forever.

XXIII

THE FLOWERY

"**WHAT STATE ARE** *you in?*"

Even if I knew whether the latest desperate question nudging me from my cell phone's screen was geographic or psychological, I couldn't have answered it. And not just because I'd only recently started paying attention to road signs again. I'd stopped checking whether I'd really removed my phone's battery a hundred miles back because this was one of the only questions I already knew the answer to. But, more importantly, there was no one left in the car to ask.

So I was ready to wrap things up. Crack my knuckles and crack this case. The big case anyway. The smaller case (which always led to the big case, if you've ever seen a movie in your life), I had left behind on the shore of the Ohio River when I crawled gasping and reborn out of that green water. I shook myself off like a dog, then found my faithful Zero sunning himself on the dashboard of the Rabbit. Two states later with the windows down, my clothing was finally drying, and Zero started sniffing the dank remnants of the river that still permeated my pores. The gunshot had grazed me, the slug gutting my secret duck pocket, rattling somewhere around the vicinity of my spine for a while but never breaking the skin, until it finally blew apart the seams of my coat and sent my stash of weapons off into the inky void to get fondled by every freshwater horror for a dozen nautical miles. Tens of thousands of miles actually, if you were into silly upside-down Earth theories like me. You'd think the loss of my brass knuckles would make me feel naked, but, kinda like Dorothy said to the Scarecrow, I missed my blackjack most of all. My eyes had cleared up, as well (or maybe I'd just grown accustomed to the infection), and the morning sun had revealed the gloomy river inlet that birthed me to be clearer than I could have imagined. So I was able to retrieve my fighting glasses from some nearby rocks easily enough, relieved to find only one new spiderweb crack in the bottom corner of the right lens. Just another tiny map, of course, coaxing me toward all the wrong towns, like another counterfeit Nashville, no doubt, a landmark city where Angie and I had our first fight when she wouldn't stop dropping change in that busker's tin cup. "Afraid of a little *change*, Dave?" she had taunted me. Wait, that wasn't Nashville, Alabama. I get mixed up sometimes. It was Smashville, Georgia, population zero!

Well, population me *and Zero now.*

So when I finally looked up, the road sign somehow said, "Welcome to Florida!" Quite the revelation, considering the circles I'd been making. This is where things would end, I realized. I found Zero's dead eyes in the rearview mirror, addressing him directly for once.

"You didn't really think it was over, did you? This is how these things go. On to the big conspiracy! Because even if we solved the mystery of her death, it is time to solve the mystery of her life. Fuck yeah! Totally just thought of that like it was nothing. Gonna put it on a T-shirt. So steal that shit, you impossible beast."

A cryptic note in my wife's yearbook had led me here, but I'd had a lot of time to think about Florida before my arrival. Florida as a concept at least. For one, it was certainly the state whose shape most resembled a guitar. A guitar with a broken neck. Which is what must have happened to Angie in order for her to fit into a guitar case.

Speaking of cases, *I told you we weren't finished with this one just yet. Bam! Remember to tip your waitress.*

I looked to my left at the acres of dead grass and bald earth, then saw what I could have sworn was a mosquito tornado. Is that a thing? When I was a kid, I remembered tons of insects swirling below the street lights, like these invisible blenders full of bugs all along the highway. But I never noticed this lately. Did the bugs get smarter? Or did the street lights? Or did they all migrate down South. My dad explained to me once how Juan Ponce de León's original christening of "Florida" meant "The Flowery" in Spanish, and I thought of how sweet and innocent this name sounded, how it didn't fit at all with the uninviting, buggy wasteland outside my window.

I tapped the most broken lens of my glasses, content that my path was just *kissing* the top corner of Florida, right where it touched that little tumor protruding from the ass of Alabama. The "panhandle," they called it, which is what Alex named his erection in *A Clockwork Orange*, a book published without its last chapter because no one wanted that adventure to keep going. Cowards!

I could have sworn I was still in Mississippi with the haze of landscape rolling past, everything all drug-addled and overalls and *Huck Finn* 'n' shit. But, no, this was definitely Florida, because the mosquito tornado keeping up with my car was now three mosquito tornadoes. At this juncture, I was grateful I'd finished Angie's dissertation, because I had some fresh stats about the joint to recite instead: 56 state prisons, and 7 creepy-ass private prisons, housing something in the ballpark of 150,000 offenders. That was more than the population of Hollywood. Hollywood, Florida, I mean. It's real (you look it up since my phone's still being weird).

My vision clouded like I was looking through gauze, and I wiped my lens to find an actual spider web draped over the newest cracks. I took this as a sign of good luck, even though Angie would have disagreed. Always plagued by mystery bug bites in the mornings, she would remind me never to get too excited if the webs in the corners of our bedroom were catching her tormentors. That just meant we were living with spiders raised on our blood.

So I decided to do an experiment to take my mind off all the barbiturate-and-socioeconomic-uncertainty-laced plasma donations that no doubt filled millions of mosquito bellies spinning round and round tornado alley like vortex mixers in the world's saddest laboratory. I tried counting sheep, to see how high I'd get before I saw my first official Florida prison. Then I switched to counting Jeeps. I only got to a hundred and one before I saw the "Don't Pick Up Hitchhikers" sign, a signal I've always known meant "prison," even though they weren't explicitly labeled as such. But when I hit a thousand and two Jeeps, I got bored with the game and pulled over at a rest stop to get Zero some food. He blinked and yawned, not as interested in these escapades since our crew had been whittled back down to me. But I knew he was hungry because I was, too.

"Patient Zero, always so patient . . . "

As I got out, a dog ran by the Rabbit, a yapping Jack Russell trailing the leopard-print leash from its harness. I froze over Zero, listening close for that elusive meow. At this point, it was only to satisfy my own curiosity (now that we had fewer distractions in the car), but I was sure I could prove he was a cat before the day was over.

The gas station was vast, cases of beer lining the floor like knee-high labyrinths, and two halves of the store divided by themes: Florida gift shop on the right, Native American gift shop on the left. A sign over the register said, "No Shirt? No Shoes? No Mask? No Problem!" and I wondered how often they got robbed. So instead of trying to sniff out the best chicken in town again, I found myself milling around the Native American side to try and seem cool, and that's when I saw something weird on a T-shirt on the "30% Off" rack that recalibrated my day. So after a quick chat with a clerk (and another surprise translation), momentum was back and I was off the ground and running for my car so fast that I almost knocked over a chubby kid on crutches. But I stumbled instead of him, skinning a knee through my jeans, and the chubby kid never slowed down at all, catching up to the Jack Russell and stomping on its cat-print leash.

A cat-print leash on a dog? I thought, remembering the *Full Metal Jacket* poster back at The Exalted, with its peace sign button and "Born to Kill" graffiti sharing space on an infantry helmet.

The chubby kid watched me brush pebbles off my legs, then trudged on, working his crutches as fast as scissors, the leopard-spotted leash gripped tight between his smile.

***

I don't think I can overstate how excited I was to decipher my first real clue. With the question of her infidelity answered, I was coming closer to solving the mystery of her "invisible prison" stuff, and, hopefully, how my wife's research on this fantastical subject could have caused her death. It's kinda convoluted, but bear with me here for a second. You remember how Angie had the word "Clearwater" written on her address book? And I assumed that must have meant "Florida," right, with all those Florida prison stats in her dissertation. Well, it *was* Florida, yes, but not "Clearwater," Florida. See, she also had that little Indian drawing next to the biggest piece of her puzzle, because "Clearwater" in Creek Indian apparently was "Shambia." And "Shambia," transformed easily into "Escambia."

And Escambia was the county I was in at that precise moment.

I won't bother telling you about the hour I wasted following an ambulance back to a West Florida Hospital parking lot, thinking this word was written on their hood in some sort of secret code. Oops, I just did. It was actually

"Ecnalubma," in case you were wondering, which spells "dumbass" backwards.

So, why had Angie come to Escambia? I'd like to say I spent hours under one of those green-hooded library lamps, brow furrowed, blowing the lid off the case with stacks of dusty books and some good old-fashioned studying. But a T-shirt screaming, "You're in Escambia! The *Real* Clearwater!" was all I needed. Well, that, and the quick history lesson from a bored, gum-twirling teenager behind the Native American gift shop counter, followed by a hip check to a chunky dog wrangler on crutches to reboot my sense of purpose. But besides this revelation saving me a thousand more highway circles, it also gave me a newfound confidence in figuring this shit out, whatever and wherever that shit may be. I knew this because, even if how I got there didn't make much sense out loud, I finally found myself staring at the gates of my first Florida prison.

***

And there it stood in all its brutalist glory. A jail that had popped up in front of my face as soon as I wished hard enough, just a couple miles from a gas station where they sold American history in the form of cheapjack dreamcatchers and Confederate flag fidget spinners and those "rattlesnake egg" rubber-band gags that never worked, but, somehow, no fried chicken, the delicious bird that built this country. Why they hadn't sold jailhouse souvenirs instead of all the Native American swag was anybody's guess, but I was about to find out.

The sign read, in reasonably large letters, "Escambia County Corrections." But above that—probably for all the PhDs—letters twice as big bellowing, "JAIL." I thought about driving up a little closer, but not having any idea what to say to whoever might interrogate me, I just parked next to the heavily fortified fence and idled.

No love locks hanging off this bitch, I thought, counting flowers on the razor wire.

That's when a muddy but bloody red '79 Chevy C10

Silverado pickup with a stained white cab rumbled in next to my car, and a huge but genial bozo in overalls and no shirt (of course) opened my passenger door and plopped down in the back seat before I could react. Zero was as confused as me, and he bumped my feet as he zipped under the seats to hide.

"Hi!" the big guy said, leaning forward and squeezing the top of the passenger's seat. I'm guessing he did this so I could gasp at the size of the motherfucker's hand, a sweaty pink mitt that compressed the headrest as easily as an office stress toy.

"How are you?" I asked. "Can I help you with something? Maybe find you a shirt?"

"Question for ya! May I ask why you're hanging around outside the gate, friend?"

"Why not?"

"You here to pick somebody up?" The man was beaming like he knew the answer. Lots of teeth on this guy, too, but goddamn if he didn't seem friendly, though, besides the fact that he'd invaded my car and was working my headrest like the tail end of the toothpaste tube. I could feel Zero sniffing my ankles in alarm.

"No, I am not. Do you work for the Department of—correction, I meant *'jail'?*"

"After a fashion." His smile was positively shark-like at this point.

"Are *you* waiting to pick anybody up?" I asked him, unable to not smile back.

"Nope. I mean, I hope not!" he said, and I realized he meant me. His smile had reached the maximum capacity before someone would have to start laughing, but we never did, though I did have to bite my lip.

"Tell me, sir," he went on. "You aren't mad about nothin' right now, are ya?"

"Mad?" I didn't know if he meant angry or crazy, so I just went with the denial. "No, man, I'm not mad. I mean, I don't think so. But, honestly, I don't know why you jumped in my car like this, and I'm kinda just waiting to see how this shit pans out."

"Okay, here's the deal. The name's Cort," he said, shaking

the headrest instead of my hand, but it had the same effect. "And I'm what you might call the V.P. of this particular prison. So, off the books, I just keep a lookout for people looking to bushwhack the new releases."

"Don't you mean V.I.P.?"

His hand came off the headrest, and his finger tapped an angry red brand that scarred his frizzy sun-burned shoulder. It did indeed read, "V.P."

"Naw, man," he said, eyes watering from holding in all his dangerous mirth. "I'm the 'Vengeance Patrol'! You like that? I just made that up."

Put it on a T-shirt!

"Great. Yeah, that's a good title, Cort. And you do what again?" My foot stroked the gas pedal, and I thumbed the ignition key, just in case.

"Well, sir, when people camp outside these gates, maybe waiting for someone to get released who wronged them, or their loved one, that's when I get them to move on out. I ask them real nice to, say, plot that vengeance somewhere else, know what I mean?"

"Why not just move the fence back to the street and put up a 'No Parking' sign?"

"What is this? Russia! No, no, that's their business. They let you park wherever you want. But I make you move as soon as you park."

"Got it. But what if I'm not here for revenge?"

"Vengeance!" he said.

"Okay, I'm not here for 'revengeance!'" I finally busted up laughing. His smile slipped.

"Ain't no such word, sir."

"Oh my god," I said. "You see that? You *are* the Department of Corrections!"

The smile was gone, but he had one foot out like he was leaving.

"So, how about you just move along now, okay, buddy? Thanks!"

"But I told you, I'm not waiting to jump anyone."

"Doesn't matter. We have a protocol."

"Do ya, though? Protocol means you have an official procedure, like a list of steps. But you're just saying, 'Move!' Which could easily be taken care of with the 'No Parking' sign I was talking about."

"I am much more effective than a sign." The big smile was back, positively radiating good cheer, so I pushed my luck.

"Okay, so you want me to move. You got it. Or . . . what if I just plant my feet here and don't do anything wrong?"

"How do you know that's the 'protocol' I was referring to?" He was back to squeezing my headrest like it owed him money, but for the first time, he seemed genuinely interested in my answer.

"I looked it up? Under 'constitution'?"

"That ain't on the internet, I hope! The internet is dangerous, bud."

"No, this was a living document. But what do you have against the internet? It never did nothing to nobody," I lied, rubbing the deep gash Greg had left dividing my eyebrow.

"Well, it has wronged me on occasion," Cort said, releasing my headrest to let it re-inflate. He abruptly stepped out of my car, slamming my door and heading back to his truck. He stopped at the bed to pop open the tool box. I got out of the Rabbit to follow, though I was listening with mounting concern as he clanked around with something heavy and unseen.

"The internet wronged you?" I repeated, confused how this high-tech topic had immediately transformed our conversation into him scrounging and banging low-tech tools.

"Oh, computers have wronged me, chief. And so many more." His voice echoed, head still buried in the gleaming silver box. "Now, those machines might be able to define a word here or there, but the real-life repercussions might just be different than what you'd expect. For example, a computer may give you a name, but it can't tell you what, unequivocally, a jackhammer could do to a person's foot. Because looking at all that information in those cyberspaces and hammering out specific details ain't really 'hammering' anything . . . "

"What are we talking about again?"

"Jackhammers."

"Well, you could ask a jackhammerist?"

"Right now?"

"I'm thinking they have their own support group online somewhere, but, yeah, why not? Call 'em up!" I shrugged, still not sure where this was going.

"Your rightful jackhammerist, while jackhammering, will have difficulty both hearing the phone or feeling it vibrate," he said, peeking up out of the tool box to lock eyes. I noticed that Cort the V.P. had one of those meaty heads—"Big Irish Face syndrome," Angie called it—but with a bit of Cuban stirred in. I took one step closer, not quite getting the angle to make out what he was wrestling with in the back of the truck.

"You know, one day someone should invent a phone app that's a picture of a jackhammer that vibrates when you get a call," I said, trying to get on his good side. "Maybe it'll be us. Instant millionaires!"

"Excellent. I love that," he laughed, showing me that picket fence of beautiful teeth. Seemed like at least ten teeth too many. Then his head shot back into the tool box like a vulture cleaning out a carcass. I thought about escape as the banging continued, but, like people probably always say right before they die, I'd come too far to turn back now.

"Here's the thing," he said, still rummaging. "Since they are designed to break up pavement, I've always suspected a jackhammer on a foot would reduce it to a bloody sack of sinew and shattered bone pretty quick. Like a sock filled with gravel . . . "

"Thanks for the visual!" I laughed, wondering if he lived in that tool box now.

"But would it really do this?" His head sprung back up.

"What if a jackhammer just increases circulation? Makes feet stronger? What we need are more volunteers."

"It would certainly make feet *bigger*," I said, thinking about the mayhem surrounding my stopover in Jasper County. "You know, I've been investigating a lot of stuff lately." Eyes trained on a fast exit back into the Rabbit, I was still feeling chatty. I guess I missed the gang. "In fact, you might say I've been born again hard when it comes to scholarly research. So I already know a sliver about all topics, and the most gruesome injury I've come across regarding jackhammers is when some drunken day laborer in my hometown of Diamond dropped one on his toe. But the thing is heavy, so it just crushes your foot anyway. So are we talking about a sustained 'jackhammering' on one spot? Or just the vibration of the tool and no hard rock under foot?"

The tool box lids slammed shut, and I backed up but kept talking.

"But, hey, I'm no expert! So I'm thinking your description is probably real accurate. I've never actually seen a jackhammering in progress, so I might be surprised."

He came around from the back of his truck and slowly held up his weighty paws to reveal nothing at all. He was laughing harder now.

"The suspense is killing me, dude!" I said. "Like, if this was a movie? The camera would pan down your body and reveal . . . surprise! Two wooden legs. Are you a jackhammer cautionary tale or what?"

"I don't understand you," he said. "But I like your moxie, kid."

"I totally thought you were going to jackhammer me just now."

"I don't need to do anything like that to send you on your way! But describing doing things like that? Sometimes that's plenty."

"You might be right."

"For example, you don't need to see a man hanging in the

air with a meat hook in his ass to understand that would hurt. Get it?"

"Got it."

"Good. And let me tell you one more thing. If you decide you really want to plant your feet here outside my gate? You may find yourself vibrating apart as easily as any rock, and we don't need to be between no hard place to make it happen."

"Nice." I had no idea why, and, as usual, I cannot justify it. But his veiled threats were making me feel like arguing. Something to do with my recent Bigfoot experience, I suppose, if you had to pin it down like a picture. "But you never know, right?"

"Never know what?"

"What if jackhammers surprised everyone when it turned out they just transform one foot into two separate but perfect feet?"

"Good *point*," he said, still humoring me for whatever reason. "It certainly depends on the point. Carbide-tipped bit, diamond point, clay, hand chisels, rock hammers, finishing hammers, wedges and shims. Now, they're all gonna do different damage . . ."

"Cort, be honest. Do you sell jackhammers?" I tried to smile as big as him, but it hurt my face.

" . . . but big feet, little feet, they always end up looking the same when I'm done."

"Magically vibrating into tiny rocks. For your head."

The smile was finally gone, with no evidence of its previous existence.

"Get the fuck out of here. You and your ferret."

"This ain't Russia, Cort. Maybe I'm not going nowhere."

"I guess we're gonna see."

"I guess. So, if you're the Vice President, then who's the President?" He said nothing to this, looked finished with our banter. I pressed on. "Have you heard the name 'Zamboni'?"

"Do I look like I play hockey?"

"You do actually."

"Git." He punctuated this by punching his own palm, and I swear I felt the shockwave vibrate my toes after all.

"You got it."

***

I'd left behind the prison gates as ordered, but I couldn't really *leave* leave. Having learned more about jackhammering than I'd ever hoped to in my life, I had taken off, but soon after started driving around in ever-tightening circles, the opposite of the chickenshit falcon in the poem. But when I ended up back at the prison, I kept my Rabbit idling closer to the road this time, the gate still within sight. Cort's red pickup was visible around an aluminum storage shed, but he was nowhere to be seen. I didn't want to push my luck (okay, I did), but after all of that loaded talk, I kinda wanted him to see someone deal out some of that "vengeance" on somebody, even if it ended up being me. The way he'd swooped in on me like that, I was hoping today was some sort of release day at the prison.

Zero rubbed a haunch against the passenger window, nostrils flaring, eyes dilated, and I looked out the window past him. I noticed a couple stray cats along the tree line.

"You want to fuck 'em or eat 'em, son?"

I watched him close for any vocalizations, then remembered cats only meowed at humans. But had anyone ever tested this with chimps? I was just beginning to think I was wrong about a release day, when a Klaxon horn made me jump, and Zero zipped under the seats. The alarm pulsed twice, followed by a buzzer, and the hulking prison gates creaked in protest as they swung open towards us. When a grown man walked out wearing a cape, I knew I'd made at least one correct decision in life.

Okay, it wasn't really a cape. It was a bundle of winter clothes thrown over his shoulder: sweater, jeans, parka. The outfit he must have been arrested in, possibly in some colder part of the country. He rejigged his gear as he walked, tying his heavy yellow cable knit around his neck, making it look even more like a big ol' cape. And with his "Remember me, world!" grin and the bounce in his step, it wouldn't have surprised me if this man flew right off into the bright blue sky. The thick bundle of his sweater knot blocked most of his face, and his eyes were buried in the natural shade provided by his Cro-Magnon, "early man" forehead, so I just assumed he did something terrible to someone, and I suddenly felt like a failure for not being there to confront a piece of shit like this ex-con. So I decided to follow him.

If that seemed a tad impetuous, consider that I grew up in the '80s, before the internet, when you had to follow people around if you wanted to peek into their private lives, specifically to ask them out. You couldn't just click a few keyboard keys to creep on a potential girlfriend. Technology be damned, you had to literally follow them from place to place, go through lockers, garbage cans, practically sniff their necks while they were sleeping. Yes, I'm saying we stalked people in the snow. Uphill both ways. And we liked it!

But I wasn't dumb enough to pull up to the prison gate again, so I backed off about a hundred yards to see who picked him up. Imagine my surprise when my new friend Cort screeched around the corner of the supply shed, his gorilla arm hanging out his window, then roared onto the highway with the prisoner's yellow cape trailing out the slider of the red pickup's rear windshield.

So I followed them both. How could I not? All sorts of thoughts went through my head. Was Crazy Cort the "V.P." mentioned in Angie's notes? When he braced me, was he waiting for this guy the whole time? What for? Was all that verbal intimidation just bullshit for my benefit, and was he there to get "revengeance" on someone himself? I had to know, and I trailed them a long time, about sixty miles along the Conecuh River, until we ended up in some town without a sign, behind a bar with a mutt-faced Harley rider circling a smashed-up barber pole, both wearily spinning their wheels out front. The roof of the bar was lined by about fifty kilowatts of flittering and struggling Christmas lights, and big swaths of white paint along the side of the building read, "The Bowery." There were even a couple horses out back, eating sticks or bugs or whatever they did when they weren't galloping majestically in midair.

Horses? Wow. Where am I? When am I?

At the end of a long row of ape-hanger choppers were a couple BMX bikes lying on their sides, and it occurred to me that I had discovered the natural end of the life cycle of the "stunted man" I had discovered back near the Kentucky border. Those shriveled, tattooed boy men in their sleeveless shirts and camo shorts rode bicycles well into their 60s, not because of an undying love for two wheels, but because their D.U.I.s kept them off the highway. This is why bicycles became more valued the further south you travelled, and why a blinged-out BMX bike would eventually become straight-up currency right around the Florida state line. Seriously, if you see a mosquito tornado nearby, lock up your Mongoose.

But I'd also heard that, anywhere west of the Mississippi, if you've lost all sense of direction (maybe due to exotic parasites in your eyeballs), these Stunted Men were no longer racking up D.U.I.s. They became "D.U.P & Ps" instead, or as my new dad Greg once called them, "Doctor P's." That's when they got busted doing meth in combination with MDMA, or methylenedioxymethamphetamine, and, you guessed it, Viagra! They found themselves with the dreaded meth boner, something even the pimpest bicycle seats couldn't cradle. Don't ask me how Angie's dad knew all this, but apparently it was a milestone that marked the official end of a man's second adolescence, and then it was on to actual motorcycles for the twilight of their wasted years. "Good work, Dirty South! Evolution in reverse," Greg would say. "But the *bi*-cycle of life is beautiful, Dave."

Out past the Harleys and the horses loomed something like an airplane hangar. Next to that looked to be an overgrown and neglected garden, full of all sorts of colorful vegetables. Cort's red pickup was nosing a tomato vine.

I rolled up my windows to keep Zero safely corralled, then walked into The Bowery. No door chimes, but I didn't feel ignored. I probably would have stood out even more if I hadn't been losing so many fights lately and cultivating so many scabs and bruises. I was suddenly thankful that the cops and bartenders and new dads (and don't forget the Skunk Apes *everywhere*) had all been so generous with their fists so that these bikers might possibly feel a little stingier with theirs. It was like I'd gotten my face immunized.

Can't say I haven't had all my shots!

Saddling up to a rustic wooden bar, also covered in stained and ragged Christmas decorations, I ordered a beer from the dead-eyed kid cleaning mugs. He slid me a glass but left my money untouched. Couldn't blame him. You always hear about how dollar bills in the United States contain traces of feces and cocaine but no one ever admits that mixing them together gets you higher. My eyes followed the smoke to a quiet poker game in the corner, and I instinctually reached behind me for my blackjack, fingers tracing the shotgun hole Greg had left behind. So I turned back around to try jawing with some bearded oldsters on the stools, mostly just listening for information. Their conversations revolved around an oil pipeline where they all worked, and their dads worked, and their dads' dads worked. Something about another pipeline coming through Florida to take it over, something else about jobs being lost, then something else about hiring all the local cons and ex-cons for cheap. This pipeline apparently treated the glut of private prisons in the state as their "farm league," and that's where I started nodding along to keep them on topic. They sure loved to hate that pipeline, and I was getting ready to probe for more detail, until one of them flicked me in my new T-shirt with his arthritic finger and mentioned that the name "Clearwater" was "pretty ironic," considering a flood of sewage that had engulfed their county jail. He went on to describe a disaster which resulted in raging fires in a prison laundry room, which blew the facility sky-high. The fire killed two inmates and injured over a hundred more, but that was nothing compared to the confusion it caused in the aftermath . . .

I slid a little closer to hear everything I could about the repercussions of this incident, but his buddy held up a hand in the storyteller's face like "slow down."

"No, that did not happen," a third old biker said from behind me.

"Fuck it didn't," the first one said, slamming his beer and splashing my face. I rubbed my eye with a knuckle and wondered if drunken parasites would make me better or worse off.

"No, no, no, it's Santa Rosa County Jail you're thinking of, nowhere near here. 600 fish missing for a day and a night—"

"You're right it was 600 inmates who lit out, but it happened here."

"How do you know all this?" I asked the first biker.

"Because they only rounded up 599," he said, smiling.

I smiled, too, not because of barroom legends of escape and intrigue, but because I was remembering how full of shit conspicuous tough guys always were, with old tough guys being worse than that, and ex-cons being the worst of all. This all helped to remind me of my reasons for coming in there in the first place.

"Have you men ever heard of an invisible prison?"

If there had been a jukebox, the needle would have scratched. Instead one of the codgers picked his ear, and stools started turning away to freeze me out. The dead-eyed bartender grabbed my wad of bills off the counter.

"Last question!" I said, standing back up to go. "Does anyone know who drives that red pickup out there?"

"There's no red pickup out there," the dead-eyed bartender said.

Red car syndrome is real, I thought. *But maybe they have the cure.*

"Are you sure?"

The rest of the bikers turned back toward me, but every craggy face had dropped.

"Why." I didn't see who asked this, but it was another one of those "whys" without the question mark.

"I'm supposed to meet him here."

"Uh huh."

One of the old men whacked me on the back, almost neighborly, but he kept gripping my coat collar afterwards. Another one pulled out my stool, forcing me to stand up. I finished my beer in one gulp and tried to shrug off the hand, but it stayed put. The man's elbow remained up high, holding me tight but letting me move around somewhat. I guessed his arms were used to a hundred years of hanging from elevated handlebars. The bartender ducked off, and bikers started multiplying. Before I knew it, I was dead center in a circle of ten or more Santas gone to seed, white beards working around their mouths all excitable. I fell back on my training, hostage negotiation.

"So all your families worked on the pipeline, huh? Sounds like hard work. Good, honest work."

A few of them squinted under their bushy eyebrows, but we still weren't moving. I switched tactics.

"You know," I went on. "If working on a pipeline didn't sound so noble, people might be more aware of how bad they were being exploited. Like imagine you guys saying instead, 'Man, our family has been sucking horses' cocks for years! My dad, and his dad, and his dad's dad, shit, all practically *born* sucking off horses. It's in our blood!'"

I caught a furry fist in the back of my skull, and the Christmas lights went out.

***

When I woke up, I marveled at how much I'd grown used to getting my ass kicked in bars, places I'd never frequented for the first thirty years of my life. I looked up at the blinking red bulbs on the curved metal wall of the airplane hangar. They spelled: "Disgraceland."

I wasn't in The Bowery anymore. I was out back. It didn't take me long to pick Cort out of the shuffling, shambling crowd around me, as he stood a good foot taller than his gang. He was still in his overalls, but now he had a leather vest framing his broad shoulders. The vest was covered in patches, including one that said, "V.P.," and this finally made sense. It helped that I'd seen the full run of *Sons of Anarchy* at least three times.

"So . . . can you get the President on the phone?" I asked Cort, grimacing as I gingerly touched the newest addition to the colony of tender spots on the back of my head.

"He doesn't make public appearances," Cort said, stepping forward and offering me a giant hand. I took it, and he helped me get my legs out in front of my body, but shoved me back down on my ass when I started to stand up. He held up a threatening finger, a reminder to sit still, then tapped his lips to signal that I also should not speak. I did what I was told and assessed my situation. Cort was the V.P. all right, Vice President of a motorcycle gang much more intimidating than the AARP rejects that populated the decoy bar out front. Through my fresh concussion and ever-watering eyes, I tried to read the crests embroidered on their leather.

The "Jobshitters"? No, wait, that jacket says, "Mobshitters." Which one is it . . .

The remaining patches surrounding me had more club names than I could process, easily dozens of gangs represented in one gathering.

The Beelzebugs, The WhyWhos, The Christ Munchers . . .

One group was brandishing a variation of the Stars and Bars on their backs, but they looked more than a little haggard, definitely the "Orphans" of the summit, really only rebelling against hygiene. I thought I recognized a former Elizabethtown student in their stinky midst, and I felt a twinge of pride masquerading as an acid burp. There was even a jacket that read, "Heaven's Devils," which, being *not quite* the Hell's Angels, seemed like a real head-scratcher for a real gang, like starting out in movies and calling yourself "Donny Jepp." I saw "The Bowery Boys" on someone else's back, and I started thinking melodramatic *Gangs of New York* thoughts instead of campy *The Warriors* thoughts, worried this wasn't some kind of summit meeting after all. More like J.R.R. Tolkien's "Battle of Ninety-Nine Armies." So I sat up a little straighter.

But what seemed clear to me was that I was witnessing the final stage of the Stunted Man life cycle Greg had always hypothesized. Back in Brickwood, Ohio, bearded men were probably patrolling the night right now, policing road kill on their BMXs, a machine built for kids but somehow shaped perfectly for the furious movement of age-burnt, sinewy bodies. But if a Stunted Man pedaled hard enough, or long enough? He would be handsomely rewarded when his husk split apart from the effort, revealing leg muscles and gleaming chrome and pumping exhaust that he would ride off into the sunset. So the army of Kris Kringles in the bar must have been an earlier stage of the Stunted Man's maturation, only appearing as a step backwards to a laymen such as myself.

Don't let wizened little men riding bicycles fool ya! They used to ride jackals!

"That's right," Cort said. "You're hanging with the Bowery Boys now, proper pukka descendents of the original Six Points Crew."

"Don't you mean Five Points?" I asked.

"Who told you that?" There was that grin.

"I can read a New York map . . . " I'd gotten real good with maps.

"Bowery Boys, let me hear you!" Cort hollered, arms out wide.

"Whooooooooooooo!"

"More like the Flowery Boys," someone muttered, but it was impossible to tell who in the press of bodies and hordes of facial hair. A dangerous hum danced through the crowd for a second, then dissipated. Cort looked like he was considering calling out the heckler, but he pulled another Mobshitter close to him and gave him a hug around the neck instead.

"Liam here? One of our Australian brothers. Ain't that right, Liam?"

"Good-o," Liam said, totally on-brand. "Australia is a lot like your Florida. A state of mind more than a state on the map. More than the sum of its parts, or its weather, you dig? Wanna picture Australia? Think of Florida, but, like, if it was the whole planet."

They stared at me, and it felt like it was my turn to say something stupid.

"You guys got a lot going on here," I said.

"Sure do," Liam said. More time ticked by.

"Welp, sorry to crash your party!" I started to get up again, and Liam and Cort quickly put hands on my shoulders to sit me back down. Cort was flipping through my wallet.

"Hang on there a second, boyo. Why did you follow me here?"

"I can't explain it." My answer to that question, as always, was 110% the truth.

"Okay, 'Davey.'" He flung my wallet between my legs but pocketed the license. "Woof. I'm gonna use this picture to scare my kids straight! So, how about, since you can't explain it, I just explain it instead. See, you've stumbled into something here, and we were thinking real hard about killing your ass, but I think we can all salvage this situation." He snapped his beefy fingers. "Jason! Come up here! Davey, I think you already met Jason . . . "

The inmate I'd watched stride out of the jail with the yellow sweater over his shoulders was pushing his way through the crowd. The bikers made a circle in his wake, now surrounding the three of us. Jason had lost the cape and was wearing the yellow sweater more like a normal person, meaning tied around his waist. He pulled his wife beater up over his head and let it drop to our feet. I noticed cracks in the floor, a strange Rorschach test of split concrete spreading out around us in all directions.

"Jason here, he was a member of The Lose Lose, a club out of Tulsa."

"Let me guess," I said, emboldened by his talk of "not killing my ass." "The mortal enemies of The Win Wins?"

"Yes!" Cort said, deadly serious, and maybe a little surprised. "That is exactly right. And we've brought him here to deal with his patch."

Cort spun Jason around to reveal an intricate tattoo on his naked back. The artwork depicted a red, plump, very butt-like apple, which was—judging by the motion lines radiating from its hearty rump—vigorously fucking the incisors of a grinning skull. I had to nod in approval, as this was the most succinct illustration of a win/win scenario that I'd ever seen.

"You already heard about the prison flood from our up-and-coming Sergeant-at-Arms back there at the bar. But what people don't know is that a lotta guys escaped under cover of that disaster. Jason here? He'd actually broken out during the flood, too, along with 900 or so gang members—accounts vary!—suddenly turned anonymous organ donors, who all had their personal information erased when the computers sparked out under that water. We all got caught pretty quick after that, so don't let the movies fool you when they act like a river is the best way to lose a dog's scent. But Jason here? He was reincarcerated under the wrong name! Just like a lot of guys. See, in the justice system's rush to wrangle us back up and cover their asses, hundreds of affiliates were incorrectly logged back into those stupid computers; names changed, numbers changed, and no amount of protests or paperwork could straighten this out, not even the all-encompassing bureaucracy of the prison industrial complex. Especially here in Florida where, as you probably heard, there are more prisons than post offices. You ever seen the movie *Brazil?* No? Well, my copy got ruined in the flood, so I don't know how it ended, but I heard it has something to do with red tape. And red tape is a secret friend to the underground. So, after a couple months of wrongful beatings and trying to convince the guards that our identities had been swapped, those 700 guys went back to just biding their time, slowly adapting to their new roles for survival, even becoming members of other clubs, rival clubs. But only temporarily! This meeting here is where we've decided amnesty. You see, these men only turned their backs on their clubs and their brothers due to impossible circumstances. *Force majeures*, all y'all! So we're here today to clean up the mess. To get everybody sorted back out. And we got some lucky lads out of jail a little prematurely, for this very purpose. Early birdies in the house!"

"Whoop! Whoop!"

"I don't get it."

"But you met Otto, right? I mean, 'Jason.' Didn't he lead you here?"

Is he saying "Otto" or "Auto"? Was Matt Fink saying "Auto" or "Otto"? Otto. As in Otto-motive. Whoever he was, he had more motive than most.

"Is Otto here? I heard he worked for a prison." I hadn't thought much about Otto after I busted Matt as the one hiding his heart flutter. Cort shook his head, then laughed loud enough to start coughing.

"'Jason,' or 'Auto,' same difference."

"What? This is Otto?"

"No, no, no, he ain't here, my man," he said, and I could tell he was lying when he saw my eyes. He composed himself. "The 'Autos' are low level. Four-wheelers. I.T. support if they're lucky. More machine than man these days."

This guy's totally saying "Auto."

"But he works for me! Not the jail, Davey. Not for you, the taxpayer. But you must have seen his website, all official-like? So what if Jason killed your wife. Or maybe she got killed by a car . . . "

"Stuck by an auto," the cop at the door accidentally got it right, I didn't say.

" . . . either way, what happens next will probably make you feel a little better about all that. But you're right, you guys crossed swords, I mean 'paths,' a couple times at least? He was actually crashing in your basement a while back. Under orders, of course."

Under the orders of peanuts, you mean, I didn't say.

"Listen, it's bigger than you know . . . "

My basement, you mean, I didn't say.

" . . . but we started there, started small, then we did some other stuff. Like take a one-hitter cell phone to email some jails receipts of bail money going through, anything to urge the release of our boys here, to straighten out these skins. And as long as it ends with those gates opening, anything is worth trying. We got about a 37% success rate when an Auto is on the case, but that's plenty. We're confident numbers will increase, right along with the *plethora* of prisons popping up along the Florida countryside. It just gets harder and harder to keep us absconders from absconding!"

Cort's explanation seemed more for the benefit of the mob than myself. There was more murmuring, but I was starting to get it, even if everybody else wasn't.

"Listen, men," he went on, arms out. "In prison, if you adopted another name, that means you adopted another patch, and that means we got hundreds of motherfuckers with the wrong tattoos. And we have all gathered here to close these chapters! To set things right!"

Wild cheers echoed around the metal walls.

"So this is like a tattoo removal thing you're doing?" I asked him.

"Sorta."

"So that talk of a Vengeance Patrol was bullshit."

"Sorta."

"And what does this have to do with me again?"

"Sorta. What? Shut your mouth, Dave! And witness a course correction for the ages!"

I noticed one of the men in the circle passing around

earmuffs. Judging by the hooting and howling, Cort was obviously more V.I.P. than V.P., no matter what his vest said. So he got his earmuffs before anybody else. And they were much bigger. Fuzzy and pink. He snapped them over his ears like the King Shit he was.

"You stumbled onto something, Dave!" he yelled, as if the world had big, pink earmuffs. "I'm not sure what you were looking for, but the moral of this story is, you throw enough at the wall and something will stick! Speaking of stuff sticking to walls, it's gonna be easier if I just show you . . . "

I had been gearing up so long listening to Cort explain increasingly complicated reasons for whatever insanity was yet to come, that I almost missed it when the crowd parted like the Dead Sea and out came the jackhammer for real.

***

Of course he's the MC Hammer, I thought. *It wasn't like he didn't warn me.*

There were only enough earmuffs for about thirty guys in the crowd, so I guessed those were the most important thirty guys. I filed away their positions in the circle, in case it became important during an unlikely getaway. I also noted the biggest guy in the room, an unaffiliated salt-and-peppered monolith wearing a black track suit and a surgical mask with a huge lopsided grin drawn on it in lipstick.

He's so big he makes Cort look like Half Court! Thank you, Cleveland! I'll be here all week! Just kidding, I'm gonna die.

One of his Mobshitters, shirtless and sweaty—with a tattoo of either Florida or a cock-eyed pistol on his back—passed Cort the terrifying tool like it was Excalibur, and it was already bucking in his arms to be let loose. It was a yellow-and-black beast with purple stains halfway up the bit and "Bosch Brute" in white Impact font on the side, a name I assumed was a preview of the squishy sounds it was about to make with my body. Cort and the jackhammer started their dance as he spun the power cord out and away from his legs with the panache of a lead-singer working a microphone stand. He started squeezing and working the handgrips with some menacing snakebites, and I fully expected him to straddle the machine and drive away into the night, or at least make some motorcycle noises with his mouth. But then the jackhammer was making motorcycle noises for all of them, and I wondered why every biker gang didn't ride these things when they were out of gas. Maybe they did.

A Jobshitter slid an open can of black latex paint in front of Cort, who dipped the tip, splashing black flecks onto everyone nearby. I spit some paint off my lip as Jason of The Win Wins, formally of The Lose Lose, arched and cracked his back, then laid himself out willingly on the floor in the middle of the circle of goons, arms and legs splayed like a martyr ready to be drawn and quartered. I didn't understand his lack of resistance and started to think maybe getting jackhammered wasn't so bad after all. I held my breath along with Jason, mesmerized as his chest inflated to present his ribs to the machine. Cort mounted him, legs wide, engine revving. The massive jailhouse tattoo was on his back, not his front, but no one seemed to care. *Maybe they have to sneak up on it*, I thought as he brought the hammer down.

In spite of the cryptic conversation Cort and I had earlier outside the prison gates, it turned out that a jackhammer's effects on a human body were not that surprising. I'd been hopeful for something less dreadful, but it did exactly what I knew it would, deep in my heart of hearts. Speaking of "heart of hearts," holy shit, you should see what's inside an actual heart! But you probably don't want to. Or is there still some confusion here? That's understandable, I guess, but who would even want a play-by-play? Great, let's move on. Whoops I lied! Here you go:

I'm no doctor, so the best way I can describe what I saw would be to compare it to the root beer I dumped on the subwoofers I installed in my Rabbit, and how I stood there watching the soda hop and bubble with the bass slapping of whatever shitty Kottonmouth Kings song was on, and when (even though I knew it would ruin my speakers), I felt compelled to pour the rest of the root beer right into that fluttering stereo ring to see what else might happen. This ruined the speakers, of course, but while the dance of root beer lasted, I'd started to picture the circular valve of my own heart, and that congenital aorta defect that always caused me to get a little dizzy when my beats were skipping, something Angie always said proved my heart was shrinking away to nothing, even though the heart monitor I wore under my shirt for a month found nothing remarkable. So down on the floor, I was thinking about of all this again, right up until the biker's own glistening pump was revealed in all its squirming glory. His ticker was bigger than I thought, certainly bigger than mine, if Angie's diagnosis was to be believed, and no doubt a lot tougher, as well, because the jackhammer seemed to have a hell of a time pinning his heart down. Cort would readjust as the tip kept slipping to the sides of the organ, over and over, possibly due to density, or maybe all the hemorrhaging, but it looked like the little sucker was protecting itself with invisible football stiff-arms or some other constant supply of almost imperceptible defensive movements. It was like there was this force field around it, finally getting its chance to be of use during what had to be the unlikeliest of all recorded "heart attacks." But whatever the reason, it was a good thirty seconds before the jackhammer tip penetrated and reduced the crux of this man to a ghastly, whiplashing water balloon. This gave me plenty of time to find the right words to paint you the following picture, because I realized it might actually be tougher than I ever thought to accurately describe such a horrendous event. And, since I already explained I was no doctor, I finally had to ask a real, live doctor what it was I was witnessing. "What would a jackhammer really do to a human body?" was the question I presented to Dr. Matthew "Ask Me Anything I Swear I'm Not A Robot" Funk, MD/PhD when I found him and his Prince avatar on a totally legit-looking online forum some time before or after all of this. And he took a "stab" at it! And the answer went something like this:

If you pressed a tool such as a jackhammer onto the abdomen of an adult male, starting centrally, say, in the periumbilical region—the most likely starting point for maximum trauma—those 1,500 thrusts per minute would essentially macerate the bejesus out of any soft tissue. So for my authentic, totally living and breathing doctor friend Matt "Don't Call Me Fink" Funk, it was really a question of how quickly the muscular abdominal wall would perforate. And he certainly gave this the most thought. Dr. Funk decided that if the jackhammer had a tip similar to a screwdriver, meaning tapered (which was exactly what this jackhammer was brandishing), combined with the weight of that particular high-end model, it would largely pound right through the body without looking back, that tapered point rushing headlong in its quest for any hard surface underneath something as insignificant as a human being. And once it was through, it would tear the floor up just as vigorously as a body, but five times as colorfully. Therefore, while it was boogying all the way down to concrete and earth, it would be a veritable shower of liquids, really nasty fireworks, given that, according to Dr. Funkenstein—who probably would have been a valuable online or offline friend if we'd never crossed paths—this would mostly be small intestine getting skewered, centrally, along with the colon, which would be shish-kabobbed peripherally. Then the hammer would find the subwoofer I was talking about earlier, a.k.a. the branching aorta, which would be cradled by the L4-5 disc, but that bow would break, and that cradle would fail.

So, from what I understood, death would come pretty quickly once things finished up in the chest. Supposedly, a person could remain conscious for maybe a minute while the jackhammer pulled a Sherman's March to the Sea through the abdomen, but once it crunched through those ribs like old toast, there would be fountains big as the Bellagio as that heart pumped geysers off into no man's land. Allegedly, there would be a sucking sound as the pleural cavity opened up with a *swoosh!* and the lungs finally popped, but who would hear such a sad symphony with a jackhammer running at full blast? Especially a top-of-the-line model like the Bosch Brute. But go big or go home, right?

But no one was going home from this. If you ever tried jackhammering a human body for a festival crowd, there were a few things that you could guarantee. There would be blood. There would be bone. There would be stool. There would be a slurry of fecal matter and pre-stool and blood and bone chips, and it would be like a stinky, red-white-and-blue Independence Day celebration. And there wouldn't be any conceivable way that the dreaded action of this tool, even tapered, even dipped in ink, could ever stain anything resembling an intact human torso with anything even close to what someone might consider a "tattoo." But the online scientific community and/or physician forums everywhere would have to concede that all of these fluids could possibly stamp a discoloration into whatever concrete floor wasn't already reduced to rubble. So maybe it *was* a giant tattoo needle after all. Only it tattooed floors, and it used humans as the real inkwells.

"Do you really want to know if someone could use a jackhammer for a tattoo?" my new doctor friend Matt Funk, stand-up guy who "never fucked my wife," but only because he was more interested in her life's work, would ask me some time before, or after, everyone's respective disappearances.

"More like tattoo removal!" I would say.

"More like soul removal!" we would both laugh.

"Little soul shaker, love removal machine . . . " he would sing.

"Fell to the red room" indeed.

I didn't know if I felt any better about the loss of my wife or Otto's life, as Cort had promised, but I'd certainly given the moment some very special attention.

Senses thrumming, teeth rattling, my skull melting over my hands like an ice cream cone, I still couldn't help screaming at the blood angel that was spreading across the floor instead of taking flight.

"Why are you letting him do this to you?!"

***

Wiping some of the dead man's bile from my eyes and spitting some of his feces from my mouth, I labored again to stand.

"I'm having a hard time following exactly what you're doing here . . . " I said to the circle of Mobshitters. I was weary and stunned, watching them press in to mill around the middle of this anatomical massacre, I gagged and kept trying to speak, but two quick jabs in the jaw from opposite directions shut me back up. I was certainly shaken, but also mesmerized by the scene. Jason had been cut clean in two by the jackhammer, and the vibrations continued to bounce and jitter those two halves of his corpse out of the way of the machine's never-ending spasms. I could see Cort working those colorful fluids into the cracks of the floor, intent on finishing what looked to be the world's largest, ugliest painting. I cocked my head at the largest tattoo in Florida, and I guessed he was trying to trace the state of Kentucky? But it came out more like Hawaii during hurricane season. When he pulled back the tip and wiped a dangling strip of errant intestine from his grin, I saw that he'd actually been attempting to draw the entire United States. Or maybe it was a dinosaur he was cracking and smearing into the floor around us. Or maybe it was a new United States of America, but made up entirely of Floridas, dinosaurs, and mosquitoes, exactly what I'd grown to expect from a throng of murderous hogsquashers with only a passing knowledge of their home state. Who needed a new map? Not me.

It's a trap not a map! I thought crazily, deciding that with enough tattoo removals like this one administered on the hangar's floor, a completed map would probably more closely resemble an elephant-shitting contest than any state of our nation. In other words, "Florida."

Since no one could hear me, I started singing a variation of the '60s *Spider-Man* cartoon theme to hang onto my sanity, or at least to go out swinging.

"Florida man . . . Florida man . . . does everything a Florida can . . . "

Cort switched off the jackhammer, and the rumbling of the metal walls revved back on down to an insect-like click as the motor cooled. He kicked a bit of torso sweetmeats out of his way and shrugged.

"The funniest thing about Mr. Lose Lose here is he never should have left that jail. He was ready to be released tomorrow."

The biggest man in the room was wiping his face with the crook of his elbows as he struggled free of his track jacket, showing off either Florida or a flaccid penis tattooed across his shoulder blades. He was suddenly laughing so hard at either Mr. Lose Lose's plight or Cort's joke that he doubled over. Then he puked right through the smile painted on his surgical mask, a flood of vomit that engulfed it completely, causing the mask to flip free of his ears and surf the pulpy waves of Cort's handiwork. I'd made it up to one knee by now and was thinking about bolting for the door, but the Alpha Jobshitter wiped the chunks from his beard and savagely shoved me back down, grunting with a more indistinguishable accent.

"Sit still or die, mate," he reminded me as Cort walked up, pink earmuffs down around his neck like a fuzzy ascot. One strap of his overalls was also hanging, and I saw either a tiny Florida or a broken boomerang drawn over his trapezius.

"So, what'd ya think?" he asked me, eyes proud. He dropped the jackhammer to the floor with a crash and held out a hand. I reached for it, but someone slapped his palm with a shotgun instead, and he cocked it and brought it up with the gaping barrel not quite trained on me, but the meaning was clear. I figured this was the end and held up a finger.

"You know, there is a tendency for people to overdramatize the moments before their final journey," I said. "But I wish they would understand it's virtually impossible to understate the importance of last words. They're not going to remember what you said. Because death means you aren't really going anywhere. And you couldn't take anything with you if you did."

"Well spoken," Cort laughed, awkwardly clapping his mitts around his shotgun, and I decided that must have saved me.

"Thanks," I coughed, having better luck keeping down my gas station grub.

"It sure was a sneaky way to get in some memorable last words, I must admit," Cort said. "If I was ever gonna kill you."

***

His arm was still twitching to the rhythm of his murderous machine as he wrapped it around my neck to lead me outside. He got in my face, beer breath and what must have been the remnants of a squirrel-shit sandwich tickling my nose hairs and fogging up my cracked and worthless fighting glasses. He told me some of his big ideas, and he seemed happiest when I agreed with him that a jackhammer, in theory, should be able to remove a tattoo, or at least create one. He told me that a tattoo needle under a microscope looks just like a baby jackhammer and that was "settled science, goddammit." He told me about flowers you could only grow in the Everglades and steered me toward the garden. He told me his master plans and his master's plan, who I "never wanted to meet." Then when I asked why he was letting me go after everything I'd seen him do, Cort said:

"Something my daddy told me once out on the river. You throw back any fish that talks."

"But why?"

"Because the littlest fish talk the most."

It sounded like an insult, but my hands were still shaking more than his. I was just relieved to be up off the killing floor of his slaughterhouse.

"We're going to use you, I think," he told me. "For a probationary period. Gonna turn that frown upside down, Davey!"

I thought about how I was officially over the big case, and wondered if I'd ever be thinking about the small case, the guitar case, my wife's final resting place, ever again.

Then he showed me his garden up close. My first true worm farm. I tried not to look, but I failed at that, too.

***

After Cort revealed what he was reaping in that plot, he brought me back into the hangar. Somehow, I'd calmed down considerably, and he was still telling me they could use a man like me. He said he needed all the help he could get "straightening out the rosters" and that this was a "win/win for everybody." I agreed, unable to stop staring at the steaming mess on the floor.

I'd sure hate to see a "lose lose," I thought.

Cort sighed but kept his million-mile smile, and I looked around for any more tangible signs of the stain formerly known as "Jason." All I saw was a yellow sweater in the corner, still knotted where his neck used to be, the sad cape he'd worn over his shoulders as he walked triumphantly out of jail. I realized a man with a cape didn't have any superpowers after all, or if he did, they didn't include foresight. But maybe omniscience, because this poor bastard was literally everywhere now, smeared as far as the eye could see, split wide open from this throat to his groin, exploded like a Thanksgiving turkey on Black Friday, viscous red numbles stretching to the far corners of the hideout. He was on our tongues, under our fingernails, even burrowing deep into our sinuses. I would taste this man forever, making him, by far, the most intimate relationship I would ever have.

The Alpha Jobshitter dragged a piece of Jason past us, and I saw there was yet another tattoo on this man's back, huge and amateurish, but fairly professional compared to the haphazard gutting and redecorating of Cort's paint-soaked jackhammer. It was hard to make out through the man's busted capillaries, but his artwork seemed to depict something long and sagging, surrounded by roses.

"Is that another state?" I asked him when he went back for a bloody boot.

"Yep, like I already said, a state of mind." No accent this time.

I'd walked right into that.

"You make me laugh, Davey," Cort said from behind me, a bit of regret in his voice. "I might have to plant you yet. And I do mean 'plant.'" He cocked the shotgun again in case I'd forgotten what I'd seen, and a still-smoking shell discharged, skipping across the concrete. I realized he must have fired it outside, when I was in shock. He retrieved it and blew in the hollow of the cartridge. "See this? Loaded with seeds instead of buckshot."

"You'll be pushing up daisies fer real!" someone shouted from a wooly, toothless maw.

"That was funny the first six times you said it, Snoopy," Cort yelled back. Then, to me, while dangerously rapping the shotgun against his own temple for emphasis, he added, "No, not daisies, Davey. Orange blossoms! Our state tree. Sounds lovely I know, but they do plenty of damage just the same. At one time, we thought filling shells with these seeds might mean we didn't have to bury the bodies! Like they'd just transform into a pastoral landscape instead, class up the joint, say to the world 'nothing bad happened here' . . . "

"'It's life . . . from lifelessness!'" someone else in the back shouted, marking the first time I ever heard a biker reference *Star Trek.*

"Ha ha, yeah! Tiny Genesis torpedoes." And that made two.

"Zip it, nerds," Cort said, then back at me again. "But our seeds never worked on people like we'd hoped. We just aren't made of soil, you see, as much as we try to keep dirty."

Cort unsnapped the remaining strap on his overalls and

peeled the denim away from his sweaty ribcage. His trunk was peppered with tiny holes in various stages of festering. Crowning his navel was a new tattoo, of course. Either another stylized state of Florida, or a broken guitar case.

"See that? Did you know they still use birdshot in Nevada prisons? Florida prisons, too. And everyone still shoots the fuck out of everybody. Even when you're outside the gate just tryin' to help." He ran a thumb along his ribs like a glissando through the keys. "And even though they've shot me with birdseed more times than I can count, nothing grows here either."

Yeah, a 'glissando,' that's what it was called. Bugging me for miles, but I knew it would come to me eventually. And here it came. Can I send it back?

"Seeds are just a bad idea all around," he said, squeezing his stomach. "And that's why I love them." A lead pellet popped from his skin and rolled across the floor, and I retched. "But our garden is getting better and better! So we're done here. Why don't you get going, Davey. And remember what we talked about, ya hear?"

On my way out of Disgraceland, I walked past their strange garden for the last time, convinced I wouldn't look back. But I couldn't help it. My red eyes traced the orange flowers lining the side of the hangar, obviously daisies and not the orange blossoms Cort had claimed. I'd only taken one semester of landscaping back in school, but I was practically an expert compared to this unit. Their garden was crammed with crown-rot afflicted Gerberas, all of them suffering from being planted too deep, but they were still sprouting strong from an artificial turn of perforated leather jackets and cracked motorcycle helmets, twisting and yearning in the morning rain as they strained to be free from the shade of the hangar and the bodies that bore them, craving a last taste of today's elusive sunshine. I couldn't look at them for long without getting dizzy again.

The shotgun blast snapped me out of it.

***

Cort sent me to another jail, just as he'd promised. And I went, ordered to sit outside the gates of Orange County Corrections until the next guy came out wearing a face that didn't match the ink under his clothes, the next sorry son of a bitch to be flying the wrong club colors after the cataclysmic identity shuffle of a flood hundreds of miles away. My job was to bring any newly freed prisoner to Cort's abattoir behind The Bowery, to an airplane hangar where there weren't any airplanes but plenty of things to declare, a Florida limbo where the mosquito tornados came on Christmas and the craziest motorcycle gangs in the land spun tales of smoking pipelines and hitchhikers with green thumbs and jackhammers asked you to dance and then sent you home with a bouquets of blossoms from a shotgun, a state of mind where the state flower would always be a blood orange.

Why not? I thought. *Could a new job, new crew, or a new life be so bad? The last life already hit bottom, then kept going straight through the floor.*

My battery-free phone buzzed under my leg, and I cracked it in half to kill it for good. But the top half soldiered on, still twitching and flickering, and I finally checked the screen. It was another list, another set of rules, sent by my new gang. It read:

You're in for life.

Don't think of leaving town.

We need to schedule a time to tattoo that patch on your back, so what works for you?

Smiley face.

I gave the message a half-second of consideration, wondering if Cort was saying he wanted to give me a smiley face tattoo. Then I decided "what worked for me" was driving past the gate of Orange County Corrections and ignoring my new obligations. I gunned the Rabbit, and me and Zero got the fuck out of Florida for good. Any adventure we had now would seem sane by comparison, and for the first time in a long time, I was almost looking forward to the future. I watched my indestructible phone hop and jump on my passenger's seat in protest, and I wondered how much of a distraction it would still be in my stomach. Then I dismissed the notion, imagining the jackhammer slipping and chasing my broken phone around a hockey rink as the device, a.k.a. the last place I existed, slid through a crack in the ice and cycled through a steaming fricassée of embarrassing ringtones and my final gas station meal. Awkward.

***

But my remaining half a phone had never worked better, and I could see a series of anguished pleas from my sister, her interrobang emoji in full force. She was saying Angie's funeral was today, and she couldn't believe I missed it. She was worried that no one would ever forgive me.

"Promises, promises," I said to her, severing the connection to the rest of that world by chucking every piece of my clamshell phone out the window. Zero nuzzled my arm, and I instinctually checked the level of litter in his box, as well as the level of worms in my vision. The sand was looking scarce, with his accidents and misfires bombing the surrounding floor mats. I didn't know why I'd ever bothered trying to corral his waste. After the first dozen roadside memorials, cat litter in a car is like sand after the beach, infiltrating every corner and seam in the upholstery and dash. If that shit did contain parasites, they were certainly integrated in all parts of my life by now, not just my eyes.

I was still celebrating possible liberation from my living dead phone when I turned to the seat behind me and the mystery creature hissed.

And I did, too.

I took my foot off the gas and stared into Zero's striped, angular face, neither of us sure what we'd really heard. I looked to the next lane and saw a Mack Truck matching speed, the logo of a brawling cat and dog painted on the flank. I realized that Zero wasn't hissing so much as he was merely expressing disappointment at the childlike interpretation of exceptional wildlife such as himself. Then our vehicles drifted closer, and I saw the cat was also chasing a spider, and an alligator was stalking the dog, making the logo eerily similar to the amalgam of animals in my signature Jr. High doodle, which in turn was almost indistinguishable to disgruntled students' caricatures of myself. And I understood that any hisses in this car, even if they did peg us as art critics, could never pin down his species any more than it could my own.

I drove on. Fast enough to blow through a toll booth before the gate came down. Almost crashing into an interchangeable specter speeding in the other direction. Though this other Rabbit was rustier, its windshield remained intact. And the clear-eyed, corresponding driver must have seen me, as well, because the second Rabbit swerved, caught the curb, then rolled, spilling the contents of its hatch onto the rumble strips, which appeared to be a large concrete frog sculpture. The frog and the driver both shattered on impact. Now pilotless, the passenger door sheared off on the crash barrier, and thousands of nickels, dimes, and pennies burst from the tumbling wreck, tinkling across the lanes. Motorists waiting their turn to pay, rubbernecked to watch the spectacle, then all those drivers opened their doors to scoop up the change, to pile coins in their glove boxes or stack them on their dashboards or possibly to drop them into the secret slots of their own doors to pay for future escapes. I watched all this chaos in my rearview mirror, marveling at who would dare drive backwards through a toll booth, and if it meant they paid you instead.

XXIV

ROAD DIRGE

IF YOU DIDN'T react badly, this is what happens . . .

All night you're typing captions for TV shows, sometimes well into the morning.

The captions look a lot like this actually. Rule number one is only one thought, or only one line, and only one at a time.

You come back part-time when she dies. It's still a grind, but there are worse jobs, and you can do it from anywhere.

You get on the road late, so you stop to eat at one of those flying saucer food stations. There's a row of five fast-food restaurants, but behind the counter no dividers separate them.

When the employees move around, it's like in the movies when the camera follows someone through the wall. You think the kids should at least switch hats or put on fake beards when this happens.

You browse the glowing burgers, chickens and tacos over your head, and you think about how the invention of dollar menus was some next-level Don Draper-type shit that changed everything. You settle on some Taco Hell as a tribute to her.

Back on the road, you pay the turnpike guy and want to ask him what drivers do if they don't have money for the booth. But you don't feel like talking and vow to get the answer on your way back to Louisville. It's the only mystery in your life you want to solve.

Back in school, when you used to take road trips from Toledo to see Angie in Pittsburgh, there was a rest stop that had a fence behind it where you could creep through with your car, take a dirt road up through some farmer's field, and then you wouldn't have to stop at the last tollbooth to pay for your exit. Except it was on the wrong side, always sending you the opposite way you intended.

It got to where you wouldn't even factor in that five bucks toll coming back. You'd count on that fence never being locked, driving home to Toledo with a quarter to your name. But back then you always took the chance, and it never once crossed your mind you might have to stop at that tollbooth without any money. Eventually, kids covered the fence in love locks, and someone else must have noticed the car-sized hole to weld it shut. You always thought the locks would disguise an invisible exit, like the colorful bookcases that conceal secret doors, only these volumes were gleaming proof of a thousand future failed relationships waiting on the other side of that unseen threshold.

You were going to call your dad so he'd know when you would be getting there, but your cell phone dies for the fifth time, like it's keeping you two apart on purpose. Pulling into his house at 5:45 a.m., the road out front that seemed so huge when you were growing up looks as small as a sidewalk now. You're about three hours later than anyone thought you'd be, but you know he's always grateful to avoid small talk, even when no one has died.

You consider sneaking in with the claw end of a hammer, like you used to in high school when you were late coming home, but that garage door has been fixed for years, ever since your brother crashed into it with his bike. In fact, everything's different. No stones in the driveway, and three security lights pop on like you're scaling the wall at Alcatraz. You ring the bell like a stranger, expecting him to be annoyed, but he opens up in a dazed stupor and goes back to bed.

You stand in a kitchen that looks totally alien to you, and you drink some water. You see they've got a fish tank now, and you sit in front of it to watch the tiny snails slide around the glass. You're not tired, but you have to try to sleep because her funeral is in three hours. Heading to your old bedroom, it feels like you're making slightly less noise than a man in a suit of armor, and tomorrow you'll be wearing your own. There's no carpet anymore. Just noisy wood everywhere, and every movement bangs and echoes like a factory floor.

You lie down on a bed that's way too small and stuff the pillow over your face when you realize you forgot your headphones. You can't sleep without music. You consider sleeping in the car and listening to the radio, but it's getting light outside, it's much too hot, and the sounds of you trying to get out of the house would be deafening. You discover that the 1940s-looking radio in this spare bedroom is not just for show. It's got a CD already in it. You push "play" on your dad's Neil Diamond mix, thinking about what songs should be played at your own funeral. You decide "Hell, Yeah" would be a good choice. You're finally starting to fall asleep when . . .

. . . suddenly it's time to go. Your dad is in the doorway. You let him say your name one more time than he needs to. You're totally swimming in nostalgia thinking about him trying in vain to wake you up so you won't miss the bus. You see your stepmom in the hall and ask her where the toothpaste is. She is too shocked to see you, but still explains, frustrated, that the toothpaste is "in the shower, of course!" like that's the most normal thing in the world, and she looks at you a bit longer to add, somewhat ominously, "So you can go ahead and spit as much as you want."

You try to brush your teeth in the shower, but the minty toothpaste foam running down your groin seems potentially dangerous, so you creep out and brush your teeth in their new perfectly polished sink. When you do spit, you find that you can do it completely silently, and you feel like you're getting away with murder. You used to try and clear your throat and sinuses in the shower when Angie was still alive, but she insisted that you do this in silence or she would be forced to leave you, something you always thought impossible.

You sit by their fish tank and wait for them both to finish getting ready for the funeral. You want everyone to feel at ease around you, so you tell your stepmom that you like all of her cool little snails. To make conversation, you start telling her how snails can no longer form hard shells because of the acid in the oceans from all the factories, and how that will screw up the food chain involving us and more than half of the creatures in the sea. But she just starts flipping out that her fish tank is full of snails.

She calls your dad over to ask how the snails got in there. Everyone debates this while your dad ties your necktie like you're a little kid. You decide the snails rode on one of the plants, and you tell them that they just eat algae and won't be a problem. You have no idea if this is true, and you imagine the fish tank months later boiling over with snails in the middle of the night. There's a huge brass snail sculpture as big as a bowling ball on the floor in the same room as the tank, and you point and say, "But it looks like you love snails!" Your stepmom just stares.

On the way to your wife's funeral, you don't even have time to dwell on the strange circumstances surrounding her death because it turns out the viewing is only two blocks from your dad's house, and you're completely unprepared to get out of the car so soon. You had at least three more Neil Diamond songs you wanted to listen to before this happened. And once inside, you suffer through condolences in various doorways with the relatives that remember you. Half ask if you've become a football fan after your move to Pittsburgh. You deflect the sports talk with, "If you lived there, you'd be sick of that bullshit after the first weekend of getting snapped in the ass with Terrible Towels."

SHE WAS FOUND IN A GUITAR CASE

In the back corner of the funeral home, you compare surgeries and jammed fingers and other injuries with your Uncle Bob. You're thinking you're winning until he one-ups you with, "The other day, they went through my leg with a wire to burn off a piece of my heart." You admit defeat and sit with your dad while you wait for your brother and sister. Your whole family's late, everywhere they go, and you know your brother will be exactly as late as you'd hoped to be. Maybe even late enough that you can sit with him in the back row out of sight of Angie's family. But Angie's family is not coming, of course. They've always had a strange relationship with each other, as well as yourself, so it was no surprise when your side of the family took over all the arrangements after her sudden death and her father's recent disappearance.

You feel small around your dad's seven surviving brothers and the fifty or so cousins who've made an appearance. You were so scrawny growing up, but they always seemed huge, always telling epic fight stories (but never epic dream stories) and towering over backyard graduation parties. You remember your cousin Mike telling you about giving someone a beating, and during the story you looked down at your fist. It looked like a girl's fist to you. And then you looked at Mike's, and it was so hairy you thought you'd just had your first Sasquatch sighting, and it wouldn't be your last. But you don't see Hairy Mike anywhere at the funeral. Against all odds, you still expect a surprise visit from Angie's dad, Greg, in spite of him being such a wildcard since her murder.

Then you do see Hairy Mike, and you've got about 3 feet and 50 pounds on him now, and not all of it knuckle hair. You wonder if he still thinks of you as that skinny little kid frying ants with a magnifying glass, always playing Vietnam Bug Hockey while everyone else threw around the football. When you threw the football it always went sideways. But you have hair between your top two knuckles, too, which you've heard only happens in 7% of the population. Since a funeral is a good time for a confession, you'll also tell Hairy Mike that you have two strays near the hole you piss out of, and that's not even the most bizarre place they're found. You fully expect a hair to be growing out of your eyeball within a year and wonder aloud what else could thrive in the inviting swirl of a human iris. Hairy Mike taps out, and you consider it a minor victory.

You go to look at pictures of Angie that are lined up all around the casket. Many of them you cut from her yearbooks, something she always collected, even from other schools. Looking at her face in the photos, you're finally as devastated as you're expected to be, and a couple of your uncles comfort you with hands on your shoulders. Drunk or sober, your uncles were always good to you. You remember one of them throwing another one into a lit grill in your back yard, then they stopped fighting to send all you kids around front. Near the coffin, there's a big board with old snapshots glued all over it, and you can remember the arguments for every party. There's also a picture of your Uncle Ron, shirtless, straddling the bow of your brother's boat, with a beer in his hand and a cigarette hanging out of his mouth. He looks like Steve McQueen. Angie is in the foreground of the photo and seems more imposing by comparison. You realize that you're standing right next to Angie's dead body. Yep, there she is. You turn away.

You hear your brother's voice when he finally shows up, and you go to sit with him in the back to hide from the photographic proof of the life you had. But your brother is so late there are no seats left at all. You want to joke, "You'd be late to your own funeral!" but you don't. You've matured a bit in the past couple years, more so in the past couple days. So you head over to sit with your dad and stepmom and watch Hairy Mike unfold some more chairs for more stragglers like your brother. You see some relatives trying to figure out who you are, but you know them all. Your grandma rolls in with your two aunts flanking her wheelchair, followed by yet another cousin. This cousin has the same ring-of-fire tattoo on his arm as your brother. Once, he said he'd have it removed "if technology made this possible." He and your brother were similar in other ways, too, lots of sports and friends. You have no trophies or tattoos, though, and you watch your grandma instead of catching up with the cousin. Your grandma is 99, and her body doesn't work anymore, but her brain is perfectly fine. You love talking to her, and you want to go to her now, but you hate to see her with her head bent down and crying. Everyone says that no one should outlive their children but your grandma might outlive everyone. She was close with Angie, though she only met her once. That was the effect they had on each other, as well as everyone else. You wonder if Angie meeting your mother would have broken the streak.

Your grandma had this nasty little Yorkie named "Mitsy" that lived to be 29 years old. Just died last year. The exact same age as Angie. You ask your dad, "What's the math on that?" He says it's something like 400 in dog years. Thinking Angie lived to 400 is oddly comforting. The dog was blind and mean as can be, though, and it wouldn't let anyone near your grandma. It just sat under your grandma's chair in her smoky kitchen and growled. It must have set some kind of record hanging on past five generations of dogs, but neither Mitsy or Angie could outlive your grandma. This is what you're thinking when they roll your grandma up to the coffin and stop. Your oldest aunt, the alpha, starts looking around the room and shouting orders. She locks eyes with you and says, "Dude, come here!" "Dude" is your nickname on your dad's side of the family, just because it starts with a "D." Your aunt renames all the boys, and all the girls are called "Sissy." Your aunt tells you that you are all now going to lift your grandma's wheelchair so that she can see your wife and kiss her goodbye. *Holy shit,* you're thinking. You used to get frustrated when your dad's side of the family would claim any tragedy as their own, but today it makes you feel loved. Your young cousin grabs one side, you grab another, your aunt's got a wheel, Uncle Chuck's got a wheel, and up goes your grandma. She's much lighter that you thought. Angie always weighed next to nothing, too.

A hundred relatives are looking at you wide-eyed now, and you feel big, like you were chosen over all these older, wiser, *bigger* cousins. You have fantasies of defending your grandma from some rival funeral next door that wants to take all your folding chairs. You still haven't looked down into the face of your dead wife. You run your eyes along the coffin instead. It's black, lacquered to a deep shine, and seems bigger than a submarine. You know she's lost inside of it, looking for exits, like she would have been trapped inside the guitar case where they found her. Then the coffin starts wobbling alarmingly on its stand because you're leaning the wheelchair over too far, and you put one arm on the coffin to keep it steady. *This is going to be a disaster,* you're thinking, but there's nothing else you'd rather be doing. Your grandma wants to see your wife's face, and goddamn it, you're going to make that happen. Struggling to let her see Angie instead of yourself is exactly the sort of task you can embrace. But everyone is straining, and the coffin is shaking, and the wheelchair is creaking, and you finally have her in there close enough. But you hear grandma saying over and over, "I can't see her." No matter how hard you strain, the angle just isn't working, and their faces won't line up. The slick, black coffin slides away from you all as you lean into it, and you think, *This thing's gonna crash.* So you look at Angie. Yep, there she is. But it's a stranger's approximation of her, so it doesn't hurt at all.

You're hoping your aunt doesn't ask you to pick up her hand for your grandma to touch instead when suddenly your grandma says, "Okay, put me down." You guess you're done. Did she kiss her like she wanted? You must have missed any goodbye kiss when you were busy keeping the coffin steady, and you think this is a good metaphor for your marriage. You turn to your young cousin and say, "I can't believe that worked," and he smiles and shakes his head. He still lives near the family, so he's seen it all. You sit back down, sweat dripping off the end of your nose, and now a preacher is up there pretending like he knew your wife, and he's doing a terrible job convincing anyone. Later you find out this saintly but self-satisfied prick was a half-hour late and only took a cursory glance at some biographical information that was handed to him 30 seconds before he started talking. Angie would have been disgusted by the lack of proper research.

Your Uncle Ron's funeral was just last week, so it's not quite the homecoming it might have been otherwise. When you were little, whenever there was a tornado warning, you and your brother and all your cousins would always end up at your Uncle Ron's house because he was the only one with a basement. The adults would play cards while the kids watched the windows, scared shitless. But it was still kind of fun, and the memory of those nights is still powerful. You wish that you were still around everyone enough that you could go up to any of them and talk about those nights of tornado sirens and cold spots in the thick summer air. But you moved away, so you find it hard to say much at all around your family these days.

Back in your car, you head to the grave site. At the last minute, your sister wants to ride with you, probably because you're the only one parked facing the wrong way. This is the sort of thing that appeals to your sister, who has always been more like you than the rest of them. As you awkwardly back out and then turn around to merge into the procession, your sister is trying to figure out a way to keep the magnetic flag they've stuck to the car. You saw her covet the tiny flag as soon as the solemn-faced funeral director smacked it on the Rabbit's roof. You look up at her wrestling with the magnet, and you are reminded of the three pizza delivery jobs you used to hold simultaneously and how you juggled their windsocks on your antenna.

On the way to Angie's grave, '90s Ex-Girlfriend herself cruises by the procession, and it's a minor thrill to see her again, and her disappointed eyes in her side-view mirror are a weirdly satisfying blast from the past. The last night you shared together was punctuated by you chasing a fly that was tormenting her around the bedroom. It was moving so fast you could barely see it, until you stood perfectly still to somehow get on its wavelength. Then you saw it so clearly you could have had a sketch artist draw its face, which had become your face. You eventually killed the fly (a lucky shot from the massive buckle of her Hot Topic belt), and you left it on a Post-it in the kitchen for her to find, with Aaron's quote from the ding-dong ditch scene in Shakespeare's *Titus Andronicus* written next to its corpse: "Do not let your sorrow die though I am dead." In the morning, however, the fly had vanished, and she became convinced you'd left a suicide note but chickened out. She was gone by sundown.

After the drive-by reunion, your slow train of vehicles cruises by a field of migrant workers who are leaning on their shovels with their hats off. You're so impressed by this show of respect from exploited strangers that you momentarily have faith in your shoestring relatives again. You tell your sister to take a picture of the workers, but she's slow on the draw and only gets one blurry photo right as her battery dies. You step out and walk over to your dad sitting on his car. He's upset, and he talks about how his brother Ron used to give him and all his younger brothers whatever money he had in his pocket so they could go get candy and pop and other stuff. He tells you how his brother would throw him his keys and let him use his car, even though he needed it for work. When your dad asked Uncle Ron about it later, he said he did this because you dad was "a good kid." You're trying to imagine someone who always thought of your dad as a kid, and you wonder how your older brother thinks of you.

Your dad's face is troubled, and that's tough to see. The photo of Ron on your brother's boat, with Angie in the foreground, must have brought back all these memories, and now your sister's crying because she can't stand to see your dad like this. So your dad lightens things up by telling another story about how they had a bench-clearing brawl at a baseball game and how your Uncle Ron had someone by the neck up against the backstop and was punching him in the face. Your dad says his brother was the strongest person he knew. He says, in awe, "That kid that he was punching and holding with one arm? His feet weren't even touching the ground." You all laugh at that, and no one is upset anymore. You feel pressure to tell them stories about Angie, but you decide you'll have to wait until the next funeral to do this, just as your dad did with Ron. You walk past another uncle and find out he recently had a grandson named after him. You wonder whether this was because he wanted a son but had three daughters instead, and you wonder how the daughters feel about this. Your brother has two daughters, and a son, a recent arrival. The boy looks just like your brother, but supposedly acts just like you. You guess this means he keeps to himself. You see that more and more, though, where the youngest child is a boy, after they've had a series of girls. You imagine someone saying, "Finally."

When everyone returns to your dad's house, you try watching *Forensic Files* for old times' sake, but fall asleep. When you wake up, your dad says your sister walked down to your grandma's house, and that you're supposed to meet her there. You change clothes and head over, and you see from the cars in the yard that there are uncles and cousins there, as always. You walk in and sit down on the floor of the kitchen next to the fridge like you're five years old again, and you can't begin to explain how comfortable this is. You decide it's because you sat in that spot for approximately the first third of your life, and no other spot on any floor could make this claim. Your grandma falls asleep in her chair, and as soon as everyone sees this, they immediately start talking about how grandma told them that she couldn't see your wife in the coffin until she turned her head to look up at you. They say that grandma told them she felt so much better once Angie turned her head, and that's why she stopped crying and told us to put her down. You don't believe in anything remotely supernatural, but you find yourself trying to remember which way her head was turned when you were wrestling with the wheelchair and steadying the slippery coffin. Your cousin says, "That cemetery's gonna be full of us one day," and you tell him that you were thinking the exact same thing, but you also can't stop thinking about the wife of your Uncle Larry who was divorced, but still has a tombstone waiting for her in the family plot. You wonder what she thinks about this—both seeing her own tombstone while she's still alive, and also knowing it's next to her ex-husband's name, who she eventually grew to hate. Someone makes a comment about the "Mexicans in the field staring at the cars all weird," and thankfully your sister defends them and explains they were simply paying their respects. "Oh," another cousin says, still doubtful. You've always appreciated their resistance to sentimentality, and, of course, their hands-off methods of grief counseling, mercifully leaving you alone to stew in the corners of this conversation. This is a trait you've adapted, which goes against your urge to lash out. It would be so natural to inflate the importance of every interaction, which in turn would make them do the same. Like Hynkel and Napaloni in *The Great Dictator* cranking their barber chairs higher and higher and higher . . . but, luckily, your family hates Charlie Chaplin. Big into Buster Keaton, though.

Back at your dad's house, you and your sister get a little punchy and proceed to eat everything in the kitchen you can find. Cereal, old pizza, some cheese poppers in a carry-out box, leftover spare ribs, strawberries, some nasty cookies with walnuts that your stepmom made. It's a leftover feast of Biblical proportions, and the blood flow to your belly helps numb and reset your brain once again and keeps you calm. You clank a lot of dishes until your dad comes out to tell you to keep it down. Your sister whispers something about that magnetic funeral flag she wanted, and you confess to her that you tried to keep one of those flags when your uncle died. But when everyone was on the way to his grave site, you realized you were almost out of gas and had to sneak out of the line of cars when they turned so you could stop at a gas station. Then, when you went to meet up with everyone after they'd left the cemetery, you saw you still had the flag, which would have been removed at the burial. So, not wanting anyone to see the flag and realize you missed going to the grave, you stopped your car, popped it off the roof, and stuck it down out of sight on the side of a small metal bridge. You try to remember where the bridge is so she can go back and get it, but for some reason you have an unwarranted fear of bridges these days.

In your old bedroom again, you try to stretch out on the plastic-covered mattress but knock over a potted planet. You lean over to set it upright and knock over an empty waste basket. It's like trying to get comfortable in the middle of a domino tournament, and you decide you're simply not meant to be in that room anymore. You turn on the light and notice it's impossibly small, and you can't understand how both you and your brother once lived in there together. You investigate the closest you both used to share, and you find the dry-cleaner's bag for the suit your dad wore to the funeral, and beneath it, an empty cage. The cage is knee-high, with a handle, and it's rusted shut. You've never seen it before, but you know immediately that it's the trap your neighbor used to capture the raccoon that murdered your dad's ducks. You're not sure why he kept it, but decide it's in your closet for a reason, so you take it with you. You creep out of the house to go see your grandpa on your mom's side of the family, because he stays up late like you. He looks like you, too, everyone says, but he acts more like your brother. No one told him about Angie's funeral. When you get to your car, two police officers are waiting for you. One offers his condolences, and another offers you a card. "If you think of anything that could help, give me a call," he says, and you tell him not to hold his breath. They drift off down the dark street like detritus.

Once you arrive at your grandpa's house, he lets you in, smiling, and you ask him where all grandma's frogs are now that she's gone. He takes you to a garden full of dying orange blossoms and insists you take a giant blue concrete frog home with you. You put it in the trunk. Then he shows you a peanut he's glued to a small piece of wood with a splash of red paint, telling you, proudly that it's "an *assaulted* peanut." You take it to keep the 100-pound frog company. Back inside, you put colorful generic batteries in his TV remote to turn on the closed-captions. He tells you that the cable guy took out the batteries so he wouldn't get his remotes confused. You suddenly feel the urge to grab the cable guy by the neck and explain to him that your grandpa isn't someone who needs things disabled like that. He shows you his new glasses and boasts about them being "indestructible." He says the optometrist recommended them after repairing his bifocals five times in one year. "Stop punching yourself!" the eye doctor said to him, and you imagine grabbing that man by the neck, too. You find an episode of *Deadliest Catch* and tell him, "See that? I typed those words." He seems disinterested, but tells you to leave the captions on anyway, then he takes the batteries out again. You tell him he can find your captions because they always seems to have an extra word hanging down into the next line of text. Sometimes two words. Even three. You tell him that, when you're working, you dream of your captions starting small, one line like they're supposed to, then slowly covering the screen from top to bottom, filling every space under the crackling glass with dog piles of words fighting each other for room to be seen. Then you say goodbye and drive around for an hour looking at the houses of people that you used to know. You think about work tomorrow, and how sometimes you type things before they happen, or how they should have happened, but mostly you just type words spoken long after everyone has forgotten saying them.

It's getting real late, and you're not sure whether to stay another night in your hometown or head back. You feel satisfied you've fulfilled your obligations to her, because there were moments when you weren't sure you were going to try. Then you turn the car too sharply, and 100 pounds of concrete frog rolls over in your trunk. It scares the shit out of you, and for a second you think you have a flat. Then you see a turnpike sign, and you decide to head back to Pittsburgh right then. Then you remember you live in Louisville now. Four hours and you'll be home. You call your sister and tell her that your grandpa gave you an "assaulted peanut," but not to get her hopes up as it was probably crushed by a frog. She's disappointed and sighs, "No fair, all I got was a 'quarter pounder' and a 'cartridge in a pear tree.'" The sadness is beginning to crush you again, but you're happy you attended the funeral, if only for your sister's sake. As you drive, you try to picture what your grandpa's gags would look like. You decide one of them would be a bullet stuck in some fruit.

After three hundred miles, you pass a long stretch of spinning windmills near Chicago and realize you went past Pittsburgh by mistake. In the light of the sunrise, you can just barely make out hundreds of dead birds littering the ground beneath the giant blades like rotten apples under a tree. You remember something a trucker told you once at a rest stop, how their forearms twitch and spasm on their days off from squeezing steering wheels, and how right turns taken much too wide always invade their sleep. Through your spotless windshield, you marvel at a landscape bathed in the warmth of the dawn. You begin counting elbow tattoos hanging out of driver's-side windows. Then you count the prisons. Then you count the crosses on the side of the road and wonder whose job it is to take them down.

You pull a U-turn and consider a spontaneous drive to Lovelock, Mississippi, a town which is split by the largest river in the United States. You figure this would be a perfect place to face your newfound aversion to bridges. During what you worry will be the final conversation you have with Angie's father, he tells you that the rivers of our country contain "the universe." You hang up your phone, not quite sure what he meant. You try to remind yourself that everyone grieves in their own way, but you notice a business card in the front pocket of your jeans, the card the two police officers gave you at the funeral, and you consider making the call. But the card is blank, except for the words "Turn Over" written in tiny script on both sides. You breathe a sigh of relief because you're no narc. Everyone continues to be surprised at how well you're taking this, including her father, and you tell anyone who asks that you find healthy outlets for your pain, usually on the highway. You tape your gas gauge and calculate the trip to Lovelock, thinking about how you need new experiences in your life to replace the old ones, how this will also help with the pain. You remember loving fishing as a child, and the bluegill you caught for your grandma, and you wonder what still swims or crawls in this river. Your grandma said that "ants were Jesus" because they could walk on the surface tension, but you don't remember what Angie once said about Vietnam Bug Hockey, how it was less of a game but "more of a map." Instead you laughed and said, "Just like everything else!" and Angie laughed even harder, but you didn't get either joke, and she knew it. You stop at a random bridge and find your lost funeral flag and secure it to your car. It remains there until you die.

You stop at a turnpike booth where a man is tuning a guitar to kill time between cars. Something in his face tells you this will be your last chance to turn around again. You remember to ask what happens if you don't have enough money for the toll. He looks surprised, laughs, and says, "You fill out a form and pay for it later. It just happened, actually."

XXV

INVISIBLE PRISONS

THOUGH WE MAY not be able to indulge in as many cinematic but melodramatic moments, such as fist clenching, hand wringing, finger banging, or knuckle cracking, our feet are actually much more crucial to mankind's ongoing existential dilemma than our hands. Consider that the word "investigate" comes from the Latin, "vestigium," which means "footprint." This is why shackles were added to prisoners' ankles. Because to the freshly incarcerated, handcuffs alone were merely a challenge, sometimes even a badge of honor, judging by the smirks of those proud men on their perp walks. And if you'd ever stumbled across a prison film, there were hundreds of workarounds to fight, fuck, or drive while handcuffed. But chain a man's legs? That was defeat. I've taken all of this to mean feet have always been, literally, our *motivation*, and so, by extension, as important to our sense of worth as wheels on a car, which is something else I've undeniably come to appreciate as more of my life is stripped away. When society is finished with us, we end up on blocks, not in stocks.

So with these things in mind, I slowed my dead red Rabbit to a stop in the gravel at the corner of the vast clearing, relieved as the sparks and shredded rubber along my rims wound down to silence. I left my broken glasses on my dashboard, and I began to walk with the cage swinging by my side, rattling with the loose skeletal remains of a cat long picked clean by whatever crawled in over my cracked driver's-side window, bones sprinkling out between the bars to seed the soil in my wake. A raccoon followed me, all the way from the Rabbit to the woods, the occasional feather trailing from its mouth. Or maybe it was fur. It certainly wasn't plumage from a haphazard plucking of a gas-station chicken in its teeth, but brilliant white tufts, maybe from the curve of a young head where the ear would have been, downy remnants of a duckling that had just barely breached adolescence before it was devoured. I thought of raccoons and their strange anatomy and how someone might consider them triply endowed. Three penises, but not positioned up-and-down or left-to-right. They were like nesting dolls, one inside the other. One of flesh. One of blood. One of bone. The bone was the weird part.

The raccoon matched my pace precisely, occasionally grunting its appreciation, until it was spooked by the sounds of children playing in the distance. It adjusted its path away from my own and disappeared into the tangle of brush and was gone.

The children in the clearing were engrossed in some sort of performance, so they didn't notice my approach. They also seemed unaware of each other, or at least following individual destinies as their hands worked hard on tasks that were so far impossible to perceive. They occasionally glanced at the sky, as if they were being watched, or judged, and I imagined a pencil with its lead sharpened to infinity piercing the clouds to pepper the grass near their shoes with bullet strikes. But this sort of intimidation was unnecessary. No sentry was apparent, or needed, and I could tell by their movements they had no intention of ever abandoning this pantomime, no apparent desire to make a dash for the road behind me or escape to the woods that surrounded us. And as far as handcuffs, or leg irons, these children were bound by neither.

I was close enough to hear the slow crunch of their feet through the brambles and drifting deadfall, and, consequently, their lack of motivation for decampment. Their steps would occasionally stop just short of a clear trajectory, and they altered course due to borders or limitations I could not comprehend. They still hadn't seen me, and I continued to study them from afar, but I got the distinct impression of confinement without force, combined with a willingness or indulging of restraint. Then I saw their mouths move, and no sound came out.

I watched those bodies reacting to unseen forces, and I thought of bugs playing hockey, and blue lines turning into hash marks, and red lines turning into fence lines, and the moment when an ant riding the puck would reach the goal and the gates would swing open and a cell door would roll back in its track with that deafening clang, and the red siren on the top of the net would begin to sing, not in alarm but in triumph.

This was the invisible prison. And I knew these kids well. Because we've all seen a movie at some point in our lives, we could safely assume they would each have one defining characteristic, from the wide-faced bully to the victimized twerp. We knew that, to begin any miraculous society in the woods that emulated imprisonment, they would have abandoned complications, problematic memories or associations, and they would have acquired completely new identities, likely based on prison films, prison novels, or prison songs. Sure, there might be one boy who actually spent some time in jail, but he wouldn't be in charge here. That would be whoever saw the most films. I'd trained for this all my life, so maybe I'd have a chance joining such a community. Just like the generations of red harvester ants, who thought they could leave a farm where nothing was ever harvested any time they wished, they remained trapped within transparent boundaries, invisible fences with no locks, and unseen trails I should be able to follow. Like the ants, I could make the most of the short time we had left.

Soon they would notice the bundle of roadside crosses in my arms, and I would start matching their names with their memorials. But until then I watched. Something swooped over my head, and I flashed back to a night on our porch back in Kentucky, when, without prompting, Angie reassured me that the eyes staring down from the awning of our house wasn't Mothman after all, and, therefore, nothing to worry about. "I saw it in the light," she said. "It's just a day-old barn owl, as awkward and helpless as a duck out of water." I pictured a splayed Cornish hen, plucked raw but bulbous, maybe something like the generous but ratty young bowerbird, the bottom rung of the avian ladder when it came to the more traditionally alluring or "calendar-ready" species. But then I saw the universe in its eyes, and they spun around, hopefully along with its head, and it spread its wings a mile wide to swallow the rest of the starlight. "Calm down, it's all feathers and lies," Angie said when I jumped. "Feathers and lies."

That night, we walked through Cave Hill Cemetery, a block from our house, and we searched for Colonel Sanders' grave. We ended up kicking around the line of high grass near the unmarked plots of the neighboring graveyard instead, weaving through this neglected annex covered in beer bottles and paper bags and other trash which had aligned itself along one perfect row on the edge where the caretaker had stopped mowing. It was in such disarray that I'd hoped to find a forgotten ribcage, at the very least. And Angie remarked that this second graveyard was somehow comforting, that "we exist in a transitional time." I lied and told her I'd had a dream about a near future where anyone looking for a dead body found one, just like kids who look for arrowheads are almost always rewarded, and she reminded me that no one ever wants to hear about dreams. We held hands and walked around graves and garbage, and I told her I wanted to be the first person to discover a body, and then, when the authorities asked how I found it, I would explain that it was simply because it was exactly what I was looking for.

But that day, we found nothing, not even the grave of Colonel Sanders, which was almost as disappointing as his renowned chicken, which was now sold at gas stations. Later we learned that all throughout Cave Hill Cemetery were yellow arrows on the roads and walkways to lead tourists to his grave instead of their own. But until we crossed that line of uncut grass, we had never looked down past our feet.

I found a patch of dirt in the clearing where even the weeds refused to grow, and with the heel of my shoe I chopped a line around my body. Eventually, I drew a square in the earth, then connected the lines so there was no exit. I sat down in my invisible cell and waited for acknowledgment.

"Hello, Dave. It took you long enough," someone laughed. "I hope you're here to do some real work."

At first, I didn't look up. But the faulty valve of my heart hiccupped at the familiar voice, and I shielded my eyes, looked to the sky, and I called in the air strike. Then I was silenced by her shadow as her body took form. She stood there blocking the trees, blocking the sun, a huge ring of keys jangling on her hip, and she asked me two questions disguised as one.

"Did you miss me?"

I covered my face with both hands and rubbed the beautiful worms behind my eyes and began to serve her sentence.

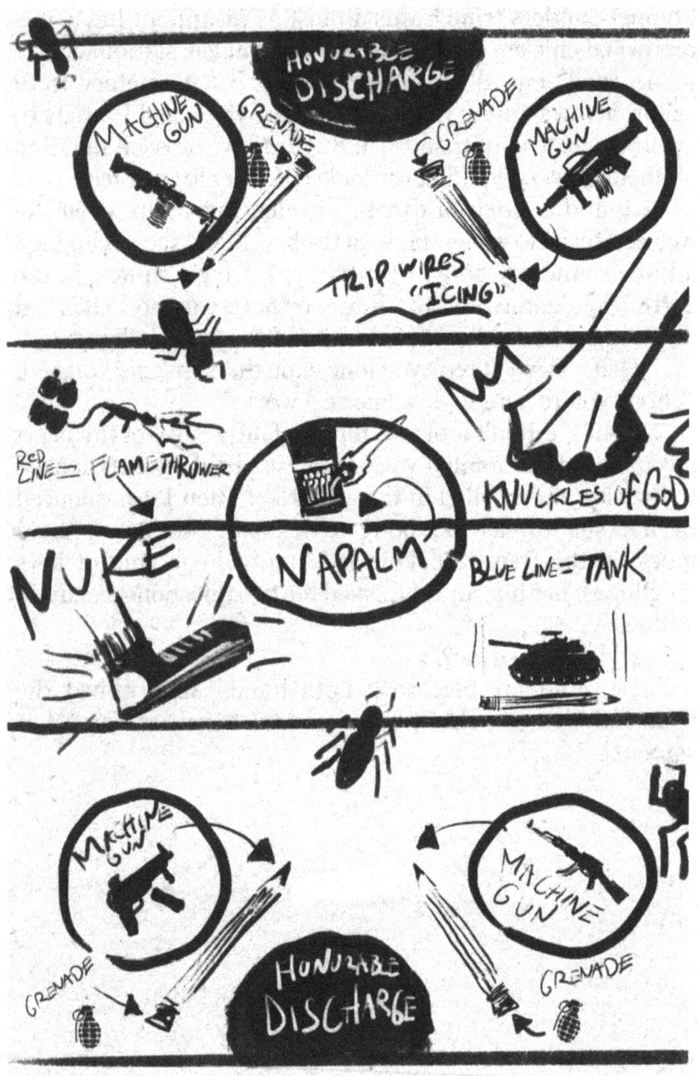
HONORABLE DISCHARGE
MACHINE GUN
GRENADE
GRENADE
MACHINE GUN
TRIP WIRES "ICING"
RED LINE = FLAMETHROWER
KNUCKLES OF GOD
NUKE
NAPALM
BLUE LINE = TANK
MACHINE GUN
MACHINE GUN
GRENADE
HONORABLE DISCHARGE
GRENADE

ACKNOWLEDGEMENTS

Thanks, Not Really Amy ("NRA"?), Hazel, Under the Bleachers Cat, Next to the Bleachers Duck, and Sorta Near the Bleachers Lizard. Thanks, Tony "The Famous Mr. Dead" McMillen for his amazing interior illustrations and Joel "Why Did You Send Me A Knife?" Vollmer for another incredible book cover that both interpreted and abandoned my wacky concept as only he could. Thanks, Max "Why Did You Send Me Brass Knuckles?" Booth III and Lori "Why Did You Send Me Another Revision?" Michelle for working construction here. For reading what I wrote, thanks, JDO, JRJ, SGJ, William, Alison, Kelby, Pat, Benoit, Jessica, Sean, Cody, John, Fred, Jarrid, Elizabeth, Liam, Sarah, Chris, Geoff, Sal, Brian, Ron, Holly, Mike, Jason, Jason, and Jason. And thanks, Robb and Livius, for hating acknowledgements pages and ensuring your inclusion. Oh, and thanks to my boys from high school, Steve, Glen, Jerry, and Dave for letting me purge our lives for material. Also, thanks to everyone who published some of these chapters early, including Cheryl, Randy, Eddie, Adam, Kelly, Matt, Cameron, Ryan, Paul, and Jason. Thanks, Harley, for the theme songs, and Nate, for always being game to build something. Thanks, Jed and Scott, for letting me hang in your St. Louis scene, and Joe, Nick, and Ross, for letting me hang in this West Coast scene. Thank you, all those '90s ex-girlfriends with the glorious Kool-Aid flavored hair. And big thanks to all of the family who lived alternate versions of these chapters with me. And finally, a huge thanks to *Forensic Files*, for teaching me how to caption TV shows, and, at the same time, how to spiral about every possible way a loved one might die and then fantasize how it would be up to me and me alone to fail spectacularly at solving their murder.

ABOUT THE AUTHOR

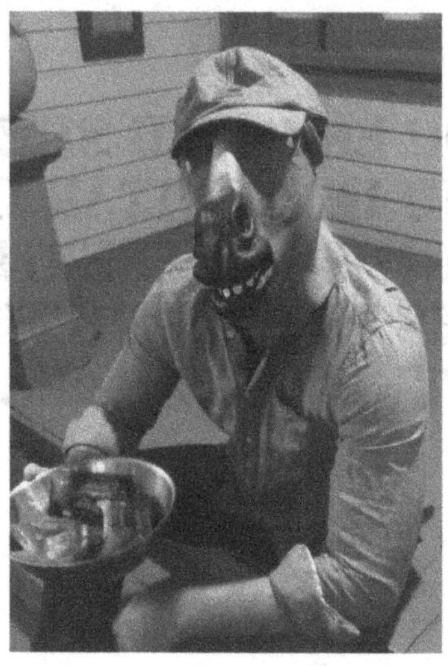

David James Keaton's award-winning fiction has appeared in over a hundred publications. He lives in San Jose, California, home of the Sharks (with thumbs) and the final resting place of a calico cat (also with thumbs).

IF YOU ENJOYED SHE WAS FOUND IN A GUITAR CASE, DONT MISS THESE OTHER TITLES FROM PERPETUAL MOTION MACHINE . . .

STEALING PROPELLER HATS FROM THE DEAD

BY DAVID JAMES KEATON

ISBN: 978-1-943720-00-2

$14.95

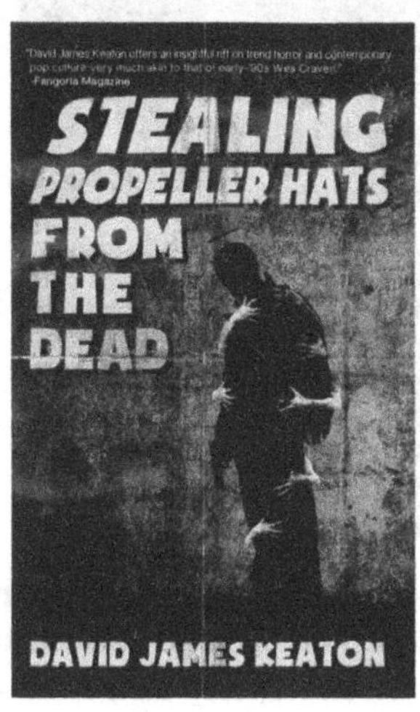

A collection of horror fiction that's both a love letter and a middle finger to the zombie saturation of our culture. It's the backlash to the backlash, as zombies are finally unfashionable enough to be cool again. Inside, you will rehearse end-of-the-world scenarios with the staff of a tourist trap, follow an undead love triangle struggling to survive a tipping point of post-modern, pop-culture references, and enjoy one small apocalypse after another as the living continue to adapt to a new world of the dead, where they'll finally discover who is hungrier. Don't let these poor souls dine in vain.

TALES FROM THE CRUST

EDITED BY DAVID JAMES KEATON AND MAX BOOTH III

978-1-943720-37-8

$18.95

**The toppings: Terror and torment.
The crust: Stuffed with dread and despair.
And the sauce: Well, the sauce is always red.
Whether you're in the mood for a Chicago-style deep dish of darkness, or prefer a New York wide slice of thin-crusted carnage, or if you just have a hankering for the cheap, cheesy charms of cardboard-crusted, delivered-to-your-door devilry; we have just the slice for you.**

Bring your most monstrous of appetites, because we're serving suspense and horrors both chillingly cosmic and morbidly mundane from acclaimed horror authors such as Brian Evenson, Jessica McHugh, and Cody Goodfellow, as well as up-and-coming literary threats like Craig Wallwork, Sheri White, and Tony McMillen.

***Tales from the Crust*, stories you can devour in thirty minutes or less or the next one's free. Whatever that means.**

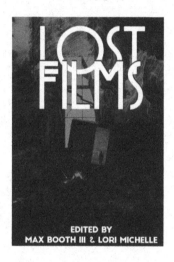

The Perpetual Motion Machine Catalog

Antioch | Jessica Leonard | Novel
Baby Powder and Other Terrifying Substances | John C. Foster
Story Collection
Bone Saw | Patrick Lacey | Novel
Born in Blood Vol. 1 | George Daniel Lea | Story Collection
Crabtown, USA:Essays & Observations | Rafael Alvarez | Essays
Dead Men | John Foster | Novel
The Detained | Kristopher Triana | Novella
Gods on the Lam | Christopher David Rosales | Novel
The Green Kangaroos | Jessica McHugh | Novel
Invasion of the Weirdos | Andrew Hilbert | Novel
Last Dance in Phoenix | Kurt Reichenbaugh | Novel
Like Jagged Teeth | Betty Rocksteady | Novella
Live On No Evil | Jeremiah Israel | Novel
Lost Films | Various Authors | Anthology
Lost Signals | Various Authors | Anthology
Mojo Rising | Bob Pastorella | Novella
Night Roads | John Foster | Novel
Quizzleboon | John Oliver Hodges | Novel
The Ruin Season | Kristopher Triana | Novel
Standalone | Paul Michael Anderson | Novella
Stealing Propeller Hats from the Dead | David James Keaton |
Story Collection
Tales from the Holy Land | Rafael Alvarez | Story Collection
Tales from the Crust | Various Authors | Anthology
The Girl in the Video | Michael David Wilson | Novella

The Nightly Disease | Max Booth III | Novel
The Train Derails in Boston | Jessica McHugh | Novel
The Writhing Skies | Betty Rocksteady | Novella
Touch the Night | Max Booth III | Novel
We Need to Do Something | Max Booth III | Novella

Patreon:
www.patreon.com/pmmpublishing

Website:
www.PerpetualPublishing.com

Facebook:
www.facebook.com/PerpetualPublishing

Twitter:
@PMMPublishing

Newsletter:
www.PMMPNews.com

Email Us:
Contact@PerpetualPublishing.com

CPSIA information can be obtained
at www.ICGtesting.com
Printed in the USA
LVHW040212010721
691622LV00004B/23